# CLAIMED BY HER TWO ALPHAS

## A PARANORMAL SHIFTER ROMANCE

### SEDONA VENEZ

# WANT FREE SEDONA VENEZ BOOKS?

Sign up for Sedona Venez's Newsletter and receive FREE BOOKS. In addition to the free stories, you will also get special pricing, exclusive previews and news of new releases.

**GET A FREE SEDONA VENEZ BOOK!**

Join Sedona's mailing list to be the first to know of new releases, free books, special prices and other author giveaways.

https://sedonavenez.com/free-book

# DOUBLE TROUBLE

## A PARANORMAL BEAR SHIFTER MÉNAGE ROMANCE

# CHAPTER 1

I PULLED OPEN the door to the Blue Moon Tavern and stepped inside. While New Fane, Montana, boasted more sheep than people, it still managed to support a couple of nice bars, along with a few dives. This was one of the nicer places.

Tonight, it was more crowded than I expected and far more casual than I was dressed for. I could blame Peyton for that. My best friend had sent me out on this adventure in a dress that, as far as I was concerned, exposed more of my curves than I was comfortable with revealing in public.

"It's hot, Sadie. Lighten up. You want them to notice you, and you want to stand out in the crowd, not be a shrinking wallflower."

We'd been in my room, a mound of dresses she'd brought over piled on my bed, some of them actually wearable. But she'd sent me out in this dark-blue wrap dress, complete with towering heels and a tiny clutch purse, which ironically, I was now clutching tightly.

*Breathe, Sadie... Just keep breathing. It's going to be okay.*

*It's only a date, not a lifelong commitment. It's just a date... just a date.* If I said it enough, maybe I'd believe it.

I ventured farther into the bar and grudgingly had to admit Peyton might have been right about the dress. A few guys were giving me long, appreciative looks, most smiling at me as I walked by. The nerves that had threatened to make me walk right back out the door faded a little. But the reason I was here still had my heart racing and my palms sweaty, making for a rather unlovely combination for a blind date.

None of the guys seemed more interested in just looking, though, so I crossed them off as not being my date—dates.

Yes, *dates*. Plural. This wasn't just a blind date with one guy; it was a blind date with two guys. I was still trying to get my head around how this was going to work. Again, it was all Peyton's doing. She had recently met the love of her life, Alex, who just happened to have two close friends who were looking to meet someone. Instead of choosing who to set me up with, Alex suggested I just meet them both, and his friends, strangely enough, not only agreed, but they thought it was a great idea. I wasn't sure what I had gotten myself into.

I thought back to that unusual conversation with my best friend.

"You can't be serious? You let Alex set me up with two guys? On the same date?"

Peyton smiled at me in a way that made me feel we were co-conspirators of some big secret. But if she knew what this secret was, she wasn't letting me in on it.

"I am, I have, and I did." She grinned. "It's going to be okay, Sadie. They're really good guys."

"I'm sure they are... It's just... it's a little awkward."

She giggled, the bracelets on her wrist clanging together, the soft musical clink of gold accenting her words. "I promise you it won't be awkward at all. Jackson and Dane are looking to settle down with someone, and Alex thinks you're the kind of girl they've both been looking for. He just figures the easiest way about it is for you to go out with both of them and see if one stands out to you." She shrugged, her lips drawn into a wide smile. "Worst case, you don't like either of them but you've made some new friends."

"Yeah, but, Peyton... two guys who want to date the same girl? That sounds... unreal. And honestly, a little perverted."

"Sadie, they're the best of friends who grew up together. They know each other better than brothers, and come on... They told Alex they're serious about finding their perfect mate. Why not just go?"

"I don't know, Peyton. It just seems a bit crazy."

"Not crazy at all. It's going to be fun. You've had a couple really crappy relationships, Sadie. You need to try something new. Face it; your taste in men is pretty suspect. Like the last guy... What was his name?"

"Peter." I resisted the urge to spit on the floor and cross myself. It hadn't been a relationship to remember.

"Yeah. Peter. I didn't even get to meet him. You two only dated for, what? A couple months? And then he was gone, just like that. And before him, it was Brad... and David—"

I held up my hand. "I'm perfectly aware of who I've dated and why we broke up." Again, Peyton was closer to the truth than I wanted to admit. I was bad at choosing men.

"So, you know, here's a chance to try a different way to find a man."

"But a blind date? Really? And two guys on the first date? It's a little out of my comfort zone, to say the least. And it's not like I'm a big believer in love anymore."

Peyton nonchalantly waved her right hand in the air, the big diamond in the ring on her finger catching the light, and I rolled my eyes. "Yes, I know. Alex is a great guy, so his friends are probably just as great, but it's still just a lot to take in. Why can't I just meet them sometime when you and Alex are there? Like at a party or something?"

"Stop overthinking this. Just go with it. For once, just let go and see what happens." Peyton leaned forward, giving me that look that told me she knew what was best for me and I should listen. "What have you got to lose? At best, you'll meet the man of your dreams. At worst, you'll have gotten all dressed up for no reason."

In the two weeks since that bizarre conversation with Peyton, one snippet kept running through my head. These guys were looking for their perfect *mate*. Not mates, plural. Not one guy wanting one and the other guy wanting... something else. Both guys were looking for the same thing, and according to Alex, that thing was me. But I was only one girl, and even if I'd gotten past the weirdness of two guys wanting to share one blind date, I still hadn't wrapped my head around how I could be the perfect mate for both of them.

Yet here I was, trying to figure out how I was going to find not just one, but two blind dates in a crowded bar. I should have backed out.

*No. You shouldn't have. It's not going to kill you to do this. If it backfires, you can tell Peyton I told you so.*

At least I should have figured out some way to recognize these guys, like carrying a rose or wearing a bow in my hair. Or maybe a nametag, so instead of standing in the crowd, turning in useless circles, I could find these guys.

I made another sweep of the room.

*You're overthinking. Just take a breath and let go.*

I closed my eyes, wavering slightly in my heels, did my best imitation of someone poised and collected, and concentrated on my breathing. Then I opened my eyes. The crowd parted, and there he was. Or there *some* guy was, some really hand-some guy.

He was sitting at the bar, and he was looking right at me. For a split second, I thought maybe I'd hallucinated him out of desperation. Even sitting down, he was big and broad-shouldered, taking up more physical space than anyone around him. Or maybe he just looked like he was. He should have been imposing, scary, but he radiated an all-American boy kind of feel, the hunky guy next door who helped you with your groceries or changed your flat tire. *A nice, safe guy.*

Until I got to his eyes. Blue. Even in the dim light of the bar, I could tell they were blue. The all-American hunk had just turned the tiniest bit dangerous. There was a fire in those eyes that woke something deep and primal, something I'd thought didn't exist in me. Or at least I'd never experienced it. I wouldn't go as far as calling it love at first sight. Lust at first sight maybe. Whatever it was, it was pretty amazing.

I really wanted to take a step forward, but I was rooted in place. His eyes held mine, never looking away, and it was like a magnet drawing me closer. Something held me back, though.

*But wait... What about my dates? Just because this guy likes looking at me—and I like looking at him...*

I turned away, the act of breaking from his gaze doing nothing to lessen the heat that had built up inside me. I was supposed to be here looking for my mystery men, not falling for the first guy who caught my eye.

*Turn around. What if it's him?*

That thought came out of the blue. And for once, I listened to the voice in my head and did a slow turn. The guy was smiling at me, and something inside me simultaneously clenched and loosened up. It was a physical sensation, a thud deep and low, and I took a step back, shocked by my body's reaction.

When he stood, I saw just how tall he was, well over six feet. He cut easily through the crowd with a grace that belied his size. He stopped just in front of me, and I looked up into those piercing blue eyes.

"Hi, Sadie. I'm Dane. Dane Hastings."

I stared. Just plain unattractive, open-mouthed, deer-in-headlights stared at this amazing specimen who'd just told me he was one half of my blind date.

Saints preserve me, maybe I'd gotten lucky.

Then it hit me.

*Where the hell is the other guy?*

The logistics of the whole thing really confused me. So, if I hit it off with both of them, how did that work long term? Did I travel from house to house for each date? Was it an every other weekday and alternate weekend kind of schedule?

Then it hit me, and I could have kicked myself for being so naïve. I knew the term ménage. Peyton was a romance novel junkie, and her latest kick was multiple partner stories. She'd been raving about her newest favorite author and the deft touch she apparently had with describing three-way sex.

But this wasn't a book; this was real life—*my* real life. I'd agreed to something so far out of my range of experience it hadn't even registered on my radar, and now I was jumping at anything that might make this make sense. *But a threesome?* That seemed too far-fetched and certainly not something I'd ever even considered doing before. Certainly, Peyton or Alex would have told me that was what these guys wanted if they were into kink.

*Wouldn't they?*

I had to be wrong about them, about what Jackson and Dane wanted from this... from me. It had to be something less weird than a fantasy ménage. The whole thing must be some kind of bizarre misunderstanding, probably on my part.

But underneath all that confusion of their motives, I was curious. I wanted to meet these guys, to see just what kind of men—best friends—would be interested in dating me.

*What the hell was I thinking?*

Maybe I wasn't thinking, and maybe that was the whole point. Peyton was always telling me I overthought everything. I'd remind her I was a Virgo and it was written in the stars. She'd laugh, and we'd agree to disagree.

Maybe I was being offered a chance to live outside my boring little life. It was out of character, sure, but... when would I ever have a chance like this again?

And now I was standing in front of a gorgeous mountain of a man, heart jumping around in my chest, hands and knees shaky. He knew my name, so he was the one. Or one of the ones.

"Hi, Dane."

He stuck out a hand, and I resisted the urge to wipe my palm on my dress. If he was that interested, he'd have to take me just as I was, sweaty palms and all. I put my hand out and watched it disappear into his. His grip was strong, but restrained, and I had the distinct impression he could crush my bones if he wanted to. I had to admit that delicious sense of controlled danger lurking just beneath the handsome exterior was quite a turn-on.

"It's really nice to meet you, Sadie. I have a table reserved in the back if you'd like to sit with us. It's easier to talk back there."

"Yeah... sure. That would be great." I did a mental hand-to-forehead. *Us? I'm such an idiot. Best friends. They came together. Duh.*

It all seemed so easy, so natural. He moved aside, letting me walk ahead of him, his hand coming to rest on the small of my back, barely touching me. But the heat of that almost-touch was searing, and for a moment, I lost track of where I was headed.

"This way." He guided me toward the rear of the bar. I remembered now from a long-ago visit that there was a section in the back with tables and booths. It was quiet, dark, and sort of on the romantic side for a bar in New Fane.

The tables around us were full of couples, but Dane was steering me toward a booth in the far corner. I saw a man slide out and stand, and for a moment, it was déjà vu as our eyes met. There was a visceral thud between my thighs, and I stumbled in my heels. Dane caught my elbow, saving both my dignity and my ass.

"Jackson, this is Sadie. Sadie, this is Jackson Taylor."

"Nice to meet you."

Jackson was almost as tall as Dane, but the resemblance ended there. Jackson was black-haired and dark-eyed, with a sensuous curve to his lips that gave me the distinct impression he had undressed me with his gaze and he liked what he saw. While that would usually be a turn-off, right now, right here, it was incredibly sexy. We stood for a longer-than-necessary moment, Dane's hand at my back, Jackson standing before me. The word ménage popped into my head, and for the first time since this whole thing started, it didn't seem perverted at all.

*Sign me up.*

"Sorry, I've lost my manners. Here, have a seat." Jackson stepped aside, and I slid into the booth, Jackson moving in beside me.

"Would you like something to drink? I think I'm ready for another."

I looked up at Dane. "Something... not too strong. White wine, if they have it."

"One white wine coming up. Jackson?"

"Another beer. Thanks."

Dane moved off through the crowd, and I got a good view of the backside of the man. He was toned with broad shoulders, narrow hips, and if I had to admit, had a really nice ass. I sighed. And then I remembered I was sitting with the other half of my blind date.

With a touch of guilt, I turned to Jackson.

I expected to see jealousy or at least irritation on his face. After all, the girl he'd picked as his perfect mate had just been caught eyeing up the competition. But he smiled at me with something like approval.

"I've got to say I'm really glad you agreed to meet us. It's not easy to find a girl who's open-minded enough to put herself out there like this. Alex was pretty insistent that we should meet you, and I'm glad we agreed."

"I... It's not my usual dating experience; that's for sure."

Dane was back, setting a beer in front of Jackson and a glass of wine in front of me. He slid into the other side of the booth, and for a minute, I sat in wonder. I was literally in the center of a whirlpool of masculinity, in the midst of something way beyond anything I'd ever experienced, let alone dreamed of.

These were the kind of guys who'd never paid attention to me. Back in high school, they were the ones who dated the cheerleaders. I had been told by Tiffany Webster—head cheerleader, prom queen, and top of the social structure at Everest High School—that this type of guy was totally out of my league. Although that was years ago, her words still stung.

But I didn't want to think about high school or ex-boyfriends or Tiffany Webster. I wanted to concentrate on Dane and Jackson. That wasn't hard. Both of them seemed very eager to get to know me.

The conversation flowed just as easily as the wine they kept bringing me. It was good—almost too good—and I finally made the conscious effort to slow down. I got giggly and silly when I drank, and the last thing I wanted to do was give these guys a reason to doubt their decision to meet me.

Somehow, past relationships got brought up, a comment about a former girlfriend from one of the guys. They laughed over it for a minute and asked an innocent question, if I'd ever had the same experience, but I brushed it off as gracefully as I could. They exchanged a look, then deftly changed the subject. They seemed sensitive to the tone of my voice, how I answered, and I was supremely grateful.

Dane asked where I worked.

"I'm a vet tech at Mountain View on Broadway." It was a pretty simple statement and a pretty mundane job, but both guys seemed inordinately pleased that I worked with animals.

"It's just that we grew up with... pets of different kinds. So, you know, we love animals."

They exchanged a look that I couldn't quite read, but my expression-reading ability was never that great to begin with and it diminished even more when I'd been drinking.

"Do you have any pets now?" I'd learned that the guys shared a cabin in the woods, somewhere out past the highway, practically in the next county.

Dane shook his head. "Not so easy when we work twelve-hour days and neither of us are home much. Maybe someday..."

"What do you do that has such long hours?"

"We're on the New Fane police force."

The pride was unmistakable in Jackson's voice, and I turned to look at him. There were those dark eyes again, that seductive smile. He sported a hint of stubble. I liked clean-shaven men, but with Jackson, that hint of roughness perfectly accented his strong jaw and hinted at something a little dark lurking just below the surface.

*He's too perfect. I'm probably drooling.*

I pulled my eyes away, turning to Dane. I was getting a

little dizzy, pivoting back and forth between the two, but I wasn't sure I could handle looking at both of them at the same time.

"We're both detectives. Although, our agency is so small, it's hard to specialize. So, if we have any major crimes, like a homicide, we all get involved. Those are few and far between, knock on wood."

Normally, the word homicide would have sent a chill down my spine, but it was looking into those intense blue eyes that made me shiver. I could picture Dane rescuing a kitten from a tree or helping an old lady across the street. I couldn't quite picture him investigating murders.

"Sadie?"

I'd drifted off again into a little daydream. "Sorry... you were saying?"

"Does that bother you? Us being in a line of work that's sometimes dangerous?" Dane set down his beer, and I lost myself a little in his eyes. Then I shook myself mentally and made myself answer.

"Oh, no. I have an uncle who's a policeman back east, although he's not a detective. Just an Irish beat cop in Boston."

"There is no such thing as 'just' a cop in Boston. That's a tough town."

We talked a little more about family, just general things, and the silences between topics grew longer. It wasn't that the conversation was lagging. The chemistry between the three of us had reached some kind of fever pitch. What had started, for me, as a slow burn from the minute I'd met them was taking over both my mind and body. I was fumbling for words, lost in whoever's eyes I was looking into.

It was oddly hypnotic to stare into either vivid blue or darkest brown and hear my words trail off into nothing.

Neither Jackson nor Dane seemed to notice, or if they did, they didn't care.

It was Jackson who first let his eyes move to my lips, his gaze like a warm caress. He leaned just that much closer, and I responded, drifting toward him. He was irresistible, and his look told me that quite possibly, he thought the same about me.

*I want to be kissed.*

His lips touched mine, and the sizzle was instantaneous. My first—and totally illogical—thought was Pop Rocks. Sparks flew and the gentle pressure increased, a tease of his tongue against my lower lip, the hint that I was kissing someone who had the power to possess me, body and soul and heart.

Jackson moved away, and I sat for a minute, eyes closed, probably looking like a dreamy schoolgirl. I opened them to look into Jackson's dark eyes, heavy-lidded, lips curved into a sensuous half smile. I looked down at those beautiful lips that had just created magic with mine in that brief kiss. I wanted more.

There was a noise behind me, and I swear it sounded as though Dane were growling. I turned toward him, a hurried apology ready. I'd just kissed his best friend right in front of him.

But any words I wanted to say were never uttered. Dane slipped one hand behind my head, fingers winding into the hair at the nape of my neck. No one had ever set off fireworks in me by just caressing the back of my neck, but Dane's touch did just that. He pulled me toward him, eyes locked with mine. There was no heavy-lidded passion, just a direct look, an I-want-you-now gaze that had me almost nodding in silent agreement.

His kiss was just this side of aggressive, his mouth claiming mine as if it already belonged to him. He pulled me in close, his lips moving over mine, the kiss deepening, intensifying. It was lush and hot, wild and a little messy. The kiss took my breath away, and it was perfect.

Dane released me, and I gasped, swallowing hard.

"Oh, well..." Words failed me. I ran my tongue over my lips. I could taste both men. It was far more intoxicating than any wine, and it made me just as confused as if I'd drunk an entire bottle of the stuff. This wasn't right—or it shouldn't be right.

I sat back, shaking my head.

"I'm sorry... This is... Like I said, it's pretty much beyond my dating experience. I have to admit I've never gone on a blind date with two guys at the same time. I'm not really sure how I'm supposed to act. It's like I'm cheating on both of you, one in front of the other."

"There's nothing you could do that's wrong, Sadie. It's not that we're intentionally trying to confuse you." Jackson looked over my head at Dane. "It's an unusual situation. I've got to agree with you."

"But we're not competing with each other."

I turned to Dane. "Not at all? Not even a little bit?"

"Trust me. If we were competing, Jackson wouldn't be here." Dane's slightly wicked chuckle contrasted with his boy-next-door good looks.

Jackson growled at his friend.

It was a relief to laugh, and some of my confusion dissipated. I still didn't understand these guys or what they wanted, other than me. But if they said they weren't competing, I had to take them at their word.

"It's a first date, Sadie. We're all getting to know each other. Right now, I... We like you. A lot. And we hope you like us, at least enough to want to see us again."

"Well, as far as first dates go, it's been one of the most interesting I've ever been on." I looked between the two guys. "Yes, I'd like to see both of you again." I wasn't sure if I wanted them together or apart, and I let the sentence trail off. It was just a first date, not a lifetime commitment. I'd heard that from someone tonight, more than once.

Jackson took my hand, strong fingers wrapping around mine. Dane slid his arm around my shoulders. I should have felt confined, invaded, with these big guys crowding my personal space. But it wasn't like that. Sure, I was surrounded by a whole lot of gorgeous masculinity, but there was a gentleness behind all that power, and I felt cocooned, safe. Protected. And I liked how that felt.

"Then we'll call you. If that's okay?"

I took Dane's other hand and raised both their hands to my lips, brushing a kiss across their knuckles. It was more assertive than I'd ever been on a first date, but then again, this wasn't any typical first date.

"It's more than okay, no matter who calls or how many of you call." I giggled again and felt a blush rising up my cheeks.

But then I was being kissed on those blushing cheeks, and nothing else mattered except being here, sandwiched between Dane Hastings and Jackson Taylor.

# CHAPTER 2

"WELL, HOW WAS IT?" Alex leaned into the gap between the front seats of the Jeep. "Come on, Dane. Jackson's been just as tight-lipped as you've been. What's up?"

Dane drove around the last curve on the old logging road, the cabin coming into sight. Jackson was sitting beside him in the Jeep, Alex in the back seat.

Dane glanced at Jackson.

He shrugged, and Dane caught the look he gave him in return. "I didn't want to talk about it unless we were together."

"Yeah. Probably a good idea."

There was one aspect of their lives they'd neglected to explain to Sadie. And they knew that would be one of the first questions Alex would ask them. They also knew from experience what one of them said to Alex got back to Peyton, sort of like a feedback loop. And now that loop included Sadie. So, they needed to tread cautiously, at least for a little while.

The Jeep crunched across the gravel parking area, and Jackson jumped out before Dane had even turned off the engine. He finally got out, stretching, scenting the cool air. It smelled clean and fresh, heavy with pine and an undercurrent of ripening berries. The cabin was on the end of an old, abandoned logging road. They were secluded, and it suited them just fine.

Alex grabbed two bags of groceries from the back of the Jeep, and Dane took the other one. Jackson was already unlocking the door, pausing at the threshold, drawing in a deep breath. He turned, nodded, and went inside.

They could never be too careful. Being werebears might make them powerful, but sometimes it made them a target.

Dane watched Alex walk up the path ahead of him, following Jackson into the cabin. He was more brother than friend, even though he was a wolf, his long blond hair and lean, lanky frame so very different from his two friends.

He'd been a part of their lives since they were cubs. He'd shown up one day in wolf form, tail wagging, a scrappy little pup dragging a big stick, practically begging them to play with him. They'd looked at him and each other, and without a second thought, they took off into the woods after him. They'd been inseparable ever since.

His clan's territory was nearby, and even though there were occasional boundary disputes, their clans had more or less gotten along. Recently, though, they'd bonded in a more formal alliance to protect their world from the outside. Much of the public land around them was being sold to timber and mining interests, and there was a mad scramble to purchase as much of their territory as they could before they were run off their ancestral land.

Dane set the bag of groceries on the counter. Jackson already had out three bottles of beer, and Dane took the one he held out to him.

"Come on, guys. Give me something. I am the one that you

set you all up, after all." He looked between the two friends. "I know Sadie's a really nice girl. Don't tell me something went wrong."

"No, nothing went wrong," Dane replied and took a swallow of beer. He struggled to think of exactly how to explain what happened—or didn't happen.

"Actually, it went really well." Jackson boosted himself onto the counter. He sat with elbows resting on his knees, beer held by the bottleneck, momentarily forgotten. "You know it's damn hard to find a woman we both connect with. Hell, you had a hard-enough time finding Peyton."

"So, she's okay with how things are? That she's going to be sharing the two of you?" Alex leaned against the counter.

Dane took steak, bread, eggs, and milk out of the bags, stalling, hoping Jackson would explain the rest. Dane looked at him over the top of the open refrigerator door. Jackson looked back at him, and Dane knew by the look on his face that he'd have to do the talking.

"Not really." Dane tried to will Jackson into helping him out, but he was suddenly interested in the label on his beer.

"She's not okay with sharing?" Alex laughed. "I can't imagine a girl who wouldn't want to share the two of you."

"Funny, Alex." Jackson took a swallow of beer without looking at him. "That's not the problem. Well, it's not the real problem." He fidgeted, shot Dane a glance, and went back to scrutinizing his bottle.

"Wait. You told her, right? You told her you're shifters? How does she feel about that?"

Dane looked at Jackson, then back to Alex. He shut the refrigerator door and shrugged. "I don't know. We didn't tell her that either. That we're shifters. Or that it's our plan to share."

Alex stared at Dane in shock. "You're kidding. You've got

no time to waste. You find a girl who's perfect, and you fumble the ball at the one-yard line? Come on, guys. You know how important this is. I told you when I set you up that you had to tell her. That was the deal. It's not fair that you keep this from her."

Jackson jumped down from the counter, boots thudding on the wood floor. "Listen, Alex, we know exactly how important this is... she is. We were handed the title of alpha—both of us—and ever since then, the pressure's been on to find a mate. But it's not that easy. If we tell her too soon, it might scare her away. It's a pretty big deal when she doesn't even know shifters exist."

"If knowing the truth will scare her away, how is she supposed to be your perfect mate?" Alex asked, his forehead crinkled, a scowl on his face.

Dane and Jackson ignored his question, though it was a good one.

"Sadie isn't like Peyton. She's a little more..." Dane tried to find the right word to sum her up, besides alluring and enticing and arousing. He felt a surge of heat at the thought of her. Just being with her had opened his senses like no other woman had. He could still smell her, still feel her lips on his...

Alex's voice interrupted Dane's thoughts. "She's what? Weak? Fragile? Goldilocks... easily frightened of bears?"

Dane shook his head. "None of the above. Reserved maybe. I don't think she's had that many great relationships. So, she's got a few insecurities, some walls built up. Dumping everything on her all at once—who... what we are, that we want to share—on the first date would have been too much. She would have pulled back."

"We made the right decision last night by not telling Sadie anything." Jackson glanced at Dane, and he nodded in agreement.

Dane took a swallow of beer. "You know how hard it is to date non-shifter women, Alex. You got lucky in meeting Peyton, and we're hoping that luck holds with Sadie."

Alex pulled out a chair and sat at the table. "You guys have a reputation for dating any woman, shifter or not. I'm surprised there are any women left in town that you haven't seduced, either on your own or together."

Dane shot a look at Jackson, pretty sure had a smartass retort ready. He frowned, raising a fresh beer to his lips.

"Yeah, well, that was before we were handed the role of alpha. I can't deny it was fun..." Jackson smothered a chuckle with another drag of his beer, looking away from Dane.

Jackson had earned the reputation as a womanizer. At least Dane had been a little more discreet.

"But all that's over. We're looking for a mate now, and I'm pretty sure we found her in Sadie. Thanks to you."

"So, when are you going to tell her your secret? Or secrets, I guess." Alex leaned back in his chair. "You can't hide any of this from her for very long."

Jackson set his bottle on the counter. "I'm starting the steaks." He opened the refrigerator, looking at Dane over the top of the door, but his reply was meant for Alex. "The sharing... we're working up to that. The shifters... we're not sure she'll accept what we are."

"How do you know if you haven't said anything? If she's so incredible, isn't she worth the risk?"

"We don't want to hurt her." Jackson set the steaks on the counter and turned to face Alex. "We got the feeling that she's been hurt enough already."

Dane grabbed an onion and a knife, chopping the onion, ready to agree with Jackson, but Alex cut him off.

"You realize that's not your decision to make, right? I mean, of course you don't want to intentionally hurt her. But she agreed to meet with you both, and that's not exactly something just any girl would do. Give the girl some credit. I think you're underestimating her."

Dane dumped the onion in a pan and looked at Jackson. He saw the same realization on his face that Dane had just come to. Sadie had taken a big risk just coming on the date. She might have been hurt in the past, but she showed up.

The steaks were sizzling in the pan, the smell of sautéing onions making their stomachs rumble.

Jackson stirred them, his back to Alex. "You might be right."

His words were mumbled, but Alex heard him, and he smiled. "I'm what? Come on, Jackson. Say it louder. I'm right... and you know it."

Jackson turned, brandishing a knife, teeth bared, giving his best impression of a snarling bear. "Don't cross the cook, Alex. I've got a weapon."

Alex waved away the threat, laughing.

Jackson's façade dropped, and his deeper laugh joined Alex's. "Fine. Write it on the calendar: Alex McKenzie was right."

They spent the rest of the night drinking beer, eating steak smothered in onions and mushrooms, and generally working their way through pretty much the rest of the groceries.

It was somewhere near dawn when Alex stood, stretching. "Well, guys, it's been fun. Thanks for the food and the beer. You must be off work tomorrow, right?"

"Normally, yeah, but it's a swing shift, patrol duty. There's a big anti-mining rally starting in the afternoon at city hall, and they're short on manpower. Seeing we're anti-mining, too, we thought we'd volunteer to help keep the peace."

"Well, I hope you have a diplomatic rally. How did Sadie

react to both of you being police officers? Or did you forget to tell her about that part of your lives as well?"

Jackson started clearing the table, dishes clattering in the sink. "Actually, that didn't faze her in the least. Some women, they hear what we do and they're gone. Either they have a past or they're hiding something in the present. We let them go. But Sadie said she had family who was in the force somewhere back east, so it was familiar to her."

"So, when are you going to tell her what you are?" Alex shrugged into his jacket, tugging up the zipper. The night had gotten cooler, a full moon rising in the east.

As always, he would walk home. As the crow flies, it wasn't more than a mile or so. It was over rough terrain, and the Elk River ran between here and his house. But as a shifter, none of that mattered. Like Jackson and Dane, being outside was the important thing.

Jackson glanced at Dane. The truth was they hadn't really discussed the details. "Not yet. She agreed to see us again... so the door's open."

"So, you're all on the same page. She likes you; you like her. I'm assuming the sexual attraction was there?"

Dane shifted in his chair, a flash of memory and a whole lot of pent-up sexual frustration rushing through him. "Yeah, more than I imagined."

Jackson grunted, and Dane knew he was replaying his kiss with Sadie as well.

"Then it's cold showers for you guys tonight? Or a swim in the lake?" Alex laughed.

Jackson gave a halfhearted chuckle, and Dane managed a weak smile. Alex was righter than either of them wanted to admit. The energy they had both felt from that one kiss hadn't dissipated. If anything, it was stronger now that Sadie wasn't here with them.

"And your bear? There's a connection there, too?"

"There's an incredible connection." Jackson leaned against the sink. "It's all good, Alex. Human, bear... they're all equally frustrated right now."

Alex chuckled. "Okay. On that note, I'll leave you frustrated bears to figure out your next step." He let himself out the cabin door.

Dane walked across the room, thumbing the lock, setting the deadbolt. He turned back to Jackson. "He's right. We do need to decide when to tell her."

"Yeah. But before that, I think we need to make it clear she doesn't have to choose."

Dane nodded. "This isn't going to be easy."

They gathered up the remains of dinner, going through the usual nightly routine. The light was breaking on the horizon when they finally had the kitchen cleaned.

"I think she needs to get to know us—as individuals—before we tell her and before we see her again together." Jackson flicked off the kitchen light. The moon was setting in the west, casting a silvery light across the rug.

Dane sucked in his breath, letting the air escape slowly through his lips. "Good plan. So, who goes first?"

Dane saw the flash of Jackson's teeth in the dim light.

"Like old times... Want to arm wrestle for her?" He turned away, heading for the living room, and Dane followed.

"We're not kids anymore, Jackson."

But he had Dane smiling. Jackson was really just a cub at heart, and that playfulness was contagious.

"Besides, I don't want to embarrass you."

"When was the last time you won? I can't even remember." He plopped down on the couch, resting his elbow on the coffee table. "Come on, Daney. Just like old times."

He'd taunted Dane with that hated nickname since they

were kids. More than once, Dane had tackled him, rolling them both through the dirt and pine needles until one of their parents dragged them apart. He couldn't very well do that now, but he could accept his challenge.

Dane pulled up a chair on the other side of the coffee table, his lips curled into a smirk of confidence. "Fine. Just don't be a sore loser."

▭

Work was challenging. I mean, my job as a vet tech was challenging. It was a walk-in clinic and we served a pretty rural population, so we got dogs that had tangled with coyotes or cats who'd gone a round or two with a raccoon. Plus, Dr. Beckley did large animal practice, and when he was out on calls, I took care of what I could at the office.

But in the two days since I'd met Jackson and Dane, it was a challenge just to get my head on straight enough to be useful. Dr. Beckley needed, more than once, to say my name a couple times to get my attention. He'd finally asked me if I was sick. I'd shaken my head, mumbling something about nothing, and he'd gone back to his office.

There was so much to think about. First of all, for a blind date, it had been good.

*Better than good. Admit it. It was amazing.*

It had shattered all my expectations. Granted, I'd set the bar pretty low, but still, Dane and Jackson were pretty damn perfect. And then there was that kiss... or those kisses.

My cell phone went off, interrupting my hundredth replay of the kiss with the guys, and I burrowed through my purse to find it. Dr. Beckley shouted from the back that he was heading out, and a moment later, I watched his pickup truck pull out of the parking lot.

*Please be them. Please be them... or one of them.*

"Hello?" Even to my ears, I sounded breathless.

"Sorry to disappoint you. It's just me." Peyton's voice punctured my little balloon of hope. "Didn't you look at the caller ID?"

"I was watching Beckley drive away."

"Great. Then you've got time to tell me about the date. You've been avoiding me. I tried calling you the next day, but either you were dead to the world or busy..." Peyton's voice trailed off on a hopeful note. She loved nothing more than regaling me with the details of her dates—and overnights—with Alex. While I was happy for her, it was a bit frustrating to listen to the ins and outs—no pun intended—of her sex life.

"I got in late, and I was a little loopy. I'd had wine." I heard Peyton's snort of laughter. She'd known me a long time.

"And then work and then groceries, laundry, sleep... work." I didn't want to admit I had been avoiding her just a little. Somehow, talking about the date, at least right away, didn't seem right. It was private. Mine. Sharing would make it... shared, like giving away the best of my Halloween candy when I was a kid. I was greedy; I wanted all the memories for myself.

"That's avoiding me. No one does laundry before calling their best friend with all the details."

"Okay. It's just... I wanted to think about what happened for a few days. You understand?" I knew she wouldn't, but that's how we were different.

"No. But I know you. So, are you ready to talk about whatever it was that happened? Can you at least let me know if it was good or bad?"

"Good. Better than good. Really good." I closed my eyes. *Really good wasn't even close.*

"Anyone get naked? Anyone go home with anyone else? You had the chance to double the fun."

"Oh, for crying out loud, Peyton. I'm not that kind of girl."

I held the phone away from my ear as Peyton's laugh cut through the air. For a pint-size girl, she had a loud, bawdy laugh.

"I know what kind of girl you are, Sadie. Which is why I thought this was such a good idea for you." Her laughter died away to a few chuckles. "Seriously, hon. Are you going to see them again? Either of them?"

"We... They said they wanted to see me. And I'd like to see them, yeah. Either one of them... or both."

"But? I hear a but in that sentence."

"It's just that they seem interested, and that's good." I sat back in my chair. I felt like a slacker, but there were no walk-ins and I could finish the paperwork in the morning. It felt good, now that I'd started, to talk this out with Peyton. "But they *both* seem interested, and I think they want to see me... *together*. Again."

There was dead silence from Peyton. "Like both at the same time again? I thought this was just a one-time thing, for the first date... and then you'd figure out if one of them was a good match. That's what Alex and I figured would happen anyway."

"I don't know. It's all confusing... and a little fuzzy around the edges. Let me tell you what happened on the date. You can tell me what you think."

"Please, by all means."

I could practically hear her drooling on the other end. I made a face she couldn't see and went on. "So, near the end, Jackson kisses me—"

"How was it? Is he a good kisser?"

"Can I finish first, please?" I smiled.

"Okay. Fine. Have it your way." Peyton was pouting. I could hear it in her voice.

"Okay. So, Jackson kisses me. And then Dane kisses me. They kissed me in front of each other. How many guys do you know that would willingly sit there and let their best friend hit on the girl they're on a date with?"

"Yeah, but how many guys do you know that go on a blind date with their best friend with only one girl between them? You've got to admit, from the start, they're not your usual New Fane type of guy."

Most New Fane guys would have punched the other one, friend or not, if they'd kissed the girl they were with. But no guy in New Fane would have done the double-blind date either. The guys in this town were old school.

"You're right. So, I'm confused."

"I can't say I blame you, Sadie. Do you think they want to share you, like a threesome?"

I frowned at the ceiling, listening to Mrs. Warner's dog, Mitsy, barking in the back. She must have woken from her dental cleaning. I'd have to go check on her soon.

"I don't know. Maybe. Maybe that's their whole scene. Did Alex ever mention anything like that to you? All you guys told me was that they were both looking for their perfect mate. I still don't know what that's supposed to mean, by the way."

"Alex would have said they were into kinky stuff, like multiple partners or something, if that were the case," Peyton replied. "And he'd never set up my best friend with two guys that just wanted to get laid."

The barking grew louder, another voice adding to the chorus. I'd have bedlam if I didn't go back and enforce the peace.

"Listen, I've got to go."

"No, you can't go yet. You didn't tell me about the kisses—"

"I really have to go. I'll call you later. I promise." I tapped the end call button on Peyton's pleading.

The kisses... I still wanted to savor those in my mind. They were my favorite Halloween candy.

I'd just gotten the door to my apartment unlocked, fumbling with keys and groceries, when my cell rang. I dropped the groceries unceremoniously on the kitchen counter, oranges rolling into the sink. Ignoring them, I dumped my purse on the table, the phone sliding away. Scrambling around the table, I finally corralled it and tapped the screen.

"Hello!" There was more bark in my voice than I intended, and I winced, hoping it was Peyton or even my mother. But I wasn't so lucky.

The deep voice on the other end was male.

"Sadie? This is Dane. Did I catch you at a bad time?"

"Oh, no... sorry. I just walked through the door." I dropped into a kitchen chair, took a breath, and counted to three. *Calm down... It's just Dane. Right... just Dane.*

"I just carried groceries up three flights of stairs, and I'm a little winded." This time I shook my head. *Enough play-by-play.* "I'm glad you called. I wanted to thank you for the other night. I had a wonderful time."

"So, did I. That's why I'm calling. I know it's short notice, but if you don't have plans, I was wondering if you'd like to go out tonight. Nothing fancy. Maybe we can go bowling, have some pizza?"

I stifled a giggle. "It's not short notice, and yes, I'd love to go." No one had asked me to go bowling since high school. Brandon Something-or-Other, and it had been a disaster as far as dates went. But I'd discovered I liked bowling.

"Great." I heard the smile in his voice. "I can pick you up in an hour. Is that enough time for you to get ready?"

"That would be perfect."

I gave him my address, and we chatted for a minute or two, the kind of conversation that meant pretty much nothing except neither of us wanted to hang up first. We finally managed to say good-bye, and I ended the call. In a little bit of a hazy panic, I fished the oranges out of the sink and put the melting ice cream in the freezer.

Jeans and a nice T-shirt with a sweater would do tonight. This wasn't a dressy date. I could be myself and not feel self-conscious in my clothes. I changed and then took a look in the mirror. My hair was still back in a ponytail, the way I wore it at work. Yanking out the tie, I shook my hair out, brushing it until it hung in a fairly organized way over my shoulders. I couldn't say it was a style exactly, but it was presentable.

Dane had said 7:00 and at 6:59, the doorbell rang. I gave myself one last look in the mirror and opened the door. And then adjusted my gaze up a few notches. If anything, he seemed taller than he had on our first date.

Dane smiled, the kind of smile that made the corners of his eyes crinkle, and it was impossible not to return it. He took a step forward, leaning down to plant a kiss on my forehead.

"Come on in." I stepped aside, and he walked into my apartment.

"Are you ready? Not to rush you, but I'm starving. I was hoping you'd say yes, even though it was short notice. I hate eating alone."

"Where's Jackson?" I grabbed my sweater from the back of the couch, and Dane took it from me, holding it while I shrugged into it.

"There's a new case. He'll probably stay with it overnight."

"Does that happen often?"

Dane closed the door of the apartment, and I locked it before we started down the hall to the stairs. "Not usually. This is a pretty quiet area. But there's been a rise in... Listen, our work is boring, and I'm sure you don't really want to hear about all that."

He held open the downstairs door, and we stepped into the cool night air. I was out of practice, being treated nicely by a guy, and I had to remind myself to stop and let him open the door to his Jeep. It was a nice change, something I could get used to.

"I can't imagine your work is boring." The seatbelt clicked home as Dane started the car.

"Maybe not boring, but it's not always the most cheerful topic. Especially on what's officially our first date."

*First date...* It was officially our first date, at least just Dane and me. It was a novel feeling, although I couldn't push back the tiny sense of guilt that while I was going out with one friend, I felt as though I were cheating on the other. I wanted to ask Dane if Jackson knew we were going out. After a brief struggle, I managed to fight back the urge.

But having fought back that urge, I couldn't think of a single thing to say. Making small talk on first dates—or second or third—was sometimes a challenge. And this was apparently one of those dates. With Jackson and Dane, there'd always been someone talking, there'd been wine, which lubricated my tongue, and everything had been easy. Being in the car alone was more like my typical few-and-far-between first dates.

Dane pulled up to a stoplight. "You've been to Stubby's before?"

Stubby's Bowl was the only bowling alley in town. Actually, it was the only bowling alley in the county.

"Not since high school."

"I have to admit I never went there during high school. I heard it was the place to be on Friday nights, though. Most of the kids I knew practically grew up there."

I hadn't. Not many of my Friday nights were spent on bowling dates or any other kinds of dates, for that matter. High school dates had been scarce, and they'd not always been successful. Peyton's assessment of my failure at dating had a long history. I sighed. I hoped it was also ancient history.

"Were you a townie?" I used the term for the kids who went to the high school in town.

Dane laughed, and I relaxed. Making someone else laugh was my defense, and I liked the sound of his laughter.

"No. Most of us—Jackson and I, that is, and some other kids —we were far enough out that we were homeschooled. My mom and Jackson's dad are teachers. So, they dragged us in from outside and managed to pound enough knowledge into us to make us productive members of society."

"I always heard homeschool kids were antisocial." I grinned in the dark. I knew that wasn't true. "Was it hard going off to college? After spending all that time with the same kids at home?"

There was that laugh again. "We seemed to do okay. I think it was harder on our parents, trying to control all of us wild things. But Jackson and I went to State and then the Police Academy."

"Did you always know you wanted to be in law enforcement?"

Dane turned into the parking lot, grabbing a spot in front of the building. Being a weeknight and not Friday, the lot held only a few cars.

"Looks like we won't have to fight for a lane."

I stepped inside, and a wave of nostalgia and a little apprehension washed over me. The thud and crash noises and the smell of pizza and burgers were oddly familiar, even though it had been a long time since I'd been here.

Dane turned suddenly, and I stopped, looking up.

"I never thought to ask... Do you know how to bowl?"

I laughed. "I do. My granddad used to take me when we'd go visit him in Billings. He taught me everything I know."

"Oh, so you've been holding out on me. You're really a pro, and I'm going to get beat by a girl."

I giggled, shaking my head. "I think your male ego is safe. I can manage to keep the ball out of the gutter, more or less, but not much else."

We got shoes, and I searched for a bowling ball, testing the grip on the lighter weights. I took my time, watching Dane out of the corner of my eye as he changed into bowling shoes. He really was a good-looking guy, and not for the first time, I wondered what the hell I was doing here.

He'd been wearing a decent pair of cowboy boots, nothing over the top, no exotic leathers or spurs, just a well-worn and obviously well-loved pair. He stood, grabbed his ball, and took a practice throw.

I was pretty sure my jaw sagged, and I almost dropped the ball I was holding.

He was graceful, powerful, the simple black T-shirt he wore stretching across his broad shoulders and chest. I got another good view of his ass, and for the first time, I had a legitimately dirty thought about what I'd like to do to him in the parking lot.

Then he turned around, smiled at me, and I felt myself blushing from my neck to my hairline. He stood, waiting for the ball return, and I took the neon-pink ball I'd been holding over to our lane.

"Find one that fits? That's always the problem with using a lane ball."

I nodded, dropping mine onto the return. His came back, and he reached for it, walked up, and neatly cleaned up the seven-ten split he'd left behind.

"Want to take a practice throw?"

I did, but I didn't. I'd just watched this gorgeous hunk of man, and now he'd be watching me. From behind. While I'd gotten past a lot of my insecurities, I had a moment of body image panic.

"I'm going to…" I pointed in the vague direction of the ladies' room. "I'll be right back."

I dipped around the corner, breathing hard, and dodged into the bathroom. The mirror showed that I looked as panicked as I felt.

*Breathe… You made it through a blind date with two guys, for heaven's sake. This is just bowling. Breathe… breathe…*

I ran cold water over my wrists, willing myself to calm down. There was no way I could hide in the bathroom for the whole night, so I took a deep breath, smiled at my reflection, and reminded myself there was this amazing guy out there who had asked me on a date.

Dane had set up the electronic scoring thing that always confused me, gotten me a beer, and was waiting for me. He smiled, and I smiled back.

*This is going to be one kick-ass date.*

And it was. I gave up being insecure and self-conscious and threw the ball down the alley. I missed more pins than I hit, but I didn't care. Dane and I talked, laughed, and drank beer. It was a little slice of small-town heaven.

After the second or third gutter ball, Dane walked up behind me as I stood on the approach.

"Here." He put his arms around me. I could feel the warmth of his body behind me, and I closed my eyes for a second as he placed his hands over mine.

"Relax a minute." His breath was against my neck, and I didn't think I could get any more relaxed. It wouldn't take much more contact before I'd melt into a puddle at his feet.

"Like this." He took the ball from my right hand, shifting it to his left. In his big hands, my little pink ball looked light as a feather. He slid his hand along the back of mine, fingers twined between mine. He gently pulled my arm back, his body moving forward slightly.

"Let your arm go straight back. You're swinging it, making an arc." He brought my arm back, then slowly pushed it forward. It was like a dance, albeit a strange dance on a bowling lane.

"Feel the difference?" He was pressed against me now, his chest against my shoulder and other parts of him brushing against my ass.

I drew a ragged breath and nodded. "Yeah. I think I do. I might need another lesson, though."

He laughed, more like a soft breath against my hair. "Anytime, Sadie. Anytime."

The pink ball appeared in front of me, and I reached for it, fitting my fingers in the holes. Dane moved away from me, and I did my thing. I was ever so slightly trembling from his touch, but by some miracle, the ball went straight down the alley, knocking over more pins than I'd left standing. I watched them fall, then turned around to Dane's smile.

"You're a good teacher, Dane." I skipped off the approach. Impulsively, I stood on tiptoe and threw my arms around his neck. I wasn't sure if I was going to kiss him or was just being playful, but then the next thing I knew, I was eye to eye with him, his hands on my waist. I looked into his eyes, and I knew he was going to kiss me.

It was soft at first, his lips against mine, not tentative. Not at all. But gentle, inquisitive. There was a flick of a tongue, and I responded, flicking back with mine.

He slid one hand up my back, cupping the nape of my neck, fingers working into my hair. The sounds around us faded, and every bit of me focused on Dane, on his lips against mine, his hands on my body. Finally, reluctantly, I pulled back.

"Thanks for the bowling lesson." Out of nowhere, I had a sexy little rasp to my voice.

"Like I said, anytime."

We reluctantly stepped apart and finished the game. Somehow, small talk came easier, and I found myself laughing and making Dane laugh. We put away the bowling balls and then sat in the little area behind the bar, waiting for our pizza. We talked about the differences between my dismal high school experiences and his seemingly idyllic homeschool ones. The pizza arrived, and despite one of my idiosyncrasies—okay, insecurities—of not wanting to eat in front of a date, I dove in. It was hot and spicy, the cheese thick and gooey, and I was starving.

I finally sat back, thoroughly full. Dane appeared just as satisfied, and we looked at each other and then the empty pizza pan. And burst out laughing.

"I like a girl who enjoys her food. It's hard, on a date, when a girl picks through a salad and I want to devour a steak. I feel like a big... bear or something, trying to be delicate."

I shrugged, trying to seem nonchalant. "Stubby's has great pizza, and I worked up an appetite."

We held each other's gaze for a moment, and the moment spun out as whatever chemistry or heat or electricity we had built exploded. Dane leaned over, and I did, too, and we kissed right there in the back room of Stubby's. My heart did a lovely little stutter step, and when he sat back, it was like a little piece of me went with him. I smiled, probably something crooked and ditzy. Dane's grin was confident, and sexy, and pretty much said he knew what he'd done to me.

"Sadly, this is a work night for me. I'd really love to stay out..." He looked a little sad, I thought, but he was right.

"I know. Me, too. I mean both... work and I'd love to stay out."

I got my sweater and purse, and Dane settled our bill at the bar. The forecast was right, a foggy mist hovering over the parking lot. We drove back to my apartment in comfortable silence, Dane holding my hand until he pulled up in front of my building.

"I really had a great time. Thanks for coming out, Sadie."

"Thanks for asking. It was fun."

Rain misted the windshield, making the world outside seem far away. It was cozy in the car, and I didn't want the date to end. But I wasn't sure I wanted to take this any further, at least tonight. The vibe I got from Dane told me that if I invited him in, things would get really hot really fast. As much as I wanted that, and him, I wasn't sure this was the right time.

He seemed to be waiting for me to make a move, to either take this further or end the date now. I sighed. It was a tough call, but...

"Like I said, I have work tomorrow... so..." It sounded like a brush off. "But you know..."

"Yeah. I know." There was a beat of silence before he squeezed my hand. "There's no rush, Sadie, really. What we have, it's not going away. At least not for me. The last thing I want is to force you. When the time is right..."

He leaned over, catching my lips with his, the gesture saying everything. I responded, grateful he understood but aware of the longing and desire in his kiss.

After a minute, he sat back. "It's all good, Sadie. All of it."

He walked me through the rain to the downstairs door. We stood under the outside light in the doorway, another kiss lighting a fire inside me that I'd have to deal with alone. Then I watched him drive away, taillights blurring in the dark.

My apartment was dark, and I dropped my sweater and

purse on the couch. I was a little buzzed from the beer, more buzzed from kissing Dane. A little hum of electricity ran through me, that wonderful feeling of expectation when everything is fresh and new and perfect.

I fell into bed, thinking of Dane, his hands, his lips, replaying the kisses we'd had, dreaming of more. Always more.

# CHAPTER 3

THE ALARM YANKED me out of the most erotic dream I'd ever had. It was of Dane, Jackson, and me doing things I never even knew could be done. I flailed in the direction of the clock, knocking it to the floor, where it continued to beep at me.

"Oh, shush." I reached down, turning it off, leaving it lying on the carpet. I fell back against the pillow. "Damn."

It was Friday, and there was work. But first, there was staying in bed, trying to catch the fragments of the dream, to stitch them back together, at least for a minute. But they wouldn't cooperate, and I was left just a little frustrated. But beneath that was the warm feeling of last night's date with Dane. I smiled, threw back the sheets, and went to take a shower.

I grinned my way through work, smiling at the dog that barfed on the waiting room floor, smiling at Mrs. Wilmot who called with her obsessive worry over her cats, all six of them. Everyone and everything was tinged with the afterglow of my date. At one point, I wondered how deliriously happy I'd have been if Dane had actually come up to my apartment. I laughed out loud, startling Dr. Beckley, and I decided I'd probably be insufferable.

After work, I was standing in front of my refrigerator, trying to decide if it was worth actually making a salad or if I should just nibble my way through the ingredients. I opted for putting the lettuce in the bowl and eating it with my fingers, sans dressing, and taking that and a container of cherry tomatoes into the living room. I wasn't a social pariah anymore, so I could watch reality TV and call it an early night. It might be Friday, but that sounded good to me.

The phone rang, and I set my deconstructed salad on the coffee table, rummaging through my purse. I'd learned my lesson. I squinted in the dark at the caller ID. It was Jackson. I took a deep breath.

"Hello." I thought I sounded fairly normal, for once.

"Hey, Sadie. How are you?"

"I'm good." I was suddenly aware I was slouched on the couch in an old sweatshirt and pajama bottoms. I sat up, raking my fingers through my hair. *He's on the phone, silly, not in the room.*

"Glad to hear." There was a pause, and my mind went in eight million directions, all of them coming back to, *He's going to ask me out on a date tonight, and I look like a wreck.*

"I was thinking, if you're free tomorrow, I'd like to take you to a movie, maybe dinner afterward. I'd ask you out tonight, but I just got off a twelve-hour shift and I'm absolutely exhausted. I don't think I'd be very good company."

"Oh, sure." I sat back. *He'd be great company, awake, asleep... Okay, get a grip.* "Tomorrow would be great. What movie?"

New Fane may have had a bowling alley, but the nearest movie theater was one town over in Jenner's Falls. It never had first-run showings, and the late showing was always an old classic.

"You know, I'm not sure. I can find out."

"No, let's go and be surprised. They have some offbeat stuff sometimes. But most of it's good."

We talked about work for a few minutes, but I could hear the exhaustion in his voice, so after we decided on a time for him to pick me up, we hung up the phone so he could get some rest.

I went to bed happy, looking forward to dinner and a movie. It seemed like such a simple thing, but it was perfect. Like bowling had been with Dane.

*Dane...* I thought about what a nice time we'd had, how easy the night had gone. I wanted to have the same experience with Jackson, but somewhere in my heart, I kept coming back to the fact that I was dating best friends. *At the same time.*

But they knew this. It wasn't a secret. Maybe I was the only one who didn't get it. I rolled over, set the alarm clock, and turned out the light. I'd just focus on the date with Jackson, on having fun, on just being myself. And try not to overthink everything as I always did. At least for now.

<br>

I was expecting Jackson to pick me up in his Jeep, but when he walked me to a cherry-red '67 Mustang, my mouth dropped.

"Not what you expected?" He opened the door with a flourish.

"When did you get this?"

"I borrowed it from a friend who collects classic cars. Figured if we were headed out to see a classic movie, we should ride in a classic car." He started the engine. The motor purred like the proverbial kitten, but that was as far as my expertise on cars went.

"Do you know what's playing?" I sat back in the seat, feeling like New Fane's version of a rock star.

"*Casablanca.*"

"You're kidding?"

"Bad choice? We can always drive to..."

"No. Perfect choice. I love *Casablanca.*"

Jenner's Falls was about twenty minutes down the highway. Besides a movie theater, it also had a fairly decent Italian restaurant. Jackson had asked if I liked Italian, so I wasn't surprised when we pulled into the parking lot.

"We've got plenty of time to have dinner and catch the last showing." He held the door open, and I stepped inside Claudio's. From the outside, the place looked like a dive housed in an old brick building. But inside was fantastic, with mellow old wood floors, marble statues, and a huge carved bar with a mirror behind that reached almost to the ceiling. It should have been kitschy, but somehow it all worked. And besides that, the food was excellent.

Jackson had a table reserved even though the place wasn't crowded. We sat in the back, and the waiter came to take our order. I always had linguine with clam sauce. Jackson made a face at that and went with a classic spaghetti and meatballs, along with a bottle of white wine.

"White doesn't go with spaghetti." I took a sip of the sparkling water that arrived.

"No, but you like white. And I want you to enjoy your dinner."

I think I blushed a little. "I'm not used to being the center of attention. Or at least, I'm not used to guys who actually pay attention to what I say... or said. Or drink." I took another drink of water, wishing for a rewind button for my tongue.

"Not a criticism, but I think you've been dating the wrong kind of men."

I couldn't argue with him. "I haven't had the best luck, no. Nothing ever seems to work out for very long." I didn't really want to talk about old boyfriends on a date with Jackson. But it was so easy talking to him, and I found myself opening up, giving him the *CliffsNotes* version of my dating history. He sat back, a half smile on his face.

"It's not easy, putting yourself out there, looking for the right one. It's frigging hard. I've had my share of wrong turns and bad luck, too."

"I can't believe you've had bad luck dating." He was drop-dead gorgeous, easygoing, with a heart of gold. All the things a woman could ever dream of in a man.

"Well, I'm still single." He leaned forward and took my hand. "But hey, if it weren't for all the bad, we've had to go through, we wouldn't know how good *this* is." He emphasized the word *this*, and I felt myself holding my breath.

I'd always thought staring into someone's eyes was corny. At least, any guy's eyes I'd stared into hadn't made me feel like I did looking into Jackson's. My heart did a wonderful little stutter step, and for a minute, all I could do was give him a deer-in-the-headlights stare.

We were still holding each other's gaze when the waiter arrived. With a discreet cough, he waited until we sat back and broke the connection. I caught the little smile on his face as he set my plate in front of me, and I felt my cheeks growing warm. Public displays of affection, aside from the kiss with Dane at Stubby's, weren't usually my style.

The food was delicious, as always, and I resisted the urge to lick my plate, using instead a piece of bread to mop up the tasty clam sauce. It occurred to me, after I'd finished, that a dish made with garlic probably wasn't the best thing to have eaten, considering this was my first real date with Jackson. Somewhere along the line, I'd have to find a mint or a toothbrush.

The waiter came by to remove our plates, and I thought we'd be leaving for the theater. But instead of the check, he returned, setting a single plate with a beautiful piece of chocolate cake between us. With a flourish, he laid two forks on the table and then, with another smile, departed.

"Dessert for two." Jackson picked up a fork and scooped up a piece of cake. He held it out to me, the fingers of his other hand resting lightly beneath my chin. I let him feed me. It was rich and decadent, full of dark chocolate, with ganache between the layers and crème anglaise drizzled over the top. I closed my eyes as it all but melted in my mouth.

"Oh my God... that is heaven on a fork. Here..." I picked up the other fork, took the next section of cake, and held it out to Jackson. He sat back with the same rapt look I probably had on my face.

"That's almost better than sex. Not quite... but almost."

I laughed with him, and we finished the cake, trying hard to savor each bite, but it was too good and it was gone in no time.

"Was that your idea? Dessert for two? I don't remember seeing that on the menu."

We walked down the street to the Mustang, holding hands like high school kids.

"It was. I called ahead, and the waiter was in on it."

"It was very sweet and romantic. Thank you."

"Sweet and romantic? Huh. I was going for sexy and charming. I'm going to have to work on that."

I laughed as he handed me into the low-slung car. It was a far cry from my battered VW, and I thought I could seriously get used to this.

The first showing at the theater had just ended, and there

were groups of people clustered on the sidewalk outside. We threaded our way through and into the lobby.

"It's been a long time since I've been here. But it still looks the same."

The lobby was old school, red velvet, brocade, niches in the walls with carvings of Greek or Roman statues. It all looked a bit worn, a bit tired, just this side of seedy. But the popcorn was hot and fresh, and they still used real butter on it, not artificial oil.

Jackson carried our drinks, and I hugged the big tub of warm popcorn as we walked into the theater. I always got a thrill of excitement walking down the faded burgundy carpet, deciding on the perfect seat, hoping no one would sit in front of me.

"How about this row? Center seats?"

I nodded and made my way down the row. There were only a handful of couples scattered about, all older, all looking like married couples out to see an old favorite movie. I wondered if some of them were married and if this was what they did on Friday nights. Or if *Casablanca* was a sentimental favorite, maybe the first movie they saw together. I sighed and settled into my seat.

"Penny for your thoughts." Jackson scooped out some popcorn. "You've got a very wistful look on your face."

"I was just wondering who these couples are, what they're doing. If they come here all the time or just for *Casablanca*."

He leaned toward me and put his arm around my shoulders. "And I'm sure they're wondering the same thing about us. If this is how we spend Fridays, at the movies, or if we love Ilsa and Rick."

"You're a romantic at heart, aren't you? You just try and hide it under that tough-guy exterior."

"You found me out, Sadie. My cover's blown." He didn't seem too upset as he grabbed another handful of popcorn.

The lights went out, and the music started. I sat back, watching as the movie unfolded. I cried when Ilsa did, agonized with her when she learned Victor was alive, and I felt the pain as Rick watched her plane disappear into the fog. The movie ended, and I sniffled a little.

"I get the feeling I'm not the only romantic."

I turned to Jackson. "Would you have gotten on that plane? Or would you have stayed behind?"

"Well, Rick's not my type, so... there's that."

I laughed and punched his arm. "You're no fun."

"What would you do?" We stood, making our way to the lobby. "Would you have stayed with Rick?"

"I don't know. Every time I watch it, I think something different. Tonight..." I shrugged. "Tonight, it doesn't matter."

"Why not?"

We walked the short distance to the car. "Every time I've seen this movie, I was by myself. Tonight—" I shook my head. "It's silly, really. Tonight, is the first time I've seen *Casablanca* with someone I... with someone else. So Ilsa can make up her own mind. I don't have to." I wound my arm through Jackson's. "I have my own guy."

He stopped on the sidewalk in the middle of Jenner's Falls and kissed me. The kiss had all the passion of Ilsa and Rick— more because it was real. It was Jackson and me.

We finally stepped apart, and I looked up at him. It was dreamy and romantic and everything I'd never had on a Friday-night date.

"I'll take you home now." His voice was low, a little rough. I heard the longing I also felt, but I knew there was this unspoken agreement. We stepped farther apart, and it felt as though part of my heart went with Jackson.

We were quiet on the drive home, but it was a comfortable quiet.

He pulled up in front of my building, and I turned to him. "You're not coming up." It wasn't really a question since I knew the answer.

He shook his head. "It's not that I don't want to. Believe me. But I think we should take it slow."

"Doesn't one of you want to get the advantage over the other?"

He gave me a rueful smile. "No, we don't. It's not like that. We—you, me, Dane—I think we all need to take it easy with this. Take our time."

I nodded. Dane had said the same thing essentially. And I knew they were right.

"Thanks for a wonderful night. I had an amazing time."

"I did, too. Even if you found out I'm not the rugged man you thought I was."

He walked me to the door, and we stood under the light where I let him kiss me again. I watched him drive away in the cherry-red Mustang, and I wondered how long taking it easy was going to take. They were only dating one girl each, but I was getting double-teamed here. And I was suffering double the temptation and double the frustration.

I went up to my apartment, the feel of Jackson's lips still on mine.

▭

"So just how many dates have you had now, Sadie? You're never home anymore." Peyton's pouty voice caught me off guard.

"You have Alex, Peyton. I thought you were talking about moving in together."

"We are... but it's no fun if I can't talk to you about him."

"So, talk about him. What are you guys up to?" I curled up on the couch, pulling the afghan over my knees. I figured I'd get comfortable and have a good hour of listening to Peyton talk about Alex.

"I don't want to talk about him. I want to hear what you've been doing with Jackson and Dane. It's been weeks. Alex says they're never home, so he doesn't know anything either. They're always out with you." There was a big sigh on the other end. "I guess I just really miss my best friend."

"Okay, okay. I miss you, too." I realized I did as soon as I said it. "This whole thing has been just so out of control. In a good way, but it's been crazy. To answer your question, I've been on six dates, three with Dane and three with Jackson. They've all been so great. I honestly never expected anything like this to happen to me."

"You still think they're interested in sharing you, like a ménage?" I heard the voyeuristic side of Peyton in her voice.

I sidestepped the implied request to discuss my sex life. "You know, that's one thing that never seems to come up. We've talked about home, growing up, school—did you know they were homeschooled?"

"Um... no. Is it important?"

"No, I just... Anyway. It's interesting. But no, they don't bring it up. We really don't ever talk about the other one either. So maybe I had this whole thing wrong. Maybe they aren't into kinky three-way sex. Maybe between your dirty mind"—there was a snort of laughter from Peyton—"and my overactive imagination, we misread the whole thing."

"Do you like one more than the other?"

I chewed a fingernail. "No. I like them both... a lot." I liked both of them more than a lot. *I am falling in love with them... both of them.*

"I think I'm falling in love with them."

Peyton's silence told me more than any words could. "What? So quickly? Oh. Wow."

"Yeah, I know. It's not like me at all to fall so hard, so quickly, and it's freaking me out. I have no idea what I'm going to do, Peyton."

And I didn't. I'd fallen in love with two guys at the same time. How was I supposed to tell them that?

*Or worse... How am I supposed to choose between them?*

# CHAPTER 4

I WAS at work a few days later when my phone rang. Dr. Beckley was with Mrs. Wilmot and one of her cats, and the waiting room had several walk-ins, all with non-emergency requests. I was handing out flea and tick drops and hesitated. I didn't like talking on the phone in front of clients, and while Dr. Beckley was pretty laid-back, there was a limit to his patience.

But I couldn't resist. I slipped my phone out of my purse, catching it on the last ring. I saw the caller ID. It was Jackson, and I scrambled to answer.

"Jackson?"

"Sadie. Did I catch you at a bad time?"

"I'm at work. But I have a minute." I ducked into the small office off the waiting room.

"I'll make this quick, then. We'd like to take you out on Friday. There's a decent band at the Crystal Corner. We thought we'd have dinner there. They make a mean steak. And then some dancing. If you like doing the two-step."

I was already nodding, a wide smile on my face. Dr.

Beckley walked by, glancing at me, the same bemused expression on his face I'd grown used to.

"I'd love to. Friday. What time?"

"We'll pick you up around seven. Would that work?"

"Seven would be great."

Dr. Beckley said my name, and I stepped into the hall.

"I've got to go. I'll see you then." I tapped the screen.

Three cats and one dog later, it finally hit me. Jackson had said *we*—as in Dane and him. I stopped with a gasp in the middle of writing out a rabies certificate.

*I am going on a date with both of them again.*

I'd agonized over what to wear, alternating between comfort, with dancing in mind, and looking sexy, with the date part in mind. There had to be a middle ground.

I called Peyton.

"The tightest jeans you own, the tiniest tank, and that black sweater with the sequins. Flats so you can dance and not fall down. I've seen you dance." She laughed, and I cringed.

I wasn't known for my grace, but I loved to dance.

"You think that's going to be sexy enough? I wore jeans and sweaters for the other dates. How about cowboy boots? It's the Crystal after all."

"Sadie, you in tight jeans with those curves, you're sexy enough to turn on any guy. Trust me. And yeah, if you're going country, wear the boots."

I did. Peyton knew guys—and apparently me—better than I did. I dug out a pair of jeans that clung to my hips and thighs and a simple white blouse, leaving a button or two undone. I wasn't quite as confident as Peyton's clothing choices required.

And from the bottom of my closet, I grabbed a well-worn pair of cowboy boots I'd bought ages ago.

The doorbell rang just before seven. I gave myself one more quick look in the mirror. I'd put on makeup, just some eyeliner and a bit more mascara. I hoped I looked alluring and not like someone trying too hard. The glance I caught showed a girl who looked deliriously happy.

Jackson and Dane were in the hall, dressed in clean faded jeans and button-down shirts, and I saw both wore nicely worn but well-loved cowboy boots. I breathed a sigh of relief. We looked as if we belonged together. I liked that feeling.

I grabbed my sweater and locked the door after me.

"Ready?"

I nodded, and Jackson led the way down the stairs. "I am. I've been looking forward to this since you called."

"Do you like to dance?" Dane held the door open, and I stepped outside. It was humid but cool. Fall was in the air, and everything smelled like damp leaves.

"I do. But I'm out of practice. I haven't been to the Crystal in ages." I remembered one date who'd taken me there, and I'd managed to stumble through an awkward dance or two. My date was even more uncoordinated than I was, and after he stepped on my toes, we decided to just sit and listen to the band.

"We usually go down on Fridays for steak if we're not working. They make the best steak around... except for ours at home."

I climbed into the cab of the Jeep, Jackson driving, Dane on the other side. I liked how this felt, both guys here at the same time. The individual dates had been great, but this seemed more natural, like it was somehow supposed to be this way.

The Crystal was busy, the bar crowded, most of the tables full. Jackson cut a path through the crowd and found us a table in the corner. Dane held my chair, we got settled, and a waitress appeared.

The guys ordered steaks with the works. I was starving, and for a moment, I looked at my usual dinner choice of salad. But the aroma of steaks and onions and watching the other people eating changed my mind.

"Steak, rare, the works."

Jackson and Dane exchanged smiles.

The waitress brought our beer, and we settled into a nice comfortable talk, the kind that fills the time while you're waiting for something. In this case, it wasn't just dinner we were waiting for. The chemistry between us was almost setting the room on fire. Individually, these guys were hot; together, I was afraid I was going to spontaneously combust from lust.

Dinner was pretty damn good. The works consisted of a baked potato, vegetables, and sautéed mushrooms smothering a perfectly cooked sirloin. For a moment, I found myself totally engrossed with the delicious flavors on my plate. When I finally came up for air, the guys were watching me with satisfied smiles.

"Did you like your steak?" Jackson sat back.

I noticed his plate was as clean as mine. "As much as you liked yours."

He laughed, and the waitress appeared, clearing our plates.

On the stage at the end of the room, the band started setting up. I excused myself and made my way through the crush to the bathroom.

It was just as crowded there, girls pushing up to the mirror, checking lipstick and combing their hair. I managed to wedge myself between two of them and washed my hands. I looked up at my reflection and decided there was nothing wrong with the way I looked. Jackson and Dane seemed to like what they saw, and for once, I saw myself through someone else's eyes. I was pretty. I looked happy. I *was* happy. And the most beautiful thing in the world right now was the smile on my face.

The band was set up when I got back, and as soon as they swung into their first song, Dane stood, holding out his hand. "Can I have the first dance?"

I nodded and took his hand. He led me onto the wooden dance floor, and I found myself being expertly turned about in a two-step. I found the rhythm, the flow of the steps, and it wasn't long before Dane was whirling me out in a spin.

The song ended far too soon, and we made our way back to the table. Jackson was there waiting, and before I had a chance to take more than a swallow of beer, I was back out on the floor.

Each guy took a turn with me, and each one was a fantastic partner. I was dancing and spinning, laughing, having a wonderful time.

A slow song started, and rather than taking me back to Dane, Jackson pulled me close and we moved in a much slower, much more sensuous dance around the floor. I closed my eyes, resting my head on his chest, letting him move us through the couples on the floor.

The song was over, and he returned me to Dane. There was a fresh bottle of cold beer, and even though I was a wine drinker by habit, this was the best tasting beer I'd ever had.

We danced again, fast, slow, everything that played. It was the most fun I'd had in a long time.

The band played their final set, and when the last dance was done, we clapped for them. Jackson took me back to our table, and I grabbed my sweater.

The fresh air felt good on my warm face. I was slightly buzzed, in a good way, and I didn't want this night to end. Though, I wasn't brave enough to ask them back to my little apartment. If they asked me back to their cabin, I'd say yes in a heartbeat.

*Ask... ask... ask...*

But then, if they asked, who? Which one? Either one? Both? I shook my head, my thoughts jumbled and confused from the beer and from the sheer joy of being with Jackson and Dane.

I linked arms with the guys, and we walked across the parking lot to the truck, breaking into an impromptu two-step on the way. I fell laughing against the Jeep while Jackson unlocked the door.

"Sadie..." Jackson was on one side, Dane on the other. I was trying hard not to giggle. "There's something we wanted to ask you."

"Yes." The word burst out before I had a chance to think. "I'd love to."

The guys exchanged a look. Jackson coughed, and Dane looked confused.

"Well... that's great. But I'm not sure you understand," he said.

"Oh. Sorry. What did you want to ask me?" I looked between them.

"We wanted to make sure you understand this... what we're looking for from this relationship... and from you," Jackson added.

"Oh..." I was confused. The beer didn't help, but there was something very odd going on. "What are you looking for?" Then the light bulb went on, and my heart sank. "Oh, you're asking me to make a decision. A choice." All the fun went out of the evening. They wanted me to pick between them.

"A choice?" Jackson looked as confused as Dane. "What choice?"

"Between you. You want me to tell you which one I want to date." I sighed. "I knew this was going to happen sooner or later. I just wanted it to be later."

Dane's sudden laugh startled me. "Oh, Sadie. You've got it all wrong. We don't want you to choose. That's the thing. That's what we wanted to ask, to make sure you understood."

Jackson took my hand. "You don't have to choose. We want you to be with both of us."

I blinked at him. "Like a threesome?"

"Well, yeah... if it comes to that. And honestly, I hope it does."

"Jackson." Dane scowled at him and then looked down at me. "What we want you to understand, Sadie, is there is no choice to be made. This is exactly the way we want this relationship to be. The three of us. For always. Just like this."

I was dumbfounded, blindsided, and I didn't know what to say, so I awkwardly asked them to take me home. On the ride back, they'd talked a little more about how there was no competition between them, that they were willing to be equal partners in this relationship with me. But for some reason, I couldn't say yes. So, I'd gone home. Alone.

▭

"I can't say I want to go through that again." Jackson scowled with clenched teeth.

Dane and Jackson drove down the old logging road, heading toward home. They'd come from a clan meeting where they'd been bombarded with questions about Sadie, about how she'd reacted to being told they were werebears. When they'd explained to them that they hadn't yet told her, they erupted in a flurry of comments, not all of them polite.

"We did the best we could, Jackson. We were honest. There's not much else we could have done."

"Well, it's not any fun explaining your love life to anyone, especially the clan, especially when so much is riding on this whole thing."

The two men rode in silence until the cabin came into view, the headlights of the Jeep splashing across the front door. Jackson turned off the Jeep and they sat, listening to the ticking of the cooling engine, half watching the shadows. And knowing Dane as well as Jackson did, he was half lost in his thoughts of Sadie, just the same.

"How do you think she's going to take hearing we're shifters? That we can change into bears at will?" Dane's question was the same one running through Jackson's mind.

"I don't know, Dane. I hope she at least gives us a chance to explain and doesn't demand to be taken back to civilization."

Dane was quiet, and Jackson knew what he was thinking. If this didn't work, if Sadie didn't—*couldn't*—accept them, they'd be lost, no further ahead in finding their perfect mate, in finding someone who would accept them for who... *what* they really were.

Jackson ran his fingers through his hair. "Right now, I want a beer and some cereal. We can talk about this later. Nothing's going to get solved tonight."

"Beer and cereal... You must be stressed out." Dane climbed out of the Jeep, his laugh cut off as he slammed the door.

Jackson followed, clicking the lock button on the key ring. "Why? Because of what I want to eat?"

"Because when you're stressed, you want beer and cereal... alcohol and comfort food. You've been like that since you were old enough to drink. Remember, I've known you your whole life."

"Yeah, well, I guess I'm not as good at hiding my feelings as you are." Jackson unlocked the door. They both waited, out of habit, sniffing the air. It was clear, clean, and cold. It smelled good; it smelled like home.

"I'm not trying to hide my feelings. I'm just as worried as you are that Sadie will run screaming for the hills as soon as we tell her what we are. Just telling her what we want in a relationship made her shut down."

Jackson dropped his keys in the bowl by the front door and headed for the kitchen. He opened the cabinet, took out the most sugar-laden cereal he could find, and poured a big bowl. Behind him, Dane opened the refrigerator. A carton of milk and a bottle of beer appeared at Jackson's elbow. Maybe he really was predictable. But desperate times called for... beer and cereal.

Jackson thoughtfully chewed, thinking about Sadie, what it had felt like to dance with her, to have her in his arms. A rush of heat flooded through him, and he set the cereal on the table. It wasn't really what he wanted, no matter how sugary. What he wanted was sweet, sweet Sadie.

Dane watched Jackson, who was lost deep in thought, a grimace on his face. "You really can't blame the clan, though. It's been confusing for them, suddenly having two alphas."

Jackson got up and set his half-eaten bowl of cereal in the sink. "No, I guess not. I'm not sure how I'd react to being told there are two alphas. It's the first time it's ever happened."

The beer tasted better than the cereal, and he took a long pull. "Times are changing. At least the purchase of the tract of land on the western boundary went through. We've got another fifty acres that belong to the clan now."

Dane nodded. The sale had gone through the day before, and it was one of the better pieces of news to come out of the meeting. But there'd been rumors of more humans crossing over into clan territory. For the most part, the bears gave hikers a wide berth, sometimes showing themselves at a distance, just close enough to gently persuade them to head in the other direction. They usually went, sometimes snapping a few pictures but almost always moving off quickly.

But poachers were a different story. Any man with a gun was considered off-limits. Enough of their numbers had been shot in bear form. It was up to Dane and Jackson now, working through official channels, to track down poachers. It was surprisingly easy for them to find their vehicles, take down license plate numbers, and then run background checks. Many times, intruders would find themselves with fines or a date in court.

"It was nice to shift, though. Seems like it's been ages since I've let my bear out."

Dane was right. They'd ended the meeting the way most meetings ended—shifting and going out into the forest. It was a release they couldn't enjoy every day, even isolated out where they lived.

"Yeah. It was. There's nothing better. Between work and Sadie, truth be told, I needed that."

Dane laughed, finished his beer, and stood. "Well, I'm ready to turn in."

"Yeah. I'll clean up here."

"Okay. Good night."

Jackson listened to the sounds of Dane heading upstairs and smiled. He loved this cabin, loved every odd corner and crooked window. He finished off his beer, looking around the kitchen. He tried to imagine Sadie here, sitting with the two of them, talking over the day, making dinner, laughing. Mostly laughing.

Jackson wanted this to work, not only for the clan. They were last on his list of priorities. He wanted this to work for Dane and himself. They'd been playing fast and loose with women too long. Even without being handed this dual alpha role, it was time to settle down, to find a mate. And as odd as it might sound to others, sharing his mate with Dane didn't seem all that strange to him. Unconventional maybe. But it didn't bother him, and he knew it certainly didn't bother Dane.

Jackson tossed his bottle in the recycling bin, took one last look around, and turned out the lights. The third stair creaked, and he smiled. It would be good to hear the stair creak when Sadie came up here for the first time, to them... to their beds. Or bed. Jackson chuckled.

"What's so funny?" Dane stuck his head around the doorframe of his room.

"Nothing. Just thinking."

"Well, don't hurt yourself."

The door closed, and Jackson found himself alone in the hallway.

"Yeah..." He smiled. In his heart, he knew it would all work out. They just needed to give her time. But then he thought about telling Sadie they were shifters, and his smile faded.

That was a whole different story, and he wasn't sure of the ending.

Calling guys was never my thing. It made my palms sweaty and my heart race. But then again, everything about Jackson and Dane made my palms sweaty and my heart race.

This was different, though. My life had changed because of these guys, and even though I'd basically left them hanging, with no clear answer to their questions, I couldn't see living my life without them. If they wanted to share, then I'd learn to live with that. It really didn't seem like all that much of a sacrifice when I got right down to thinking about it. It was just... different.

I punched in the number to the cabin. It didn't seem right to call either one or the other since this was a group thing. Despite my butterflies, I laughed. *A group thing... Sadie is part of a group thing.*

"Hello?" Dane answered the phone, and for a second, I just let the sound of his voice wash over me.

"Hey. It's me."

"Sadie. Hey..." His voice went gentle, as if too many words spoken too loudly might be the wrong thing to do. "Hey..."

"Is Jackson there? Can I talk to both of you?"

"Oh, yeah. Just a minute." There was a muffled bellow, then some other noise, and then the sound echoed and faded for a minute.

*I must be on speakerphone.*

"Sadie? Hi, it's Jackson."

"And Dane."

"Okay, hi. I'm glad you're both there. I wanted to apologize for the other night."

There were two men suddenly telling me I didn't need to apologize, that it was all right, everything was okay, fine...

"Hey... guys?" There was quiet on the other end. "I wanted to tell you that I've thought about what we talked about—what you're... proposing, I guess would be the word."

*Proposing? No, wrong word.*

"I mean, what you suggested."

*Better... sort of.*

I took a big breath. "I'm saying it's okay. Whatever you guys said, I'm okay with it."

There was silence, this time of the stunned variety. Then there were two men laughing, telling me how great this was, how happy they were, hoping I was just as happy. I let them have their moment of relief, smiling at their enthusiasm.

"Okay... well, you know, that's..."

"Hey, sorry. We're just—" I could hear the smile in Jackson's voice.

Dane cut him off. "We're just happy you understand."

"Well, I can't say I really understand. But I'm willing to give this a try. You guys—both of you, I mean—this is probably the happiest I've been in a long time. I don't want that to go away just because this relationship—relationships... I'm not sure what this is. But I want things to go on."

There was more laughter, more talking over each other.

Finally, Dane was the only one talking. "Sadie, we wanted to ask you if you'd like to go camping with us, both of us, this weekend. It's supposed to be the last really good weekend of warm weather, and we'd like to take you out to a place that's kind of special to us. Maybe just an overnight."

"Camping?"

*Camping? Sleep-in-the-woods camping? Peeing-in-the-woods camping?* I hadn't been since I was a kid.

"Sure. Great. I mean, it's been a while." I'd just agreed to an odd-numbered person relationship. What was risking a little poison ivy or snakebite?

"Great. We'll pick you up early Saturday morning. It's a drive and then a hike."

"You'll love it." Dane sounded far more enthusiastic than I felt, but I smiled. Maybe I'd work up the enthusiasm between now and then.

"Okay. Crack of dawn on Saturday. I'll see you then."

*What have I just agreed to? A three-way relationship and camping all in one week?*

Peyton would never believe this. I barely could believe it myself.

# CHAPTER 5

JACKSON DROPPED INTO A KITCHEN CHAIR, exhaustion lining his face. His body ached, and his mind was numb. He and Dane had both just come off a twelve-hour shift, working a case together. That didn't happen very often. Crime in New Fane was usually limited to things like cattle breaking loose and trampling through a neighbor's cornfield or traffic accidents. But there'd been several break-ins, some assaults, incidents that were out of character for their sleepy little town. They didn't know if it mirrored what was happening in other small towns across the country or if something bigger was afoot. But right now, both of them were too tired to even think straight.

"Want a beer?" Jackson pulled open the fridge. "Or something to eat?" There wasn't a whole lot to choose from. They'd been gone so much that the refrigerator was pretty barren. But there was always beer.

"Beer. And then bed. I'm beat."

Jackson nodded and sat across from Dane. They looked at

each other for a minute, knowing they'd have to talk about Sadie.

"We need to tell her, Jackson. She's getting invested in us, in this whole relationship. She understands we want to share. Now she needs to know why."

"Yeah. I know. It's just... I'm happy right now, you know? Happy she's agreed to give this a chance. I want to enjoy that for a little while." He knew he sounded selfish, but at the moment, he was. He was tired, and he wanted to think about good things, not problems.

"Do you think we should still push through with the camping trip? It's going to be a beautiful weekend. I was thinking we could hike up to the waterfall, camp in the spot under the pines. If it's hot, we can go for a swim, let her cool off after hiking up the mountain."

Dane knew Jackson was changing the subject, but he left it alone. "Yeah. It should be beautiful with the leaves changing. I think that's a good idea. It's isolated, quiet... We'll really be alone. It'll give us a chance to get to know her better."

There was something else on Dane's mind besides the obvious elephant in the room. He leaned forward, elbows on the table, eyes down. "So, I haven't been with her yet. Have you?" He looked up at Jackson, who frowned, then shook his head.

"No. We agreed not to... sort of. And I figured you wouldn't be able to keep it a secret if you did." Jackson laughed.

Dane scowled. "Yeah, well, that's not my point. My point is I can't be around her without my bear—and my human—much longer without something happening. I'm just letting you know being in the woods with her... I'm warning you. I'm not sure I can control myself."

"I know, Dane. It's the same for me. Our hot water bill for the month should be zero with all the cold showers I've taken."

Dane stifled a laugh. "There's that... and I'm pretty sure she feels the same way. The chemistry between us—her and me, you and her—it's pretty intense."

"So, what you're saying is no holds barred? If the occasion arises, then go for it? I assume we're only taking one tent."

"One tent, one sleeping bag." Dane shook his head, laughing softly. "I don't want to be that obvious, but..." His voice trailed off.

It was going to be a challenge in more ways than one. Far away from everything, their bears wanting to be set free, and the girl of their dreams all together. It was going to be one hell of a ride.

True to their word, Jackson and Dane were at my door before the sun had officially cleared the horizon. It didn't matter. I'd been awake for hours, anxious, excited, wanting to go, terrified to go. This was probably the watershed moment in this relationship, the event that everything pivoted on.

*Oh, for heaven's sake, stop thinking about it. This is overthinking to the max.*

So, I'd gone over the stuff the boys had said to bring. I had shorts and T-shirts and jeans in case it got cold. I didn't have hiking boots. Peyton had lent me a pair, and I hoped they would be all right. They were a little big, so I'd added a few pairs of socks to my backpack. Or Peyton's pack. I'd never known her to be a nature girl, but her closet yielded the boots, a pack, and a rain poncho. The girl was full of surprises.

They'd said we could swim in the river if it was warm enough. I'd let that comment slip by. Swimming with boys was something I strenuously avoided. But I kind of warmed to the idea of swimming with Jackson and Dane. A moonlit swim with lots of darkness to hide me. A few of my high school insecurities had surfaced, chief among them: wearing a swimsuit. I'd never really gotten comfortable in my own skin, and the idea of being in a suit around those two perfect specimens of manhood rattled me.

I thought back to the afternoon at Peyton's when the topic had come up.

"Get over it, Sadie," Peyton said, buried in her closet, tossing out things she deemed suitable for me to take along. She swore she had a swimsuit I could use.

"Here." She emerged, triumphantly holding what looked like two handkerchiefs with strings attached. "This will be perfect."

"You're kidding, right? Even if it was close to my size..." I took what was supposed to be the top and held it up to my chest. "Look. It barely covers one side of me."

"Yeah, well, they're not interested in how much it covers. They're interested in how much it shows."

I put the top aside, hoping it would get lost in the rubble on Peyton's bed. "I'm not risking getting arrested for indecent exposure. They are cops, you know."

Peyton flopped down on the bed, picking up the discarded bikini top. "You think you're going to finally fuck these guys? You think it's going to be one at a time or—"

"Peyton! Seriously?" But those were the same thoughts I was having, even if the thoughts in my head didn't include R-rated language. "I don't know, honestly." I threw myself back on the bed. "God. I hope it's going to happen. I'm about ready to tear their clothes off. I'm not sure how they're managing to not do the same. I thought guys had impulse control issues. These guys are masters at control."

"I thought maybe they were gay."

I grabbed the nearest pillow and hit Peyton with it. She

*raised her arms, laughing as she fended off the attack. "Oh, come on. You can't believe that."*

*She sat up, grabbing the pillow from me, hugging it to her chest. "No, not really. They're a little too rough around the edges. But it's odd they haven't made a move yet."*

*"Maybe they were waiting for me to get over them asking if I wanted to be shared... or share them... or whatever it is we're doing. So, one didn't have an advantage or something over the other?"*

*"Maybe. Maybe they want your first time to be a group thing."*

*"Oh..." Oh, right. "Group thing."*

*"You do realize that's probably going to happen for real, right, Sadie?" Peyton got off the bed, looking down at me. "I think peeing in the woods is the least of your worries this weekend."*

The doorbell rang, and I jumped, suddenly jolted from my thoughts. I dropped the itsy-bitsy bikini that Peyton had forced me to take. There really was no way in hell I was going to wear that in public or private. I'd just have to wing it if the occasion arose. I zipped the pack and went to open the door.

Dane and Jackson were standing in the hall, looking even more ruggedly handsome than usual. I blinked, then wished someone would come out of their apartment just so I could introduce my boyfriends.

*Boyfriends, plural.* I was kind of getting used to the idea.

"Hey, Sadie." Dane kissed my forehead, his typical greeting.

Jackson, as usual, pulled me into a hug and kissed me full on the lips. It seemed so long since I'd been around both guys, and I stepped away from Jackson, suddenly shy.

"It's okay. Remember, we're all in this together." Dane looked at me, then Jackson. "No competition, like we said."

I took a deep breath, then blew it out. "I think it just hit me what I agreed to."

"Camping? It's not that bad. The weather's nice..." Jackson glanced at me, then at Dane, who shook his head. "Oh, right. The other thing."

"It's going to take some getting used to. Whatever it takes—however long—it's okay. We're not pushing you. If we are, just tell us to back off a little, give you some space."

Dane nodded, and a little of the tension in my body left. I managed a smile. "Deal. I'll tell you when you're pushing, and you can just take a step back."

"Sounds good to me." Dane looked past me at the pack on the floor. "You got all your stuff?" He reached down, lifting the bag. "Anything else?"

I glanced around the apartment. "No. Just my phone and keys." I jammed the phone in my pocket and picked up my keys. "Lead on, and I'll lock up."

There was a lot of laughter and jostling in the narrow hallway and down the stairs. Old Mr. Pinkton stuck his head out of his door, scowling at me. I gave him a cheerful wave as I disappeared down the stairway.

The sun was just coming over the horizon, coloring the sky with pinks and yellows.

"Oh, this is pretty. I can't remember the last time I was up this early."

Dane opened the door of the Jeep, stashing my pack behind the seat. "The drive is several hours, then a hike up the mountain. It's easier to set up camp if we're there before dark."

I climbed in, Jackson behind me. Dane was behind the wheel. I buckled myself in, and we were off.

The drive was beautiful. We took little winding highways and back roads, heading toward the mountains in the distance. Breakfast was in a little diner, the kind with one booth by the window and six stools at the counter. Between Dane and Jackson, with me sitting in the middle, we took up most of the space. But the waitress was nice, and my order came on a plate the size of New Mexico, pancakes hanging over the edge, with bacon and hash browns with onions and cheese. I cleaned my plate almost before the guys did. And for once, I felt no guilt.

We were back on the road, driving the rest of the morning. Around noon, Dane pulled over just as we started up the mountain, and we ate a snack of apples and trail mix. I was still full from breakfast and eager to get on the trail.

"Not much longer. You can see where we're headed." Jackson stood behind me, pointing over my shoulder, one hand wrapped around my waist. I followed his arm, spotting a stand of dark evergreens on the side of the mountain. They looked impossibly far away, but I knew distance could be deceiving in the mountains.

Jackson pulled me into a quick hug, and we climbed back into the Jeep. An easy rhythm had developed, with hugs and touches, kisses happening spontaneously. Nothing seemed odd or out of place. There were a few awkward moments when I got mushed between them when everyone went for a hug at the same time. But we turned it into a group hug and laughed about it.

But while the rhythm might have appeared casual on the surface, the tension and fire running beneath those touches and kisses was anything but. There was a sense of moving toward something, and I knew damn well what that something was. We all did. And it was pretty clear that we all wanted the same thing.

"Here's where the trail starts." Jackson had been driving for about an hour, and he pulled over to a wide spot at the side of the road.

There was a marker for a trail that curved up the side of the mountain, disappearing into the deep shade of the trees. It looked dark and exciting, and a little thrill ran through me.

"I can carry your pack if you want." Jackson held it in his hand. It looked tiny beside his and Dane's huge packs.

But I was determined to carry my weight on this trip, and I held out my hand. "Nope. Nothing doing. I can carry it."

He handed it to me, and I managed to shrug the thin straps on without too much trouble. Jackson and Dane shouldered their packs, and after locking up the Jeep, we faced the trail.

"It's a pretty steep climb for a couple hundred feet, so don't get freaked out at first. Then it levels off and runs along that ridge."

I craned my neck up to where Dane was pointing. "Oh... right."

"We'll stop if you need to. We do this all the time, so we're used to it. But if you want to stop, just give a yell."

"Okay."

We stepped over the low split rail fence that separated the parking area from the forest. The path was dirt and soft under my feet. The guys started up the trail, and I watched them for a second, marveling not for the first time at just how damn handsome they were—how handsome *my* guys were. With a smile, I set off after them.

---

We had finally stopped, me winded and sweaty, the guys as fresh as if they'd just stepped out of the truck. I hadn't really wanted to stop, not just because I wanted on some level to prove myself, but because I had found that once I started hiking, I really liked it.

"This is fun." I sat on a log, struggling out of my pack. "You know, I really didn't think I would like it this much." I was surprised and happy about that.

"You look like you're enjoying yourself." Jackson handed me a bottle of water. "We were hoping you'd at least give this a try. We like being outdoors, camping, fishing for salmon, stuff like that, as much as we can. If you like this..." He glanced around the clearing where we sat. "Then that would be icing on the cake."

"Oh, so I'm a cake now?" I grinned at him, enjoying the momentary look of confusion on his face. It had been only recently that I'd discovered Jackson was incredibly easy to tease, and he fell for it every time. Behind me, I heard Dane's laugh, and then he stepped over the log, sitting down beside me.

"Cake... ice cream... cookies... dessert." His arm went around me, and he pulled me against him.

He was warm and smelled like sunshine and sweat, a good kind of sweat, the kind you get from walking up a mountain. It was a nice, manly smell. But it was doing all kinds of things to my emotions and hormones.

*Manly and dangerous.*

"Oh, yeah... all the good things." Jackson dropped on the other side of me, hand resting on my leg, but only for a minute before he moved it in a gentle caress.

So now I had them on either side, adding more than just kindling to the fire inside me. If I didn't pour water on them, or me, that fire would be raging out of control in no time.

"So how long 'til we reach the campsite?" I took a swallow of water, the cool liquid doing absolutely nothing to put out the blaze that burned inside.

Jackson's hand stopped moving, and Dane shifted away just the slightest bit. The temperature between us dropped a couple degrees, and I took a breath.

"About an hour. There's a river to cross—actually, a small waterfall really. It's an easy crossing, and the pines are just on the other side."

"Oh, wait... Are there bears in these woods?" I'd heard stories of hikers being attacked, especially near rivers that had fish. It seemed a likely place for bears to be.

"I... don't think so." Jackson's voice had taken on a strained tone.

I glanced at him and found him looking over my head at Dane. I turned, looking up at Dane. His expression was just as opaque as Jackson's.

"Is there something you're not telling me? There are bears, aren't there?"

"No. I mean, there are bears all over the place... just not here. Or there are..." Jackson shot a panicked look at Dane.

"What my not-so-eloquent friend is trying to say is there are bears in these woods. But no hikers have been bothered by them this year or for the past several years. Down lower, where the river widens, there have been some sightings, but no one's been attacked. It's a valid concern." Dane glanced at Jackson. "But nothing you need to worry about."

"Oh. Okay. I guess you'd know, being who you are."

Jackson stood up from the log, and Dane made a strangled noise. "Who we are? What do you mean?"

Both of them looked at me as if I'd grown two heads.

"I mean, being on the police force. You'd know about bear attacks and stuff, right? What did you think I meant?" I stood up, screwing the top back on my bottle of water. "Did I say something wrong?"

The guys shot another opaque look at one other, and then both smiled rather strained smiles. "No, we just... I mean..." Dane coughed, and Jackson knelt down, suddenly interested in a strap on his pack.

"I think we should probably get going, right, Jackson?" Dane picked up his pack, shouldering it with ease. "We still have a long way to go."

I picked up my bag, shrugged it on, and winced. My shoulders were sore.

Jackson stepped toward me, reaching for it.

"Here. I'll carry it for a while. You're not used to this. It's no fun if your shoulders are raw." He slung it over one shoulder, and again, I was in awe of just how strong these guys were.

The rest of the hike was much more enjoyable without the extra weight. I was free to wander a bit, look at flowers, ferns, and I saw a deer watching us from the forest, big, dark eyes staring into mine. Then, with a flash of white tail, it was gone, just a few leaves moving to even show she was there.

I heard the waterfall before I saw it. Dane was ahead of me, a mountain of a man walking up the path, Jackson behind me. I caught up to him on the narrow path, and he stepped aside.

"It's right up ahead, just around the next turn. Go on. You'll love the view."

I walked past him, following the path. I turned the corner, and there it was. It was like something out of a fairy tale, a long plume of water cascading from a cleft in between dark rocks, spilling into a clear pool that appeared bottomless. Where the water hit, it sent up a spray that caught the afternoon light, projecting a moving rainbow over the surface of the pool. It was breathtaking, a glorious aquatic amphitheater. Even from here, I could feel the dip in the air temperature. The combination of the warm sun on my shoulders and the cool breeze from the falls was a sensuous feeling, and I understood right then and there why the guys loved being outdoors.

"What do you think?" Dane stood on one side, Jackson on the other. "Pretty, huh?"

"Oh... it's beyond pretty. It's beautiful." I couldn't take my eyes off of it. "It's amazing."

"If you want, we can go for a swim. I'm hot, and I know Jackson can use a bath."

"Funny... You're a little sweaty yourself."

"Yeah. I think a swim would be great." As soon as the words left my mouth, I cringed. *Swimming... with boys?*

"Great. There's a side trail over here." Jackson was already heading into the thick brush, pushing aside overgrown brambles and ferns. "Watch it here. These blackberries are wicked." He picked a few, popping them into his mouth.

I struggled through the berry patch, coming out onto a narrow path. We walked down toward the pool, my mind racing through every possible scenario it could to get me out of swimming in daylight. Then it struck me: I hadn't brought the suit. It was lying on the couch.

"Oh, hey. Shoot. I forgot my suit."

Jackson was at the edge of the pool, pack on the gravel, already stripping out of his T-shirt.

"No problem. We'll just go without."

I watched as Dane joined him, pulling his shirt over his head. Jackson was undoing the snap and zipper on his jeans, and then the next thing I knew, I was watching these two guys, totally naked, walking into the water. Jackson dove below the surface, Dane following him.

*Oh shit. So much for best-laid plans.*

"Come on in. It's not as cold as I thought it would be." Jackson ran his hands through his hair, pushing it back from his forehead.

Dane surfaced a few feet away, standing up. The water came to just above his waist, so I knew if I waded out there, most of me would be below water. Just not all of me.

"Okay. Um... I just... I've never gone skinny-dipping before."

Jackson grinned, looking over to Dane. "Okay. Tell you what. We'll turn around, and you can get undressed and wade out. We promise not to look until you say it's okay. How does that sound?"

I thought it sounded less like a solution and more like an invitation to a whole new set of problems. But I was hot and the water looked wonderful—and to be honest, so did Jackson and Dane.

"Oh, to hell with it." I yanked my shirt over my head and reached for the snap on my jeans. *Damn, I'm not even wearing a pretty bra.*

I had them halfway down when I looked up. Both guys hadn't turned around, and I thought they probably wouldn't now, judging by the looks on their faces.

Neither of them looked very upset that I was sporting a mismatched set of white cotton bra and blue cotton panties. They didn't look as if it was going to bother them that I'd missed a few sessions at the gym or that I really liked desserts.

In fact, both of them seemed to be utterly and completely enjoying the view. Maybe it was the altitude or the fresh air or the sense that I had control over these guys right now. A brand new, totally untested sense of feminine power rose up in me, and everything changed in a heartbeat.

I slowed my mad haste to tear off my clothes and took my time with my jeans. I straightened, reaching behind me, undoing the clasp on my bra. I let it fall forward, catching it just before it revealed all my secrets. There was a hushed gasp from Dane and stunned silence from Jackson.

It was pretty obvious I had their attention. I let the bra fall to the ground, lazily reaching for it, picking it up, laying it on my pack. When I turned back, it was to two guys who stood, mouths open, eyes glued on me.

I'd never done a striptease, but I was empowered to do a little shimmy as I pulled off my panties. I dropped my eyes as I dropped my panties on top of the bra. Then I walked as gracefully as I could into the water.

I was met with two very happy-to-see-me hugs, Jackson wrapping his arms around me from the front and Dane from behind. And I wasn't totally surprised to find two very-happy-to-see-me erections beneath the surface of the pool.

"You didn't turn around." I looked up at Jackson, tracing a wet finger along the stubble on one cheek.

"I'm sure as hell glad we didn't." Dane's deep voice was very close to my ear, and I looked at him over my shoulder. "I wouldn't have wanted to miss that for anything."

"Well, I'm happy to have made your day." All that feminine power was melding with the fire they'd lit before, and there was nothing more I wanted to do now than take this further, to explore and touch and give in.

"Sadie..." My name on Jackson's lips was heaven. "Sadie, we just want to make sure you're ready."

"Oh, hell yes, I'm ready. I know you're sharing—or I'm sharing, or being shared—and I know you don't want to rush things. But frankly, I'm tired of waiting. I've been ready. And you've been ready. And I don't think there's any more reason to wait."

There was a beat of silence, and then Dane's laugh was tickling my hair and his lips were on my ear. "Then by all means, let's do as the lady says."

And they did do as I said. Jackson caught my lips in a kiss that was primal and wild and beyond words. He tasted of the berries he'd eaten, and I flicked my tongue over his lips, suddenly aching for the feel of his against mine. I was instantly rewarded, and our tongues danced between our mouths.

There were hands on my breasts. If I thought about it, I'd have to guess they were Dane's, hands that were gentle but firm, covering most of my breasts, caressing and fondling them, making my body sing with pleasure.

Jackson's hands slid down to my hips, pulling me against him. His erection pressed against my stomach. The heat of him against me was surprising in contrast to the cool water. But the contrast and the heat was singularly the most sensual thing I'd experienced in a long time, and I thought if the world ended now, I'd be happy.

Behind me, Dane moved closer, his cock resting against my ass. It felt incredibly long, and there was blip of shock in what remained of the logical part of my brain, wondering if it was true about the size of a man's hands and the size of their... Because Dane had the biggest hands I'd ever seen.

But rational thought was not what I wanted. I wanted feeling and sensation, and both of them were giving me almost more than my brain could register.

They started this devilish game of turning me around between them. I gave up trying to decide who was touching me where, whose lips were on mine, whose erection was in front or behind me. It all blended into feeling loved and cherished and wanted.

Things went pretty quickly from kissing and touching to hands and fingers exploring my most wickedly sensitive areas. I finally moved myself sideways between them so I'd only have to turn my head for kisses and so I could caress both of them at the same time. It was a distinctly erotic feeling to be holding their cocks, wet and slippery, moving my hands over both at the same time while they kissed and nibbled at my lips and neck.

Dane was the first to venture lower, his lips sliding down

over the curve of my breast. I wrapped my fingers in his hair, watching as he licked and kissed his way to my nipple. They were puckered from the cool air and all the attention, and as he pulled it into his mouth, I gasped. The feeling was intense, little electric sparks running through me.

I turned to Jackson, aching to be kissed, and found him watching. The residual sense that they were in competition rose up, and I tensed. But the look on his face was one of blissed-out pleasure, a look that told me he was enjoying this as much as Dane or I.

Then it hit me. This could work. They weren't going to suddenly punch each other out because the other was kissing me.

And then I stopped thinking about anything except the feel of them kissing me, touching me, of me touching them. They took turns licking and sucking my breasts—until they stopped taking turns and both of them were in front of me and I was looking down at Dane and Jackson, watching as they each lavished a breast with full attention.

I didn't think I could stand it anymore. The ache to have them make love to me was too strong. I tugged at one handful of hair, then another. I got a dreamy, unfocused look from each guy as they came up for air.

"Is there somewhere we can go?"

They smiled, and I blushed. I'd never been the aggressor in sex, or in relationships, but with these guys, it was so easy. And they were so obliging.

"Yes, ma'am. Right this way." Jackson stood, taking my hand.

I looked up at him as Dane waded out to the edge of the pool.

"Towels. There's a sandy cave behind the waterfall."

"Oh, sand. Yeah. Towels. Good." *I've been reduced to single word sentences.*

I ducked under the waterfall, for a brief instant totally engulfed in rushing water. It was exhilarating and something I thought I'd want to do again. But later.

Dane was back, holding several thick beach towels. He spread them on the sand, then knelt, holding out his hand.

For one surreal moment, I saw myself from the outside, as if I were standing in the opening to this sheltered cave. Here I was with these two gorgeous men—two gorgeous *naked* men— who were clearly eager to follow my lead. And who were more than willing to share me. Not compete for me, for my attention... or for my love. They both wanted me, completely and without reservation. It was beyond my wildest expectations.

Jackson was behind me, his hands on my hips. I stepped toward Dane, took his hand, and knelt on the towel. He leaned forward, lips brushing against mine. The touch was gentle, but my reaction was immediate and intense.

I pushed him down until he was on his back on the towel. I caught a glimpse of white teeth flashing as he smiled up at me, but then I was kissing him, claiming his mouth, my tongue dancing with his. He grabbed my waist, and I moved over him until my knees were on either side of his hips. I wanted him, badly, and I quickly lowered myself onto his erect cock.

I broke away from our kiss as he slid into me, thrusting up to meet me. It was heaven to finally have him inside me. I sat back, feeling like a goddess, a rush of sexual power flooding through me.

Hands came around to cup my breasts, and I leaned back into Jackson's embrace. He nuzzled my neck, his lips and tongue flicking over my skin, nibbling at my earlobe. I reached up, winding my fingers through his hair, turning my head. His lips rose, finding mine, the kiss powerful, searing, taking my breath away.

Dane's hands clutched my hips, his rocking up, thrusting into me with more force, more impatience. I looked down, watching him as he watched me, Jackson's hands kneading my breasts, pulling and rolling my nipples between his fingers. I gasped as a combination of pain and pleasure rocketed through me, and I almost bent double as a thud of arousal hit me low in the belly.

I started moving, sliding up and down on Dane's thick cock, rocking my hips, grinding down against him. Jackson moved with me, his breath rasping in my ear, his hands squeezing me. His cock rested against my back, the hardness and heat exciting me just as much as Dane's inside me.

Things took off, rising to a fever pitch in a matter of minutes. All of the pent-up sexual frustration between the three of us had an outlet, and once the gate opened, there was no stopping it.

I lost control first, my body taking on a life of its own. I writhed against Jackson, one hand sliding down from my breasts, his fingers moving between my legs. I screamed as he found my clit, and then I was coming, hard and fast, my body shaking, Jackson holding me, Dane thrusting into me as I shook and rocked.

Then I was moving, Jackson pushing me forward, Dane sliding out of me as I planted my hands on either side of his shoulders. Jackson grabbed my hips, pulling me up to my knees, his cock sliding against the inside of my thigh. I arched my back, almost begging, knowing it would be only a matter of seconds before he would thrust home.

When he did, it was beyond anything I could have imag-ined. The breath went out of me in a soft exhalation, and I closed my eyes as he sank into me. Everything else left my mind as he pulled back, then drove in again.

I was still on the edge, my body still pulsing in a way I'd never felt, alive like never before. I moaned, and before the sound was finished, Dane pulled me down, kissing me hard. I almost devoured him in a wet, messy kiss.

Everything spun out of control. At some point, Jackson pulled away from me, Dane thrusting up to take his place. They took turns, driving me into a seemingly endless orgasm, my body shaking so hard Jackson had to hold me up or I would have collapsed on top of Dane.

On some level, I wanted them to stop, and I tried to tell them I couldn't take it. But as much as it was over the top and out of control, I wanted it to go on, to take me higher, to see how far, how much... how long.

Dane's thrusts grew sharper, more erratic, his grunts and moans louder. He grabbed my hips, forcing me down onto him as he came. I felt every nuance of movement inside me, every pulse that sent molten heat into me, through me. I was consumed by them, by my own body.

I slumped forward, but Jackson pulled me back upright, thrusting into me hard and fast, filling the space where Dane had been. I was a boneless, quivering woman at that point, barely able to focus. But in Jackson's arms, I didn't need to. I could give in, let him use me, pummel me until he came. It was a heady sensation, to lose control, to give it over to someone else and enjoy it so much. I screamed, head back, my body arching against Jackson. Then the cave and Dane below me, the feeling of Jackson's arms around me—everything faded. I gave in to the blackness.

I woke up on the sand, cradled in Dane's arms, Jackson holding my hand. I gave them a hazy smile because they looked worried.

"I'm okay. Really..." I sat up, still smiling. Whatever they'd done to me, my body felt leaden but as though I could float away at the same time.

"We thought we'd... done something wrong." Jackson was still holding my hand, and I gently took it away from him. I was slightly self-conscious, sitting naked in one guy's lap with another manly hunk kneeling across from me. I scooted a towel out from beneath us and managed to cover my womanly bits.

"Nothing wrong at all. Everything was perfect."

"But you... fainted."

I gave them my best I'm-a-woman-of-the-world smile and rose as gracefully as I could on wobbly legs. "I'm fine. I think I'm going to go for a swim."

I left them sitting in the sand and walked to the edge of the cave. I dropped the towel and lowered myself into the pool, wading beneath the cascade of water. And then I screamed, the water drowning out the sound. I had never in my life been—as Peyton would say—so thoroughly fucked.

*And I loved every second of it.*

# CHAPTER 6

"I HAVE RETURNED."

I looked up as Dane came up the path from the pool. He had a stringer of fish, big fish, dripping water on the pine needles. It seemed he'd hardly been gone. Jackson had gotten a fire going and he and I had barely gotten the tent set up and the sleeping bags unrolled, and now Dane was back.

"Salmon?"

"The best. Fresh caught. If the fire's ready and the pan's hot, we can have dinner in no time."

"Everything's all set. There's butter, lemon, some dill."

"You guys really make roughing it seem like a four-star hotel." I watched as Jackson started unpacking what looked like a whole kitchen's worth of cooking supplies.

"Anything I can do to help?"

Jackson handed me a small canvas mess kit. "You can unpack the plates and stuff, set up..." He looked around, then pointed. "There's a log over there. Dane, can you give us a hand?"

Dane nodded and picked up what looked like half a tree, easily carrying it across the clearing, setting it down by the fire.

"Table, chair, all in one."

I watched the whole thing with wide eyes and an open mouth. This was the guy whose touch was so gentle, his kisses so soft, with what looked like super-human strength.

"Okay. Let's get this show on the road. I'm starving." Jackson set the pan on the fire, dropped in a chunk of butter, and watched as it melted.

Dane laid the fish in the pan, and I heard the sizzle. It took only a few minutes for the aroma of frying salmon to reach me. My stomach grumbled, and I realized just how hungry I was. I watched, almost drooling, as Jackson expertly turned the fish, adding lemon and dill.

I passed plates to Jackson, who served up the fish, and I gave a plate to Dane. I took mine and a fork and sat on the log. Jackson plated the last portion, and we sat in the gathering dark.

I took a bite. "This is... amazing." The meat was excellent, rich and buttery, the bright tang of lemon the perfect compliment.

"We've cooked a whole lot of fish out here, right, Jackson?"

"We have."

The guys dug in. And I gave up any illusions that I was a dainty girl and tucked into that meal with both hands. I don't know if it was the fresh air, the swimming, or being with Jackson and Dane, but I was ravenous.

We finished the fish, and from somewhere, Dane produced blueberry tarts and a thermos of white wine for dessert. "It might be a little warm." He poured the wine into the cup of the thermos and handed it to me. "A little unconventional, but then again... so are we."

"I'll toast to that."

We sat around the fire as the sun went down, the dark closing in around our little clearing. It was beautiful, romantic, mysterious. I loved every minute of it.

I had no idea what time it was, but both guys suddenly raised their heads, looking out over to the west... or east. I was never good with directions, but they were. Something was out there.

A flash of lightning and a deep rumble of thunder told me what that was. Before I had a chance to say anything, Dane was heading for the tent, grabbing his pack and mine. Jackson followed him, his pack in one hand and my hand in the other.

We had just crawled inside when the first fat drops hit the tent. Lightning lit up the space, followed almost immediately by a crack of thunder.

"It's come in pretty quickly. I thought we'd have a little more time before the storm broke."

"Did you know it was going to rain?" I pushed my pack to the back of the tent, sitting cross-legged on my sleeping bag.

Dane shook his head. "No. Not really. Just a lucky guess."

The only light was the increasing flashes of lightning. It was eerie but strangely exhilarating. It didn't take us long to continue where we left off at the waterfall. We'd all been just a little shy, a tad awkward with each other. I think their world had been rocked just as hard as mine, and none of us really knew quite how to act.

But now, in the dark, we were right back at it, hands pulling at clothes, unbuttoning shirts, tugging down zippers. There was a giddy moment where I was sandwiched between them, a rigid cock in each hand, someone kissing me, another hand palming my breast. I was lost in a sea of masculinity, and it was wonderful.

They took turns again, each giving me their full attention, every movement bringing me closer to another orgasm. I wanted to pace myself, but then I realized that was impossible. So again, I gave in and let them make love to me, my body reacting without thought, moving instinctively in some primal way I never knew existed.

It was all heightened by the rush of wind outside, the rain pelting the tent, the thunder booming around us. I was just as wild as the weather outside, arching and bending, licking and sucking, taking and giving.

And then, like the storm outside, it was over. We lay in a tangled heap, arms and legs—more arms and legs than I was used to sleeping with—wrapped around me. I fell asleep to the sound of the wind in the pines, a few scattered raindrops hitting the tent, shrouded in an aura of contentment. The last thought I had before sleep claimed me was, I wished it could always be like this.

Jackson woke in the middle of the night, Sadie's rich, wild honey scent surrounding him. It was everywhere, and it was driving him mad. She was curled beside the two of them, her sleeping bag open, her arm and one lush breast exposed. Jackson's beast rose, swift and hot, demanding to be satisfied, and he was suddenly flooded with desires and needs he could not control. It was all he could do not to shift then and there.

Dane was sleeping on the other side of Sadie, and Jackson wondered how the hell he could manage to sleep with her lying between them. How was she not affecting him the same way?

Moving as slowly as he could, Jackson eased out of the tent, padding silently across the carpet of pine needles to the edge of the clearing. The pines rose around him, and he moved quietly into the darkness of the forest. There was no place he felt more comfortable than out here in the wilderness.

Jackson closed his eyes, letting the sounds of the night wash over him, the cool air brushing against his skin. Every part of him came alive, the hairs on his arms—every hair on his body—stood up. His bear was alive, and he wanted to come out and play.

Standing in the dark beneath the stars, he spread his arms wide, embracing the night, letting the ancient energy of his people flow into him. He felt it rising from the earth, coming down from the sky, swirling through him in a cloak of power and strength. He felt the change start in his very cells, that first rush of adrenaline followed by euphoria, something so charged with emotion he'd never put words to it before.

But now he could. It was the same euphoria he felt with Sadie, the rush, the high. That connection—knowing it in his heart—filled him with incredible power.

The hairs on his arms started to lengthen, grow coarser, darker. The bones in his arms and legs stretched, the muscles pulling, snapping. It hurt, but the pain was familiar and welcome.

Jackson fell to the ground, his body changing from a two-legged human to a four-legged ursine. Nascent claws appeared, grew longer, extending from the thick pads of his toes, digging into the soft dirt. His jaw lengthened, thickened, fangs growing to replace teeth.

He opened his eyes slowly, breathing in the world around him. He could smell their campfire, the fish from dinner... and Sadie.

It was dangerous, he knew, to show her his true self before they'd had a chance to tell her what they were. But the desire was too strong. He had to see her, to show her to his bear, to let him know she was really a part of their lives.

He crossed the clearing, nosing open the tent flap. Her

scent washed over him, and he lifted his muzzle, breathing deeply, imprinting her into his mind, his heart... his very soul.

The tent flap moved in the breeze, the zipper scraping against the fabric. Sadie stirred, and Jackson froze.

"Jackson? Dane..." She groggily reached for him and found empty space.

Dane rolled over, sitting up. "It's okay, Sadie."

"I heard a noise."

Sadie turned and looked at Jackson. Their eyes met, and he backed out of the tent, turning and running through the woods. Jackson's exit was less silent than he hoped for. Behind him, he could hear her panicked voice and Dane's reassuring tones.

Jackson scrambled through brambles, heading for the cover of the pines. Then suddenly, he stopped, listening to the night. Sadie's voice faded away, and he cursed his impatience, the impulsive nature of his bear. He dropped to the forest floor, looking over the valley below, the faint sound of the waterfall rising on the breeze. He closed his eyes, letting himself change back, the process reversing. There wasn't any pleasure in this shift, only regret.

"What the hell were you thinking?"

A shaft of light cut through the dark. Jackson turned, watching Dane push through the shrubby undergrowth. He was dressed in jeans and boots and carried a flashlight and a pair of sweatpants. When he saw Jackson, he trained the beam on him.

"Here." He held the pants out to Jackson.

He rose, took them, and pulled them on.

"You scared her enough to want to go back."

"You left her alone?"

"She wanted me to go check, make sure you were all right." Dane waved his hand. "We should go back."

They walked in the dark for a few yards. Dane was angry, and Jackson couldn't blame him.

"Why, Jackson? What happened?"

"It's... I couldn't help it. You know what it's like."

"Yeah. I do."

"Finally, being with her out here. And then having her so close, being able to touch her whenever I wanted to. And her scent..."

Dane grunted. "That's the hardest."

"Yeah. It just got to be too much."

"So, what do we tell her?"

Dane stopped. Jackson could almost feel his thoughts, the turmoil, the confusion. "I think we tell her. Now. Here."

"In the dark? In the middle of the night?" Jackson couldn't believe what he was suggesting.

"You got a better idea?"

"We tell her it was a bear, but not that it was me. Tell her it was after berries, not us. Tomorrow, in the daylight, we can tell her it was me."

There was a beat of silence. "Okay. We'll try that."

Dane turned on the flashlight as they entered the clearing. "Sadie? It's us. It's okay."

The tent flap opened, and Sadie crawled out. Her eyes were wide, and guilt ran though Jackson. It was his fault she was so afraid, simply because he couldn't keep his bear in check.

"Was it a bear?"

She looked tiny and frightened, and they both knew they couldn't tell her now that they were shifters. Jackson reached out and pulled her into a hug.

"Yeah, I think it was." She trembled in Jackson's arms, and he glanced at Dane over her head. "Probably came for berries. They like blackberries."

"But why did it come into the camp? Would it attack us?"

"It probably smelled food." Dane pointed back down the trail. "It's why we hung the food back there. But our clothes might smell like our dinner."

Jackson shook his head, and his voice trailed off. "It just wanted the berries, Sadie. That's all. It didn't want us." He kissed her forehead.

*Except it did want you, more than you can know.*

The sun was coming up, filling the tent with an eerie greenish light. I rolled over, stretching, reaching for Dane or Jackson, finding only empty sleeping bags. I opened my eyes, and then everything that happened last night came rushing back. I sat up, panic surging through me.

The tent flap was open, and through it I could see the guys, Jackson sitting on a log by the fire, cooking what must be breakfast. Dane came into the clearing with an armload of wood. Everything seemed normal, like any ordinary camping trip.

I dug through my pack and found clean clothes. In the confines of the tent, I got dressed, raking my fingers through the tangles in my hair, finally deciding there wasn't much I could do without a comb or mirror. *They're just going to have to love me with elflocks and no makeup.*

"Hey, morning, Sadie." Jackson stood, crossing the clearing. I got my usual hug from him and, when Dane walked over, my usual kiss on the forehead. It was familiar, and it made me smile.

"What's for breakfast?"

"We have eggs, bacon, pancakes... pretty much the contents of our kitchen."

"I'll have whatever's easiest. I don't want to make work for you."

Dane laughed. "Sadie, food is never work for us. You should know that by now."

I sat on the log by the fire and took the coffee Dane offered. It was hot and black and tasted better than any I'd ever had.

"About last night…" I didn't want to sound like a baby, but I wanted to make sure the thing I saw was really the thing I saw, that I wasn't suddenly becoming prone to nightmares.

Dane and Jackson exchanged a look I couldn't read, and my heart skipped a couple beats.

I set the coffee on the ground, sloshing some into the dirt. "Something happened that you're not telling me, right? It was a bear, and something happened."

Jackson pulled the sizzling pan off the grill, and the guys took a seat on the log on either side of me.

"You're right. It was a bear." Dane took my hand. "But it didn't do anything except look into the tent. It didn't want to attack you."

"You know that how? How the tracks looked in the dirt? Maybe you scared it off before it could attack. I heard if you startle a bear—"

"Sadie. It didn't want to attack. Trust me. I know."

I turned to Jackson. "You can't know what it was thinking. It's a bear, not…"

My words died in my throat. Something in Jackson's eyes told me there was a whole lot more to this. Gently, he took my other hand, laying it palm down on top of his big hand. Mine looked tiny, the ends of my fingers far from the ends of his.

"Do you trust me, Sadie? Do you trust us?"

I looked from our hands into his eyes. "I do. But what—"

He stood, pulling me with him. "I want to show you something." We walked across the clearing to the edge where there was a swath of bare ground. "Here... look."

He pointed, and I looked down. There, in the dirt, was a track.

I looked back to Jackson. "That's a bear track? It's huge..."

"It's a bear track." He knelt, placing his hand in the indention, softly, almost reverently. "It's also my track." He looked up at me. His eyes held so many emotions: sadness, fear, hope.

"I don't understand."

"He's telling you he's the bear, Sadie." Dane was behind me, not touching me, but close enough that I could feel the warmth of his body. "We're bears, Sadie. We're shifters."

The world tilted in a sickening way, and I closed my eyes. I'd met guys who were a little off-center and held some strange beliefs, but this took the cake.

"You mean you run around in the woods and pretend to be bears?" I wanted to believe they were just nature boys, that they really just enjoyed nature. "Right? Or like a totem animal? A Native American thing?"

"No, it's not pretend." Jackson stood, towering over me. For the first time in a long time, I was afraid. I was afraid of Jackson and Dane.

"We're shifters, beings who can turn—shift—into an animal form. Our clan—that's what we call our family—are bear shifters." Dane's voice was totally rational, but his words were crazy talk. No one could turn into an animal. It wasn't possible.

I made a sound like a laugh, and Jackson's brows drew together. "You're making this up. You're trying to scare me, making a joke out of me being afraid of the bear." I stumbled away from them. "You're mean, if that's what you're doing. I thought after... I thought I could trust you." I turned, tripping over a tree root, the earth coming up fast to meet me, knocking the wind out of me.

Dane was there first, hand on my arm, helping me up. But I shook him off, scrambling through the pine needles.

"Don't touch me. I want to leave." I finally got to my feet, breathing hard. "I'm heading back."

"Sadie, listen. We're not making this up. If we show you, if Jackson shows you what he is, will that make it easier to believe? Please, Sadie. You have to know it's not easy for us either, keeping this a secret."

"We didn't know how to tell you." Jackson stood at the edge of the clearing, and I watched as he toed off his boots. "If I show you—"

"You can take your clothes off. You can run around and pretend to be a bear and then get dressed if that's what it takes to get you to take me home." I folded my arms. My chest was tight from holding back tears, and my heart literally hurt.

Jackson pulled his shirt over his head and then undid the snap and zipper on his jeans. I'd seen this performance before, and a thrill of desire zipped through me as he pulled off his pants. But I shook my head. This was the guy who was trying to get me to believe he was a bear.

"Sadie, this is going to be intense. I can't tell you it's going to be easy to watch, but if you want to know us—the real Jackson and Dane—this is part of the deal."

I had this image of Jackson dropping to the ground, running around on all fours, and then we'd laugh about it. But instead, he stiffened, arms and legs going rigid. He closed his eyes, head back, and I watched as the most bizarre thing I'd ever seen began.

Coarse dark hair sprouted, grew long and thick, covering Jackson's skin. It was like a time-lapse photo or something, and for a moment, I was totally engrossed in whatever the hell this was. It took me a minute to realize his arms and legs were contorting beneath the pelt that grew over him. They somehow grew and thickened at the same time, taking on the rough proportions of a bear standing on its hind legs.

I stood, frozen in place, shocked and terrified at the scene unfolding in front of my very eyes. This couldn't be true. It couldn't be happening. But it was. Jackson—*my* Jackson—was shifting into a bear. A real, live bear.

He dropped to the ground, and for the first time, I really looked at his face. His jaws changed, thrusting forward from his face, turning into a short muzzle. Fangs were visible behind the snarling lips, long fangs, very white fangs.

Where there had been hands and feet resting on the ground, there were thick paws with huge claws extending from them.

Then it was over. Across the clearing stood a huge bear, dark-brown fur catching the morning sun. It was beautiful in a strange, otherworldly way. I swallowed, my dry throat clicking. Behind me, there was movement. It was Dane, and I wanted to move away from him, but I was rooted to the spot.

It, or *he*—I couldn't call it Jackson anymore—opened its eyes, looking at me. I blinked, then blinked again.

In those brown depths was Jackson, the same man I loved, looking at me intently from behind the face of the bear. The same hope, fear... and love I'd seen on Jackson's face was reflected in the gaze of this huge beast. The world took another sickening spin and everything went gray around the edges, and from a distance, I heard Dane's voice calling my name.

*This can't be real. This can't be real. It's not real. Please...*

Then I was falling, gravity pulling me down in slow motion. The bear was looking at me, saying my name.

*But bears only talk in fairy tales.*

And then gray went to black.

I opened my eyes and screamed. The bear was looking at me. I screamed again, and the bear was gone. Then it was Jackson, concern etched in his face. Dane appeared over his shoulder. I tried to sit up, but one or the other pushed me gently down.

"Just lie still. You're okay. Okay? Just lie still." Jackson's voice sounded strange, and he looked pale. "We're going to take you home soon." He disappeared from view.

"What happened?" My voice was just as strange, weak and shaky.

"You fainted." Dane sat down and held my hand. I wanted to pull away, but it felt good. The contact felt normal. "I don't think you hit your head. I caught you before you hit the ground."

I tried again to sit up, this time managing to struggle past Dane's protests. "I'm fine. Really."

Jackson sat a few feet away, barefoot, wearing just his jeans. He looked as shaken as I felt.

It came back to me. Jackson taking off his clothes, changing...

"You turned into a bear."

The guys were silent, exchanging worried looks. Finally, Jackson stood, walking tentatively toward me as if I were going to bolt back down the mountain. The thought crossed my mind, but the fear I'd felt earlier had faded, dulled around the edges. Right now, it wasn't fear as much as betrayal that filled me.

"Yes. I did. It's... like I said. It's what we are."

"And it didn't occur to you that I might have wanted to know this, oh, like when we first met?" My voice rose with each word, and I took a deep breath, trying to quell my rising sense of panic. This was all so unreal, and I was totally out of my depth.

"We wanted to tell you..." Jackson shrugged. "Between both of us wanting you... wanting a relationship with you, and the shifter aspect, we thought it would be too much all at once, that it would scare you off before you got to know us."

"Well, you were right. This is all..." I stood. The world got really bright, and I covered my eyes with my hand.

"Sadie, sit down. Please. You're upset, and you fainted. You need to at least—" Jackson took my arm, but I shook him off.

"Stop telling me what I need! I need to get away from you, both of you. I need to go home."

The guys stepped back, exchanging glances. I walked on trembling legs to the log by the fire. The bacon in the pan was burned, the coffee pot turned on its side.

Dane picked up the pot, pouring out the cold coffee. "We'll pack up, head back down, and drive you home."

"Fine. I'll get my stuff."

The tent was warm now that the sun was higher. I gathered the few things that weren't in my pack and crammed them inside. I looked over the tangle of sleeping bags and thought about last night, right before the bear showed up. *Before Jackson showed up. Jackson as a bear.*

I'd managed to adjust to not one, but two amazing guys wanting to date me. I'd even gotten past both of them wanting to have a relationship with me at the same time. But I was pretty sure I'd have to draw the line at... shifters. Men were men, not bears.

Suddenly, desperately, I wanted to talk to Peyton, to tell her about all the strangeness of this trip and to have her tell me everything was going to be okay. I desperately needed my best friend.

My mind raced in a flurry of thoughts. *Does Alex even know the truth about his two friends?*

I fished my cell out of my pocket and prayed there was some kind of service up here. But there were no bars, nothing. Sighing, I stuffed the phone back in my pocket.

The guys broke camp quickly, and we left the same way we came, heading down past the waterfall. Our tracks had been washed clean by the rain, at least the ones outside the cave. But I knew if I went beneath the waterfall, I'd find footprints, and more, in the sand, mute reminders of what had happened.

I turned my back on the pool in the forest and headed down the path after the guys. All of that was in the past. I was headed toward my future. A future without Jackson and Dane.

# CHAPTER 7

IT WASN'T until we were almost home that I reached Peyton. We'd stopped for gas about an hour away from New Fane. It had been a tense, silent ride, and the relief at hearing her voice was almost a physical sensation.

"Sadie. Are you back? How was the great wilderness?"

"I'm not back. I don't really know where I am. But... can I have them bring me to your house? I need to talk to you." Tears choked my voice.

Dane looked up, and I turned my back on him, walking away.

"Yeah, sure. Are you okay?"

"No. But I can't talk about it now."

Dane and Jackson were watching me, looking worried. They'd tried to talk to me while coming down from the mountain, but the last person—people—who could give me any perspective on this was them. They were the reason I was confused, scared. They were swirling around in all this mess with me.

I told them where I wanted to go, and Dane, who was

behind the wheel, nodded. The rest of the drive reverted to silence.

"Sadie..."

I shot Jackson a look that meant I wasn't interested in what he had to say, but he went on. Dane kept his head forward, eyes on the road, but by the tense way he held his shoulders, I knew he was just as anxious to add his thoughts.

"No, listen. I want to say this. I want to apologize for how this weekend went. More than anything, I want to tell you how sorry I am you were scared. That I frightened you. It wasn't what I wanted to do at all."

I sat, arms crossed over my chest. I counted to three... five... "Well, how the hell did you think I was going to react to a bear sticking its head into the tent? Did you think I was going to jump up and embrace you?"

"No... of course not. I shouldn't have done that. And I'm sorry. Sorrier than you can know."

"The last thing we wanted was to ruin this relationship." Dane glanced at me, then back to the road. "What we have... how far we've come..."

"*Had*... what we had." I shook my head. "I don't think I can see either of you again."

"Because we're shifters?" There was an edge to Jackson's voice.

I frowned. "You act as though this is something trivial. But you're a bear... bears. Besides that, which is crazy enough, essentially, you lied to me. You let me fall in love with you, with both of you, and then you drop this... this *thing* on me. How do you expect me to feel?"

"You love us?" Dane's voice had taken on a hushed tone.

"I did." That undid the floodgates, and I let the tears I'd held back since that morning run down my cheeks. "I loved you too much for my own good."

Dane reached for my hand, but I pulled it away.

As we pulled up, I could see Peyton watching out of the window of her apartment. Dane parked at the curb, shutting off the engine. There was a moment that stretched on, and I knew they wanted to say something else. I felt trapped between them, and it made me angry. Or I wanted to be angry. These were the two men I'd decided I could love, both of them at the same time. They'd made feel safe, and now they scared me.

"Let me out, please."

Dane shifted behind the wheel, turning to look at me. "I just want to say I'm sorry, Sadie. Once more. And to ask that you at least think about giving us a second chance."

"You said you loved us. That has to count for something."

"I also said that you lied to me. You had a secret and it affected me, and you kept it a secret until I'd gotten in too deep. How can I trust you? How do I know there aren't any other secrets you're going to throw at me?"

There was that look between them again. This time I knew something was up. I was learning, finally, to read their expressions.

"What? There's more, isn't there?" I held up my hands. "I don't care. I don't want to know."

"You're right. There is something else. It has to do with our clan."

I shook my head. "No. I don't want to know. Really. Just let me out." I pushed against Jackson, but it was like pushing against a wall. "Please. Let me out."

He sighed, but he opened the door, stepping out of the Jeep. I slid across the seat.

Dane had gotten out, and he came around the front,

carrying my pack. I held out my hand, but he held on to it. "Sadie..."

"Give me my pack." I grabbed a strap, pulling hard. He let go, and I took a surprised step back. I wrapped my arms around the pack like it was a life preserver and I was sinking. I was, but I wasn't going to give in to my feelings here on the sidewalk.

I turned, looking at Peyton framed in the window. I expected a look of righteous anger or something equally powerful. Peyton had never been one to hide her feelings.

But as I walked up the sidewalk, I realized she wasn't even looking at me. She was focused on the men on the sidewalk, and she looked... not at all as I thought she should.

I looked over my shoulder. Dane and Jackson stood there watching me. I looked back to Peyton. And in this bizarre triangle, she was looking at them. Something was wrong with the geometry in this picture. This had gone from a threesome to a foursome... from a triangle to a square.

*Something is wrong here, very, very wrong.*

Peyton was holding the door open for me, and I walked into her apartment, dropped my pack, and burst into tears. She pulled me into a hug, patting my back in a distracted way. With her arm still around me, we sidestepped awkwardly to the couch, where we plopped down on the cushions.

My tears trailed off, and I looked up at Peyton. The look on her face as she'd watched Jackson and Dane was still there, and it was still out of place.

"Peyton?" For a minute, I almost forgot about boys and bears. "Peyton, what's wrong?"

She let go of me and stood. "I'm having tea. Do you want some?" She disappeared into the kitchen. I could hear water running, the bang and clatter of cupboard doors and tea mugs, then her muffled voice. "What happened? You scared me when you called."

Boys and bears came rushing back in my head. "Sorry. I was... emotional." *That's an understatement.* "I didn't mean to scare you."

Peyton came back with two mugs of tea, setting mine on the coffee table. "I thought you'd been attacked..." Her voice trailed off, and she suddenly found something very interesting in her tea.

"I was, sort of. At least it felt like an attack." I took the tea, something Indian, full of spices, heavy on cloves, sweetened with organic honey. There wasn't much in Peyton's life that wasn't organic.

She sat in the cane chair across from me. "What's going on, hon?"

I shook my head. How could I even begin to explain? I'd seen something I didn't understand, that I didn't think anyone could understand. I wanted to tell Peyton, to have her freak out with me so I didn't feel so alone knowing this... *thing* about Jackson and Dane. I leaned forward, the cup rattling on the coffee table as I set it down.

"Sadie, what's wrong? You're white as a ghost. Are you sick?"

I shook my head. "No. Nothing like that. It's something that happened... something with Jackson and Dane."

"What is it?" Her eyes went wide, and she spilled a little tea on her skirt.

I ran my fingers through my hair, my head pounding. This was harder than I thought it would be.

"Jackson changed into a bear." I sat forward, waiting for Peyton to freak out the way I had. The way any normal person would react when she heard full-grown men turned into full-grown bears.

But Peyton didn't freak out, and somehow that was almost as bad as watching Jackson morph into a bear. Because if Peyton wasn't freaking out, that meant she knew something I didn't.

"Peyton?"

She looked away, out the window, down at the floor. Anywhere but at me.

"Peyton..."

"What do you want? Yes, I knew. Alex knows. He's their best friend."

"And you're *my* best friend. When were you going to tell me?" I shivered, pulling the throw on the couch around my shoulders. "Was it everyone's idea to keep me in the dark about this?"

"It was originally Alex's idea, yeah. He thought it would be too much..."

"Unbelievable. Does everyone think I'm fragile or something?"

Peyton laughed. "Well, you know, you pretty much freaked out when they told you they wanted a joint relationship. You had to think about it, Sadie." She leaned forward. "You had to think about having a relationship with two guys who are crazy about you."

"Don't give me that. You thought it was a bit strange yourself, Peyton."

"Yeah, but I didn't tell you to give up on them."

"But this is a little more extreme, don't you think? They change into bears, for crying out loud. Jackson changed right in front of me." I shivered at the memory. I still couldn't believe I'd watched it. Who did that? "But you knew that already. How did you know?"

"Alex told me after you went out with them a few times. He's known them forever, and he was so happy for them... and you. He... I don't think he meant to tell me before they told you. He was just so excited about the whole thing."

"You've known all along? And as my best friend, it didn't occur to you to tell me who... or *what* I was dating? It all seems so crazy to me. I can't believe you'd keep this from me."

Peyton shifted in her chair, shaking her head. "Do you want the truth? I thought they'd have told you by now. I really did. I think they messed up by waiting. And they sure as hell messed up by springing it on you in the middle of the woods." She bit her lip. "But it wasn't my secret to tell, Sadie. Can you see that? When I found out you were actually interested in them, I was so excited. Our boyfriends being close friends, and us... I couldn't believe it. I was so happy for you. For all of us."

"Did you know from the start they wanted to share me? That they wanted to make this a threesome?"

She shook her head. "Not that, no. That took me by surprise."

"You're surprised they wanted to share me, but not that they change into bears?"

She made a face but didn't answer.

As soon as I saw her face, I knew why. Alex was their friend. They were bears.

*Oh my God...*

"He's a bear thing too, isn't he? You're dating a bear guy?"

Peyton rolled her eyes as if I were three-quarters simple. I hated when she did that. "They're called shifters, not bear guys or whatever. And Alex isn't a bear shifter, no. He's a wolf shifter."

I stared at her. "You're kidding. And you're okay with that?"

"Yes, as a matter of fact, I am. I love the guy, Sadie. He's the best thing that's ever happened to me. The fact that he's a shifter?" Peyton shrugged. "It's sexy, to be honest. It just makes him even more different from anyone I've ever known before. There's all this controlled power and his beast and then..."

For the first time since I'd known her, Peyton blushed. Then she cleared her throat and came to sit beside me on the couch.

"Sadie, I'm sorry. If I could turn back time, I would. If I had known how this would play out, I'd have told you in a heartbeat they were shifters." She took my hand, squeezing it, but I didn't return her gesture. I wanted to be mad for a little bit longer. "I wanted the best for you... I still want the best for you. And Jackson and Dane, I think, *are* the best for you. But I'm sorry, really sorry you got hurt by all of the secrecy."

Something unclenched inside me, a bit of the hot anger cooling, and I squeezed her hand. She was my best friend, and yeah, she'd made a mistake. But if I couldn't forgive my best friend, then where was I? I'd be without any friends, best, boy, or other.

"It's okay, Peyton, sort of. Not the best, but better. You got stuck with a secret that wasn't yours to tell, I guess. Mostly, I'm confused, and I'm still mad at you, for now at least."

"You can be mad. It's okay. I have thick skin." She hugged me, and I hugged her back. It would be okay between us, but not right away. We both knew that, and for now, it was good enough. "Besides, I deserve it."

My head hurt. My heart hurt. Nothing made sense anymore. Everyone had a secret life, and my best friend knew more about the guys I was dating than I did.

Peyton drove me home, and I walked up the stairs, dragging my pack behind me. It seemed like an eternity since I'd been here. My life had changed, been turned sideways, upside down. The people I trusted—loved—they all had secrets.

I took a shower, washing away the scent of being in the woods and being with Dane and Jackson. I smelled like sex, and before the whole bear-in-the-boyfriend surprise, I was enjoying the wild, erotic scent of the guys that surrounded me. But now it made me feel icky, and it was just a reminder of how this whole relationship had failed.

After that, all I wanted was sleep. I was drained, emotionally and physically. I tumbled into bed naked, pulling the blankets around my shoulders. The room was dark and cool, and I should have dropped off to sleep.

But I tossed and turned, fighting with my pillows, my mind playing over every word everyone said. I rolled over, squinting at the alarm clock. I'd been in bed for only an hour, but it seemed like an eternity.

I rolled onto my back, staring up at the ceiling.

I didn't want to think about Jackson and Dane, but there was a stubborn part of my mind that refused to give it up. Like a toothache when you can't help poking that tooth with your tongue, I let my mind wander, let the thoughts surface.

The first date... confusion, then nerves, then relief. More confusion. What the hell did they want?

They told me what they wanted; they wanted *me*. And that had confused me even more. Guys were supposed to be competitive. They should be trying to one-up each other or outdo the other for my attention and affection. But they both wanted me. It wasn't a competition. It was something else.

When I'd finally stopped fighting the idea and gotten my head around how this just might work, it seemed perfectly logical. It also seemed magical and wonderful, and it was certainly the most sexually charged relationship I'd ever experienced.

I fell in love with them then, heart and soul, and I sure as hell hoped at some time soon, body. They'd been extremely restrained in the sex department, and at times I wondered if there was some ulterior motive behind the lack of, for the lack of a better term, real sex. The chemistry between us was intense, and I wondered how many cold showers they were taking.

For one shocking afternoon, after reading an English historical book, I wondered if they were gay and I was a ruse to the world. But this wasn't repressed England, and if they were gay, why hide behind me? That idea got tossed out, and I put away the book.

The past weekend had shattered any illusions that there was a problem with sex. It had blown my mind. They were attentive and assertive, gentle and forceful, and obviously confident enough to let me, for the first time in any relationship, take control for a while. It was a heady sensation, and I felt like an equal partner. That had never happened before.

Lying in the dark, I realized I was smiling.

But then this whole bear-shifter stuff happened. I rolled over onto my side, anger and betrayal flooding through me in a toxic mix. All my trust had been destroyed. How the hell could two grown men keep that a secret from the woman they said they wanted to spend their life with, the woman they claimed was their perfect mate? They should have told me.

*And how would they have done that?*

I hugged my pillow. For the first time since I'd woken to the sounds of a bear—Jackson the bear—outside the tent, I thought about how Jackson and Dane must have felt. I didn't want to. I wanted to nurse my broken heart, to whine to Peyton, to cry over this betrayal.

But those thoughts started working their way to the surface. I didn't want to see their side of it. They'd kept a secret, a big one, from me. They should have told me.

*How?*

I sat up, throwing the pillow to the end of the bed. How do you tell someone you can change into a bear? When would have been the best time to tell me? On our first date, when I discovered there were two guys who wanted me? Later, when they told me they wanted to share me equally?

*We want a threesome, and oh, by the way, we're bears.*

I didn't want to admit it, but it must have been hard for them, wanting me to know, but not knowing when or how.

Then it hit me, the proverbial bolt of lightning. They must have thought the camping trip would be the perfect place. For one thing, I was stuck there with them. I couldn't very well run away or drive away. I'd have to listen—or watch.

Something must have gone wrong. Jackson wasn't mean; neither was Dane. There must have been a reason he changed. That couldn't have been how had they had planned to tell me they were shifters.

"Shifters." The word sounded strange and foreign. I said it again, and it echoed in my bedroom. My empty bedroom.

I could be in a tent with Dane and Jackson. Or somewhere else with them. We could be together, instead of me alone here and them there.

Maybe I'd made a mistake, reacted too quickly, acted rashly.

I reached for my jeans, finding my cell phone. I sat with it for a minute, fingers floating over the buttons. Did I want to call them and tell them I'd thought about it? Or did I want to sulk in my room in the dark, nursing a broken heart?

"Should we call her?"

Dane sat across from Jackson at the kitchen table. He had a can of soda, and for once, Jackson didn't want a beer. Or cereal. For some reason, he wanted to experience the welter of emotions that burned inside him, and he had the feeling Dane was going through the same thing. They knew Sadie was out there, either at Peyton's or at her apartment, feeling a thousand times worse than they did. They'd broken her trust in them, and they'd broken her heart.

"No. Not yet. She needs space."

"Yeah, okay. But..." Dane took a drink of soda and made a face. He stood and poured the rest of it into the sink. "I just feel... like I should be doing something."

"I know. But she's got to work through this. The more we push, the more we push her away."

Jackson knew Dane was right, but that didn't make things any easier. His mind was going in a million directions. They'd messed up the whole thing. They couldn't blame her for wanting to get as far away from them as she could.

"I'm going for a walk." Dane opened the front door, the soft late afternoon air moving past him.

"You want some company?" Jackson stood, but he shook his head.

"No. Not really. I need to think... or not think."

The door closed, and Jackson was alone. It wasn't a nice feeling at all. He wanted someone.

No, not *someone.*

He wanted Sadie.

# CHAPTER 8

I WAS STILL SITTING with my phone in my hand as darkness fell outside. I'd been at war with myself, the part of me who was betrayed and hurt wanting to roll around in all that pain, playing victim, feeling sorry for myself.

The other part wanted my guys back, regardless of who or what they were. I missed them, and somewhere inside, I'd started feeling bad for them as well as myself.

Something Peyton said—well, a lot of things Peyton said—kept running through my mind.

*"When are you ever going to find another man, much less two, who are going to love you like they do?"*

She was right. I'd never find anyone like Jackson and Dane. Ever.

Peyton had also said I was making things too complicated, overthinking like I always did. And after lying here in my bed for the better part of the afternoon, I had to agree. I'd thought of this from every angle, and it all came back to the fact that I missed them.

I hit send, and the phone rang on the other end. Before I'd even really thought of what I wanted to say, Jackson was there.

"Hello?"

"Jackson? It's Sadie."

"Sadie. Hi... Let me get Dane." There was the now-familiar underwater sound of the phone going to speaker, the rumble of Jackson's voice calling Dane's name.

"Sadie? We're here."

There was a weighted silence on the other end, and I suddenly felt like I did in high school, standing before my English class, expected to discuss hidden symbolism in the novels of Flannery O'Connor. My mouth went dry, and my hands trembled.

"Sadie? You still there?" Dane's voice brought me back.

"I'm here. I... It's... This is hard. I want to say... I want to say so much, but I don't know where to start. So please just listen." There was no reply, so I forged ahead. "You guys really blindsided me with the whole bear thing."

That's not how I wanted to start this. *What the hell?*

But I seemed to have opened a floodgate, and there was no stopping me. "I trusted you guys, and you held out on me. And you scared me. You could have told me in so many different ways who... what you are." I stopped for a breath. "But you did it in the worst way possible."

"We know that now. And we're sorry."

"I know that. But sorry doesn't fix things, at least not yet." I swallowed hard. "You guys broke my heart. It's going to take time for that hurt to go away. But..."

I could practically feel them pulling the phone closer. Despite everything, I smiled. I wanted my broken heart to mend, and I wanted them to help me.

"But... I'm willing to think about letting you guys back into my life. On one condition."

"Anything... Whatever you say." There was a babble of voices, and I waited for them to stop talking.

"No more secrets. Ever. If you have something to tell me, some other part of your life you think I need to know about, then I want to hear it. Now." I waited, praying there was nothing else. But as the longer it took them to answer, the more I knew there was something else.

"Well, there is something else." Jackson sounded serious, and I could imagine the look of concern on his face.

I closed my eyes, bracing myself for the worst.

"Can we do this in person? We can come over..."

I opened my eyes. "Is it that bad? God, what now?" A horrible thought broke through everything else. "You're going to change me into a bear thing, too? That's it, isn't it? I'm going to be a bear?"

"No... no... Oh God, no." They both were almost shouting.

I held the phone away from my ear. When they'd settled down, I raised the phone again. "So, what is it?"

"We need you to come meet our clan. It's part of the reason we were looking for a mate in the first place." Dane's voice was patient, and I waited. "Jackson and I are the alphas for our clan. We needed a mate, so when Alex met you and liked you so much, he thought you were someone we should meet. He thought maybe you were exactly what we were looking for."

"To be honest, it was a surprise for us." Jackson took over. "We didn't think we'd feel so much for you."

"But we did... from the very first moment we saw you." Dane finished the thought. "We have no doubt that you are our one true mate, Sadie. That we're supposed to be with you."

"But what about the clan thing? Why do I need to meet them?"

There was a sigh, and I recognized it as Dane's. "The Clan has never had dual alphas before or alphas who aren't mated.

They're anxious for things to settle down, to return to some-thing like normal. And part of getting the clan under control is..."

"Showing off our new mate."

"So, it's like meeting the extended family? Except all of them are bears?" It seemed odd, but then again, most of my life at the moment seemed odd.

Jackson laughed. "Yes. You pretty much got the picture. It's not as bad as it seems. You won't be meeting a bunch of bears, if that's what's worrying you. It's a gathering of our clan. You get to meet them, and if I know the clan, there's food and beer, probably dancing. Some of the guys like to cut loose and shift."

"But you'll be with us, and we promise not to change into bears in front of you."

I tried to imagine a family picnic suddenly full of beer-drinking bears, and the whole surreal aspect of it was too much. Better to stick to one thing at a time. And that was getting this relationship back on track.

"I'd like to see you both." I got suddenly shy. "I miss you."

"We miss you, too. We can come there."

I looked around my apartment. It seemed... wrong for them to come here. It was too small to contain them. "Can I come to the cabin?"

There was silence again, this time charged with energy, excitement. I felt the same way. I waited, but I was pretty sure the answer would be...

"Yes. I'll come get you now." It was Jackson. The call lost the underwater sound. I was off speakerphone. "I'll be there in half an hour."

I'd only meant to go see Jackson and Dane and stay overnight to make sure we were all on the same page, to seal the deal on this relationship.

But that one night stretched into two, then a week. Then they were driving me to work and picking me up afterward. And pretty soon, I'd packed up my apartment, given my landlord notice, and moved into the cabin.

There was pleasant confusion over bedrooms and sleeping arrangements. I did feel like Goldilocks, trying out each bed. The cabin had four rooms upstairs, and even though this cabin was what I wanted and Jackson and Dane were who I wanted to be with, I discovered I wanted a room of my own, someplace private. The guys were a little mystified by this seemingly peculiar request, but I got my way, and I was installed in the biggest bedroom. I was happy.

But that first night, we never got past the living room. Dane met Jackson and me at the door, and I'd done nothing except drop my purse on the floor before I was swept up in an embrace, quickly followed by Jackson, and I was back in that wonderful crush of masculinity, both of them pressed against me.

We managed to get to the living room, where Dane had lit a fire. The cabin was cozy and warm, and in the soft glow, I let them undress me. I was perfectly content to let them take the lead, one of them undoing the buttons of my blouse, the other teasing down the zipper on my jeans.

The kisses they gave me were soft and gentle, each one holding me, caressing me, passing me to the other. They gradually shed their clothes, and as they held me, I felt more warm skin and hard muscles beneath my hands, against my body.

Someone lowered me to the floor, to the thick rug in front of the fire. It warmed my skin, but I was already hot from their kisses and caresses. I knew being with both of them at the same time had the potential to send me on a wild ride, and for a moment, I wondered if I could learn to handle both of them. I decided it was worth it if it meant I could stay with my guys.

This night was slow, relaxed, each of them taking their time, lighting a slow fire inside me and then fanning that flame until I was moaning under their touch. And all they'd done was kiss me, touch me. But they'd kissed and touched every inch, lingering over breasts and nipples, each taking a turn delving between my legs, teasing me until I arched against whoever was there.

Finally, they let me come, or else, they were as heated as I was. Dane rose over me, sliding into me, and I came instantly, almost violently, pushing up against him. He growled and thrust hard, and as I moaned and cried beneath him, his sounds combined with mine, reaching a crescendo as he came.

Jackson held me as I came down from my high, and I turned to him, pulling him down to me, kissing him, then moving lower. He lay back, and I took him into my mouth, sucking him, gently at first, as he'd done to me.

I worked my tongue around the shaft of his cock. He moaned deeply as I pulled him deeply into my mouth. I held him there for a long moment, waiting until he started bucking up against me. I pulled him from my mouth, moving over him, holding him in my hand as I lowered myself.

He thrust up to meet me, hands grabbing my hips. I met his eyes and watched the emotions that played across his face. Then he closed his eyes, planted his feet on the floor behind me, and thrust up hard. I leaned forward, and he wrapped his arms around me, slamming inside me over and over as I held on for the wild ride.

Jackson came with a harsh cry, one hand on my back, the other pressed against my ass. I buried my head against his neck, my body reacting to him, coming again, my hips rolling forward to meet his final thrusts.

We slowly came apart, and Dane was there, pulling me against his chest as Jackson lay on his back, breathing hard, one hand resting on his chest, the other on my thigh. We didn't talk, at least not for a long time. Slowly, we moved and shifted, pulling the blanket off the couch, fitting our bodies together until we were lying in a contented tangle on the floor before the dying fire.

Dane was slowly combing his fingers through my hair, a sensation that was lulling me into sleep. I closed my eyes, letting myself drift away.

"You're okay with everything? With us and this unconventional arrangement?"

"Um-hmm... it's all good."

"And with us being shifters?" Jackson wrapped an arm around my waist.

"Uh-huh... yes." I wanted to sleep—and to wake up and do this all over again.

"So, meeting the clan, you're okay with that, too?"

I opened one eye. "You're pressing your luck, Jackson. I'm happy and sleepy. I'll meet your clan and watch bears drinking beer. And I promise, at least now, to try not to freak out when they shift."

I felt more than heard Dane's deep rumbly laugh. "Okay. Fair enough. You've earned your sleep."

I felt myself drifting off, my head on Dane's chest, Jackson's arm around my waist. Somehow, despite it all, this was going to work, the sharing, the shifting, and everything that was to come.

Right at the edge of sleep, it came to me that I'd finally found my own clan of sorts in these beautiful men... my two men.

*My two bears.*

I RESISTED the urge to twirl in front of the mirror. I was wearing a beautiful white dress, sheer and light, with enough satin to remind me that it was a wedding dress. Well, sort of a wedding dress. For all intents and purposes, today was my wedding day.

Except I wasn't marrying just one guy. I was mating with two. The two loves of my life, Jackson and Dane. And it wasn't a wedding as much as an introduction to their family and to my place in their lives. Because it wasn't enough to simply fall in love with two guys. I had to fall in love with two bear shifters. And their family was their Clan. Add to that the fact they were both alphas of their clan, and things went beyond complicated.

*Holy shit, well beyond complicated.*

"Tell me again how this mating ceremony works. There aren't really public displays..." I turned around.

Peyton was sitting on my bed, grinning at me.

"No public displays of anything, except maybe a kiss."

"Knowing Jackson and Dane, there'll be more than a few kisses. Those guys can't keep their hands off you." She got off the bed, walking around me, tweaking the dress here and there. "Let me do your hair before we run out of time. You've been glued to the mirror long enough."

Peyton was my best friend, through thick and thin, through all the trauma and drama with my two bears. Today she was also makeup and hair, moral support, and bridal attendant all rolled into one.

I let her take my hand and pull me down into a chair.

"You know, you really got it made here. It's actually a little much fairy tale for me." Peyton giggled and winked at me.

I looked at her in the mirror as she looked around my room. "You've got two great guys. You've got this great house in the middle of the woods. Plus, you have your own room."

"You sound jealous. Things not going so well with Alex?" I grinned at her reflection, teasing her as I always did, waiting for the reaction.

It earned me a punch in the shoulder. "We're fine. If we weren't, you'd be the first to know. And since Alex can't keep a secret, Dane and Jackson would be the next to know."

Now that I knew Alex was a wolf shifter, there was a certain symmetry to the whole thing, and I was grateful for how it all came together.

"So up?" Peyton twisted my hair into a loose knot at the nape of my neck. "You have this flower thing, right?"

I nodded. I'd made a braided wreath with greenery from around the yard.

"No flowers, just ivy and some holly so nothing will fade."

"You didn't pick any poison ivy, did you? You know you're not all that much of an outdoors kind of a girl."

I sighed, rolling my eyes for effect. "No, no poison ivy. And yes, hair up and you can put the flower thing on if you want."

"Consider it done."

She worked on my hair for a few minutes, putting it up, pinning it in place, pulling a few tendrils loose to frame my face. When she set the headpiece on, I watched in amazement as I changed from my usual rather nondescript self to something out of a fairy tale.

Peyton rested her hands on my shoulders. "You look amazing, Sadie. Really amazing."

"Thanks. I feel amazing." I stood, pulling her into an impromptu hug. "Is it time to go down yet?"

Peyton shook her head. "No. Alex said he'd come get us. We've still got a few minutes."

"Oh. Okay." I was excited, wanting to start this new part of my life. I'd been living with Jackson and Dane for almost a month, and while nothing would change in our relationship, this was a public commitment, an affirmation of our love.

And I wanted to see my guys.

"Are they gone already?" I went to the door, but Peyton got there before me, all but throwing herself in my path. It was dramatic and theatrical and pretty much in Peyton's usual style.

"They're already downstairs. You know that. You heard them go down."

"Okay... okay. I'll just go sit quietly in the corner." But I couldn't sit. I shook out my hands, a flush of goose bumps rising up my arms. I wanted to dance, to spin around like a little kid. I satisfied myself with pacing back and forth at the end of my bed.

"So, you know, I'm confused." Peyton perched on the chair I'd been sitting in. "Alex is no help with this since it's not his clan and they don't do things the same way. Why are there two alphas? Why not just one like other clans?"

I stopped pacing. There had been more than one conversation between the guys and me about shifters and clans. It was foreign to me, so the fact that there were two alphas hadn't struck me as anything out of the ordinary. But it was.

I sat on the edge of the bed. "Dane said there were two clans. The one the guys grew up in and another much smaller clan that was on the fringe of their territory. When Dane's clan's alpha died, he was the next in line. I think he said he was the nephew of the old alpha?"

I scowled. I felt as if there was going to be a quiz on family clan history after the ceremony. Like Jeopardy but with bears instead of Alex Trebec. But sometimes it was hard to follow lineages and who was related to whom and why someone was in line for alpha.

"So? Why two?" Peyton made that gesture with her hand, the one that said I'd drifted off somewhere and wasn't answering her question.

"Oh, sorry. The other clan didn't have a next-in-line blood alpha and they'd made a request that Jackson become their alpha. He agreed... and then the fracking people started buying up land, basically pushing the other clan off its territory. The clans decided to merge, but neither wanted to give up their alphas. So, they ended up with the two."

Peyton shook her head. "Sounds convoluted and complicated."

"It is. Believe me, if there's any group that's wedded to tradition and ritual, it's the shifters." I raised an eyebrow. "You should know that from living with Alex."

"Yeah. I do. But his clan's a little more modern—or organized or less archaic or something."

There was a knock on the door, and I drew in a breath. Peyton crossed the room, tossing me a wink as she did. She opened the door a crack. I heard a male voice, and my heart took off at a breakneck pace.

Peyton closed the door and turned to me. "They decided to call off the ceremony."

I stared at her, my heart dropping into my stomach and a shiver racing down my spine. Then she smiled, and I jumped off the bed, swatting at her. She ducked out of my way, laughing.

"You're just mean. You know that?" I landed a hand to her butt, and she scampered away.

"You should have seen your face." She rubbed her backside, grinning. "Sorry, you should know by now that there's no stopping those fools from making you their mate. But it was funny."

"Yeah, hilarious." She was my best friend, and I should have expected nothing less. "But promise. No more. Okay?"

"Promise."

"Pinky swear?" I held out my hand, little finger extended. Peyton crossed the room, linking her finger with mine.

"Pinky swear. No more playing around." We stood like this for a moment. "Seriously, Sadie. You are one lucky girl. And I am jealous, just a little. I love Alex with all my heart. But I'm still waiting for him to make it official."

She leaned forward, pulling me into a hug. I closed my eyes, inhaling her scent of patchouli and lemongrass, so very thankful I had her here, even if she was a pain in the ass.

I stepped back in time to see her wipe her eyes. "Why, Peyton, is that a tear?"

"You tell anyone and you're in big trouble."

I shook my head. "And you say I'm the romantic."

She brushed a hand across her face. "Come on. You're going to be late to your own ceremony." She reached out, adjusting something in my hair. "I pronounce you ready."

"Then let's do this."

I walked down the hall, down the stairs with the big peeled pine bannister, and into the living room. The front door was open, and from inside, I saw sunlight filtering through the pines and a whole lot of people gathered where we usually parked my car and the guys' big trucks.

I was getting the chance to make a grand entrance, right through the front door and onto the porch where Jackson and Dane waited. Or at least I hoped they were there. From my vantage point, the crowd was all I saw. I hesitated, my feet slowing down.

Peyton put her hand on the small of my back. It was comforting to know she was here for me.

"Come on, Sadie. Everyone is here to show their support." She gave me a push, propelling me through the open door. I caught myself just as I stepped onto the porch.

Jackson and Dane were there, standing on either side of me. I was used to seeing them in jeans and T-shirts or their police uniforms. But today they were resplendent in crisp white shirts and dark slacks, no ties. I glanced down. They were wearing dress shoes, not boots.

I suppressed a small wave of giggles that threatened to spill over. There had been no end of discussion over what they were going to wear. Both balked at the idea of tuxedoes or suits of any kind, and I'd given up trying to coerce them. It might not be a wedding, but I wanted everyone to look good in the pictures. The last I'd been told was they'd show up looking presentable.

But they were more than presentable. Dane to my left, with his clean-cut, boy-next-door good looks, all blue eyes and sandy blond hair. And Jackson on the other side, with dark eyes and black hair, rugged and brooding, sexy and mysterious at the same time.

They stepped forward, planting a kiss on each cheek. Excitement welled up inside me, and for a minute, the group on the lawn disappeared. I was here with my guys, exactly where I wanted to be.

"You look amazing, Sadie." Dane took half a step back, holding my hand. "You're absolutely beautiful."

"Of course, she is. She's our girl." Jackson grinned down at me, one eyebrow raised. "She's always beautiful."

There was a discreet cough, and we turned to find Buck walking up the steps toward us. Buck was something of a character, which was saying something since there seemed to be quite a few characters among the clan. I wondered sometimes if it was genetic, coded in their DNA, because I had yet to meet a bear that wasn't a bit more interesting than the average human.

"We're ready if you love birds are." He winked at me, one bushy eyebrow rising and falling. Jackson had explained that Buck was sort of the clan's master of ceremonies.

He cleared his throat. The little eddies of talk died down, and we all listened intently.

"We are here today under the heavens to welcome a new member to our clan." Buck's baritone carried to the farthest corner of our yard, rich and deep, mesmerizing all of us. It was pretty clear why he held the role he did. "Sadie has graced us with her presence, uniting with Jackson and Dane and bringing our clans together."

Buck paused, and I looked out over the group. There was a divide, a subtle space between Dane's larger clan and Jackson's smaller one. I hadn't met anyone from Jackson's clan. They'd seemed not so much standoffish or unfriendly as distant or apart, separate. I supposed it was hard losing their land, moving from where they'd always lived.

I saw them looking at me, and I smiled. They were my clan now, too.

"We start a new chapter in our clan's history today, a new

beginning. This new beginning is written in bright ink, big letters, starting with Sadie's name."

The crowd murmured, a sound like a running stream, a happy sound.

"We welcome her as the mate to Jackson and Dane, our alphas. And as a member of this clan."

*This clan.* His words hung in the still air. Not two clans: one clan.

I knew what I was. I was glue, double-sided sticky tape, intended to bond these clans together. I knew this. We'd talked about it many times before. But hearing it here in front of the clans—*clan*—in front of all these people... Well, to say it was overwhelming was an understatement.

But then Dane swept me up in a tight, secure embrace and then passed me on to Jackson, who squeezed me so hard I thought I'd burst, kissing me hard in front of everyone. He set me on the porch, and I forgot about responsibility and clans and everything else. I was officially one of them, and no matter what might happen, right now I was in the place I loved most: between my two bears.

Everyone broke into applause, and I caught sight of Peyton and Alex, the only non-bears here. Peyton waved, and I flashed her a bright smile that told her just how thankful I was to have her here on this special day.

"Come on. We have a party to go to." Dane took one hand, Jackson the other, and they led me down the stairs and around to the back of the cabin.

The clan had done everything. Setting up tables, bringing food. I felt like a princess as they escorted me to our table. There were flowers everywhere, in Mason jars, in vases, and everything looked beautiful.

"This is amazing." I turned to Jackson. "They did all this for us?"

He pulled me against him. "They did this for *you*, Sadie. This is all for you."

The clan gathered around us, Buck front and center. Someone handed me a glass of champagne, and everyone went quiet.

"To Sadie, the newest addition to our family... our clan. Our newest alpha female." Buck raised his glass. "And to Jackson and Dane for finally having the sense to know a good thing when they saw it."

There was laughter and the clink of glasses. I took a drink, bubbles tickling my nose. Then people were coming up, shaking my hand, a few hugging me. Jackson and Dane and I got separated, and for a minute, I was swept up in swirling groups of people, introductions, hearing names that I probably wouldn't remember. But it didn't matter. I was happy. I had a family, a really big family.

The afternoon was filled with food and drink, and just as the sun began to set, someone started playing a banjo. I was sitting between Jackson and Dane, eating a piece of cake—or maybe my second piece of cake. It didn't matter. I'd learned that this clan really knew how to throw a party. The food had been amazing and the desserts beyond description.

Music filled the clearing, and a few people got up to dance. Someone else joined in with a guitar and a fiddle, and pretty soon, most of the clan was dancing, twirling and stomping their feet. I clapped along, watching the people dancing. The music was a combination of folk music and modern, and I wondered if their music grew along with the clan.

Dane grabbed my hand, pulling me up, breaking my train of thought. "Come on."

The music had changed to a Texas two-step. This was a dance I could handle, and I knew from one of my dates with Dane and Jackson that they were terrific dancers. I followed him out into the group, looking forward to having him spin me around. As much as I loved to dance, I wasn't known for my coordination. But dancing with Jackson and Dane made me feel light and ethereal and totally graceful.

By the time we were done, I was breathless from exertion and laughter. Dane brought me back to our table, and I had only long enough to take a swallow of champagne before Jackson had me back out on the floor.

Alex appeared between dances, asking if he could have a turn. I nodded, and Jackson relinquished me to him. I saw Peyton on the edge of the crowd and smiled. She gave me a thumbs-up and big grin. I'd barely been able to say two words to her, but I was pretty sure she'd stop by in a day or so and we'd rehash everything that had happened.

"You've made my buddies really happy, Sadie." Alex was just as good of a dancer as Jackson and Dane, and I was being expertly spun around the floor in a breathless whirl. I wasn't sure what to say. Even though Alex was Peyton's boyfriend, I didn't see him all that often. I was glad we had this little bit of time together.

"And they've made me happier than I've ever been before."

Alex shrugged. "It's more romantic-sounding than glue." He laughed, and it took me a minute to get his meaning.

"One clan, two alphas?" I looked up at him, and he nodded.

"Yeah. Something like that. It's been hard for Jackson and Dane, with pressure from the clans, looking for a mate. They're lucky to have found you. You're one in a million."

I wasn't sure what he meant about pressure from the clans. But there wasn't time to ask, and being spun and flung around the floor, I really couldn't carry on an in-depth conversation. I'd have to ask the guys later.

Our dance ended, and Peyton appeared, winding her arm through Alex's. He gave me a quick kiss on the cheek.

Peyton leaned over, kissing the other one. "You're a beautiful bride, Sadie."

"It's not a wedding..." But she knew that. She and Alex disappeared into the crowd, and I found myself back in Dane's arms.

The rest of the night went by in a whirlwind of dancing and laughter, meeting other Clan members, and being taken for a turn on the floor with some of the other guys. One older man solemnly escorted me to the floor, bowed in a very gentlemanly fashion, and then took me through a very spirited jitterbug. When we were done, he returned me to Jackson and Dane.

Jackson took my hand, but I shook my head. "I'm done for a while. That last guy..."

"Fergus." Both my guys replied in unison.

"Fergus. I'm no match for him or his energy." Someone had brought water, and I greedily drank a glass. "Let's just watch for a while, okay?"

Jackson dropped into the chair next to me. Dane nodded, and then someone came up, catching his attention. He rolled his eyes, letting himself be pulled into a conversation. That had been happening more and more, and I frowned as he walked away.

"It's the ranch fire case. Everyone's been on edge, asking if there are any new leads."

I nodded. The fire had been at the Stone's Throw Ranch, between New Fane and Jenner's Fall. Someone had burned down a barn, then tried to shoot the woman who owned the ranch. Jackson and Dane had been working the case for months, but everything seemed to have gone cold. The man—a shifter—they thought was responsible seemed to have vanished.

"It's hard when the guy's seemingly vanished into thin air." Jackson took a swallow of beer. I caught the worried look on his face, but then he turned to me, his usual good-natured grin on his face.

"But this is our night, not the time to talk business. You ready for another dance?"

The musicians had slowed down the pace, and a waltz was playing. I took his hand, and we went back to the dance area.

I snuggled against Jackson, resting my head in the vicinity of his shoulder. Both guys were so tall, but I loved being in their arms. Jackson moved me in slow, dreamy circles, my arms around his neck, his hands on my back. He held me lightly, but there was a possessive quality to that hold, and I closed my eyes. For the first time in my life, I knew what it felt like to be loved, completely and utterly, with no strings attached.

There was a soft cough nearby, and I opened my eyes to see Dane standing beside us.

"May I have this dance?"

Jackson kissed my forehead, then let me go. I watched as he walked back to the table, stopping to shake hands with a few people. Dane took my hand, then spun me out in a slow circle, bringing me back into his embrace, drawing me tightly against his hard, broad chest.

"Having a good time?" The words were murmured over the top of my head. Dane had a few inches on Jackson, and I'd long since given up trying to crane my neck during conversations.

"I am." I rested my cheek on his chest, the thump of his heart against my face. "I'm in heaven."

I heard him sigh. "I wish we could just stay here like this forever."

I did look up at him. "You're starting to sound like Jackson. He's the romantic among us. You're the logical one. Remember?"

His soft laugh rumbled deep in his chest. "I guess it's rubbing off on me. Or it's just the day." We stopped dancing as he reached down, set a finger under my chin, and tipped my face to his. "Or it's just you."

I felt myself tremble at his touch, at his heated words. The fire that burned in his eyes intensified, and my body ached to feel him inside me.

"This has been the happiest day of my life, Sadie. And it's all because of you." He leaned down, lips brushing against mine. I stood on tiptoe, kissing him back.

When he let me go, I looked past his shoulder at Jackson perched on the edge of a table, watching us intently. He smiled, and I gave him a little wave.

Dane started us moving again, less dance and more a prelude to what I knew was going to happen later tonight. A not-so-subtle shift in how he held me, how his hands moved over me, the way he looked at me told me we'd be leaving the party soon and heading inside. His sudden impatience only turned me on more, knowing that he wanted me.

I was still amazed that these two men, best friends since childhood, could share me, share their love for me... and share their bed. There'd never been any competition between them. I'd never even seen either one jealous. If anything, both seemed happier now that I'd moved in the cabin.

Sometimes it brought me to tears to realize that I'd found not only the love of my life, but the *loves*. Other times, I felt silly and possibly a bit greedy. Who was I to think I should have not just one, but two wonderful men?

I shook my head, not wanting to let my insecurities ruin the evening. This was an important night, not just for me, but for Jackson and Dane.

"You okay?" Dane's voice brought me back to the here and now. "Everything all right? I know it's been a big day for you."

I smiled up at him. "I'm wonderful. Really happy..." I tried to blink away the tears but succeeded only in making one slide down my cheek.

"Tears of happiness I hope?" Dane reached out, brushing one away with his thumb.

I nodded. "Only happiness."

"Then let's make a wish." He brought his thumb to his lips. "That any tears you shed are only tears of happiness, never pain." He flicked his tongue over his thumb.

"Is that a shifter thing? Or a bear thing?" I'd never heard of wishing on tears, but it touched me deeply.

Dane shrugged. "Not sure. My mom used to do it when I was a kid. If I hurt myself, she'd wipe a tear away and then wish all my tears would be happy tears."

People began drifting up, saying good night, wishing us all the best. I wondered if some silent signal had been given or if everyone had seen Dane and me on the dance floor. As much fun as this had been, it had to end, and I was looking forward to the night with my guys. Sure, we'd been living together, but this was an occasion, something that marked a new chapter in our lives.

The last of the guests drove away, and we stood on the porch, watching as the headlights faded down the mountain. The night had gotten a little cool, and I shivered. Instantly, two arms went around my shoulders, and the warmth of their bodies did more than just warm my skin.

"This has been an amazing day. Really." I looked between them.

"I agree. It's been pretty damn perfect." Jackson hugged me tightly, and I wrapped my arms around him briefly.

I turned to Dane, hugging him.

"But the night's still young... at least for us." Dane leaned down, and I lifted my face to his. He kissed me softly, tenderly, but with such longing I melted into him. "You're not going to sleep anytime soon."

I finally broke away with a soft gasp. "Sounds good to me."

I reached for their hands, and we stepped into the cabin. In minutes, Dane had scooped me up into his arms and headed toward the bedroom. *Our bedroom.* The one I now shared with my two bears.

▭

I woke in the late morning, Jackson curled on one side, Dane stretched out on the other. I blushed, remembering what had happened in this bed last night—and this morning—and could do nothing to control the huge grin that was suddenly sprawled across my face.

*Damn, the things they did to me.*

It was just starting to get light outside, the curtains glowing a pale yellow. I stretched, loving the feel of the sheets against me, the erotic scent of sex rising around me, the warmth of the men in my bed. *My guys. My bears.* I pulled the sheet over my shoulder and snuggled against Dane's. I smiled, closed my eyes, and dozed off.

A cell phone started ringing, breaking through the half sleep I'd drifted into. Dane moved away from me. Then a second phone rang, and Jackson jerked awake, throwing off the sheet. I sat up, groggily pulling the sheet up to cover me.

"What is it? You're off work today, right?"

Dane had disappeared down the hall. Jackson was pulling on sweats. He glanced back at me, and I heard Dane's voice across the hall.

"Something's up." He leaned forward, kissing my forehead. "Stay in bed. I'll be right back." He was gone, and I was alone.

I hugged my knees, looking out the window. The light had

gotten a little brighter, moving farther into the room, but it was still early. There was movement in the hall, low voices, and Dane was back, dressed in his uniform.

"There's been another fire." The look on his face told me everything, and I nodded.

*There hadn't been any more fires. Until now.*

"Is it bad?" I hugged myself tighter. No one had been injured yet.

"Not sure." Dane sat on the edge of the bed, brushing back a strand of hair from my forehead.

"Be careful, okay?" Tears welled up, and I blinked them back.

I knew going into this relationship that there would be times like this, that they'd be dealing with things that could be dangerous. But until now, it had only been routine stuff. The Stone's Throw case had become background noise, something the guys talked about less and less. Now it all came back, the emotions and feelings of dread fresh and intense.

"We always are." He leaned forward, kissing my forehead. "We'll call when we can."

He stood, and I saw Jackson in the doorway. "I'll keep an eye on Dane, you know. Make sure he doesn't get into any trouble. Don't worry, okay?"

I rolled my eyes. "Always the joker. Give me a kiss."

Jackson crossed the room, and I hugged him. But I could tell he was anxious to get going, so I released him.

"Call, okay?"

Dane was already in the hall, and Jackson turned, shooting me a gorgeous smile. "You bet. We love you, baby."

And then they were gone.

I listened to the trucks leaving the yard. They'd taken both, leaving me with the car. I sat back, pulling the blankets up to my chin. I should go back to sleep, but I was too keyed up to even try. Maybe today would be a good day to play domestic goddess and tackle the towels and sheets situation in the cabin.

Jackson and Dane had been living here long enough that their mothers had long ago stopped sending care packages. And they'd lived here long enough that whatever they'd brought from home was threadbare and frayed. I'd decided new sheets and towels for everyone was in order.

I'd told Dane and Jackson about my plan. There had been bemused looks between the guys, but they said I could do what I wanted as long as there were no frills or lace on their sheets. I'd rolled my eyes, but agreed. No lace or frills for the guys. Deal.

Peyton had said she'd come with me to the nearest mall. I knew she was far less interested in helping me with sheets and towels than she was in buying new clothes for herself. But I was looking forward to spending the day with Peyton. It seemed we never hung out anymore.

When it was finally a decent hour, I called her. She said she'd be right over.

"You're committed now, so I never see you." Peyton was driving, and I was tightening my seat belt. Her driving record was a bit tarnished, but she had asked if she could drive my car, so she was at least trying to stay close to the speed limit. Her car was iffy over the long haul. Mine was just low on gas.

"You're committed. What's the difference?"

"You've got two guys, and that takes twice the time."

I laughed, gripping the door as we rounded a curve. "I think it's more that I don't live around the corner from you anymore."

"Well, whatever the reason, I miss you. We need to do this more often."

"If we survive the trip, sure. We'll plan a girls' night once a week."

The car screeched to a halt, more or less in a parking space. She grinned at me. "I think that's a great idea."

We spent the better part of the day wandering through the mall. Peyton had gotten only half a dozen things, and I'd found non-frilly sheets for Jackson's and Dane's rooms and a gorgeous set of pristine white sheets with lace, soft as a kiss, for the spare bedroom. I had all kinds of images running through my head of Jackson and Dane and me on these sheets, arms and legs tangled in white linen, doing things, wicked things...

"Sadie! Earth to Sadie." Peyton poked me in the arm.

"What?" I stopped walking. "What did I miss?"

"You missed... Never mind. I know where your mind was. You're turning into a dirty girl, you know? It's about time."

I shot her a look, but she just laughed.

"And I made you blush. You're so cute."

"I'm a dirty-minded cutie?"

We were in the food court, and I wanted ice cream. Peyton wanted Chinese, so we split up. I was standing in line, trying to decide between Madagascar Chocolate Supreme and Death by Chocolate when someone bumped into me. I gave a vague sorry and then stepped up and gave my order. Death by Chocolate won by a nose, and I turned, searching the crowd until I saw Peyton waving at me. I made my way through the crowded tables and dropped next to her, piling my bags on an empty chair.

"So, did you give that guy a piece of your mind?" She talked around a mouthful of something pungent and full of noodles.

I frowned. "What guy?"

She frowned back. "The guy who was either trying to cop a feel or steal your purse. Didn't you notice?"

"Someone bumped into me, but that's all." I took a lick of

my cone, almost swooning at the lush taste of the dark chocolate. "No big deal."

Peyton's frown deepened. "Sadie, he didn't just bump into you. I saw him. He either made a swipe for your purse or your ass. The guy behind you in line told him to back off. So, he walked away."

I'd stared at Peyton during this whole recitation of events. "You're kidding."

She shook her head, handing me a napkin. "You're dripping."

I looked down. Melted Death by Chocolate was running over my hand. I took the napkin, trying to wipe the sticky ice cream off my fingers. Finally, I gave up, took one last disappointing mouthful, and dropped the rest in Peyton's discarded rice container.

"I guess I was preoccupied." I'd been fixated on ice cream, but I didn't want to admit that.

"Jackson and Dane on your mind?" Peyton smirked, spearing a piece of chicken and twirling some noodles around her chopsticks.

"Actually, no." I narrowed my eyes. "I do think about other things besides them, you know."

"Oh, so the honeymoon's over?" She sat back, pushing her plate away. "You're an old married woman now, and the shine has worn off the penny?"

I gathered up my bags. "Where do you come up with this stuff? There's no shiny pennies and nothing's gotten dull." A flush crept up my face as an image from last night surfaced. I turned away, rearranging the perfectly arranged packages.

Peyton's laughter pealed out. She had a big laugh, and she wasn't afraid to let loose. Most times, I didn't mind, but right now, right here, it was a little much.

"You're holding out on me, aren't you? You had some wild

monkey sex with the bears last night. Come on. Dish the 4-1-1."

"Oh, for crying out loud, Peyton." I stood, grabbing my stuff. "You have sex with Alex, and I don't ask for all the details."

Peyton gathered up her used dishes and dropped them into the garbage. She slung her big bag over her shoulder. It was woven out of some native fabric with bells and beads worked into the fringe, and it tinkled and rattled as she adjusted it.

"I don't have sex with two scorching hot guys at the same time."

"Shh... Peyton, please."

An older woman turned around, gave me a look, and then hurried off.

Peyton's laugh rang out again. "Come on. Let's go before security tosses you out for being a wanton woman." She linked her arm though mine, and mercifully, we left the food court and then the mall.

"You want to drive?" She held my keys out to me, and I shook my head.

"No. You can be my chauffeur a little while longer for being mean in the mall." I dumped my stuff in the back seat, got in the passenger side, and fastened my seat belt as Peyton got in behind the wheel.

"Sorry, but you're just so much fun to tease. Especially now." She started the car and jammed it in reverse, flinging her arm over the seat as she backed up. "I never thought you'd be the one with two guys, doing whatever wicked things you do up in that cabin." She stopped, put the car in drive, and looked over at me. "And you know I can't pass up the chance to tease you."

She floored it, and we shot out of the parking lot and onto the frontage road. I hung on to the handle above the door, eloquently dubbed the "oh shit handle" after my first ride with Peyton.

"But this is my car, remember? Take it easy, okay?"

"Gotcha." She hit the brakes, or at least I think she did. The car slowed a little as we merged into traffic. Peyton was doing her usual bob and weave across lanes, but at least she was doing it at a reasonable speed.

We'd cruised along the main street for a few blocks when I realized Peyton had stopped talking.

"Peyton?"

She was gripping the wheel, glancing between the rearview mirror and the road, biting her lip.

"What's wrong?"

"There's a car back there, a shit-colored sedan, that's been following us. I swear the guy driving is the guy from the mall."

I turned around, trying to see what Peyton saw, but there was a bus behind us. "You mean the guy who ran into me?"

"Yeah. Same baseball cap, same dark glasses from what I can see. He never gets close enough, but he's been on my ass since we left the mall. Makes every lane change I do, every turn. Can't be coincidence since I've been trying to lose him for the last fifteen minutes."

"You have?" I sat back. I hadn't been paying attention.

Peyton's driving was always erratic, and there were many times I'd swear we were lost, but she claimed she knew exactly where she was going.

Now I saw we were in a vaguely industrial area of town, someplace I'd never been before. "Do you know where you're going?"

"No, actually, I have no fucking clue where we are. I'm lost."

"Oh my God."

Peyton's colorful language only pointed out how tense she was.

I looked behind us again. There was less traffic, and now I could clearly see a beige sedan a few blocks away, pacing us, not getting closer but not falling back. I could just see that the driver was wearing a baseball-type hat and sunglasses. I had no idea what the guy in the mall looked like, so I'd have to take Peyton's word it was the same man.

"What should we do?"

"I think I should get back to where there's more traffic and then lose his ass."

"Where's there more traffic?"

She jerked her head to the right. "This way."

Peyton suddenly cranked the wheel violently to the right. The car shuddered through a ninety-degree turn, the wheels chirping on the blacktop. Before I'd recovered, she did it again, and I slammed into the center console.

"What the hell, Peyton?"

"Hang on."

She flung the car into another right turn, and I wondered why she'd bothered warning me this time.

"Like I said, what the hell?"

"You always make three right turns to shake a tail. Alex said that once, so, you know, I thought I'd try it out."

"Did it work?" I looked behind us. A big truck was pulling out of a warehouse, and my view was blocked. "I can't tell."

"We're kind of back where we started. Hang on."

I did, and this time she made a left, a little less aggressively, and I was only lightly slammed into the door. I sat up, looking back.

"I think that did it."

We were back on the main road, two lanes in each direction now starting to fill with the first rush hour traffic.

"I can't see him anymore. Holy shit, that scared the hell out of me. Creepy!"

"Then let's get the hell out of Dodge."

Peyton floored it, and we were off, sailing through yellow lights that changed to red as we passed beneath them. The exit for home came up, but she kept going.

"Another evasive maneuver?"

"Oh shit. No. Fuck, I missed the exit." She glanced over her shoulder, flicked on her blinker, and got in the right lane. "We'll take the next one, double back, and go home."

"All right." My stomach was in knots, not just from Peyton's driving, but from whatever was happening. It was frightening as all hell being followed by some stranger. What the hell did the guy want with us? With me?

"Oh shit. I should call Dane... or Jackson. Or someone." I unbuckled my seat belt, twisting around in my seat. The incessant beeping of the restraint alarm started up, but I didn't care. My purse was buried under bags of linens. I rooted around, finally coming up with my purse. I turned around in my seat, fumbling for my cell phone.

"There's got to be something..." I punched speed dial for Dane's number. It rang once, then dropped to voicemail, and then inexplicably cut out.

"Crap." I hit Jackson's number. "Voicemail and then nothing."

The call didn't even go through this time, just made a weird beeping sound.

"They must be out of range." I tapped the screen. "Should I call Alex?"

Peyton shook her head. "No. He's out of town today. The exit's just ahead. I promise not to miss it this time, and then we'll be headed home. Everything will be fine. Just put your seat belt back on. That beeping is driving me crazy."

I wasn't really convinced, but I didn't say so. I clicked my seat belt back on, yanking it tight. Peyton took the exit, cutting across a lane or three, and then made a quick left, driving on the overpass toward the on ramp. The light was red, and Peyton fidgeted as we waited.

"I'd kill for a cigarette right about now."

"You quit, right?"

"Yeah. Wish I hadn't now."

The light turned green, and she turned left to a chorus of horns and screeching brakes from oncoming traffic as she cut in front of them. We went down the ramp and merged with traffic, sticking in the right lane. Our exit sign appeared, and Peyton flipped on her blinker. We took the exit, got on the highway, and got the hell out of town.

I sat back in my seat, finally breathing normally. "Great evasive driving, Peyton. I think you missed your calling in life."

She gave me a tight smile, eyes glued to the road. "Just wait 'til we're home before you congratulate me. We still have thirty miles to go."

The ride was very quiet, extraordinarily tense. I realized only after my palms started to hurt that I was clenching my fists. I shook out my hands.

We'd left the highway, taking the main road to the smaller one that led to the cabin. I could see our mountain, the dark stand of pines above the house. But it wasn't visible from here.

"We're almost home. Don't worry." She reached over, patting my leg. I turned to look at her, then everything seemed to go into slow motion.

Peyton was looking forward, and her eyes went wide. She took her hand off my leg, grabbed the steering wheel, and wrenched it to the left. I opened my mouth, either to ask what she was doing or to scream... or both. Nothing came out but a strange breathy sound. It was like in a dream where you want to scream, but you can't.

I looked back out the front of the car. The beige sedan was coming at us, in our lane. Or the lane we'd just been in. We were now in the wrong lane, headed for the ditch. The driver's side wheel hit the shoulder, sending a shower of gravel against the side of the car. I watched the beige sedan pass us on the right, the driver looking over at us. I was struck by the impassive look on his face. And by the gun that was pointed at me.

Our car skidded along the shoulder, and for a second, I thought Peyton would be able to get it under control. Then she screamed, a strangled sound. There was a strange popping noise, and the car was filled with sparkling fragments of glass as my window shattered. A fine red spray of blood hit my face, and I jerked back.

Then everything sped up. We were heading down an embankment, sliding sideways through long grass, the car shuddering violently. Then it hit a culvert, tipped to the left, and rolled over. I had a dizzying view of grass, then sky, then grass as my arms flew up over my head, limp, out of control, the seat belt pulling painfully across my stomach. Then the car slammed down, right side up, coming to an abrupt halt at the bottom of the embankment.

I was dazed, my head hurt, and my stomach felt like I'd been sucker punched. But I wasn't so out of it not to notice that Peyton was unconscious and bleeding from her arm. I punched the seat belt button, swearing at it until it released.

"Peyton? Hey, Peyton?" I tried to remember anything and everything I'd learned in Girl Scouts about what to do—or not to do—with someone who was injured. I didn't want to touch her head or move her neck. But I wanted to see how badly she was bleeding. Gently, I lifted her arm.

She'd been shot. I'd never seen a gunshot wound, but I

knew instinctively what this was. There was a bloody hole on her forearm, and when I turned her arm over, there was a ragged wound on the underside. Both were bleeding, and beneath my hands, I could feel the sickening sensation of bones moving.

I started to shake, and the world went a little green. I closed my eyes. This wasn't the time to be sick. Peyton needed me. I took a deep breath, then blew it out.

"You're going to be okay, Peyton. Okay? Do you hear me?"

I reached into the back seat. The sheets and towels were tossed about, and I grabbed a thick terry cloth towel. I wrapped it around her arm, then reached back and found a pillow case. It was brown, meant for Jackson's room. I managed to tear off a strip, tying it around the towel. As I pulled the ends tight, Peyton mumbled something.

"Peyton? Wake up... Oh God. Peyton!" I reached out, grabbing her shoulder.

"What the hell?" She turned her head, wincing. "My head hurts." She looked out the windshield. "Oh fuck. I wrecked your car, Sadie." She started to cry.

"No worries, Peyton. Really. We need to get out of here."

She turned unfocused eyes toward mine. "The guy..."

"Yeah, the guy. From the mall. He..." Somehow I couldn't bear to tell her she'd been shot. "He ran us off—"

She shook her head. "Sadie... the guy from the mall..." Her eyes widened, and she reached out with her good hand. "Behind you..."

I'd turned my head just as the passenger door was pulled open behind me. Hands grabbed me around the waist, pulling me from the car. I screamed, but the wind tore the sound from my lips. I kicked, flailing against him. But he was built like a brick, solid and immovable, and he lifted me off the ground.

"Hold still. I have a gun, remember?" Something hard was

jammed into my back. "So, behave. I don't need you alive, or your friend."

I stopped struggling, and he set my feet on the ground. Peyton was moving around in the car but didn't seem to be having any success with the seat belt. She looked up and our eyes met, and where she'd been fuzzy before, her eyes were now filled with panic.

"You're coming with me." He shoved me toward the back of the car. "Sit down." He pushed me down on the ground. "Don't try anything. I'll shoot again, no hesitation." He waved the gun in my face, then jerked open the back door, rummaging around in the back seat. "You were supposed to be alone today."

I craned my neck, looking into the car. Peyton was turned in her seat, looking between the guy and me. He grabbed a sheet—one of my new, pristine white sheets—and tore off a long strip. I let out a strangled cry.

"Sorry to ruin your honeymoon sheets. But the way you guys go at it..." He laughed, an ugly sound that made my skin crawl. "You're way past the virginal purity of white sheets."

"Hey—"

"What?" He reached down, grabbing my arm. "Don't like to be told you're a little slut?"

I stared up at him, mouth open, as he pushed me down onto the ground. He stuck a knee in the middle of my back. He wrenched my arms behind my back, wrapping the sheet around my wrists, pulling it tight, way too tight.

"She's not a slut, you bastard." I heard Peyton's voice, and for once, I wished she would keep quiet. But I didn't think that was going to happen.

"And I have a gun, bitch." He took his knee away, then pulled me up by my hands. That hurt my shoulders, and I cried out. He set me down hard on my butt, and I scrambled around, rising onto my knees.

I tried to listen for traffic on the road above, a car, a truck... someone on horseback, anything. But it was eerily quiet, too quiet.

"Stay here."

I watched him move around the other side of the car. For a big guy, he moved very quickly, with that strange grace large men sometimes have. The insane thought that he was a good dancer crossed my mind, leaving as quickly as it had arrived.

He opened the door, and I saw Peyton take a swing with her good arm. He slapped her across the face, and she spit at him. It hit his shirt, and I cringed. It was bloody.

"I don't have time for this." He held the gun out, pointing it at Peyton's head.

She froze. I screamed.

There was noise up on the road, the sound of a truck going by. I screamed again. The truck didn't slow down and it certainly didn't stop, but it must have been enough to give the guy second thoughts. He took the gun away from Peyton's head. From somewhere, he pulled out a knife, slicing through her seat belt. He grabbed her arm, dragging her out of the car. I couldn't see them, and I struggled to get to my feet, leaning against the car. But all I could see was the top of the guy's head.

Then he stood, pulling Peyton to her feet. "Like I said, I have a gun." I didn't see it in his hand, so I assumed he had it shoved into her back. He dragged her around to the rear of the car. He'd tied her arms in front of her, rather than behind, and I could see blood seeping through the towel.

"She needs help."

"You need to stop telling me what to do." But he reached inside the car, grabbing another towel and the rest of the ruined sheet. He wadded it all up, jamming it into the pillowcase I'd ripped up.

"You're going to do exactly what I tell you, exactly the way

I tell you. I have shot people before, and I'm not above shooting you now."

Peyton sagged against me, and I felt her shaking. It must hurt like mad to have her arms tied like that. I wanted to say something, but at the sight of his gun, I bit my tongue.

"We're going to walk up the embankment and get into my car. You..." He pushed Peyton forward. She stumbled, almost falling, catching herself on the rise of the ridge. "In the back seat."

He turned to me. "You, in the front. If there's a car coming, you don't do anything. No screaming, no jumping around. Play it cool and you might make it out of this alive."

We started up the embankment. It was hard with my arms behind me, and the guy periodically pulled us upright, propelling Peyton and me up the slope. He was slightly gentler with her, but not by much.

It seemed to take forever before we reached the shoulder of the road. I looked desperately in both directions, but there was nothing as far as I could see, except big, blue Montana sky. Across the road was a field of big black beef cows looking at us over an electric fence. They were no help.

The beige sedan was parked at the side of the road, engine running. It would have been nice if the truck that passed had stopped. Must not have been a local. Locals always stopped, even for strange cars.

The guy opened the back door, pushing Peyton forward. She fell against the side of the car, hitting her arm on the fender. She slumped forward, and for a minute, I thought she had passed out. I took a step toward her, but the guy waved me back.

"Get in. Stop faking." He put his hand on her head, guiding her into the car. She fell limply across the back seat.

He tore another strip of fabric off my sheet and tied it

around Peyton's ankles. He did something else with more strips of sheet. She didn't move anymore.

"Come on, lady. Move your ass."

I walked around the car, hoping, praying—willing—someone to drive by. I walked as slowly as I could, but the man was there, pushing me along, opening the door. He shoved me inside, then reached across me, fastening the seat belt. He jerked it tight, and I sucked in a breath as pain radiated across my stomach.

"What do you want? Why—"

He backhanded me, the suddenness of his action and pain cutting off my words. I blinked back tears of shock and surprise. No one had ever struck me before. For a minute, I was speechless, scared, bewildered. Then a wave of anger rose up, hot and fresh, totally foreign, but it cleared away the last bits of fog in my brain.

"Ask me questions again and you'll regret it."

My words hung in the air. He was either going to hit me again or shoot me. But I was pissed, and I'd had enough.

The guy turned, looking at me through dark glasses. I looked at his face, as much of it as I could see. For the first time, I saw him, really saw him. He had bad skin, pockmarked. Greasy black hair stuck out beneath the baseball cap. Dirty gray flannel shirt, black leather jacket. Dark jeans.

"I've had enough of you." He grabbed my hair, pulling me toward him through the open passenger door. "Now shut up."

He had another strip of sheet, and he wedged it into my mouth, tying the ends behind my head. I panicked, trying to breathe through my nose, but it seemed like there wasn't enough air in the car.

"Finally, no more noise from either of you."

Then he wrapped another strip of fabric over my eyes. I struggled frantically as the cloth slipped over my nose. But he jerked it up, tying it tightly. I saw patterns against the darkness of my closed eyes.

The passenger door slammed, and then I felt the car move as he got in. His door slammed, and then the engine started and I felt him shift into gear. He pulled onto the highway, the tires spinning briefly on the gravel shoulder.

We drove for I don't know how long, taking turns, slowing, speeding up. I'd only lived with Jackson and Dane for a little over a month, and I'd only driven back and forth on the same roads to the cabin. They lived in the middle of nowhere, and I hadn't been adventurous in exploring the area. I tried really hard now to remember how many turns we made or where the sun was warming me, but I couldn't do it.

The car slowed and turned again, crunching across gravel. It grew colder. Then we stopped. The guy turned off the car. He opened his door, and a cool breeze washed over me.

He opened the door on my side, grabbing my arm, pulling hard. But I was still belted in. It hurt, and I grunted in pain. He let go, leaning across me, undoing the clasp.

"Come on." He pulled me out, and I stumbled after him. We were someplace in the shade or in a building. A breeze blew, carrying a bad smell. It wasn't familiar.

We hesitated, and there was the creak of a rusty hinge. He pulled me forward, and the temperature dropped another ten degrees. It was damp and smelled like dead mice.

"Sit."

There was the scrape of a chair on the floor, and he pushed me down. My butt hit the seat, and it wobbled. He grabbed my shoulders, steadying me.

"Don't move. Do and that'll be the last move you ever make."

I heard footsteps walking away, then nothing for a moment or two. I tried to stand, but it was hard with my hands tied behind me. Then there was the slam of a car door and more footsteps coming back. He'd brought Peyton, and apparently, she was walking on her own. I was pretty sure she was gagged, too, because if she wasn't, there'd have been a tirade coming from her. There was another scrape of a chair and the thump of someone being pushed into it.

"Okay. Here's the deal. Blindfold off because I want to see your face when I tell you what's going to happen to you."

There was a tug at the back of my head, brief pain as my hair was pulled, and the blindfold came off. I blinked, even though the space we were in was dim. I wanted to look around, to look for Peyton, but I forced myself to focus on the man in front of me.

The man with the gun. The man who had kidnapped us.

He took off his dark glasses and crouched in front of me. His eyes traveled over my face. "You're prettier than I thought." He looked lower, and I tried turn away. "But I'm not into that kind of thing, even if you are tied up."

I clenched my teeth, biting down on the gag in my mouth. Hot, acid anger flooded through me, pushing aside the fear.

"Your friend, though..." He looked past me to where Peyton must have been sitting.

I bit down harder, breathing roughly through my nostrils. He curled a lip in what I thought was supposed to pass for a smile.

A sudden burst of static made me jump. He snorted out a brief laugh and then stood, reaching for a walkie-talkie on his belt. Holding it to his ear, he turned away, but not before I caught the unmistakable sound of Jackson's voice. I tried to listen, holding my breath so I could hear what was being said.

"Roger. They found the car..." Static flared, and I sat forward, frowning. "...no sign..." More static. "...out..." The radio went silent.

I shifted in my chair, looking at Peyton. She looked more dazed than I thought she should be, and I wondered if she had a concussion. The man turned, shoving the radio into the back pocket of his jeans with a noncommittal sound. Was it my car they found? How often did cars go in the ditch around here?

The man certainly didn't seem worried about what he heard, and that bothered me. But then he pulled a chair in front of me, turning it backward, swinging one thick leg over the seat. He leaned on the back of the chair, settling in like we were going to have a friendly chat.

"I figured they would. Your friend here…" He nodded, and I heard Peyton shifting in her chair behind me. "She's got some talent when it comes to driving. If you'd been driving, Sadie…" He reached out, finger stroking my cheek.

I jerked my head away and he laughed.

"I have a feeling I'd have gotten you back at the mall. But…" He shrugged. "Life's not always easy. I lost you there but found you closer to home. It all worked out for the best."

I wanted the gag out of my mouth. I wanted to talk, ask questions, ask why he'd kidnapped me. But he seemed to enjoy my silence a little too much.

"You have questions." He nodded. "I can almost read your mind." He leaned forward, voice dropping.

"You're going to be my ticket out of this godforsaken country. I hate it here, and I want out. But I'm a hunted man. You know that." He nodded as though this should mean something to me.

I scowled, shaking my head.

"You know me, Sadie. At least you know what I've done." He reached into his pocket, pulling out a gold lighter. He flicked it, the bright flame casting a circle of yellow light over his hand. I watched the flame as he brought his hand between us. "Got it now?"

I looked at him closely, at the flame reflected in his dark eyes. There was something not quite right about him. Not just that he'd kidnapped us. His eyes followed the flame with more excitement than I understood, and I had the strong sense for a minute that me, Peyton, and wherever we were was totally irrelevant to him. I watched him—and the flame—intently, hoping he wasn't planning to light me on fire.

Then it hit me. I pulled abruptly away from his hand and the lighter, almost overturning my chair. He laughed, a nasty sound that chilled me. He reached for me again, and I pulled back, shaking my head violently. But all he did was pull the gag out of my mouth. I sucked in a huge breath.

I think I intended to scream, but my words came out in a desperate whisper. "You started the fires."

He looked pleased, way too pleased that I'd figured it out. But then his face darkened.

"And I got sold out by my companions, left behind... abandoned in the middle of nowhere with nothing. I don't know how you survive out here."

"You don't know anything about me."

He shrugged. The flame was still dancing between us, and he looked at it wistfully before closing the lighter, then slipping it into his pocket. "I don't really give a fuck about you, though you'd be wrong to think that way. I want out, and you're my ticket, like I said."

"You're going to ask for money?" I tried to think how I could get his radio, how I could call Jackson or Dane. He must have it turned to the police channel. If I kept him talking...

"I have money. I need freedom—a way to escape."

"Oh. Okay. Well..." My mind was spinning, trying to make sense, trying to keep panic from overwhelming me.

"So, if you don't want money, what?"

"You're a bargaining chip. I trade you for getting out."

I shook my head. "No one's going to let you go free. You started those fires. You tried to kill someone." My voice trailed off. I wanted to believe what I said. I didn't think this guy was very stable, and I started to think maybe I should just stop talking.

"Don't underestimate the pull on the heartstrings, Sadie. Those bears are wild about you. Don't think I haven't been watching."

That got my attention. A sudden chill wracked my body. "Watching?" My voice was just above a whisper. "You've been watching us?"

"You think because you live in the middle of nowhere, you're safe? Isolation doesn't bring safety." He pushed away from his chair, standing over me. "Besides, you don't have curtains in your bedroom."

The blood drained from my face, and I realized I was gaping up at him. He reached out, set a finger under my chin, and gently pushed up. I closed my mouth.

He stepped around me, pulling the ties at my wrists painfully tight. I realized he was tying me to the chair. Then he was moving away, and I craned my neck. He was tying Peyton, who was leaning unsteadily on a wooden stool, to a center post in the room. Her arm was still bleeding, and she looked shaky and pale.

"She needs a doctor or..."

He jerked her arms forward, and Peyton gasped out a sharp cry. I winced.

"She's not going anywhere." The man turned to me. "Neither of you are." He tied Peyton's hands around the post, tugged the ends of the sheet again, and then went to the door.

"I've got things to do now that I have you here. I'll be back."

He went out the door, slamming it behind him. I heard the snap of what must have been a padlock and then footsteps crunching across the gravel. The car started, then drove away.

I turned to Peyton. Her head sagged between her extended arms. I thought maybe she'd passed out.

"Are you okay?" I wondered briefly why he'd left me ungagged. We were probably in the middle of nowhere, as he called it. If I screamed, no one would hear me. Not a comforting thought. "Peyton?"

She looked up at me, her face contorted with pain, tears running down her cheeks.

"Oh fuck. Peyton... I'm sorry."

She shook her head back and forth, slowly at first, then almost violently. I thought she was going to throw up, and I panicked, knowing she'd choke with the sheet in her mouth. I tried to turn the chair, pushing with my feet, sliding it over the broken floorboards until I got hung up on one that stuck up sharply from the rest.

To my amazement and relief, she managed to spit the gag out of her mouth. She took a breath, then another, and then gave me a smile. It was a weak one but a smile nonetheless.

"He was sloppy with the gag. Guess he thought I'd be out longer."

"Are you okay?"

She sat up against the post, wiggling on the unstable stool. "Not by a long shot. My arm hurts like a bitch. What the hell happened?"

"He shot at us... Hit you. And I guess broke your arm. Or you broke it when the car rolled over."

Peyton stared at me. "Last thing I remember was driving down the road to your house."

I frowned. Maybe she really did have some kind of head injury. "Do you remember driving home from the mall? Some guy following us? Missing the exit?"

Her face brightened for a second. "Oh... yeah. Okay." Then her eyebrows drew together, and she got that fuzzy look again. "Then we were coming home."

"He came at us. You drove on the shoulder to get away."

"And I went in the ditch... Oh, Sadie. I wrecked your car." Her tears started again. "I'm so sorry."

I didn't know what to do with this, with her tears. Peyton wasn't supposed to cry. I was the teary-eyed one. She hung her head again, sniffling quietly. This was a complete mess.

"Peyton, hey... it's okay. He had a gun. You tried to get us out of his way. It's okay." Okay wasn't what I wanted to say. I wanted to tell her she'd saved our lives.

She looked up at me. "Yeah. Okay. It's sort of there, you know? But like someone else's dream." She looked down at her arm. "He shot me?"

"Yeah. He did." I wasn't sure if I wanted to tell her I thought he'd been aiming at me. It's what I'd been thinking before he'd started talking about using me as a bargaining chip. Now I thought maybe he had been aiming at Peyton, trying to get her out of the way. The thought made me physically ill.

"So now what?" She sniffed dramatically. "Where did he go?"

I scooted the chair around the board in the floor. If I pushed with my legs and twisted, I could walk the chair awkwardly forward, at least a little bit. Finally, I ended up facing Peyton, panting and sweaty. I hitched the chair forward once more, almost toppling onto her.

"Oh, Peyton." I was close enough to see blood seeping through the white towel I'd wrapped around her arm. "You need a doctor."

"Yeah. I need a lot of things." She lifted her chin, looking past me. "Do you know where we are?"

For the first time, I looked around me. The room was small,

messy. There was broken furniture in the corners, what looked like the remnants of a primitive kitchen along one wall.

"Someone's hunting cabin maybe. Do you remember anything about the ride here? He didn't blindfold you."

Peyton shook her head. "I don't remember much of anything. Nothing about wrecking your car... just getting dragged in here."

"Outside... did you see anything outside?"

Peyton frowned, then closed her eyes. She was quiet for a long time. "The backside of Saddle Mountain. To the..." She turned her head away from me, opened her eyes, and nodded. "That way."

"So, we're north of the cabin." I did some mental geography in my head. "I think."

Peyton shifted, giving me a look, I didn't like. I couldn't say it was hopeless, but it was less hopeful than I wanted to see. My own store of hope was at a pretty low point.

"Does it even matter? Even if we got untied..." She shrugged, winced, bit her lip. "Do we make a run for the hills?"

"You hit your head, so I'll pretty much ignore anything you say." I swiveled in my chair, looking for something, anything I could pick up.

"We don't know how long he's going to be gone. I'd rather be ready when he comes back, even if that means..." I didn't know being ready meant. "I just don't want to sit here and wait for... whatever."

Peyton shook her head, briefly closing her eyes. "Yeah. Okay. My head hurts." She put her head down on her arms. "I feel sick."

This was bad. "Okay. Just breathe... Take deep breaths. Keep talking, okay?"

She nodded. "Yeah. Okay." Her voice sounded small. It

wasn't how Peyton was supposed to sound. I'd always been the one needing to be held up, not the other way around.

I wanted to hug her, but that wasn't possible. Leaning forward, I briefly rested my forehead on her shoulder. She sighed but didn't look up.

The cabin was small, but there were all kinds of things in it. Most of them looked broken, but there had to be something, anything...

Broken chairs were tossed in one corner. I hopped my chair toward them. After a small eternity, I was sitting with my back to the pile, fingers reaching for a broken leg that stuck up from the rubble. I wasn't sure what I was going to do with it, but at least it was something. But when I pulled it out, I lost my grip and it clattered to the floor, rolling into the corner.

"Shit... fuck." I kicked the floor.

"Sadie, you swore." Peyton raised her head. Her face was pale, and her eyes were heavy-lidded.

"Peyton? Hey, talk to me."

"I don't want to... My head hurts." She closed her eyes, swaying against her ties, then jerked upright, eyes wide. "Ow... my arm hurts. What happened?"

"It's broken, Peyton. You got shot, remember?"

She stared at the bloody towel around her arm as if it were all new. "Oh... yeah. You told me that."

I needed to do something. Peyton had a concussion; I was sure of it. She needed a doctor, an emergency room. Panic welled up, along with tears. I sniffled them back, frustrated beyond all reason.

"Okay, here's what we're going to do." I worked my chair back toward Peyton. My legs ached, and they shook every time I stopped to rest. I finally got myself where I wanted to be, in front of Peyton, my back to her.

"Can you reach my hands?" I craned my neck, trying to line up my hands with the post. "Can you try?"

Peyton looked at me with glazed eyes, then down to my hands. She shook her head, groaned, and then dropped her head again.

"Try, Peyton. Dammit. Do something." I wanted her to at least try.

"Can't... can't move them." Her voice faded away.

"Why the hell not?" But she didn't answer.

I moved the chair a quarter turn, and then I saw the reason. The man had tied Peyton's hands not just around the post, but around a spike that stuck out from the side. She really was tied more securely than I'd originally thought.

"Okay... okay. Sorry." But she didn't answer me.

We were stuck, tied to a chair and a post. We were at the mercy of an arsonist slash would-be murderer.

It didn't look good.

# CHAPTER 10

I LOST TRACK OF TIME. Peyton faded in and out, mostly out, and each time she came back, I had to explain where we were, what happened. Finally, she stopped talking, hunched over with her head resting on one arm. I waddle hopped my way back to her, sitting close enough to listen to her breath without bumping her arm.

Jackson and Dane had to know by now I wasn't home. I'd heard them on the radio. But my mind started playing tricks. What had I heard? Was it someone talking about my car or someone else's? Did they think I was just hanging out with Peyton? They weren't the clingy, overprotective type, and I kind of wished now that they were.

I looked at Peyton once more. It was getting dim in the cabin... and cold. She was still the same, still sitting with her head down, but she was breathing. I sat for a long time, tears running down my cheeks, watching the light fade from the dirty window by the door.

There was a cold breeze, and I sat up. The man slammed

the door behind him, flashlight in hand. The window beside the door was black.

I must have dozed off. A violent shiver raced through me, and I belatedly realized my hands were numb.

"Well, I see you've had the tour of the place. Sorry it's such a mess, but I had to fire my maid. She stole all the kitchen knives."

Mentally, I kicked myself. I'd gotten distracted by Peyton and panicked and never even thought about the kitchen. If I were in one of Peyton's trashy romance novels, I'd be considered TSTL—too stupid to live.

"Anyway, things are looking good." The man took the radio out of his pocket and set it on the table. "No chatter about you. They probably think you went to Billings or something. This is perfect."

My heart sank. They didn't even know we were missing. No one was looking for us.

"I'm sure you're dying to find out what happens next."

The tone of his voice, his words alone, chilled me more than the night air. In the erratic shadows cast by the flashlight, he looked beyond crazy. The only consolation was he was waving the flashlight, not the lighter with its dancing flame, between us. Because with that dancing flame in his hand, I had the feeling he was only seconds away from setting me on fire.

Before I had time to really think about that fresh fear, he grabbed the back of my chair, dragging me away from Peyton. I tried to dig my heels into the floor, succeeding only in having my heels banged against the wood. The noise roused Peyton, who looked up in fuzzy alarm, blinking in the shadows.

"You two... double trouble."

He set me back closer to the door, turning me away from Peyton. I twisted around, trying to see her, but between where he'd dropped me and the lack of light, she was just a dark shape.

"I think you want to pay attention to me. Your friend…"

I turned back to the man. He was waving his hand in a vague sort of way toward Peyton.

"She's not core."

"Core? What the hell does that mean?"

"It means she's a peripheral, not core. You're core." He pulled the other chair over again, settling down in front of me like we were going to have a friendly chat. "Core is freedom, me getting as far away from here as I can. And you're core because you're my ticket. But I told you that already."

"Yeah. Okay. I'm core."

He nodded, smiling. "You're getting the picture." He shifted on the chair, reaching beneath his jacket, and pulled out a gun, something shiny and silver and very wicked-looking. I tried not to gasp or throw up or lose control of other bodily functions as I stared at the weapon.

"Being peripheral, she's not necessary." He waved his hand again, this time holding the gun. My breath caught in my throat, and I cringed, expecting the worst. But the guy was looking back at me.

"It's not time for that yet. Or I should say again? Missed before." He shook his head. "She's a damn good driver. Shame to lose that talent." His shrug told me he didn't really care at all.

I blinked at him, horrified. He was going to kill her; he'd *tried* to kill her. Tears gathered in my eyes, and I started shivering again, so hard I could feel the sheet biting into my wrists. For a moment, I thought I was going to be sick, and I swallowed hard.

"But you can do this… core thing without her. You don't need to—"

"Yeah, I do." He absently rubbed the barrel of the pistol

against his head before pointing it at Peyton. "She's not necessary... peripheral." He was looking at her, his eyes shadowed by the bill of his cap, but it was clear she'd caught his attention.

My heart thumped painfully in my chest. I needed him to stop looking at her. I needed him to look at me. Focus on me. "But you need me, right? I'm core."

Slowly, he pulled his gaze back to me, looking at me for a minute as though I were a total stranger. As much as I hated having him look at me—and basically hated him—I didn't want him even thinking about Peyton.

"Yeah. You are."

"And I'm your way out of here."

He nodded, a half smile curling his lips. "Yeah. Right. You are."

I was running out of things to parrot back to him. The word core was starting to sound ridiculous, but it seemed to hold his attention.

"And it's dark, so that's when you... we... when we..." I floundered, not sure how to ask what he was going to do next.

"Soon, yeah. Dark is when I make my move." His voice had dropped to a whisper, like he was a kid with a big secret.

When he leaned forward, I automatically pulled back.

"I like the dark." One hand reached out, touching my cheek.

He flicked the flashlight off, and in the afterimage, I saw his leering face, felt his fingers on my cheek. My world as I knew it was being turned on its head.

# CHAPTER 11

THE WORLD WENT DARK. My only sense that seemed to
work at that moment was touch, perceiving the gross feel of his
heavy fingers on my skin as he stroked my cheek. Then I
smelled cigarette smoke, the odor of the man across from me,
and the rancid air of the cabin.

Then another sense kicked in. Hearing. I jerked my head
up, the man's fingers slipping away from my face just as the
door burst open, filling the cabin with intense light.

Everything came into sharp relief. The light was so bright it
seemed to split right through my skull. I closed my eyes and
turned my head away.

There was yelling, a man's voice saying, "Put the gun
down!"

I opened my eyes and looked back to the door just as
Jackson charged through. His eyes met mine, and for a split
second, he was all I saw.

Then the side of my face exploded in pain, and I fell in
slow motion, hitting the floor hard, landing on my side. The
breath went out of me in a whistling grunt, and I struggled to

pull in more. It felt like the time I'd fallen off Zephyr, our neighbor's pony, and had the wind knocked out of me.

From the unique vantage point of the floor I saw Dane in the door behind Jackson and another man in dark clothes, holding a gun, moving quickly into the room. There was noise behind me, then the sound of breaking glass. I struggled to look over my shoulder, but the chair made it impossible to move.

The man in dark clothes knelt in front of me. I struggled to look past him, to find Jackson and Dane, but the room suddenly seemed very empty. There were more noises outside, shouts, and then the terrifying sound of a single gunshot. I kicked my legs in panic, trying to get away from the chair, to see where Dane and Jackson were.

"Sadie... Easy. Lie still." The man reached behind me, trying to untie my hands.

"I can't. I need to find them. Where are they?"

"Hold still." More fumbling with my hands.

I turned my head and saw New Fane P.D. on his billed cap. "Oh, for fuck's sake. Don't you carry a knife?"

His eyes widened briefly, and then I swear he tried to cover a grin. "Yes, ma'am."

There was something cold against my skin and then the amazing feeling of my hands being free. But that was quickly followed by pain as I tried to move my arms. I swore under my breath, trying to sit up without moving my arms.

"Here... let me." The New Fane guy lifted me bodily to my feet. I swayed, and he put out an arm to steady me. "You should really sit down..."

But I was already headed to the door. I looked back at him and pointed to Peyton. "She needs you more than I do."

Outside was just as bright as inside. The full moon overhead cast its own silvery light, along with several big police cruisers and a giant black truck, all with headlights and spotlights on high beams. I squinted, raising a hand to shield my eyes. I had to find Dane and Jackson. I had to know if they were okay.

There were no more gunshots, but somewhere close by, there were deep growls and the sound of something—or things, big things—crashing through the underbrush. I ducked between the truck and a squad car parked at a crazy angle, out of the bright lights, just in time to see the unmistakable shape of a bear charging from the edge of the woods—straight for me.

It wasn't Jackson or Dane. They were just as familiar to me in bear form as they were in human. This bear was the kidnapper.

My body protested as I threw myself down on the ground. It was cold and damp, and the gravel dug into my hands as I crawled under the truck, banging my head on something mechanical beneath the vehicle.

The bear skidded to a halt, gravel rattling against the underside of the truck, hitting me in the face. From here, its paws looked huge, the claws extending out and down, digging into the dirt. I wasn't sure if it knew I was here, and panic surged through me, urging me to get away. But I curled my fingers into the ground, holding on, trying to root myself to the spot. There was no way I could outrun a bear, and I had no idea where Dane or Jackson were right now or if the guy looking after Peyton was out with his rifle.

There was a growl, and the bear dropped its head, looking at me under the truck. Our eyes met, and I knew given half a chance, he'd kill me.

He swiped a paw under the truck, claws ripping my shirt. Pain seared my skin, and I screamed. That got me an answering roar and another swipe of the giant paw. But I was already scrambling out the other side, gravel digging into the palms of my hands. A panicked look over my shoulder showed me the bear was already moving around the truck. If I could get up, maybe I could get into the truck.

I stuck my head out from beneath the truck. The bear was coming around the bumper to my left. Fear ran up my spine, and a strangled scream escaped my lips.

Pulling myself upright, I turned away from the bear, reaching blindly for the door handle. But instead of metal, my hand hit thick, dense fur. I jerked my hand back and froze. I was standing face to face with a bear. Jackson.

Before I had a chance to do more than breathe out, Jackson pushed me aside, roaring as he moved past. I was spun against the truck, banging hard into the fender. He roared again, and this time there was an answering roar, far too close for comfort. The other bear was charging toward Jackson. All this was happening in the narrow space between the vehicles, and I was at ground zero.

There was nowhere to go but up, and I reached high, managing to grab the side of the truck with the tips of my fingers, and with legs kicking, I hauled myself up before falling awkwardly—and hard—into the bed. I got to my knees, peering over the edge.

I'd gotten out of the way just in time. Jackson rammed into the other bear, hitting him in the shoulder with his head, momentum carrying Jackson past him. The bear hit the side of the truck with enough force to knock me sideways. I got my balance and gripped the edge, watching in horror as the bear spun, mouth open, already charging at Jackson. He lunged, biting at Jackson's flank. There was nowhere for Jackson to go. He was trapped in the narrow angle between the truck and the crazily parked police cruiser with a crazed bear shifter clearly intent on killing him.

The bear hit Jackson hard, massive jaws open wide, huge fangs sinking into his thick fur. I bit my lip, wanting to do something, anything. I knew Jackson's fur was thick and beneath that was tough skin, but this was a cornered bear, unstable, driven by an insane need for self-preservation.

Jackson turned, snapping at the bear, but he couldn't maneuver his body in the tight space.

I spun around, looking for something to use as a weapon. All I saw was a toolbox, and I dropped to my knees and wrenched it open. There was a hammer on top, and I grabbed it.

I jumped up, flinging the hammer at the bear—and instantly wanted it back. Out of the corner of my eye, I saw another bear, this time Dane, barreling toward the others. The hammer flew over the heads of all three, shattering the window of the squad car. Both the sound and the hail of shattered glass went unnoticed by the trio.

Dane hit the bear low, knocking him off balance. Jackson pulled away and I looked for blood on his fur, but he was moving fast, bellowing as he turned back.

The bear was pinned between Jackson and Dane, and he knew it. For a moment, he stood, eyes rolling wildly in his head as he looked between the two. Then he stood up on his hind legs, front legs outstretched, and lifted his open mouth to the sky. The sound he made was neither human nor bear, growl nor bellow. It was frightening and desperate, completely mad, and full of rage.

He dropped to all fours and swung his huge paws at Jackson and Dane, his claws slicing the air. But he was no match for Jackson and Dane. They kept their eyes on the bear, dodging the increasingly erratic swings he made, ducking beneath the razor-sharp claws, always moving forward. They closed the distance between them and the bear until there was nowhere for him to go. Jackson made the first final move, Dane following his lead. I knew what was going to happen, and I turned away.

It was over quickly, but the sounds of the fight still hung in the chilled night air. I sat in the bed of the truck, my body shaking, my mind swirling with so many conflicting emotions there was no way for me to process any of them. My bears had saved me, but they'd killed in the process. I knew it was the only outcome, and it would have been the same if they'd have been in uniform and shot the man in a gunfight.

I put my head on my knees, dragging in ragged breaths. There was movement, car doors slamming, voices around me. I heard my name, and I looked up. Jackson was standing at the end of the truck, his face pale in the cold white lights. He undid the tailgate and climbed up beside me. He was barefoot, dressed in gray police sweats.

"Sadie? Are you okay?" He knelt down, not touching me. "Did he hurt you?"

I looked up at him through a haze of tears and shook my head. "No..." The word caught in my throat, and I reached up for him. He pulled me into his arms, and I broke down, sobs wracking my body. I was dimly aware of the truck shifting and then another pair of arms going around my shoulders.

"Is she okay?" It was Dane, his voice close, the warmth of his body closer. There was no answer from Jackson, but Dane's arms tightened against me. I saw he was wearing the same gray sweats, and he was barefoot, too.

I pushed away from them, sniffling. "Peyton? She's hurt... She needs a doctor."

Dane nodded. "The ambulance is on the way. Should be here any minute. Matt's been with her. He's an EMT."

As he spoke, the thin wail of a siren rose in the distance. "If she can hold on just a little longer..." I didn't want to finish that sentence or that thought.

Dane wrapped a gray wool blanket around my shoulders, and I clutched it tightly. "She's okay, Sadie. She'll be fine." He rubbed my shoulders.

I shook my head. Until I saw her, until she was out of this terrible place and in a hospital, it wouldn't be true.

"Come on. You need to get out of here. Get checked—"

I shook my head again. "I want to see Peyton. And then I want to go home."

Jackson shot Dane a look, but before they could argue me out of it, I stood.

"Please. I'm fine, really. But I want to see Peyton."

Jackson jumped out of the truck and then turned, holding out his arms. "Come on."

I sat on the tailgate, and he grabbed me under the arms, lifting me and setting me on the ground. Dane jumped down beside me.

The ambulance was closer now, coming up the rutted road, swirling red lights casting chaotic shadows over the surroundings. The siren cut off as it pulled up in front of the cabin. Before it had even stopped, the back doors opened and men in EMT uniforms jumped out. They disappeared into the cabin.

"Wait here." Jackson moved away, following the EMTs. Dane wrapped an arm around my shoulders, and I rested my head against him. What I really wanted was for him to pick me up like a child and carry me away from here. But we stood in silence, waiting.

Someone pulled a stretcher out of the ambulance, dropped the legs, and wheeled it through the door. A few minutes later, it reappeared, this time carrying Peyton and moving much more gently.

"Come on." Dane walked me forward as they carefully maneuvered the stretcher over the rocks and gravel.

Jackson said something, and they stopped just shy of the ambulance doors.

Beneath a pristine white sheet, Peyton looked small and vulnerable. Her eyes were closed, and I reached under the sheet for her hand.

"Peyton? Hey... it's me."

She turned her head toward me, squinting in the bright lights. "Hey, yourself."

"You're going to be okay, okay?" I squeezed her hand and got a weak squeeze back.

"Sure, the hell am." She closed her eyes. "Tell Alex I'm going to need round-the-clock care when I get home... I want to be waited on hand and foot." Her lips curled into a little grin.

"Yeah. Okay. Will do." I was reluctant to let go of her, but I tucked her hand back beneath the sheet.

The EMTs lifted the stretcher, sliding Peyton into the ambulance. Dane pulled me away toward the police cruiser, and I tried not to trip over my trailing blanket. Jackson followed behind.

"All right. Home it is." Jackson reached for the door of the police cruiser, then stopped, and I walked into his back.

"I think we have a problem, though." He turned to me with a wicked little smile twisting the corners of his mouth.

I didn't understand until he pointed at the shattered window, the one I'd broken with the errant throw of the hammer. "Oh. I broke your car."

"Yes, you did." His smile deepened. "You know, I could arrest you for damaging police property. I might need to use handcuffs on you if you resist."

Despite having been shot at, kidnapped, and worried beyond all distraction about Peyton, a little giggle escaped me. I felt disloyal to her, but it felt so good to breathe, to let go, to finally let myself feel safe. I *was* safe. Jackson and Dane were here. The man was... gone. It was over.

We ended up in the truck, leaving Matt to deal with the shattered window. Sitting between Dane and Jackson, I was overcome with exhaustion. I slumped against Jackson, closing my eyes, letting the warmth of the blanket, the heater, and most of all, the warmth and strength of Jackson's body comfort me. I was asleep before we'd even gotten to the main road.

"Sadie, wake up. We're home." Dane's voice sounded far away. I tried to snuggle closer, but he seemed to be getting farther and farther away. "Come here."

I opened my eyes as he pulled me across the seat. And then I got my wish. He picked me up and carried me into the house and up the stairs. I nestled against him, eyes closed, already falling back to sleep.

He set me on the bed, and I blinked my eyes open. Jackson was there, and they gently got me out of my clothes.

"Do you want a bath, Sadie?"

My head was on the pillow, and it was the softest thing I'd ever felt. I shook my head. "Later."

Someone kissed me and then someone else kissed me, and I let myself stop thinking, stop feeling, to welcome the exhaustion that had come back to claim me. I took a deep breath and gave in to it.

CHAPTER 12

I WAS RUNNING IN A FIELD, and a bear was chasing me. I
was laughing because Jackson and Dane would never hurt me
and chase was part of the game. I ran and ran, and then I
tripped. Falling, I saw the bear, blood on its teeth. It wasn't my
bear. This bear had a gun.

I sat up, heart pounding, gasping out a scream. Something
moved in my room, a shadow rising over me. This time the
scream was loud. I lunged across the bed, tangling myself in the
sheets.

"Sadie. Sadie... it's okay. It was just a dream."

I looked up from my mad scramble from one shadow to
another standing in the doorway. But this wasn't a shadow. It
was Jackson. I turned around. Dane stood on the other side of
the bed, looking scared and oddly helpless. He reached over,
turning on the bedside lamp.

My heart thumped painfully. I sat back, still clutching the
sheet to my chest. The remnants of the dream clung to me,
tendrils of fear wrapping around my mind.

"Oh... yeah. Okay." I settled back against the pillows.

The guys looked at each other, then me.

"Can we sit with you?" Jackson sounded tentative.

"Yeah. I'm fine. Just a dream."

They perched on the edge of the bed as if too much movement would break me.

The curtains were pulled, but I was pretty sure it was dark outside. I was so disoriented. "How long have I been asleep?"

"Twelve hours, maybe more. We got back just before dawn."

I realized I was naked under the sheet and pulled it up under my chin. "And you've been sitting in here with me?"

Jackson ducked his head. "Well, one of us has been."

"You must be exhausted."

Dane shrugged. "We got some sleep. We've been working, too. There's been a lot of cleanup to do after... after what happened." He dropped his eyes.

"Oh God." It all came back in a rush—the night illuminated by harsh lights, the gunshot, and then the sounds of bears fighting. I closed my eyes, but that only made the images more vivid. Then I remembered I hadn't been alone. "How is Peyton?"

Jackson nodded. "She's okay. They're keeping her in the hospital at least for a few days."

"That long? She's not okay if they're keeping her that long."

Dane took my hand. "It's her arm, Sadie. They need to do surgery to fix the break, but they needed to make sure she was stable first."

"Oh... and she is okay?"

Jackson breathed out a laugh. "She's tough. You know that. She's been driving the hospital staff—and Alex—crazy. Yeah. She's okay. They'll do the surgery tomorrow morning."

I settled back against the pillows. "When can I see her?"

"Sometime after her surgery."

"Okay."

The silence between us was a little less comfortable than usual. We all seemed to have something to say, but no one knew how to say any of it.

Jackson shifted restlessly, but it was Dane who made the first overture. "Sadie..."

I held up my hand. "There's a lot we need to talk about. But for now, can you just tell me what happened? Who was that guy?"

Dane frowned. "His name was Faull. He is—*was* the man who started the Stone's Throw Ranch fire."

"And shot at the owner?"

"Yeah. He did."

I shuddered. It might have been the same gun he shot Peyton with. And it was my fault she'd been hurt because she was with me.

"So, he's the one you've been looking for?"

"He is—was. We knew he was somewhere in the area, but we had enough pressure on him that he couldn't—or wouldn't—leave."

"But he was a shifter. He could have just... shifted and left?"

Jackson grinned. "We're shifters, and most of the police department is, too. Matt..."

"The EMT?" I blushed, remembering how I'd yelled at him.

"The EMT. He's a wolf. Best tracker we ever met. He's been working almost nonstop on this case, following leads, sometimes literally with his nose."

Dane was still holding my hand, and he gave it a squeeze. "But this... all of what happened—" His voice broke and he looked down.

Jackson picked up the thread. "It's our fault. We didn't realize how... what he was like."

"That he was batshit crazy?"

Dane winced, and Jackson arched an eyebrow. "You could put it that way. No criminal operates the same as everyone else, but this guy seemed to have gone off the deep end."

"He said he'd been abandoned by his partners or something."

"He had. We had his vehicle. The one he was driving was stolen from Jenner's Falls over a week ago. We knew it was him, and we thought he'd be on the run. But then..."

"How did you find me?"

"We found your car in the ditch on Leader Springs."

"But the police radio..."

"We had a suspicion he might be listening in, so..."

"Radio silence." Jackson sat back against the head of the bed. "We tracked him—and you—the old-fashioned way." He tapped his nose. "As shifters."

"Alex was part of it."

"Where was he?"

"He tracked Peyton's scent from the car to the cabin. We'd gotten a tip from someone who'd driven by on the road, saw you and Faull, and called it in."

"The truck that didn't stop." I smiled to myself, silently apologizing for thinking bad thoughts about whoever that was and now thanking them.

"Alex had been trying to find Peyton. She wasn't answering her cell. He'd been monitoring the radio, heard the call about your car, and was there before we were. He had Peyton's scent, and we almost had to tie him up to keep him from getting to her before we'd gotten to the scene."

"But I didn't see him."

"We had him wait at the main road. He met the ambulance on their way out."

I thought about Peyton and how scared she must have been and how wonderful it had to be to have him there.

We sat for few minutes, Jackson on one side, Dane on the other. There were still so many things I wanted to say, and the tension between us was thick. I took a deep breath, even though I didn't know where to start.

"It's hard... What I saw—or what I know happened. What I heard." They were silent, my two bears, so I forged ahead. "I know you did what you had to, and it wouldn't have made any difference if you were in uniform."

My voice faltered, and Dane pulled me close. "Sadie, you went through more than anyone should have to. You saw things, heard things that no one should ever have to experience."

"It's just that... I see you one way, as my friends, lovers—soul mates. I see you in your uniforms, but it's like you go off to work and I don't think about what happens there. You come home, and life goes on. This... this was me in the middle of everything you do. Up close and personal. Way too personal."

I turned my face to Dane's chest and let the tears I'd been struggling to hold back fall. Jackson rubbed my back and ran his fingers through my hair.

Finally, I sat up.

"Sadie, are you asking us to give up our work?" Jackson's voice was strained.

I turned away from Dane and toward him. "I'm not asking anything. I'm just telling you how I feel. I'd never ask you to give up what you love doing."

Dane slid off the bed, pulling me with him. "Listen, this has been a long day, almost two days. How about a bath and something to eat, and then we'll talk? Okay? There's nothing that needs deciding today. We've got some days off. Let's just decompress and see how it goes."

I nodded. My mind was spinning, my emotions just as confused. A bath sounded wonderful.

"All right. I'll run the water, and Jackson can make you something, bring it up when you're done."

I nodded again, feeling like a small child someone was taking care of. It was actually fine. I wanted to be cared for, and I let Dane lead me to the bathroom.

He ran the water, adding bubble bath, and I stood patiently, watching. He helped me into the tub, then sat at the side.

"You want me to wash your hair?"

I looked at him over the edge of the tub, steam rising around me, and shook my head. "No. I think I want to be alone for a little bit. I'll let you know if I need anything."

He brushed a strand of hair away from my face and nodded. "Okay. We'll have soup or something when you're done. You want to eat in your room?"

"Okay. Yeah. Breakfast in bed, only it's nighttime." I managed a smile.

He reached out, touched my cheek, then stood and walked out. I noticed he left the door partway open.

I lay back in the hot water and bubbles, willing myself to relax, trying to untangle all the threads of chaos in my mind. Something that was said came back to me.

Had it been in the back of my mind to ask Dane and Jackson to stop working? I'd been honest when I said I rarely thought about what they did while they were at work. It wasn't that I wasn't interested or didn't care. Maybe I was just being naive, sticking my head in the sand, not wanting to face the fact that they faced dangerous situations—or death—on a routine basis and there was nothing I could do about it.

I shifted restlessly in the water, soaping my arms with bubbles, letting the warm water run over my skin. But it was more than that. If I hadn't seen the actual... event, I'd heard it. They'd killed someone, another shifter, to protect me.

*To save my life.*

It was emblazoned on the side of their car. To protect in their work, yes. But tonight, they were protecting me as well. They would put their lives on the line for me. They would kill —for *me.*

The realization that they loved me that much struck me so hard I sat up in the tub, sloshing water on the floor. It flowed through me, that love, the sheer intensity of it taking my breath away. It didn't matter if that was their job. They'd do the same thing no matter what. They'd kill to protect me, regardless. Why hadn't I seen this before? How could I not have seen how deep their love went?

I got out of the tub, trailing bubbles on the floor as I pulled on my robe. They were in the kitchen, and I could smell something amazing. But food wasn't what I wanted.

"Sadie? Are you okay?" Dane looked up from a sheaf of papers spread across the table. "I didn't hear you come down."

Jackson turned around, spoon dripping soup on the stove.

"I'm fine. I just... It's just..." There seemed no way to put into words how I felt. It was too big, too much, too deep to describe. "I love you. Both of you." It felt inadequate, three small words to describe what they meant to me.

Jackson and Dane exchanged a look.

"I love you, too, Sadie. We both do." Dane stood, coming around the table. "Are you sure you're okay?"

I thought they should be able to see that I was okay, more than okay, that I should look different. That what I felt inside should be visible on the outside.

"Sadie? You're scaring me just a little." Jackson set down the spoon, crossing the space between us.

"I'm fine, really."

Jackson touched my hair, my cheek.

I looked between him and Dane. "I think I figured out something about this whole thing. How I feel about it at least."

"And?"

I took Jackson's hand, holding the other out to Dane. "I want you... both of you."

Dane stood, took my hand, and I pulled them toward the kitchen door.

"You figured out you want us?" Jackson gave me a lopsided grin. "That shouldn't be news."

I shook my head, returning his smile. "Not that... Something else. About what we talked about before, upstairs." I tugged their hands. "But I want to talk upstairs. I want us in one place, at one time, preferably horizontal. And definitely without clothes."

That got a laugh from Dane. "Got to love a girl who calls the shots."

I didn't need to pull them up the stairs. They followed willingly. We went back to my room, where there was a little bit of pleasant awkwardness about getting undressed. I'd dropped my robe and climbed back into bed. Jackson and Dane looked at each other, shrugged, and peeled off their sweats and T-shirts.

We were back where I felt most comfortable, in my bed with the two men I loved more than anything next to me. I took a deep breath, blew it out, and the last of the anxiety left me.

"So, what's this revelation?" Dane, always direct, the realist, reached out and took my hand.

"That you love me." I squeezed his hand. And then I turned to Jackson. "And that you love me."

I glanced between them, both looking back at me with a mixture of acceptance, expectation, and a whole lot of confusion.

"Of course, we love you, Sadie. I don't understand..."

I grabbed Jackson's hand, holding them both in my lap. "So... what happened at the cabin. You..." I swallowed hard. "You killed that man, the shifter, and I saw it. Heard it."

"Sadie..."

I squeezed Dane's fingers. "Let me finish. When it happened, and later... it seemed brutal and violent, and it was. There's no denying that. It's part of what you do. It's your job. But it upset me very much. I couldn't understand how the men I loved could act like that, could do that."

Jackson shifted on the bed, but I went ahead before he could speak.

"But it's part of your job, to protect people. He'd tried to shoot me or Peyton or both of us. He would have killed her; I'm sure of it. And eventually, with me... who knows?" The buoyant feeling of my discovery sagged as snapshots of that day flashed through my mind. "And he attacked both of you. So, you had to do what you did. Any police officer—Matt even— would have done the same thing."

"Right. I'm not sure I follow you, though."

"Just now, it hit me—and it was so obvious. You did what you had to, both of you did what you did, because you love me. I'm so grateful for that. So happy, so very, very happy. But I don't think I knew what that meant. That if my life was at stake, you'd do whatever was needed to protect me."

Tears gathered in my eyes, and I blinked them back. "I knew when I found you two, I'd found the loves of my life, but I didn't realize how deep that love went."

They were quiet... my guys, my bears.

"You know we'd do anything for you, Sadie. There's no question about that."

"We will always take care of you. For the rest of your life."

Their words came out at the same time, the conviction

strong in each voice. I raised their hands to my lips, kissing them, holding them against me.

"I guess I'm in awe."

"You're our life. Without you..."

"We're nothing." Dane finished Jackson's thought.

I nodded, sniffling. "I love you guys so much. Everything you do to protect me, to make my life so incredible... I'm so lucky to have you both. But it was so terrifying to be there." A tear slid down my cheek. "To be so close to what happened."

"It's going to take time to get over what happened. You were kidnapped. Anyone would be upset after that. You and Peyton... you're both going to need time to heal."

Jackson pulled me close. "And we're here, whatever you need. If you're having dreams or can't sleep... if you want to talk."

"Or be left alone. Whatever. We're here for you."

I had something to say, but Jackson leaned over and kissed me. Whatever I wanted to say wasn't important, at least not now. When his lips touched mine, everything else melted away. That's what I needed—his kiss, the warmth and strength of his arms around me. All the turmoil over what I saw or what I thought or felt about what happened, it could wait for another day, another time.

Jackson broke our kiss, and I turned to find Dane there, warm and waiting. He cradled my face in his hands, his kiss no less passionate but as individual as the man kissing me. It still took my breath away, being with both of them at the same time.

Dane pushed me gently onto my back, his rising erection rubbing against my hip. I was instantly ready, almost desperate to feel him inside me.

There was no hesitation in our dance, a dance that grew more familiar and more exiting each time we were together.

Dane settled between my thighs, exhaling softly as he entered me, matching my sigh of contentment, arousal, need.

The buildup was slow, Dane rising over me, eyes focused on me, looking into some part of me no one else had ever seen. I caressed his lips and cheeks, trailing my hand over his chest.

I arched against him, sliding my legs up his thighs, his hips, loving the feel of his muscles flexing as he made love to me.

The buildup might have been unhurried, but the payout was abrupt and intense. It was never the same twice, with either of them. This orgasm washed through me like waves crashing on the beach, wiping my body and mind clean, leaving behind an afterglow like none I'd ever had.

Dane moved away, and I lay, eyes closed, gasping, after-shocks shooting through me. I'd taken a breath, maybe two, when Jackson filled the space Dane had just occupied. He thrust into me, the fading aftershocks coming to life almost violently.

My eyes flew open, and I looked up into Jackson's dark eyes, the face of the other man I loved. The man who was now driving me insane, building on the fire Dane had started, changing it, everything ratcheting out of my control.

And Dane was there, touching my face, my breasts. I turned my face to him, and he kissed me, his tongue delving into my mouth as Jackson thrust into me.

In the next moment, I was flying, my body weightless, my emotions swirling, my voice rising as I came again, over and over, an endless loop of pleasure and satisfaction I never wanted to end.

▭

I'd gone to see Peyton the next afternoon. I heard her before I got to her room. She was arguing with someone—someone who was losing—about what she could or could not eat. Apparently, what she had was not what she wanted.

I leaned through the open door, rapping on the frame. "Peyton?"

She looked up, eyes flashing. One was bloodshot and puffy, black and blue, but behind that was good old Peyton. "It's about time. Did you bring me anything to eat? They have me on some liquid diet. I'm not an invalid. I can eat real food."

I tried to suppress a grin, but she shot me another look. The nurse bustled around, checking Peyton's IV, her cast, something under the sheets. At that, Peyton slapped the woman's hand. The nurse pulled back, gave Peyton a look I supposed was intended to appear fierce, and stormed out of the room.

I looked at my best friend, and we both burst out laughing.

"So, you're feeling okay?"

"Except for this..." She lifted her arm, the cast a startling white. "And the fact that the bastard ruined my new tattoo."

She settled back against the pillows. "Come on. Sit down. Tell me what you've been up to. It's been what... three days since all that shit went down?"

"Truthfully, I think it's two." I was still confused on days. I'd fallen into a deep, dreamless sleep after Jackson and Dane left me.

Peyton waved her hand. "It doesn't matter. They had me on so many pain meds I couldn't have reliably told you my own name."

I sat on the edge of the bed. "Do you remember anything?"

She shook her head. "Not much. You were there. I wrecked your car." She winced. "And that asshole shot me."

"The cabin? Anything about that?"

"Alex in the ambulance. That's the next thing I remember. Then not much 'til I came out of surgery. What did I miss?" She reached for me with her good hand.

"Nothing. I mean, a lot. But it's a long story." I wasn't sure I wanted to get into a play-by-play with her right now.

"But there's something, isn't there? You're not a very good liar, Sadie. And you can't play poker worth a damn."

Peyton knew me better than anyone, and she was the one I told everything to. "It's just... they killed the guy who kidnapped us. I was there. They'd shifted, all three of them. And Jackson and Dane... I heard what they did to him."

She held my gaze for a minute, hers level and calm. "Jackson and Dane did what any good bear would do, right?"

I looked down at her hand in mine, the bruises and cuts on her knuckles, then at the cast on her arm. I remembered the feeling of those broken bones under my fingers when I wrapped the towel around the wound. I looked at her face, the black eye, all of it. I remembered how he'd hit her, how he'd shot at her, meaning to kill her. Not me, her. Faull had done that to my friend.

Something raw and primal rose inside me, a foreign feeling of red-hot rage, a desire to hurt the man who'd hurt Peyton. Something clicked, a lens shifted in my brain, and everything became crystal clear.

I looked at her, my friend, the one who always saw things clearly. And I smiled. It was going to be okay.

"Yeah. Jackson and Dane did what any good bear—what any good friend or lover—would do. I would do the same for you, too. We're all family now, Peyton. And we always will be."

# BETWEEN TWO WOLVES

A PARANORMAL WOLF SHIFTER MÉNAGE ROMANCE

# CHAPTER 1

SWEAT DRIPPED INTO MY EYES, but I knew if I used the half second it would take to brush it away, Jack would be on my ass. So, I kept up my rhythm, feet moving between punches, hips and legs limber, my fists slamming the big bag as hard as I possibly could.

From behind the bag, I heard Jack grunt, but I didn't lose focus. He was almost as big as the target, and I knew his grunt was one of disapproval. Not from the force of my punch. I didn't think *anything* I threw could possibly rattle him, but I still tried. He'd been an amateur boxer since before I was born, a light heavyweight with a face that bore the scars of years in the ring.

*And he is a total hard-ass.*

"Less power, Red. Breathe... and stop staring at the damn bag. You're not focusing."

I absolutely *hated* being called Red. Only Jack could get away with calling me that. My name is Risha Reynolds. Being a redhead meant, for most of my life, people went for the easy jab of Risha Red. Yeah, I also got hit with the typical ginger you-don't-have-a-soul comments, but that shit didn't bother me. Not anymore anyway. Being called Red, however, made my fists clench and my blood boil. I wasn't sure why I had such a knee-jerk reaction to it, but it just bothered the hell out of me.

Like I said, Jack was the only one who could get away with it.

I punched again, landing a hit that sent the bag quivering like it was having a seizure. It felt good. *Really good.* Some of the anxiety that had been swirling around in my chest faded, that itchy feeling at the base of my spine that had been plaguing me since... since that fucker Harrison left me.

I stayed light on my feet in an easy bounce and then imagined it was Harrison, the asshole, in front of me instead of the bag. *Harrison, the jerk that left me for a college roommate.* Bounce again. Hit again. Harrison was on his knees now. Left-right combination, and Harrison was begging for a second chance.

The bag was suddenly coming at me. I took a startled step backward, dropping my hands. Jack reached around the bag, slapping his hand against the side of my head. It stung, but I was more embarrassed than hurt.

He scowled at me from behind the bag. "Whatever you're thinking about, it isn't this."

I stared at him. "What did you do that for?"

"Because you're wasting my time and yours. If you want to pay me while you daydream, find someone else. I want to train, not stand here watching you fuck around."

"Okay. Okay." I threw my hands up. "Sorry. It's just—"

"I don't care what it is. Here..." He reached for my hand, big fingers working quickly over the laces. "I'm paid to be your personal trainer, not your personal therapist."

The glove hit the floor. I held up my other hand, and he went to work on that one.

"I'm sorry. You're right. I'm a little out of it today." *A little is an understatement.* "It won't happen again."

"Damn straight." He dropped the second glove, reached out, and tapped a stubby forefinger against my forehead. "Whatever's up here, Red, leave it out there. You got about a quarter of an hour. Use it if you want or hit the locker room. But I'm still charging you for it."

I watched him walk away. He was right; he was *always* right. I'd known Jack for a little over six months, and even though he was a hard-ass, he'd given me the best advice about Harrison by not saying a damn thing. And usually, like today, that advice had been a slap alongside the head and a refusal to let me wallow in self-pity. Or at least not wallow on *his* time, even if it was my dime.

The day was a wash as far as training went. I scooped up the gloves and my water bottle and headed to the locker room. From across the ring that dominated the center of the room, I caught Jack's eye and the slow shake of his head. I could read him from here. *Wasting time again.*

So, I detoured, dropped the gloves and bottle, and climbed onto the treadmill. I'd walk out the last of my session, maybe redeem myself a little. I punched in a short program and started walking.

But this was worse than the bag. There was nothing to distract me from myself. I tried watching the guys in the ring and focusing on their motions. The cute guy with the black hair was sparring with someone new, and for a minute, I watched them circle and dance, jab and weave. But even that wasn't enough to hold my attention. It drifted again. Back to Harrison.

*You need to get your head on straight, Risha.*

Jack was right. To still let what happened with Harrison bother me after all these months was crazy. But he'd been the guy I thought was the love of my life, my soul mate, the man I was going to marry. And I thought he felt the same way about me. That was until he told me he thought we should see other people. And then topped that off by casually mentioning he was dating my old college roommate. I called it quits.

The timer buzzed on the treadmill, and I stepped off. The cute guy was gone from the ring, and Jack had already started training with his next client. Everyone was busy getting on with their lives. I gathered up my gear and headed to the locker room.

Jack was right. I needed to move on already.

"I think getting away is a good idea, but why the middle of nowhere? Can't you get Harrison out of your system at a spa or some resort? Some place with indoor plumbing?"

My best friend, Maggie, was curled on my couch, sipping a cosmo, as usual. She'd just binge-watched an entire season of *Sex and the City*, and she was channeling her inner Carrie Bradshaw. I had to giggle. It certainly suited her personality. She was a girly girl through and through and a complete opposite of me. Maybe that was why we'd been friends so long. Opposites attract and all that bullshit.

"I like to hike and camp. You know that." I plopped down in the chair opposite her. "It's only for a couple days. Nothing's going to happen to me, other than bug bites and maybe a case of poison ivy. I'm just tired of everything that reminds me of Harrison. I'm tired of..." I waved my hand in the vague direction of pretty much everything in sight.

We'd shared this apartment, and while I'd gotten rid of most of his personal belongings, the things we bought together, like the couch I no longer sat on, were silent reminders of him— of us. Of what was no more.

"I need a vacation. And it's been ages since I've gone camping. I miss being out in the woods. And hey, it's a two-person tent if you want to come along."

Maggie was already shaking her head. "Oh, hell no. Not me. I'm a city girl, and you know it. I'm lost if there's anything other than concrete beneath my feet. If I go longer than a few days without retail therapy, I go into shock."

"And that's exactly why you need a two-bedroom apartment. Just so you have enough room for your shoes."

"And that's why I'm a very happy girl." She laughed. "Retail therapy. Works every time."

"Well, I'm glad you found your bliss. Mine is outside. Alone with nothing but nature and myself."

Maggie's laugh faded. "Yeah. About that." Her expression suddenly changed, and I knew where this conversation was headed. "So why can't you think here? Why not just hole up with a gallon of Ben & Jerry's and a bunch of movies?"

"Because there's email and phones and clients with deadlines... and interruptions." *And reminders around every corner and in every drawer and in every closet.* Basically, I lived in a haunted apartment with my ex as the resident ghost.

"But why the need to live amongst the wild? Can't you just unplug everything and disconnect from the world for a bit? Even I can do that."

"Not the same, Maggie. Do you want another cosmo?" It was hard to derail Maggie when she got like this. But she wasn't taking the bait.

I got another beer, bracing myself for what was coming next. She waited until I was back in my chair before she started up again.

"Rish, I've said this before. You spend too much time alone. You work from home, order groceries online, have takeout delivered. Who do you see besides me?"

"Jack, at the gym." I wanted to say the other guys at the gym, but I had to admit, even to myself, I really didn't even know their names. "Clients." That sounded lame to my own ears.

"Clients. Rish, you've never even met most of your clients. For all you know, Hannah in Canada might be a middle-aged man in Florida. These people are barely more than an email address or Skype name."

"That's unfair. It's not like that, and you know it. This isn't online dating; this is my business. I'm a ghostwriter. It's not like I have to know my clients personally. They send me an outline, I complete the work, and they pay me. I don't exactly have to be their friend."

But I did have to admit I had doubts sometimes about who was on the other end of the email address. As a ghostwriter, all my business took place via the Internet, so I would never really know. But quite honestly, I didn't care. I kept my head down and did the work.

"My point, Rish, is you're alone. A lot. And I don't know that it's a good idea for you go off and be even more alone than you already are."

"This is different."

"How so? Alone is alone, either here or in the middle of nowhere. You're still alone."

"I asked if you wanted to come with me, remember?" I figured that would shut her up. "Besides, I'm my own best company. I have an active imagination. And hey, there are a whole lot of people living in my head. They'll keep me company." I gave her my best smile, but she wasn't buying it.

"That's another thing. You write strange stories about were-wolves, vampires, things that go bump in the night. You asked if you could duct tape me to a chair just last week to see if I could escape!" She shook her head, and I laughed. I'd asked her to do that as research, and she'd flat out refused to be my guinea pig. I couldn't say I blamed her. "It's just that I worry about you."

"Yeah, I know. I worry about me, too, sometimes. But this is different. There's something special that happens in the deep woods... something elemental. I always feel as though I belong out there. Like I'm going home." I shrugged. "Sounds weird to you, but it's my bliss. I miss it."

Maggie rolled her eyes, but I could tell I was getting through to her. "Well, you were always the hippie chick." She grinned at me over the edge of her glass. "I suppose running naked through the woods would do you some good. At least you'll get rid of that indoor pallor, get some sun. You never do see the sun, do you? With the vampire hours you keep."

It was my turn to roll my eyes. "I'm not a vampire. I work from home. And I don't tan. You know that. Red hair..." I ran my hand through my hair, fanning the strands over my shoulders. "Freckles, all of it... I'm doomed to be pale, regardless of my work schedule."

All this flaming red hair—which only flamed brighter as I got older, not dimming as my mother had said it would as she tried in vain to console me while I'd cried over its brash color—was really difficult to manage, which meant I wasn't exactly a popular kid. It had taken *years* to finally come to terms that I would always stand out in the crowd, and through it all, somehow, I learned to love the hair and freckles that made me different.

Maggie sighed, a sound of resignation.

I hoped we'd come to the point where she just gave up, just as we did every time, we had a variation of this conversation. I didn't like the confrontation, and this was as confrontational as we ever got.

"So, when are you going off to play forest fairy?"

"This weekend, I think. If I can get caught up on work, I

can take off Thursday and Friday and be back Sunday night. I'm only going up to the hot springs at Big River."

"Oh, see? You'll be skinny-dipping, too! I've heard all about the sort of things that go on up at those secluded hot springs." Maggie giggled, finishing her cosmo. "Too bad you don't have someone to take along..." She winced. "I'm sorry. I mean some random guy you just met, you know, for a wild weekend fling in your two-person tent. Maybe you'll meet your hippie soul mate up there. Heaven knows you'd have more in common with the guys who hang out up there than the juice pigs at the gym."

"No wild weekend flings. I want to meditate, do some yoga, sit in the springs, and just think."

Maggie leaned forward, setting her glass on the coffee table, her smile fading. "You just can't do things like everyone else, can you?" Apparently, she hadn't quite given up yet. "It's the same thing with the boxing. Why not a membership at a regular gym? Instead, you go to the extreme, hanging out with a bunch of guys who like to beat the shit out of one another. And still, no dates."

I rolled my eyes, probably for the tenth time in the last hour. We'd had this conversation before, too. "I didn't join the club looking for a date, Maggie. I wanted to get in shape—"

"You can get in shape at a better place than a fight club, Risha."

"It's not a fight club."

Maggie was already holding up her hands in mock protest, but she was smiling. "I know, I know. Boxing is a great workout, great for cardio, gets you strong... I've heard the sales pitch."

She laughed as she stood and grabbed her purse, then leaned over and kissed my cheek. "Listen, Rish, you do what you need to do. You've never done the conventional thing, so if heading into the woods and bending yourself into a pretzel is what you need, then go for it. Personally, I think a weekend at

Bloomingdale's would be a great way to forget an ex, especially if you happened to still have one of his credit cards. But then again, we never do see things the same way, do we?"

"I guess not," I replied with a smile. Maggie drove me crazy at times, but I knew she always had my best interests at heart.

"Have fun," she said, hugging me. "Everything is going to be okay. Harrison was a jerk. You know you're better off without him. So, go and zen out until you feel better. I love ya, girl."

"I love you, too, Maggie."

After she left, I slumped back into my chair, avoiding the couch, shifting around until I got comfortable.

Maggie had known me since grade school. We'd seen each other through boyfriends and college, jobs and first apartments. She knew me better than anyone, even if it was clear she didn't understand me.

But she was right; I wasn't conventional, never had been. And that was fine with me.

CHAPTER 2

I WAS HEADED to Big River, which ran down the backside of Black Wolf Mountain. Most of Black Wolf, and the mountains around it, were part of the Seven Mountains State Park, but the ridge that ran north along the backside of Black Wolf belonged to a huge tract of land, over several hundred acres that stretched all the way to the Canadian border, that everyone assumed belonged to a private party.

It was crisscrossed with disused logging roads, some that ran up to the park land. Most were posted with *No Trespassing* signs, blocked off with chains and padlocks, and over the years, small trees had sprouted, further blending the roads back into the surrounding forest.

According to local lore, and then translated through stories that got passed around among hikers who used the springs, there had been sightings of big animals—wolves, mountain lions, bears—bigger than any known species. Most of those stories were told around the campfire, along with a bottle or three of wine—or something stronger—shared with novice hikers coming up the mountain for the first time.

The logging road that ran up the back of the mountain wasn't on park land, and there hadn't been any logging in the area for decades. It had always been rough, but this year, there had been torrential rains and the road turned from washboard to rutted to washed out far below where the trail to the hot springs began.

So, I parked my car, dragged out my gear, and locked up. I always worried I'd come back to find the car gone, but in all the years I'd been coming here, it was always right where I left it. The only problem I'd ever heard about was when a bear had attacked a friend's ancient Subaru to get after some food that had been left on the dashboard. He'd come back from a week in the woods to find the roof torn off the car and the food long gone.

I stopped to look around, breathing in the cool air. I closed my eyes and smiled. It felt like the first time I'd smiled in a long, long time. Or at least that the smile felt authentic, not forced for a client on Skype or a cashier at the market or a cab driver. It occurred to me that there might be more to think about this weekend besides Harrison. Maybe it was time to think about the bigger picture rather than just the missing piece to the puzzle.

After hiking halfway up the mountain to the turnoff to the springs, I was sweating, breathing hard, and very glad I'd only brought enough in my pack for a long weekend. The idea of setting up camp, kicking back in one of the hot springs as the sun went down, and then having a simple dinner by the fire with some wine was looking more and more enticing. I dropped my pack for a minute, loving that fleeting sense of weightlessness that happened after shedding all that bulk. I stretched my arms and rolled my shoulders. This was going to be a great weekend. I would be one with nature, live in the moment, stop dwelling in the past. Maybe I'd come home with my own tall tale from the forest, my own lore to add to that of my camping friends.

The forest ahead of me was deep, dark green. I always loved this part, stepping off the road, out of the sunshine, and into the cool darkness of the woods. It was magical, like stepping into a fairy tale. I thought of *Snow White, Sleeping Beauty*, and the other stories I'd read as a child. If I could build a house anywhere in the world, it would be here on the edge of the unknown, just over the line from civilization. Not so far over that I'd have to give up plumbing and shaving my legs, but just enough to ease out of the rat race.

So, I shouldered my pack and took one last look back down the road. There was no one in sight, no other cars, no sounds of traffic, nothing but a lone hawk circling overhead. I felt as though I were alone in the world. And that was fine with me.

Out of habit, I dug my phone out of my pocket, checking for messages before I remembered there was no service up here. I chided myself for bringing along this last bit of technology. I held it for a minute and considered flinging it off the edge of the mountain, but I wasn't quite ready to divest myself of all the trappings of civilization. I shut it off and jammed it into my pocket.

The woods were cool, the path covered in pine needles. I was on level ground for the next couple miles, and then I'd find a gentle descent to Big River and the springs. My steps were muffled, almost soundless. I could already feel the tension and anxiety of the past months ebbing out of my body. I was pretty sure by the time I reached the springs, got my little camp set up, and made dinner, I'd be exhausted—in a good way. A soak in the hot springs and a little wine, and I'd be too tired in body and mind to obsess about Harrison. And tomorrow, maybe a sunrise session of yoga, a nice breakfast, and then I'd sit and think.

The pines here grew so close together they almost touched overhead. The path wound in and out of shafts of sunlight, and for a time, I was conscious of the difference in warmth against my skin, then the chill as I stepped out of the light. My senses seemed heightened, every detail popping out at me. I started to notice my footfalls, the shushing sound my boots made, the wind above me. I was in my zone, living in the moment. This was going to be a great weekend.

Something was off, though. The hair on my arms stood on end. I stopped, thinking there was someone on the path ahead of me or behind me. Or in the woods. I listened carefully, but the only things I heard were the wind, a few birds in the trees. Maybe I wasn't as relaxed as I thought I was.

I did a slow circle, but I didn't see anyone. A bird sang somewhere close by. Another answered. The forest seemed just as it always did, filled with its usual flecks of color. I shook my head, laughing at myself. Maybe I'd turned into a city girl, buffered by traffic noises, city sounds, and now freaked out by a little silence.

But standing in the middle of the path wasn't going to get me to those hot springs. With one last look back, I turned around.

And stopped dead in my tracks.

The wolf stood in the middle of the path. It was big, *really* big, but also amazingly beautiful. It stared at me, and I was mesmerized, unable to look away. And then I panicked. Staring at them was a sign of dominance or aggression or something. But I'd be damned if I was going to take my eyes off the predator.

But it didn't seem vicious. *Like I would know what a vicious wolf looks like.*

It looked more curious than anything, standing in the path with its head tipped to the side, dark eyes on mine as if it were analyzing me. And it was stunningly beautiful, dark fur tipped with silver, big eyes. I stared at him and he stared back, and for a moment, I had the sensation of having my mind read or my soul searched. Or the living daylights scared out of me.

"Hey, boy... good boy." *Oh my God.* My heart was frozen in fear. The wolf tipped its head farther. *Progress.* I babbled on. "Oh yeah. Good boy..."

The wolf took a step forward, pink tongue showing in a doggy grin. I took a step back.

*No one's going to believe this. Oh shit. Take a picture.* Slowly, I eased my phone out of my pocket, eyes never leaving the wolf. I turned on the phone, dropped my eyes from the wolf for the split second it took to take the picture, then looked up.

The wolf whined, a low, soft sound. *But what does that mean? Have I upset it?*

Reflexively, I clicked off another couple pictures. The wolf whined again, and I let my arm fall to my side as it took another step forward. Every cell in my body told me to run, but I held my ground.

"Okay. Okay. I'm done. No more pictures. Good boy..."

The wolf stopped, ears pricked forward. Then it advanced another step.

I held up my hands. "Whoa... stop." The hair on the back of my neck stood up. "Please stop." My voice came out in a desperate whisper.

The wolf stopped, eyes still locked with mine. They were blue, like a husky dog.

*Maybe that's what he is, just someone's pet off its leash.* I let out a sigh of sorts.

"Would it be too much to ask you to sit?"

Behind it, the tail started to wave back and forth in slow motion. And then, to my amazement, it sat down in the middle of the path. *So, it is someone's pet.*

"Hello?"

I spun around. A man was walking toward me, wearing a park ranger uniform. Relief washed through me, along with a wave of giggles. This must be the ranger's dog.

"Boy, am I glad to see you. Your dog—" I was already pointing, and I turned back to the wolf. But the path was empty. No dog or wolf or anything else was visible in the shifting patterns of light and dark. My giggles faded away.

"Sorry, ma'am. Did you say dog?" His friendly expression took on a hint of concern. "I don't have a dog. None of us do."

"There was a dog..." I was still pointing to where the animal had been. "Or a wolf..."

The ranger walked past me, then crouched at the spot where the canine had been. "There's tracks here, ma'am, but I can't really say what made them. Hard to tell when it comes to this stuff." He brushed his hand over the spot, scooping up a handful of pine needles. I watched as he lifted them to his nose and inhaled. His face took on a strained expression, blotting out the friendly neighborhood ranger concern. I'd have to say it was a look of recognition, followed by one of pure hatred.

But when he tossed away the needles and stood, all that was gone. I blinked, not sure what I'd seen replaced by a bland expression, a noncommittal smile. Maybe I was still spooked by the phantom wolf or the light and shadows were playing tricks.

He smiled down at me. "It was probably just a coyote chasing a rabbit. The altitude, the light, the isolation... if you're not used to being out in the woods, it can play tricks on you."

I frowned. "It was a wolf or a big dog. I'm not a novice. I've been up here before—"

He cut me off. "We haven't had a wolf sighting in the park in decades."

There was something programmed about his response,

dismissive in a way I didn't like. It felt as though the guy was hiding something.

"Okay. Then it was a coyote." I shifted my pack, settling it on my shoulders. "I should get going, then. I've got a way to go before I set up camp."

"You're headed to the springs, then." He stepped to the side of the path. "Then I'll let you get on your way. Don't wander off the path. Wouldn't want you getting lost." He touched the brim of his hat, and I stepped past him.

"Thanks." I walked along the path, looking down at the spot where the wolf had been. If there had been any sign of paw prints, they were obliterated now. Somehow, the disturbed pine needles looked like a broken window in a church. I wanted to put it all back in order. But I walked on.

I'd only gone a couple yards when I had the urge to turn around to see if the ranger was walking away. But I knew he wasn't, and I knew when I turned—which I did—I'd find him watching me. And he was. He waved again, still smiling. When he finally turned away and headed back down the path, I let out the breath I'd been holding.

Some of my excitement had dimmed after the encounter with the wolf. And the ranger—something tugged at my mind about the whole thing. Something was off that I should have noticed. It wasn't until I was almost to the springs that it dawned on me. He hadn't been wearing a name badge. And he hadn't told me his name.

# CHAPTER 3

I ARRIVED at the springs in the late afternoon. The trail dipped close to the river and the springs before climbing back up to high ground. Things looked familiar, although it had been years since I'd been here. Trees had grown, some had fallen, but the whole placed felt known. The springs, as usual, were totally different. But that was normal. Nature was capricious, and nowhere was that more evident than down by the river. I dropped my pack and took it all in.

In early spring, when the snow melted off the mountains, the river that ran through the area rose, tumbling down the mountain, moving rocks and sometimes boulders. And each spring, the first hikers in, and sometimes locals, worked to rebuild the rock walls around the places where the hot springs bubbled up, creating ledges for sitting and filling in the bottoms of the pools with sand. Most years, there would be many small pools, each big enough for just one or two people.

This year, there were several smaller pools and one big party-sized area in the middle of everything. It could easily hold a dozen people, and as I set down my pack, I marveled at how many rocks it had taken to construct this beautiful creation. I walked around, noticing seating ledges, a sandy bottom, and an actual set of steps built out of flat stones. It made me think a group of engineers had shown up to create this masterpiece. It was an even more impressive feat when I thought that it would be gone next spring.

I grabbed my pack and went to find a place to set up camp. The park maintained a few wilderness areas on this side of the mountain. There was a clearing that I was particularly fond of, and I hoped nobody would be there. Since I hadn't seen any cars and since it was still early in the season, I was pretty confident it would be free.

And it was. I breathed out a sigh and set down my pack for the last time today. There was something very special about this place, the way the trees formed a lacy ceiling overhead. There were hardwoods, oaks, and maples mostly, and right now, the leaves were still that bright green that made the clear light seem magical. It was perfect.

I sat for a minute in my cathedral of trees, just breathing in the cool air, enjoying the silence and not having my pack on my shoulders. A weekend spent here would do me a world of good. I realized I was still smiling, and it felt wonderful.

*First things first.* I needed to set up the tent, which was probably my least favorite chore. But if I didn't have a tent and it rained, which it usually did, I'd be miserable. Best to just get it done.

I fought with the slippery nylon and flexible rods that held it all together. It was fiddly, and I muttered under my breath. Harrison had never enjoyed camping, and gradually, I'd stopped going on solo hikes. So over time, I'd given away most of my good gear to friends. No one had wanted this old tent, and I'd never gotten around to getting a new one. Not that I'd have ever used it while we were together.

*Enough, Risha. You came here to forget about him, not look for things to remember.*

I sighed, sitting down on a log someone had moved into the clearing, the tent in a forlorn pile at my feet. I wanted to forget, but there were so many things that reminded me of a conversation with Harrison—or more likely, an argument. The tent, a piece of art he'd left behind. *The one I bought for his birthday.* The couch. The apartment we'd shared. I'd thought about moving, but I realized there was only so far, I could go in getting Harrison out of my life and my mind.

The sounds of the river caught my attention. The sun was getting lower, and I made a sudden decision. I would go down, take a soak in one of the hot springs, and leave the tent until later. The slices of sky that showed between the trees were clear, and I could set up the tent when I got back.

Rummaging through my pack, I dug out an old pair of shorts, tattered and full of holes, indecent for any public place. But they were perfect for the hot springs. I'd learned a long time ago that no matter how carefully they tried to make the ledges and seats comfortable, the rocks could still be rough on my tender backside and would inevitably ruin any good pair of shorts I wore, so I had decided to pack my old, worn-out ones.

I cast a slightly nervous glance around the clearing. There was no one around, and I knew that. But since I'd left the ranger, I'd had the disconcerting feeling of another presence. Not exactly of being watched, but that there was someone close by. I'd done a lot of long-distance hiking in college, and I'd discovered this weird kind of sixth sense that happens when there's someone ahead of you or behind you on the trail. There's no sign of them, but you know before you hear or see them that they're there.

But there was no one here now, except for a blue jay that was unhappy that I'd invaded its territory. It cawed and carried on, scolding me loudly. I shook off the eerie feeling of being watched, tugged off my jeans and underwear, and pulled on my shorts. Reaching beneath my T-shirt, I undid the clasp on my bra and wiggled out of it, sliding my arms in and out of the sleeves of my shirt. I dropped the bra on top of my jeans. I tucked a Thermos filled with white wine in a towel under my arm. The jay scolded again from the pines, and I jumped.

*It's just city girl nerves. You're out of practice. That's all.*

The walk to the springs had one of the most spectacular views in the area. From beneath the dark branches of the pines, the path suddenly turned, and I stepped into the bright sunlight at the edge of a drop-off. Below was the river, an emerald strand tumbling over boulders the size of my car. The water was full of shifts in color and translucency from its mad rush over the rocks, churning white in some places, almost clear in slower-moving areas. It was stunningly beautiful. Everything I'd been worrying about fell away as I stood and took in the view.

There were several pools along the riverbank this year, some small ones, one or two larger ones. The water in them was a kind of cloudy blue-gray from the minerals in the water. I'd never quite understood where the hot springs came from. Every time I saw them, I vowed to find out. Then I fell in love with them all over again with the magical feeling of sitting on a rock in hot water while watching nature, and then I forgot that I cared where they came from. All I cared about was that they were there and someone took the time to make it easy to access them.

I scrambled down the path to the river and the pools, trying to decide which one to sample first. The temperatures could differ radically between pools, with some being just above the chill temperature of the river and others so hot I could only stay in a few minutes before feeling like a boiled lobster. I wanted something warm and comforting, a pool I could melt into and stay in for hours.

I dipped my toe in several, testing the waters. Some were hot, some were cool, and some were steaming. I laughed at the image, me walking from pool to pool, feeling a little like Goldilocks wandering around until I found one that was just right. Easing down the bank, I stepped into the pool. The water was perfect, almost too hot to stand, but I knew I'd get used to it quickly. Uncapping the Thermos, I poured the cup full of wine, taking a long, healthy swallow.

I sat on a rock, the water swirling around my legs, curling my toes in the heat. Across the river was the edge of the land that didn't belong to the park, and I tried to see into the darkness of the pines. Even though it was only twenty yards or so away, it seemed like another country, vaguely foreign, slightly spooky. I thought of wolves and woodsmen and witches with poisoned apples living in gingerbread cottages. I was mixing up my fairy tales. *And it's only my first glass of wine.*

Scattered all over the bank were small stones, polished smooth by years in the river. Picking up a handful, I choose a dozen or so that felt good in my hand or looked interesting or were just plain pretty. I'd learned a little ritual ages ago, something to help clear the mind. I held up one stone, wishing I'd remembered to bring something to write with. I'd have to improvise.

"This is the painting Harrison didn't like. Take the memory and wash it away." I threw the stone into the river. It barely made a sound as it hit the surface. I tried to visualize all the hurt attached to that image washed away in the river.

I picked another stone. "For the time he missed my birthday party." I flung the rock. It skipped once on the water and disappeared. I took another sip of wine. I wasn't sure if it was the ritual or the Chardonnay, but I suddenly felt better.

I went through the rocks one by one, letting go of a little pain with each one, throwing the stone into the river. Finally, I was down to the last. It was different, bigger and black, polished to a high sheen. I wondered what kind of rock it was. But again, my knowledge of geology failed me.

"For my father. I miss you, Dad. More than you can imagine." I held the rock, thinking about my father, about him and me—just him and me—for as long as I could remember. Maybe this rock should have been for my mother, who left us when I was seven. But I'd given up being angry with her a long time ago. She'd made a choice in her life that didn't include her husband or her daughter. I didn't—*couldn't*—understand why. But being angry with her had torn a hole in my heart. I'd given up the anger and tried to patch up that hole.

But my dad... missing him was a palpable thing, an ache somewhere deep inside. I didn't want to forget him, but the pain of missing him was just as sharp as if he'd died yesterday instead of two years ago. I wanted the memories, just not the pain.

I held the rock, weighing it in my hand. Closing my fingers around it, I raised my arm, ready to toss it into the river. But I couldn't unclench my fist. I brought my arm down, opened my hand, and looked at the rock through a curtain of tears. Maybe this was the wrong time, wrong place for this. I found myself crying, tears plopping onto the rock, making the black surface glisten. *Not today.* Finally, I slipped the stone into my pocket.

After a minute or two, I scooted to a lower boulder, pouring another cup of wine. The water rose around my waist, heat sinking into my core. I slouched down, stretched my arms along the rocks at the edge of the pool, and let the water rise almost to my chin. I was in heaven.

I lost all track of time as the water moved and danced around my body. My muscles relaxed bit by bit, and then all at once, it was perfect. The water was the perfect temperature, and I couldn't tell where I ended and it started. My body floated, and my mind went blank. Maybe the rock tossing ritual had actually helped.

There was a bird singing somewhere in the middle distance, a low whistle that repeated twice, then paused, then picked up again. I counted the repeats, waiting through the pauses, then started whistling back, trying to see if the bird would answer. It did, giving me a long series of whistles in response to my amateur attempts. I giggled and took another sip of wine. I was nicely buzzed from the heat and the alcohol and, by now, more than a little giggly.

"That's pretty good. You must spend a lot of time up here."

I sat up too quickly, slipped in the water, then splashed around for an awkward minute, trying to see who was talking to me. The sun was in my eyes, and all I could make out was a dark form towering over me.

"Sorry. I startled you." The form moved around to the other side of the pool. I pivoted, watching him turn from a dark, face-less shape into a man with longish dark hair and piercing blue eyes.

"You did." I'd stopped splashing now, and I sat on the edge of the rock, watching as he walked so the sun was shining on his face. My heart was still thumping away in my chest. There was always the possibility of other hikers showing up at the springs, but still, he'd scared the daylights out of me. And no matter how nice hikers could be, I was always uneasy when I was out here alone and a lone guy showed up. I liked to trust people and give them the benefit of the doubt, but I'd heard enough stories over the years to be wary. He seemed okay so far. But I sort of regretted being buzzed on wine and out here all alone.

"Sorry again. I thought you heard me walk up. I crashed

through the underbrush like a moose. Anyway, can I join you?" He dropped his pack and smiled at me.

For a minute, I lost the thread of our brief conversation. The smile was dazzling, all white teeth set against tan skin. I managed to look at the rest of his face, bright-blue eyes framed by long dark hair curling around his shoulders. The moment stretched on, and then I remembered he'd asked me a question.

"Oh, yeah. Sure. There's lots of room." Actually, there wasn't. It was one of the smaller pools, but it would hold two. I pulled myself upright, the air chilling the skin on my arms and my upper chest. It cleared a bit of the logy feeling in my head.

*Why did he have to choose my pool of all the ones around?* I suddenly felt so awkward and uncomfortable.

"Great." If possible, the smile got bigger.

He pulled off his black T-shirt and started undoing the buttons on his jeans. I realized I was staring, then quickly dropped my eyes. Some people liked to skinny-dip, and while I didn't have anything against skinny-dipping, I wasn't sure I wanted to be in a pool with a naked stranger.

*A stranger... This stranger maybe, but not necessarily a naked one.*

"It's okay. I'm wearing trunks."

My face flushed, but I looked up at him, managing a smile and an apologetic shrug. "You never know at the springs. A girl can't be too careful."

He was wearing trunks. But if he'd been naked, he couldn't have looked any sexier. It had been a long time since I'd looked at any guy with the least bit of interest, but for some reason, I couldn't look away from this one. He was all long legs, tan skin, broad chest with just enough dark hair to keep him from looking too manscaped. I swallowed hard, managing to keep the smile on my face from getting any wider.

"So, you've been here before, then?" He slipped into the

pool, the water distorting his shape as he sank below the surface. There was an eddy in the pool, and I swore it carried an extra wash of something besides heat against my body. My arms flushed with goose bumps, and I was suddenly conscious of my wet T-shirt, how it clung to my breasts. How little was left to the imagination, his imagination. I sank slowly into the water, the heat of it against my cool skin sending a shiver through me.

*Don't get all excited here. He's still a stranger. Just stay cool, okay. Don't embarrass yourself.*

"I've been coming here since college... I used to come with friends on breaks and then started coming alone after that."

"Oh, hey. I'm so rude. My name is Colt." I thought I heard an accent, not Canadian, certainly not American.

He leaned across the space between us, hand extended. I hesitated, then reached out, fingers just brushing his. I scooted forward a little more, and that's when I lost my balance.

I slipped off the boulder, going face first underwater. For a minute, the world was very hot and very murky. Water went in my mouth and up my nose, the odd taste of minerals heavy on my tongue. I flailed for a moment, unable to get a grip on anything solid, unable to get my footing. Then a hand grabbed my upper arm, pulling me out of the water.

Sputtering, I finally drew a breath. I blinked and spit out a mouthful of warm water. It tasted bitter, metallic. The guy pulled me onto his lap with a strength I found quite surprising, more than a little alarming, but strangely appealing. I wiped the last of the water out of my eyes, coughing. There could be worse places to end up after falling into the pool.

He wrapped an arm around my waist, pulling me against his muscled chest. I was at a loss as to what to do with my hands, just barely resisting the urge to run my fingers through that light dusting of chest hair. I finally ended up with my hands folded primly in my lap. If my heart had been beating hard before, now it practically shook my body with every beat.

"You okay?"

I nodded. "Yeah. Just embarrassed. I'm not usually this clumsy."

"It's okay." He chuckled, and I was immediately captivated by the sparkle in his eyes. "Do-over? I'm Colt. Nice to meet you." He held out his free hand. I took it, shook it, pulled away... but he held on. "And you are?"

"I'm Risha. Rish to my friends."

"Can I call you Rish, then? Do I qualify for friend status yet? I did just save your life, after all."

"You did. And you do. So yeah, Rish is fine."

"Or Red. I think you look like a Red." He reached up, fingering a strand of my hair between his fingers.

I stared at him. A flash of resentment at that old name rose up, but I bit back my retort and looked closely at his face. There was no malice in those dark eyes, nothing intended, other than him looking at my hair, at the strand wound around his fingers. But I was a little freaked out by the intimate gesture, even if it seemed innocent.

"Yeah. I've been called Red." *In the past.* But I didn't add that. I was moving on, and he sure wasn't part of my past. Although, I wasn't sure right now what he was or what he really wanted. Or what I was doing. I should be back on the other side of the pool. Or out of the pool.

"It suits you. You look like a Red."

I cocked an eyebrow. "And what does a Red look like?"

He tugged gently on my hair. "I bet when this is dry, it blazes like fire." His eyes moved languidly to mine. "And I bet you're just as fiery."

The hand on my waist slipped down to my hip. My T-shirt

had ridden up, and his fingers brushed over my bare skin. I gasped, then coughed to cover the sound.

Colt let go of the strand of hair and reached up to touch my cheek. "You okay? Do you need mouth-to-mouth or anything?"

I laughed. "Don't you think it's a little late to ask? I'm talking, and..." His fingers slipped to the nape of my neck. "Breathing..." I might be breathing, but those breaths were coming in short little gasps. His eyes moved slowly from mine, down to my lips. I swallowed hard.

"Yeah. But you know..." He pulled me closer. "Better safe than sorry."

I pulled back. "Speaking of safe..." His pack lay behind him, and I eyed it warily. "I'm not exactly sure—"

"You're not exactly sure if this is the right thing to do? If I'm dangerous? Or if you can trust me?" He raised an eyebrow. "I'm not dangerous. I can tell you that you can trust me, but those are just words. You'll have to make up your own mind about me." He looked over his shoulder at his pack. "If you can reach it, toss it where I can't. If that makes you feel better. I won't be offended."

I looked between him and the pack. Without too much trouble, I snagged the strap, tugging it around to the side of the pool. Colt watched, his expression open, easy.

"Better? A girl's gotta do what a girl's gotta do, right?"

Before I could answer, his lips touched mine, softly but not tentatively. Behind the gentle touch was an energy, something powerful but restrained. I'd never felt anything like this in my entire life, and it wasn't just that I was kissing a stranger.

*Oh, wow... I am kissing a stranger.*

I tried to pull back, but Colt's fingers tightened on the back of my neck. I should have been... not exactly scared, but at least a hell of a lot more cautious. I should have pulled away. But I didn't. I might regret this later, but right now, I wanted this... *whatever* this was or wherever it was going. I wanted Colt.

The kiss deepened, his lips parted, and I was right there with him, my tongue meeting his, dancing between his mouth and mine. I raised a hand from my lap, touching his neck, his jaw, moving to wind my fingers into all that dark hair. It was curly and soft.

Arousal washed through me, and my fingers tightened against his head, pulling him closer, deepening the kiss even farther. I felt Colt's lips curve in a smile against mine as his fingers worked beneath my wet T-shirt, tugging it higher up the curve of my ribcage, stopping just short of where I wanted his hand to be.

He broke the kiss, pulling back just enough to look into my eyes. "You seem to be breathing just fine, Red. You sure you need any more mouth-to-mouth?"

"You're kidding, right?" I wiggled in his lap, feeling his thighs tense and flex... feeling something else tense beneath the thin fabric of his trunks. "I think we both want the same thing, Colt. Unless there's something else..."

Colt laughed, pulling me back until my forehead rested against his. "Yeah. Okay. Just wanted to make sure. I get the sense this isn't your usual method of approach. Mine either. But—"

"I'm sure." I might not do this often... or ever. But I was sure of what I wanted, even if he was right about me.

I kissed him, moving on his lap so I could wrap both arms around his neck. He shifted in response, his erection rising against my hip. I wiggled again just to feel the hardness of it and to see what Colt would do.

Colt didn't miss a beat. Without breaking our kiss, he grabbed my hips, sliding me back off his lap. I pivoted, legs apart, so when he pulled me back, I was straddling him. I was sitting face to face on his hard thighs, his erection sliding up between my legs as the hot water swirled around us. He pulled me closer until my breasts were pressed against his chest. He slid his hands down my back as he broke the kiss, slowly teasing my lower lip between his teeth. When he released me, I was weak and shivery with desire, glad I was sitting down.

He cupped my ass, pulling me hard against his body, making waves in the pool. "You really are ready for this." I couldn't tell by his smile if he thought this was amusing or confusing, if he was asking a question or making a statement.

"Yeah... Are you?" I rolled my hips, grinding against Colt. "You want to change your mind?"

This time, his smile told me everything, his words the icing on the cake. "Like hell. It's not every day a gorgeous, barely dressed woman practically falls into my lap."

"I did fall into your lap." I ran my hands through his hair, returning his smile. "You saved my life. I'm just showing my gratitude."

"I like how you think, Red."

I wasn't sure I was thinking or that I wanted to. I wanted to feel, to just go with the flow. Somehow, as crazy as this all was, it felt right, and that's all I cared about right now.

"Yolo."

"Hmm?" he murmured, his eyes wild with desire.

"You only live once."

He pulled me back against him, capturing my lips with his. Birds sang around us, the sound of the river catching the edge of my consciousness. All of that faded as Colt kissed me, the sound of his breathing, the soft moan he made as I shifted against his erection the only things I heard. I was lost in a sea of arousal and sensation swirling through me.

Colt's hands moved up my back, tugging up my shirt farther, exposing my breasts. It was my turn to moan against his mouth as he cupped my breasts, working his thumbs over my wet nipples. They puckered hard and tight, and my moan turned into a full-throated cry of pleasure as I broke away from him, head tipping back.

"Oh God."

Spanning my torso with his hands, Colt pushed my breasts up and together. He looked down, and I arched my back, pushing against his palms. He responded, fingers tightening against me, kneading my flesh. I bit my lip, unable to stifle a second cry.

"Watch me, Red."

I looked down at him, meeting his eyes as he lowered his head, flicking his tongue over one hard nipple. Something close to an electric shock ricocheted through me, and I jerked in his arms. I saw the corner of his mouth turn up as he moved to the other breast, circling the rosy nipple with the tip of his tongue. The feeling was exquisite, sending another shock wave through me. Watching him made little tendrils of excitement curl through my stomach. Having him ask—*demand*—that I watch heightened everything.

So, I watched as he pulled the nipple into his mouth, sucking gently at first, then gradually more forcefully. I wound my fingers through his hair, holding him against me. I pretty much fell apart anytime a guy touched my breasts, and I was already miles down that road before Colt even bent his dark head to work his magic.

Watching was one thing. I needed to participate. I reached between us, fumbling for a minute with water and fabric until I found Colt among the swirling warmth. There was a brief pause in the movements of his lips and tongue as I wrapped my fingers around him. The swim trunks muffled our contact; the close proximity of our bodies limited my movements. It didn't take long for Colt to begin shifting restlessly beneath me.

Finally, he lifted his head, dark eyes meeting mine. "As much as I'm enjoying this, Red, I think we could do better."

"I agree. We need a change of venue. And a change of clothes. Or less clothes." I squeezed him through his trunks, and he grunted out a breath, the corner of his mouth curling up.

"Actually, I like the venue. You're right about the clothes, though."

He reached down, undoing the snap on my shorts, fingers working the wet fabric over my hips. But he didn't get very far. "Stand up."

I did, resting my hands on his shoulders while he tugged my shorts over my hips. They slid down my legs, sinking beneath the surface as I stepped out of them. Leaning forward, he kissed my stomach, tracing a circle around my navel with his tongue. I shivered as a breeze wafted over us, over my exposed breasts. The sun was setting somewhere behind the tall trees, the air getting cooler. I looked over his shoulder, half expecting to see a hiker or three enjoying the show.

Colt turned his head, following my gaze. "No one there." He turned back, fingers tracing over my skin. "Goose bumps. Come here."

"Not 'til you get rid of those." I pointed to his swim trunks. "I'm not going to be the only one naked here."

Colt chuckled and lifted his hips. I remained standing, hands on his shoulders, as he pulled off his trunks. I couldn't help but grin at the momentary difficulty he had in getting the wet fabric over his erection. The water was opaque enough that I couldn't get a good look at him, just tantalizing glimpses. I bit my lip, trying not to stare but failing.

He tossed the trunks onto the edge of the pool. "Better?" He grabbed my hips, fingers playing over my skin. There was an insistence, an urgency to his touch, an impatience that matched what was building inside me.

I glanced around, scanning the woods again.

"If you're worried about being seen..."

"No... not really." I couldn't help but look back into the trees. The feeling I'd had on the trail surfaced, the sense that someone was watching me... us. The last thing I wanted was company.

Colt's hands slipped around to my ass, fingers probing uncharted waters, distracting me from whatever it was I couldn't see.

"Red, if there is someone there, you're giving them a really good show by standing there—"

Before he could finish that statement, I leaned down, kissing him hard. I straddled his thighs, settling into the water. This time, with no pesky trunks or shorts between us, it was just him and me and all that warm, swirling water.

I reached between us, fingers wrapping around him, guiding him into me. He slid home easily, as if he'd been there before, as if this were second nature for both of us. There was none of the awkward fumbling of first-time sex between strangers. It was... as if we'd done this dance many times.

Any musings I had about all of that faded away as I sank down onto him. Colt flexed his hips, and I replied, rolling mine against him. I settled my arms around his neck. The water rose around us, buoying my breasts between us.

"This is nice." Colt touched my hair, brushing a strand back.

I laughed. "Nice?" I ground my hips down. "That's not what I was going for."

I claimed his mouth with mine as something wild and primal took control of me. I rocked and swiveled, grinding against him. Each movement brought a new sound of desire from Colt's lips, from moans to grunts, all of them sweet music to my ears, all of them mixing with mine.

The water around us swirled and sloshed as our movements increased. I found footing against the rocks, giving me leverage. Pushing with my legs, I had control and I could move up and back, sliding him out of me, poised over him.

He broke away with a ragged sound, hands gripping my ass. "You're a tease, Red. I thought you might be."

"Is that a bad thing?" I wiggled a bit, teasing both of us. My body wanted him with a need I'd never felt with any man. But I liked the heady sense of control I had, and I wanted to prolong this moment as long as I could stand it.

"Not at all. I like a challenge. But..."

With a rush of swirling water, Colt stood. I clutched his neck, yelping in surprise. There was no choice but to wrap my legs around his waist or risk another dunk in the water. And in that flurry of movement, he drove himself deep inside me.

"In the end, I like to be in control." His voice was a low growl. Our eyes locked as he turned, surefooted. With that strength I found arousing, he eased me down on a flat rock, his thick cock still buried inside me. He leaned over, hands planted on either side of my shoulders. "And I'll show you what nice is really like. And what it's like to be teased."

He pulled back, hips flexing in short strokes, giving me just enough of himself to remind me of what I wanted. I arched and twisted beneath him, but he held back. I tried to pull him closer with arms and legs, but he was remarkably strong and I couldn't do much but struggle beneath him.

"You're enjoying this, aren't you?" I was breathing hard, both from my efforts and mounting frustration. "You're getting off on this whole control thing."

He grinned down at me. "Of course, I am." His body

blocked out the sun, and I looked up into his blue eyes. Strands of hair, damp with water or sweat, curled around his face.

*God, he is so damn sexy.*

"Do you want me to beg?" I wiggled against him, hoping it would be the trigger that brought him home. I was poised on the edge, so close but so very far away.

"No, Red. Not that. Never beg." He lowered his head, kissing me hard. When he pulled back, I was gasping. "Never beg. Because I want this as much as you do."

When he drove himself into me, I screamed. Birds scattered out of the trees, and the sound of their startled flight was lost in my next cry as Colt thrust himself hard into me, his body coming down onto mine, pressing me into the rocks and sand. I didn't care that there was something sharp poking my ass. All I wanted was Colt. And I got him.

He thrust hard and fast for several moments, his head dropping onto my shoulder, open mouth pressed against my neck. I wrapped arms and legs around him, pulling him hard against me. We moved as one, his thrusts matching my arching and bucking beneath him.

I'd been waiting for this, waiting to move with Colt, to bring each of us together to the height of pleasure, to bring both of us to wherever this experience was leading. I didn't want to rush, but once we'd started, there was no holding back.

I came suddenly, but not unexpectedly. Clutching Colt desperately, I let go, let my body take over. The orgasm that we'd created shook me to the very core. Nothing I'd ever experienced could come close to this.

From the depths of my pleasure, I heard Colt cry out, felt his body tense in my arms. There could be no other way to say that he melted against me. Arms went around my back and waist, one hand sliding down to my ass. There was a hot rush inside me, but there was no way for me to tell what came from

Colt or what came from me. And I really didn't care. It was bliss, pure and simple.

After a long time, Colt rolled onto his back. The sun was behind the trees, shadows creeping across the river. The birds had come back to the trees, apparently over the startling experience of watching Colt and me.

I traced a finger across his chest. "That was crazy."

He lifted his head, giving me a lopsided smile. "It was." He turned, propping himself up on one elbow. "And amazing."

I sat up. It felt strange to be lying naked on the rocks. In all my years camping, of coming here, I'd never been one to go skinny-dipping or even wander around undressed in camp. But here I was, buck naked, lying under the sky in the fading light. But I was getting chilled, and even though I was lying next to Colt, looking at all that gorgeous man, the aftershocks of sex coursing through me, I wanted to be in the water.

I leaned over, kissed his cheek, and sat up. With more grace than I'd displayed all day, I slipped back into the pool. Colt sat up on the edge, dangling his feet in the water. I leaned against his knee. He, ever obsessed with it, ran his fingers through my hair. Occasionally, he met with a tangle, gently working it free.

"Figured I'd find you with a woman."

I jerked around, splashing water into my face again, and Colt's. His fingers snagged in my hair, jerking my head back. I desperately wanted to sink beneath the water, but until he let go of my hair, I was stuck above water, exposed. *And more than a little freaked out.* He finally let go, and I slid down as far as I could beneath the surface.

"Sorry. Didn't mean to startle you. Hey, Colt."

Déjà-vu washed over me. I looked up at the guy standing by the edge of the pool. I tried not to stare, something I'd been failing at miserably all day. Truthfully, I wanted to bolt, but I was hardly dressed for a dash across rocks to the safety of the woods. Even my towel was out of reach. I was pinned down.

"You two know each other?"

The other guy, a blond giant who could easily have passed for a Viking, nodded. He dropped an enormous pack on the ground and kicked off his shoes. Colt slipped into the water next to me as if it were normal for him to be naked in a hot spring with a strange woman who was cowering in the water.

"This is Jericho." He nodded at the blond giant who was still towering over me. And I noticed, with shock, that he was dropping his shorts, leaving them at the edge of the water. I didn't stare this time. I just closed my eyes, wondering what alternate universe I'd wandered into.

But then, it was the springs. Maggie had pegged it.

The water level rose, but only to the underside of my breasts. "We hiked up together. Then he went off to look at some... What did you want to see?"

"There are some Indian carvings in one of the caves on the other side of the mountain. Wanted to get some shots of it before the light left."

Someone splashed water in my direction, and I opened my eyes. "And you are?" Jericho held out a hand. "Nice to meet you, whoever you are."

"Risha." I stretched out my arm, just able to reach his hand. There was no way I was going to stand up, sans shorts and shirt. I could see the shorts snagged on a rock, just out of my reach.

Jericho let go of my hand. By sitting back and stretching out my leg, I could barely touch the waistband of my shorts. I had no idea where my shirt had gone. *If I can just hook a belt loop with my toe...*

"These belong to you?" Jericho reached down into the water, picked up the shorts, and held them out to me with a smile. A smile that told me he knew *exactly* why they were snagged on the rocks and weren't on me.

"Yeah... um, thanks." I reached for the shorts, arm stretched full length, the other arm automatically covering my chest. My fingers touched the wet denim just as Jericho twitched the shorts out of my reach. "Hey!"

"Just wondering if you're sure you want to put these back on yet."

I lunged for the dripping shorts, my feet slipping on the rocks. My head went under—again—water going up my nose, into my mouth. And again, hands grabbed my arms, pulling me to the surface. I came up sputtering—again. This time, I was face to face with Jericho.

"You okay?" He relaxed his grip on my upper arms. "You're going to have bruises here. Sorry about that." His death grip loosened, but he didn't let go.

"I'm okay." My hair hung in my face, a wet curtain obscuring my view. Jericho reached up, pushing aside the wet mass. I turned, looking at Colt for... help? Another rescue? Reassurance?

He only smiled at me. "Jericho's okay. Really. A little aggressive maybe. But I'd trust him with my life."

*A recommendation from a slightly less than stranger for a brand-new stranger.* I wasn't sure how I should take that.

I turned back to Jericho. "I'm okay."

"You said that. But that's okay. Okay is good." He shifted beneath me, and damn, if there wasn't something hard poking against me.

My heart rate was up into the triple digits. Without moving from this pool, I'd gotten enough cardio to make Jack very happy.

I stared into Jericho's eyes. His were blue, not the bright clear blue of Colt's, but a gray-blue that matched the color of the water swirling around my hips... my naked hips. *And my naked torso.*

I should have been pushing away, slipping back under the water, struggling into my shirt and shorts. Anything but sitting naked on a stranger's lap. *Again.* But the longer I looked into those eyes, the less anxious I felt. There was something calming, something almost mesmerizing about his gaze. Somehow, sitting on a stranger's lap seemed perfectly accepted, even naked.

*But then again, this isn't my first time today.*

Colt. The guy I'd just had sex with was less than four feet away, watching all of this. I jerked my head around. I expected the worst, expected to see him red-faced and angry, fists balled, ready to fight. Or if not that, at least looking annoyed.

But Colt was anything but angry or annoyed. He slouched in the water, arms spread across the rocks behind him. And he was smiling, that same sexy, wolfish grin I'd seen before.

I turned back to Jericho. "You... I shouldn't... We shouldn't... be like this. This is all wrong."

"It's okay. Colt and I are good with sharing. If you're interested." His grin was as wolfish as Colt's.

Then it hit me. "You were watching? You watched me... with him... us?"

He shrugged, one eyebrow raised. "No." He was still holding my arm with one hand. The other moved down to my hip, then slid lower, fingers playing over my ass. The movement was slow, deliberate, and I drew in a breath. "But I can smell his scent all over your beautiful body."

The feelings inside my belly, the arousal Colt had awakened earlier, all sprang back to life. *Something else he said...*

"Sharing... You mean... you share... You'd share me?" That was the last thing I expected to hear. But then again, these guys were strangers. I knew nothing about them, except they were different in looks as day and night but were both sexy beyond all expectations. And they had the same distinct accent.

"Colt and I have been friends a very, very long time... almost like brothers."

I stared at Jericho, losing myself for a minute in those gray-blue eyes, confused by his words. I felt I'd had way more than just a half a Thermos cup of wine. Some things just weren't adding up.

"Almost like brothers?"

"We're not related. Best friends, though. And we have the same tastes... in many things."

There was movement behind me, water sloshing against my back. Hands settled on my hips. Lips brushed against my ear. *Colt.* Something vaguely familiar in a very strange and surreal place.

"You, however, would be hard to share. A man could get very greedy with a beauty like you."

Jericho let go of my arm now that I was basically pinned between him and Colt—not that I was going anywhere anyway —his hand sliding up my torso. He glanced up at me, his look holding a question, but it was clear he already knew the answer.

I nodded anyway.

Colt's hands moved to my waist, caressing whatever bare skin Jericho wasn't touching. Maybe Colt felt he had a proprietary claim on my breasts, and it was fine with me if he wanted to have a return engagement with them. I was already missing my shorts, and there wasn't much left that Jericho hadn't seen. But there was something tugging at the back of my mind. Best ask the question before these two distracted me even more than they already were.

"So, you share? Like... everything?"

Colt grabbed my hips, and the press of his erection against

my ass reminded me of what we'd already done. He leaned forward again, lips nuzzling my neck.

"We share things we find... interesting. Or that we like. We share a cabin up here. We share..." His tongue slipped along the line of my jaw, lips nibbling my earlobe. "Women, on occasion."

Jericho slipped a hand between my legs, fingers moving over me beneath the surface of the warm water. There were enough residual aftershocks from my interlude with Colt coursing through me that I went a little weak in the knees at Jericho's touch.

I searched his eyes again. "Do you share all your women?" I wasn't that far gone that I missed the look Jericho gave Colt.

"Some." He thrust a finger into me. I tried to bite back a moan but was unsuccessful. "It's not like we have a different girl every night. Or week. We like women..." He added a second finger to the mix, curling them inside me. I gasped, closing my eyes as desire swirled through me. "But they need to have something special about them, something that excites us. It's not often we find that."

"You have that something special." Colt's voice was close to my ear, his breath warm against my damp skin.

A burble of nervous laughter rose up inside me. "I do?"

"Oh yeah, you certainly do. Colt and I don't sleep around. This isn't something we do on a routine basis, you know. We don't haunt the springs, looking for willing partners."

"Girlfriends? Wives?" I wanted to get this straight in my head before things went too much further. *Although, they've gone pretty damn far already.*

"Neither. We're lone wolves."

At that, I laughed out loud.

Colt's fingers cupped my breasts, pushing them up, together, fingers rolling my hard nipples.

Words were getting stuck between my mind and my

tongue. "Lone wolves..." I tipped my head back, sighing between words. "There's more than one of you."

Colt's laugh was low, sexy. "A pair of lone wolves, then."

Jericho looked up at me with heavy-lidded eyes. "Any other questions? Your curiosity satisfied?"

Not in the least, but... "Yeah... no... no more questions."

"Good. Now kiss me. Colt got a head start."

I was already leaning down, ready to kiss those chiseled lips.

He reached up, wrapping his hand around the nape of my neck. "It's my turn."

His kiss surprised me, the softness of it when I was expecting something a little rougher around the edges. It still took my breath away. I started to sink onto Jericho's lap, ready for a repeat performance with a new partner. But he grabbed my hips, pushing me back.

Startled, I broke away from his lips. "I thought you wanted your turn."

"I do. But I want something different."

Jericho stood. I took a step backward, running up against the hard warmth of Colt's body. He still held my breasts, cupping them in his big hands.

I didn't care if I stared, and I was pretty sure Jericho was perfectly happy to have me look at him. The way he stood, the way he looked down at me, he certainly enjoyed the attention. So, I gave it to him, letting my eyes travel over his gorgeous body.

Jericho was taller than Colt by an inch or so. Overall, he was less heavily muscled, leaner, built like a sprinter, where Colt was built like a fighter. But he was no less sexy for it.

I'd finally looked at everything above his waist, and now I let my eyes linger below. I wanted to gasp or applaud or... *something*. Because he was simply stunning. And very erect. I'd never had a man stand and let me admire him. Clearly, Jericho loved the attention, and I loved giving it to him.

But looking was far different than touching, and it was clear by Colt's restless movements behind me that he was a man of action. He'd gotten a little aggressive with his fondling, moving on to an almost possessive touch. The attention was welcome, but my breasts felt heavy and tender.

I reached up, setting my hands over his. "Nice and gentle, please."

"Sorry. Or not." He laughed against my neck. "You're too luscious not to maul."

"She is a luscious girl, isn't she?" Jericho reached out, pulling me against him. "Curvy and perfect for the taking."

I tipped my head up, ready for his kiss. But instead, he pulled me around so I was facing the edge of the pool, my back to him. With one hand on my back, one on my hip, he pushed me forward. I put my hands out, catching myself.

There was splashing behind me. I caught sight of Colt climbing out of the pool beside me, sitting on the edge. To say he was on full display would be an understatement. It was clear he was just as interested in looking as he was in being looked at. I couldn't help but notice he was fully erect, his cock rising from a trimmed thatch of dark hair, a long trail that ran up his stomach, melding with all that glorious hair on his chest.

With a graceful move, he slid over. I lifted one hand, and he moved beneath me. There was no mistaking his intent, and I was happy to oblige.

But behind me, Jericho was making his intentions abundantly clear. He'd grabbed my ass, fingers tightening against my skin. I wiggled in his grip, giving him a clear indication, I was ready and willing for whatever he wanted to do.

He thrust his slick cock between my legs, the thick shaft

rubbing against my already sensitive folds. I shivered from the chill in the air and from the force of Jericho's touch.

"I bet they call you Red, right?"

I caught Colt's look.

"Yeah. I get that from time to time." I looked back over my shoulder. "And yeah, you can call me Red."

His laugh was louder than I expected, and the bird's overhead chattered in protest. But I didn't have a chance to say anything else. Jericho wasted no time thrusting into me, hard and fast, more brutal than Colt.

Jericho wasn't interested in teasing. He was interested in one thing: setting up a wild pace. I rocked back and forth, teetering on the edge of falling into Colt's lap. I looked up at him, knowing I'd see that sexy smile, knowing what he was waiting for. And that I was more than ready to give it to him as soon as I caught my balance and my breath.

"Ease up, Jericho. You're going to wear her out before her time."

Behind me, Jericho growled, but he slowed his pace, at least enough so I wasn't being jolted back and forth.

Colt leaned back, giving me more than enough room to move.

I shifted my weight, reaching for him, wrapping my hand around his shaft. As I lowered my head, he flexed up into my hand and into my mouth. This was another first for me. There was a moment of awkwardness as I moved, trying to get comfortable, and Jericho countered, trying to hold on to my slippery ass. Colt shifted beneath me, trying to... well, keep himself in contact with me.

We finally got the perfect arrangement of limbs, the perfect pitch in this weird dance of ours. It was amazing, simply the most erotic situation I'd ever been in.

The heat inside me that was left over from Colt ignited

under Jericho's touch, under the force of his body slamming into me. Being taken from behind by this blond giant who obviously knew how to pleasure a woman and having Colt spread out in front of me sent me into overdrive. There was no way I could hold back this orgasm, no matter how long I wanted to keep this going. I came, and I came hard.

I lost my grip on the world, on reality, and on Colt. But he wasn't ready for that. He sat up, grabbing my head, pulling me back down, forcing himself between my lips. I wanted to scream—or tried to, all my sounds muffled against the hardness of Colt's erection. But I took him back into my mouth, even though I could barely breathe, because in that moment, all I wanted was to pleasure both the same way they were sending shivers of sweet pleasure through my body.

For a split second, I had an image of the three of us, Jericho holding my hips, forcing himself into me, his body pressed against my ass, Colt sitting, legs spread, feet in the pool, fingers wound through my hair as he held me, as he forced himself into my mouth. And in that split second, I thought about what Colt and Jericho were seeing, how this all looked to them.

And arching and bucking between these two gorgeous, rugged men, my body wracked with the most intense orgasm of my life.

From behind me, Jericho bellowed. There was no other name for the sound. It startled me out of my own little erotic world for a moment. A thrill ran through me as he gripped my ass, his body slamming into me so hard I jerked forward, almost swallowing Colt. There was no complaint from him, just a loud moan as his cock hit the back of my throat.

Jericho's next bellow was only slightly softer, but he was clearly headed for his own major experience here. He dug his fingers into my hips, and I knew there was a pretty good chance I would have fingerprint bruises as a memento of this event.

With a final cry, he drove himself to the hilt, filling me with heat as he came. I bucked against him again and again, a second —or third—dizzying wave of orgasmic joy flooding through me as he grunted and thrust into me.

Whether it was watching Jericho or me or both of us, Colt's trigger was tripped. He tightened his grip on my head, fingers digging into my hair. It hurt a little, but the pain only served as a counterpoint to everything else happening in my body.

The flex of his hips was accompanied by a low moan, almost a growl, and he came. I'd never been a big fan of oral sex... but this blew my mind. He tasted rich and salty and slightly odd and totally foreign. But at this moment, it was right, all of it. It was messy and sloppy, uncontrolled, and wild. And yeah, it was mind-blowing.

Colt finally released his death grip on my hair, flopping onto his back on the rocks. Jericho's manic thrusts slowed, his hands relaxing, until I felt him slide out of me, away from my body. I sank onto my knees, the water rising around my ass, swirling between my legs. I winced as the hot water washed against me, but it was soothing.

Jericho sat beside me, rubbing my shoulders. Colt sat up and slipped onto the rocks on the other side of me. I knelt between them, resting my head on my arms, eyes closed. We were in the shade now, and even though the air was cool, I felt heated from the inside, like I was a little glowing ember.

"You okay, Red?"

I opened my eyes, looking at Colt, although it was Jericho who was talking. I was too sated to even lift my head. "Yeah. I'm great." I smiled, and Colt chuckled.

"She seems fine to me, Jericho."

"Good."

I closed my eyes. "You guys okay? I know you do this all the time, but..."

Jericho shifted beside me, water rising gently against my legs. "We don't do this all the time. What did you tell her, Colt? That we have random sex with every woman we meet?"

"He didn't say that." I turned to look at Jericho. This was awkward, and I was getting sand in my mouth.

"I don't want you to get the wrong impression about us. When we said that we share, that doesn't mean we sleep with just anyone."

I sat back, spitting out the sand. "I don't know you guys, so... you know." I shrugged, pushing back from the edge of the pool, sinking into the water like a hippo until it was up to my neck. The rest of the pool was taken up by Jericho and Colt's long legs. I kind of nestled between them, breathing deeply, enjoying the swirl of the water around me.

Colt sat forward until we were almost eye level. "I said we share what we find interesting. And that does include women from time to time. But..." He ran a finger along my cheek. "Those have been few and far between."

"Oh." I had the sense there was a lot more than a few and the far between carried a whole lot of history. But I was willing to let it all go for now. I was relaxed, in that good way you get after great sex, but sitting in the hot water was making me sleepy. I sat up without slipping under again.

"I'm ready to get out if you guys are." For some unknown reason, I was hoping for a little privacy to get dressed. Sex was one thing, getting dressed another. It seemed oddly intimate to dress in front of guys I probably would never see again.

They took the cue, climbing up out of the pool. They were less shy about getting into their trunks, and I averted my eyes for that brief moment.

"Where are you camped?" Colt shouldered his pack. "If you want company, that is."

"Oh... yeah." It hadn't even occurred to me there might be

more to this than just... this. "Up the path, on the left. You'll see my stuff." I guess I did want their company.

"We'll walk slow, give you a chance to get dressed." Colt nodded, and he and Jericho skirted the pool, heading toward the woods

"I won't be long." I stayed in the water, the eddies and currents matching the swirling emotions inside me. I waited until they were out of sight, then climbed out of the pool. My shorts were there, but it took a minute to find my T-shirt. I was wet, the clothes were half dry, and everything was covered in sand. I smiled. *Just what you'd expect on a camping trip.*

I grabbed my stuff and headed up the trail. I could hear them talking up ahead, but I didn't make the effort to catch up. It was nice knowing I had company, even though it took away the me-in-the-wilderness-alone theme from the weekend. But what the hell? Maybe this was what fate had set up for me. Maybe this was what I needed.

As far as testing my limits and my boundaries, I was chalking up new experiences right and left. First, sex with a stranger, then sex with another... and then both at once.

*What the hell am I doing?*

But I'd thrown judgment out the window, self and otherwise. This was my weekend, and I was going to follow wherever this oddball path took me. At the moment, that path seemed to be dragging me through a whirlwind of crazy sexual adventure.

# CHAPTER 4

THE SUN WAS ALMOST DOWN by the time we reached my little campsite, if an abandoned tent and a lone pack could be called a campsite. It was much darker beneath the canopy of trees. The pines added a green bulk that seemed to soak up the last of the sunlight. We all had flashlights, and Colt and Jericho made a complete circle of the area. I stood in the middle, a little bemused. I'd never seen anyone do that before, except in rattlesnake country. But we didn't have rattlesnakes here. I chalked it up to idiosyncratic camper superstitions.

"Nice tent. You want some help setting it up?" Colt dropped his pack beside the pile of nylon and fiberglass, picking up the pieces I'd left in a heap.

"Help yourself. It was what drove me down to the springs. I'd given up trying to puzzle it out." I picked up my pack, ferreting out matches and my fire starter kit. "I'll get the fire going—"

But Jericho already had a tiny flame cradled in a bunch of pine needles, and I watched as he tenderly set it among a pile of tinder, carefully feeding it small twigs, the flame growing quickly. He glanced up, catching my gaze, grinning at me over the flickering flames. "I got a merit badge in camping when I was a kid."

"I see." I dropped the stuff back into my pack. "Is there anything you guys can't do?"

"Not if it involves living off the land." Colt stepped away from the tent. It seemed it had materialized out of nowhere. "We've been roughing it in some way since we were kids. Both of us grew up near here, spent most of our time messing around in the woods."

"Or getting into trouble." Jericho added a larger branch to the fire. The flames licked around it, turning blue and yellow. He dropped to the ground, leaning his back against the log. He gave me an encouraging smile. Hell, he gave me a smile that could have lit a fire without matches.

I stood for a moment, debating where to sit. Suddenly, I was shy, as if I were on a blind date, not sitting around the fire with two guys I'd just had sex with in the hot springs. Two guys who certainly had an effect on me and my libido. I perched primly on the log.

"I'll round up some more firewood." I just caught a glimpse of Colt as he disappeared silently into the woods.

Jericho tugged his pack closer, pulling out a Thermos. After a minute, he handed me a metal cup. "Here. Brought enough for all of us."

I took an experimental sniff, then a sip. *Bourbon*, I thought. Whatever it was, I was pretty sure it was the strongest thing I'd ever tasted.

Jericho stretched his legs toward the fire. We watched the flames for a minute. Somewhere in the woods, a night bird called, its mate answering. Then it went still, and the only sounds were that of the crackling fire.

Jericho stretched again, looking up at me over his shoulder.

"What's your game, Red? You're a good girl... You're not someone who sleeps around. So why the sudden ménage in the hot springs? Feel like taking a walk on the wild side or what?"

The fire crackled, sparks rising against the backdrop of the dark trees. Above that was the deeper black of the sky, brilliant stars just pinpricks in the dark. The fire caught Jericho's eyes, and for a startling moment, I swore they glinted red. I blinked and blinked again. But the moment was gone.

"I don't... I'm not." I shifted on the log, taking another sip of bourbon. It burned like proverbial fire. I swallowed hard, tried not to cough, and wasn't entirely successful. The last thing I wanted to look like was a lightweight in front of these guys. There was something about them that brought out my competitive edge, among other feelings or urges or desires. I shrugged, trying for nonchalance.

*Like this is normal for me. Sex in the afternoon; drinking the hard stuff at night.*

"Let's say I stepped out of my life for the weekend." I looked down at Jericho, but he was staring into the fire, for which I was profoundly grateful. I wasn't sure I could stand that piercing gaze at the moment. "I needed a change, needed to do some thinking."

"I'm all for getting away from it all, looking inward, doing a bit of soul searching. And for you, if that means a weekend fling, so be it." He took a swallow of his drink. "Anything I can do to help you..." He glanced behind me.

I turned to see Colt materialize from the forest, carrying an armful of firewood.

"Anything we can do to help, just let us know."

"Help who?" Colt dropped the wood, grabbed a branch, and added it to the fire.

"Red. She's on a voyage of self-discovery. I told her we're here for her."

Colt crouched in the glow of the fire, poking it with a stick. The fire roared up briefly, then settled back. I caught the smile on his face and was eternally grateful for the darkness around us and that if either of them noticed my blush, they'd think it was a rosy glow from the fire or the fire of the bourbon. Both of them had already gone a long way in helping me do whatever it was I'd come here to do.

"I don't want to pry, but there must have been something that prompted this weekend away. Care to share?"

I took another sip of bourbon. It was kind of growing on me, the warmth sliding through my body. The last little bit of shyness melted away. There was no reason not to tell these guys the reasons I was here. Chances were good I'd never see them after this weekend. Might as well get the truth out there, get it out of my system.

"A couple months ago, my boyfriend—my fiancé actually—cheated on me. He'd started dating my college roommate." I took another shot of liquid courage. "He wanted an open relationship. I wanted nothing to do with him."

"So, you took to the wilderness to clear your head?" Colt nodded. "Sounds like a good plan. Hard to think when you're surrounded by reminders of the guy."

"Exactly." I waved my arm, intending to point at Colt, but managed only to slosh a bit of bourbon on the ground.

Jericho reached up, gently taking the cup out of my hand. "Maybe you've had enough for now."

"Oh... sorry. I've never been good at holding my liquor." The warmth in me was making the world a little fuzzy around the edges. It was a pleasant fuzziness. "And I had some wine before..."

Jericho laughed, a nice sound. I could get used to that sound. "It's okay. You just do what you need to. We'll watch out for the big bad wolf, make sure you're safe while you sort out your life."

"Oh, hey… that reminds me. Did you guys see a wolf today? A big black wolf. Don't know if it was bad…" I reached behind the log, digging in my pack for my phone. "Here… I took pictures." I unlocked the phone, scrolling to the shots of the wolf on the path. I leaned forward and held it out so the guys could see it.

"See?" I flipped through the photos. The first one was clear. The rest wouldn't win me any awards. "He sat when I asked him to, but I didn't get a picture of that. I thought he might have been the ranger's dog, but the guy said…"

I got the feeling no one was listening to me. I glanced at Colt, then to Jericho. Neither were looking at me or the phone. They were looking at each other, and the look they exchanged was one I couldn't miss, even in my happy state. Something was wrong, very wrong.

"You did see it, right?" I slumped on the log, then slid down onto the ground between them. "I think the ranger thought I was crazy."

"Ranger?" Jericho's voice had an edge to it. "What ranger?"

Colt coughed, then turned away as he fumbled for… something. "Yeah, Jericho, there was a ranger." His voice was muffled.

I turned to Colt. "Were you on the path ahead of me? You must have been if you saw him and then showed up at the springs when you did. Or did you say you came from the other way?" Wine, bourbon, and the afterglow of sex had muddled my recollection of what he'd said when we first met.

"Yeah, I saw the wolf." Colt sat up, absently poking the fire. "And I saw the ranger."

Jericho tensed beside me, leaning forward to look past me at Colt. "Were you going to tell me? Or just wait 'til he showed up here? What the hell were you thinking? Or you weren't thinking, were you?"

I sat perfectly still between the two of them, confused, the fuzzy feeling fading. The air was charged with tension. I wasn't exactly scared, but I was no longer drifting in a comforting haze of alcohol and sex. "What did I say? Did I say something wrong?"

The tension held for a moment, then shifted. Whatever was going on between them, they'd let it go, at least a little.

Jericho finally stood, making a point of stretching, though I knew he was far from relaxed. "You're fine, Red. This is between Colt and me. Nothing to do with you."

"You're not going to fight or anything, are you?"

Jericho moved around the fire, heading for the trees. "No. Just guys being guys. No fighting. I'm going for more firewood."

I relaxed bit by bit. Maybe in my muddled state, I'd misunderstood whatever had just happened.

"So, you did see the wolf? Big, black... blue eyes..." I looked into Colt's blue eyes, at his dark hair. It had dried now, and it curled around his shoulders. In the light of the fire, it looked tipped with deep red. But in the sun... would it be tipped with silver?

Colt turned to me. "Big black wolf. Yeah, I think I've seen him before."

I stared at him, almost unable to look away. Blue eyes, black hair...

"You've heard the stories, Red. The legend of Black Wolf Mountain... the rest of it, the territory to the north, all the wild stories."

I nodded, not looking away, unable to. But I didn't want to look away. It felt like I could look into those eyes for a long time... forever. If only...

"So, do you believe them, the stories you heard around the

campfire?" Colt reached out, winding a strand of hair through his fingers, tugging lightly. "You know, I could really fall in love with this hair."

"Obsessed much?"

"Yeah. Pretty much. Is that a problem?"

I shook my head, leaning toward Colt, following my strand of hair. His gaze slid down to my lips, a look so sexy I almost felt the caress of him against me. Swoon was never a word I'd have used to describe how I felt with a guy before this. I closed my eyes, swooning. But his words tugged at me, and I stopped leaning forward, stopped swooning. He tugged on my hair, but I pulled back, the strand held taut between us.

I opened my eyes. "Wait... Stop distracting me. You asked if I believed in the stories. What stories?"

"Red... Risha, there's something you should probably know about Jericho and me. Something that might change how you think about us."

"Oh. Okay." *Married? Girlfriends? I thought we covered all that.*

He let go of my hair, watching as it fell against my shoulder. "It's not what you think... None of that."

The instant his eyes met mine, I knew it, in my heart, in my soul, in every cell in my body. I went cold, then hot, then felt that swooning feeling again. Only it was more sickening than sexy this time around.

"You're the wolf."

He didn't answer, didn't have to. It was written clear on his face. My heart took off like a racehorse out of the gate, and I dug my fingers into the sandy dirt under my hands. This was worse than a girlfriend or a wife.

*Oh, my fucking God.*

"It's okay, Red. Really. I'm not the big bad wolf of legend. Neither is Jericho."

That snapped me out of wherever my head had gone. "Jericho? He's a... thing like you?"

"Don't say it like that. We're not things." He actually sounded hurt. And I felt bad for... What? Insulting his heritage?

"Then what are you?"

"Right now, I'm just a guy. Like I was before, at the springs. Just a guy sitting around the fire, enjoying your company."

"Then who or what were you before? On the trail?"

"That was also me. Only in wolf form. We call ourselves shifters. We can change shape. And in our case, it's from human to wolf and back."

"Are you serious? This sounds crazy." I could barely breathe, my head swirling in colors of black and gray, and I felt as though I might pass out.

I looked closely at Colt, at the face of the man I'd had sex with just a few hours earlier. I thought having sex with a stranger was way outside my comfort zone, but what he'd just told me pretty much blew all that right out of the water. My instincts kicked in, and I felt just as I did on the path. The urge to run was almost overwhelming. He was either telling the truth, or he was completely insane. At the moment, either or both was just as chilling to think about.

But this wasn't the wolf... or it was. But it was also Colt. And I happened to like Colt. I liked Colt very much. It was obvious the dynamic between us had changed; the lighthearted banter was gone. The sexual tension was still there, but it was overlaid with something a lot like fear.

"Okay. So, let's say I can suspend disbelief long enough. You're a wolf in human clothing?"

He cracked half a smile. "You could say that. It's a little more complicated. There's a history with Jericho and me and a backstory that's a bit long in the tooth." His smile widened. "Sorry. Couldn't resist the pun."

I managed something of a smile, I think. I wasn't sure. Most of me felt numb. "Why were you a wolf when I saw you?"

"I wasn't sure who you were yet. Friend or foe. When I'm in wolf form, I see things differently. Literally. My senses are heightened—smell, hearing, sight. I get a better view of who I'm looking at. A more accurate view, in most cases."

Some of the tension seeped out of me, despite hearing Colt explain that he was a wolf shifter. Listening to him, hearing his voice, the calm way he was talking to me, somehow made it seem okay. Maybe even believable. Somehow, someway.

"You're hypnotizing me, aren't you?" I made the effort to shift my gaze to the fire. "That's a thing you can do, right? I watch television, you know. I know how this works."

He laughed softly. "Red, if I were into mind control, my life would be a whole hell of a lot easier. And television usually gets it wrong. Vampires don't sparkle; shifters don't use mind control. At least not all the time." He stretched his arms over his head. "Believe me, life as a shifter isn't easy. This has been one of the better days of late."

"Oh." I wasn't sure if that included me or something else. My mind was spinning, too many questions piling up, fighting to be the first one asked. But before I could pick the front-runner, Colt stood.

"Something's wrong. Jericho should have been back by now."

Bewildered, I scrambled to my feet, tripping over the little pile of firewood. Colt was already on the other side of the fire, heading toward the gap where Jericho had gone.

"What do I do?"

"Stay here." He turned back, face set in rigid lines. For a

moment, the wolf played over his face, eyes glowing in the light of the fire, his hair catching the slight breeze.

"But what...?"

A howl cut through the soft night air. The sound chilled me to the bone. I stepped backward and tripped over the big log, landing hard on my ass, the wind knocked out of me. Colt stopped, half turned toward me, half turned toward the forest. If he saw what was coming out of the forest almost on top of him, he never flinched.

All I saw was a ball of gray fur wrapped around what looked like a big rag doll. I screamed and struggled to sit up, to catch my breath, to get my bearings. Suddenly, everything was obscured by the fire, the figures blurred, red-tinged. I finally got to my feet, and what I saw wasn't any less chilling from that vantage point.

The figures separated, the rag doll taking the shape of the nameless ranger. The gray fur resolved into a different wolf. From the way Colt swung around, teeth bared at the ranger, eyes narrowed, I knew this wolf wasn't just any wolf. *This is Jericho.*

The ranger and Jericho faced off briefly on either side of the fire. Jericho snarled, exposing brilliant white fangs, advancing stiff-legged around the flames. The ranger crouched, moving in the opposite direction, keeping the fire between them. There were rips and tears in his khaki uniform, some of them edged with blood. Colt looked strangely hesitant, poised between Jericho, the ranger, and me.

I realized a split second too late that the ranger and I were on a collision course. He realized it a moment before I did. I went left. He went right, but I couldn't avoid him. He slung an arm around my neck, pulling me against him.

He smelled awful, not just of dirt and sweat, but of something rotten. I wondered vaguely if he was some kind of shifter as well. But it was getting hard to breathe, and the world was going gray and fuzzy. I struggled, but the man was much stronger than I was. Struggling just got harder and harder, so finally, I gave up, concentrating on breathing. And even that was getting harder by the second.

"Let her go, Weatherly. She's not the one you came for."

"No, but she's the one I've got." Ranger Weatherly jerked me upright so hard my feet left the ground. That just made everything worse, made breathing next to impossible. I went limp, and not by choice.

"Back off. And call off your dog, Colt. You know what I want, why I'm here. And if I can't have you, then I'll take this one. You know I can snap her neck in a heartbeat, so don't fuck with me."

Something cold tickled the skin below my jaw. Colt's eyes narrowed, and Jericho whined. I guessed Weatherly had added a knife to the mix to back up his promise to break my neck.

The world was going black now, the ranger's voice getting faint. My head fell to the side, and through half-closed eyes, I saw Colt on the other side of the fire. Jericho stood by his side. Their expressions were identical, anger mixed with fear mixed with confusion. Those weren't looks that instilled confidence in me.

But I couldn't blame them—*didn't* blame them. I tried to tell them that, tried to talk, tried to send telepathic messages. I was leaving the conscious world, and the last thing I wanted them to feel was responsible.

*Silly thought...*

# CHAPTER 5

I JOLTED AWAKE. My neck hurt, and I tried to lie still until the zings of pain in my body stopped, not sure what, if anything, was broken. I tried to open my eyes, then realized they were already wide open but I couldn't see. For a long, horrible moment, I thought I'd died and this was purgatory, that I was stuck in a place where I was unable to see or hear or speak. But then I realized I wouldn't have this much pain if I were dead.

Slowly, bits and pieces came back to me: the fire, Colt and Jericho—sex—the ranger. Weatherly. It occurred to me that I finally knew his name. I was on something soft, and something was stuck in my mouth. So, I was blindfolded, gagged, and lying on a smelly mattress.

*But I'm alive.*

"Hey, you're awake." The voice was close, sounding absurdly happy about that fact.

I jerked again, another wave of pain shooting down my arms. My hands were tied behind my back, but I could wiggle my fingers. They worked. The pain meant I was alive and that even if I was injured, I wasn't paralyzed. It might have been a small thing, but I was suddenly very happy to feel pain.

But why Weatherly had me and what he intended to do—that, I wasn't very happy about.

"Let's get better acquainted."

Hands touched me, my face, pulling my hair hard enough to make my eyes water. I grunted. I was pretty much over reveling in pain now. All I wanted was to see and to be able to sit up.

The blindfold came off. I looked up at Weatherly.

I wanted to laugh, which was impossible with the gag. Weatherly looked far worse for wear than I felt. Whatever happened before they tumbled into the clearing, Jericho had gotten in few good scratches and bites. Weatherly's uniform was shredded in places, the edges caked with dried blood, torn skin visible beneath a few of the bigger tears. And if he smelled bad before, he smelled even worse now. Sweat, old and new, dirt, and blood. And I sensed the sharp tang of fear on him. Not a pleasant combination. *But what the hell does he have to be afraid of? I'm the one tied up and gagged.*

Weatherly wrenched the gag out of my mouth, pulling my hair again, my scalp aching. I glared up at him, mustering as much bravado as I could.

"Listen, Weatherly... I don't know what your game is, but I'm pretty sure Colt and Jericho aren't going to just let you take me. They're probably on their way here right now." At least I hoped they were. *How much loyalty does an almost stranger garner?*

"I'm sure they are. And that's just fine by me. The more the merrier."

"What do you want with me?" The whole disjointed conversation by the fire, the part about Jericho and Colt—all that could wait. I wanted to know what my part in this was. And I wanted him talking so I could find a way to get my hands free or get him to untie me. I wanted to take a swing at him so bad I could taste it.

"I don't want you... or I didn't. Until I saw you on the path. But then that damn wolf showed up." He loomed over me for a minute, then must have decided it was awkward bending over to glare at me. Grabbing my shoulders, he yanked me upright. I had no balance, wavering from side to side. And then I fell backward, my head hitting the wall. I closed my eyes as a new pain added itself to the mix.

"The wolf showed up." I heard a footstep and opened an eye, watching as Weatherly turned, pacing across the small room.

It gave me a chance to look around. There wasn't much to see. The room was bare, just the mattress I was sitting on, a few chairs sitting at random angles, a table shoved in the corner. All in all, not someone's permanent residence. Probably a deserted rental cabin from the '50s, long forgotten, long abandoned. *Perfect place to keep a hostage.*

"The wolf showed up. The wolf I was after. One of them anyway."

"So why bother with me?"

Weatherly paced a few steps toward the door, twitching open the tattered curtain that hung on the window. He stared out at whatever was out there, whatever he could see in the dark. Then it struck me. *He's a wolf... a shifter.* He could see in the dark just like Colt and Jericho. And that meant he could change just like they could. And with him as a wolf, I didn't stand a chance.

I wiggled my hands, turning my wrists. The ropes bit into my skin, burned like hell. But I thought there was some play in them. Maybe it was my imagination, but it was the only thing I had to hold on to right now.

Weatherly moved to another window, looked out, then turned back to me. I froze, my wrists screaming in pain, my shoulders rotated at some unnatural angle. Something changed in the way he looked at me, something darker crossing his features.

"You were going to be collateral damage at first. Get you out of the way, nasty hiking accident. Didn't matter if you knew what any of this meant. You just needed to go away. But then... you hooked up with those two. How the hell did that happen? I tracked them forever, and there's never been a woman. But now there's you."

"I'd be happy to just bow out right now. No harm, no foul."

"Not so fast. Plans change." He crossed the little room, almost standing on my feet. "I can use you."

He grabbed me again, pulling me upright. "Those guys used you. I can use you, too."

I was pretty sure his idea of use wasn't going to be anywhere as fun as what happened with Colt and Jericho. I struggled, trying to disguise my attempts at freedom with frantic wiggling. Something loosened in the ropes around my wrists, one loop slipping. Weatherly apparently wasn't very good at knot tying.

"Use me how?" *Do I really want to know?*

"I can make you one of us, like me." He leered at me, baring his teeth. They were the same brilliant white as Colt's and Jericho's, a little longer than normal, far sharper than any human teeth should be. I jerked back, trying to get away from him.

"Bite you, mark you, make you mine. You'll be mated to me, and I can have what they have."

Whatever he was saying was lost on me. I'd stopped paying attention after the mention of a bite. I didn't want to be bitten, not by Weatherly or anyone else. My heart galloped wildly in my chest, and I struggled not to go into full-blown panic mode.

Another loop of rope fell away, and for a surprised second, I felt hope that I might stand a chance of getting away. Then I let fear replace exhilaration. It wasn't hard. I heard Jack's voice in my head, telling me to wait, look for my opening, to keep my eyes open. That I just needed to focus, to be patient.

But Weatherly had other ideas. He pulled me against him, his big hand grabbing my hair. For an instant, I wished I'd chopped all this hair off, given myself a buzz cut. That way men wouldn't be able to yank me around by it.

He pulled my head back, eyes drifting from my face to my neck. He smiled, if that's what it could be called. My body had gone numb, limp, partly by design, mostly out of my control. The only thing moving was my heart, thumping along at a dizzying pace.

"It's not going to hurt." He was focused on my throat, his arm slackening against my back.

*Just stay cool... Don't telegraph...*

Weatherly dropped his head, and I was out of options. I brought my knee up, aiming for his crotch. I hit his thigh instead, and it was like kneeing a tree. But it gave me an opening. I pulled against the hand holding my hair, setting my scalp on fire, and swung for the moon with my left. I hit him hard in the side of the head.

The blow didn't do much damage, but it did startle him. He took his arm away from me but held on to my hair. I swung again, a wild right that whistled through the air past his face. I could hear Jack's snort of disapproval in my mind. Waste of energy, throwing useless punches.

"Knock it off, little girl. I'm not impressed with your little hissy fit. Just accept it." He pulled me up by my hair until I was standing on my toes. I sucked a breath through my teeth, trying hard not to scream at the pain. "Not so tough now, are you?" He dragged me backward toward the mattress. "I think there's a better way of doing this. Giving you swinging room is dangerous."

He pushed me down onto the mattress, following me, his big body covering mine, finally letting go of my hair. I hit him wherever I could, pounding his back, his shoulders. It was like punching stone. I wanted to scream, but he was crushing my chest with his, and getting air was growing harder.

I brought my knee up again. This time I connected with something that got a reaction from Weatherly. He grunted, his hands stopping in the middle of the act of tearing off my clothes. I tried again, but he reared back, slapping me across my mouth. I tasted blood, and for a horrible moment, everything went black.

"You know, I like a fighter, but this is ridiculous. You're being downgraded to collateral damage again." Weatherly fumbled at his belt, and the cold sharpness at my throat snapped me back to reality.

"I've been chasing these bastards long enough. They're the last of their clans, and I'm the last of mine. They've taken everything from me, my land, my clan, and left me out in the cold. I'm tired, and I'm tired of you. You're not worth mating. You'd be nothing but a thorn in my side."

He slid the knife against my throat, and for an instant, I wondered if he was joking or if this was just some weird sort of foreplay. But he pulled back, grinning, a terrible expression full of lust send hate and so many clashing emotions that I had to look away. I tried to turn my head, and then I felt the warm rush of blood seeping from the place he'd cut.

"There. Just lie there and die." He pushed away from me.

I wanted to sit up, to scream, to do something. But a tiny

part of my brain told me I was probably better off just being still, and for once, I listened to that little voice.

I reached up, almost tenderly, touching my neck. When I pulled my hand away, there was blood, so much blood. Too much blood, it seemed. I closed my eyes, putting my hand over the cut, praying to every deity I could imagine to let me live, to end this nightmare.

The door crashed inward, and I opened my eyes, watching as it shattered into a thousand rotten splinters. Behind it was Colt, as wolf, followed by Jericho, as human. Colt shook himself briefly, eyes locked on Weatherly. Weatherly still held the knife, and he rushed the wolf, bringing the blade around in a big arc. It all looked like slow motion.

*His footing is off... Wild punch... Won't connect...*

It didn't. Colt ducked easily, coming around, snapping at Weatherly's legs. He bit hard, teeth sinking into his thigh. Blood ran down his dirty uniform, mixing with old blood and dirt. I took grim satisfaction in Weatherly bleeding, too. But I didn't have the energy to do much more than think about it.

Jericho circled Colt and Weatherly, kneeling beside me. Weatherly's grunts and Colt's growls filled the air. Jericho met my eyes, and it was pretty clear from the look in them that what he saw frightened him. I smiled, or tried to, attempting to sit up.

"Stay still." Jericho's voice was low. "Just stay still."

There was a crash behind him, and I didn't stay still. I wanted to see, to watch Colt. To know he was okay.

Jericho sat near my head. He'd torn off his T-shirt and held it to my neck. I wasn't sure if it was to stop the blood or so he didn't have to look at whatever damage Weatherly had inflicted.

Weatherly was down on the floor, Colt standing on his chest. One massive front paw held down his arm, now a bloody and torn appendage but still clutching the knife. The other paw was on Weatherly's neck. I gave a silent cheer at the sight of it.

"Give it up, Weatherly. You're done for." Jericho's voice seemed far away, really far. The room's perspective seemed stretched somehow.

*Blood loss... You're losing it... Hold on...*

"Fuck you. Fuck both of you. And your hellcat." For being pinned by a wolf, the man had spunk.

Colt growled, shoving his face into Weatherly's. I was sure the growl was a returned fuck-you. Then he lunged.

"Don't watch." Jericho reached down, covering my eyes. I closed them, not because he said so, but because it seemed easier this way, to just lie here and rest. Suddenly, I was tired.

*Sleep... Just go to sleep...*

There was a terrible crunching sound and a gurgle that filled my ears. Then there was nothing, just the sound of my heart beating out its last rhythm.

*At least you met some cool guys... had a good weekend...*

"She's not going to last long. We can't take her back to the cabin." That was Jericho. My blond Viking.

There was a snuffle and a wet tongue licking my hand. I opened an eye, almost on the same level with Colt. He nudged me again, whining low in his throat. I wanted to tell him I was sorry, that I wished I'd met them under better circumstances.

*Maybe when I wake up...*

"Colt, you have to do it. Before it's too late."

There was movement, someone lifting me, holding me upright. I opened my eyes to see Colt beside me. He nuzzled my face, his wet nose in my ear. I wanted to laugh because it tickled, but it seemed like a whole lot of work. So, I tried to smile.

I was cold, bone cold. I knew I was sitting on Jericho's lap, his arms banded around me, but I couldn't feel anything. Not the warmth of his embrace or the solid presence of him behind me. It seemed everything was growing colder around me, and I half expected to see my breath puff out. But it was still summer.

Colt's muzzle brushed against my neck. He whined again, a tentative sound.

"Do it... now, Colt."

There was a blinding flash of pain. I squeezed my eyes shut, trying to scream, succeeding only in making a muffled groan. Then, again, more pain and Colt's body pressing me back against Jericho.

*What the hell are they doing to me? They're supposed to save me!*

Heat flooded through me, intense, almost unbearable. I could feel everything—arms, legs, fingers, toes—in a way that I didn't like. It was like being dumped head first into one of the steaming hot springs. I wanted out of my skin.

"Red? Hey... can you open your eyes? Look at me."

I forced my eyes open, looking up at Jericho. "Yeah... okay."

The room was brighter now, things coming into focus. But there was a roaring in my head that made his words garbled, indistinct.

"Can you hear me?"

I nodded. "Yeah... shh..." His voice only made the roaring louder. "I'm okay. Just don't talk right now."

"You're not okay. But we need to get you to our cabin. I'm going to pick you up now, okay?"

But I didn't have a say. I was lifted in the air, flying, I thought, even though I knew that was impossible. People didn't fly. But then we were out in the forest, the cool air a blessed relief against my feverish skin. Maybe I was dead and an angel, flying through the forest.

I closed my eyes again, or they were still closed. I wasn't

sure. I decided I'd completely lost it and that taking that nap now might be a good idea.

I let go of reality and let myself go someplace else, someplace far away. The roaring faded, and everything went silent and black.

CHAPTER 6

THE ROARING in my head was gone, replaced with a migraine. I could tell, without opening my eyes, that it was light outside. But eyes closed was preferable right now.

I was in a bed, so that must mean I was in Jericho and Colt's cabin. Some snippet of conversation came back, something about bringing me here after... After what?

"Oh, geez..."

After Colt had killed Weatherly. After Weatherly had tried to kill me.

I reached up, touching my neck. There was a bandage wrapped around my throat, a big bandage. Weatherly must have done quite a number with his knife. I let my hand fall back onto the bed.

"Hey... you awake?"

I opened my eyes enough to look toward the voice, toward Colt. He stood in the doorway, hair pulled back in a low ponytail.

I smiled. "Yeah." My voice came out in a weak little croak. "I'm awake."

He crossed the room and sat on the bed. "You've been out for a few days." He took my hand, chafing my fingers in his. "We're glad you're back with us."

"Me, too." I tried to sit up, but my body didn't really want to cooperate.

"Here... you're going to be weak for a while." Colt helped me sit up, propping pillows behind me. "Better?"

"Yeah. Better." A wave of vertigo sent my head spinning. I swallowed, my dry throat clicking. "Can I have some water?"

"Yeah. Here." He poured a glass from a pitcher on the bedside table. "Drink slow. Your throat's probably a little bruised."

The water was cool and felt like heaven, but he was right. It reminded me of having my tonsils out as a kid. All the ice cream you want... except you can't swallow it.

"What happened?" I handed him back the glass.

"Hey, you're awake."

I looked past Colt at Jericho. He smiled, crossed the room, and sat on the other side of the bed. Same thing. He took my hand and held me as if I were made of fine china.

"She wants to know what happened."

I wasn't so out of it that I didn't catch the glance between the guys. There was a long moment of weighted silence.

Jericho finally blew out a sigh. "Yeah. Okay. It's complicated. I don't know what Weatherly told you... And you should probably eat something first. You've been out for days. You're weak."

"I'll eat in a bit," I replied. Right now, I needed to know what happened and why I felt so different. "He said a lot of stuff about you guys. None made much sense, though. I got the feeling he thought you two had something he wanted. And then..."

The feel of the knife was back, the pressure, the non-pain of the cut. "He wanted me, but then he didn't." I shrugged, at a loss to explain anything else.

Colt nodded. "Weatherly's been after us for a long time. We live here, on family land... Jericho's family, to be honest. The land that's not part of the park. I was raised on the other side of Black Wolf. The mountain is named after my clan. But shifters lead a very dangerous life, even on land that's virtually inaccessible. Weatherly's from north of here. Long story short, clan rivalry, clan betrayal. Jericho and I teamed up. Weatherly decided he'd rather be the proverbial lone wolf than join a clan that's not his."

"So, he's—*was*—a shifter, too?" I was relieved that I used the right term this time.

"Yeah. We're all that's left of three different clans. I think being alone took a toll on Weatherly, sent him off the deep end into some dark place that he couldn't get out of. There was some really nasty stuff that happened in his clan near the end. From what we heard, it wasn't good."

"What happened to your families?" It hurt to talk, but I wanted answers. "You're the last of your clans?"

Jericho nodded "Yeah. We're it. We decided a long time ago that two against the world was better odds than going it alone. This land, my clan's land, has never been part of the park. It goes back a long, long way in my family, further than even Colt's claim to his lands. The deed's structured in a way that whoever occupies the cabin, as long as they can prove they're part of the family, owns the land. Someone was smart a long time ago." He gave me a crooked smile. "Smarter than the average wolf, I guess. Colt wasn't so lucky, though. Or Weatherly."

"My family's land ended up being taken over by the state.

Eminent domain. Turned Black Wolf into a park. I still think of it as my land, even though it's full of hikers and backpackers. Ruffles my fur to see them, present company excluded." He squeezed my hand and smiled at me, and I squeezed back.

"Thanks for that. So, he's been after you just because..."

"Because he could. Because he'd gone around the bend? Because he was jealous, wanted something he thought was better than what he had? Who knows? Weatherly was just plain crazy, either from isolation or because he drove himself there on his own. The man was full of hate." Colt shifted on the bed so he was sitting beside me. I moved a little, sharing the pillows. Jericho took the cue and sat on the other side.

Sandwiched between them, I felt safe and warm and less out of my body. But something was still off. "So, Weatherly tried to kill me, right? With a knife?"

"Yeah," Colt said. "We got there too late..."

"And saying we're sorry is never going to make that better." Jericho squeezed me hard enough to almost pull me over. "We messed up big time. But we'll never do that again."

"You didn't get there too late. You got there in time, or I wouldn't be here, right?" I touched my neck again. "You saved me."

From the silence between them, I knew there was more to the story.

Colt was the first to say anything. "About that... You're right. We saved you. It wasn't exactly what we'd planned, but it was the only way to save your life."

Something inside of me clicked, words that Weatherly had said coming back to me. "He said he was going to bite me... bite me, mark me, make me his." It sounded like a demented chant. "What did he mean?"

"Red..." Colt coughed, starting again. "Red, to make

someone who isn't a shifter into one, we bite them. Bite them while we're shifted. It... does more than just make you one of us. It also can save someone. Like you."

"Save me? From Weatherly?"

"No. Save you from dying. Weatherly cut your throat. You were bleeding to death when we got there. The only way to save you was to change you."

I twisted around, ignoring protests from both of them. I faced Colt. "You bit me? In that shack?"

I'd never had anyone look at me like Colt did. There was a hopelessness to that expression, but there was something beneath that, a stubbornness that said he'd do it again, given the chance. And a lift to his chin that dared me to challenge what he'd done.

"You saved my life." No question about it. No challenge to his actions. His face relaxed, his smile returning. "I'm one of you now. A shifter?"

"Yeah. I did. You are."

I looked at Jericho. "I'm part of his clan, right? Not yours. Does that change anything between us?"

Jericho shook his head and chuckled. I could see the look of surprise and relief on his face that, of all possible questions, that was my main one. "It doesn't have to. I just want to be with you. I don't care about anything else." He looked a little confused. "You seem awfully calm for someone who's just been told she's been bitten by, mated to, and turned into a shifter. Most people, from what I've heard, tend to be a little more... agitated maybe... with that much information."

I sat for a minute, looking out the window. I could see trees and what I thought was probably the top of Black Wolf. It was nice, this room, this view. I could do worse.

"Red? You okay?"

I looked back at Colt and Jericho. The guys I'd met yesterday—or the day before or the day before that. I wasn't sure when, really. My head hurt worse than any migraine I'd ever had. But I knew they'd risked their life for me, and they'd done what they felt was the best thing for me. It seemed only logical that I take it on faith that it was the right thing.

"If you haven't figured it out by now, I'm not like most girls." That got a laugh from Colt and a sound from Jericho that just made me shake my head. "Could be because I've written stuff that's stranger than fiction. Although, this is right up there with strange. But I've thought about what other kinds of lives would be like. Obviously, I thought they were all fictitious, just stuff I made up. This is like finding out the fairy tale is real."

I sank back against the pillows. Exhaustion swept through me like a summer breeze. I yawned, a rather inelegant gesture, considering. "I'm tired. Is that normal?"

Jericho slid out from beside me. "Yeah. You lost a lot of blood. And Colt's bite was on the aggressive side."

"Hey... I've never done this before. And it wasn't under ideal circumstances," Colt replied, defensively. He sat up, easing me back onto the pillows. I sank into them, breathing out a sigh. I could feel consciousness dissolving, sleep taking over.

"Are you able to eat something? We can make you some soup," Jericho asked, clearly concerned about me. "I'd rather you eat before you go to sleep again."

"I can't eat yet... I'm just so tired. I'll eat when I wake up. Please don't worry. I just need to sleep a little longer, and then I'll be good as new."

"Just rest, Red. We'll be around, checking on you. If you need anything, just let us know." Colt's voice was deep and soothing, and I found myself drifting off quickly.

"How will you hear me?" I closed my eyes.

Hands tucked the blankets around me, pulled the curtains, and doused the bedside light.

"Red, we're wolves. We can hear you breathing," Jericho replied.

I smiled, imagining them sitting somewhere close by in the dark, counting my breaths, my heartbeats. It put my mind and heart at ease, and I fell asleep knowing I was safe.

# CHAPTER 7

THERE WERE NOISES... crashing... things breaking. The scent of rotten wood, splinters in my fingers. Splinters in my neck. Clawing to get them out... Someone cutting them out with a knife. My Dad used tweezers when I was a kid...

*Everything hurts... My neck... My body. I want Colt... Jericho... Teeth.*

I thought I was awake. Or that I was dreaming.

I screamed. And again. And then fell into something not close to sleep, but further from death than I had been.

---

The next time I woke up—really woke up—it was dark. Someone was sitting in the chair in the corner, snoring softly.

"Jericho?"

"Hey..." He sat up, the chair creaking. "How do you feel?"

"Tired. But better. Not so wiped out, though. My head is all fuzzy. I think I had a bad dream."

"You mumbled a lot, screamed sometimes. We've been

taking turns sitting with you to wake you up. But you were really out of it."

I nodded. Out of it was a pretty good description.

"Are you hungry yet?"

I sat up, adjusting the pillows.

Jericho turned on the lamp beside his chair. There were dark circles under his eyes, and I wondered how long he'd been sitting there watching me sleep.

"Starving. What time is it?"

"Late... not far off dawn, I think. I lost track of time. I do know you've been sleeping for the better part of twenty-four hours."

I stretched, easing the kinks out of my shoulders and neck. "You know how you feel when you go to the movies in the afternoon and it's dark when you come out? Kind of disoriented? I feel like that."

Jericho laughed, stood, and crossed the room. "Yeah. It's been a long time since I've been off the mountain, but I know what you mean."

"Can you get Colt? I want to talk to you guys. Together."

"Yeah, sure. But then you need to let me make you something to eat."

I sat in the dim light, listening to Jericho going downstairs then outside, to his and Colt's voices. I could hear them from up here. The guys came in, and then there were footsteps on the stairs, louder as they came down the hall.

"Red. You okay?"

"I could hear you, hear almost everything you said, even outside."

Colt broke into a big grin. "See? You are one of us now."

I started shaking uncontrollably, my mind spinning. "One of you? I thought... That was all true? I thought I dreamed all of that... stuff about being bitten... being changed."

Jericho sat on the edge of the bed. "It's true, all of it. Do you remember the rest of it? Weatherly..."

"Yeah. I remember him, the knife, blood..." I touched my neck.

"And Colt biting you?"

I stared at Colt. "Yes..." *Teeth...* "Yes. You bit me after Weatherly..."

"Tried to kill you. With a knife." Jericho said the words so carefully, as if saying them again would actually hurt me.

Tears welled up in my eyes. "Yeah, he did. Then there was a lot of crashing..."

"Colt broke down the door."

*Splinters...* "As a wolf. And you were there." I reached for Jericho's hand. "But not as a wolf."

"No. I didn't shift, in case we needed to get you back here. Which is what happened."

"You killed Weatherly."

Colt was still standing in the doorway. I held out my hand, and he crossed the room, dropping onto the bed beside me, taking my hand.

"Yeah. I killed Weatherly." His voice was low, almost inaudible. "I've never killed anyone before."

His hand trembled, and I squeezed back. "Thank you. You saved my life."

"He saved your life by biting you. By making you one of us."

I glanced at Jericho. "That's the part where I lost the thread. The part that I thought I dreamed. But that's true?"

"It is. I bit you... It was the only way to save you. You'd lost so much blood. We thought we were too late. It was the only thing we could do. You can't know how hard it was... knowing that you didn't have a chance to decide yourself. That we decided your fate."

"But you saved my life. I can't be angry over that. I can be confused—and I am—but I can't be angry."

Colt squeezed my hand, then slid his arm around me, pulling me against his chest. "You're one of us now. Part of the clan."

I let him hold me. Jericho rubbed the spot between my shoulders, and we stayed like that, all wrapped up in each other, until my mind started coming up with more questions.

I pushed away from Colt. "And I'm part of Colt's clan, right? I remember asking you this already, but I feel like I need to make sure I understand."

Colt nodded. "Yes, that's right."

I turned to Jericho. "And you're sure we're okay?"

Just days ago, these two men were complete strangers, and now it felt as though they were the most important people in my life. The thought of being away from them made me panic.

Jericho nodded, his lips curving into a bright smile. "You're a shifter, a wolf. Right now, that's all that matters. Your blood line isn't pure anyway since you were created, not born to this." He shrugged. "Frankly, the least of my worries is which one of us bit you. The only thing we care about is that you're alive and in one piece."

"Weatherly called it a what? A bite to make me his?"

"Mating mark. And you're mine, if you want to get technical." Colt leaned back, the sexy half smile I loved turning up the corner of his mouth. "But I'm not one to get too hung up on technicalities."

I punched Colt lightly on the shoulder. We sat for a long time, watching the darkness outside, me hearing things I'd never heard before. I was getting sleepy again, a good kind of sleepy, not the zoned-out feeling I'd had before.

But there were things that needed to be figured out, at least for me. I was changed, marked... a radically different girl than the one who had arrived to spend the weekend doing yoga. I was a completely different animal now. But I was an animal who didn't know where she belonged.

Finally, Colt gave words to the thoughts running around in my head like a caged squirrel. "You're welcome to stay if you want. I want you to stay."

I punched him harder this time. "You said you don't use mind control."

"I don't." He rubbed his arm, winking. "But I can read them. You don't know where to go... what to do. Stay here. Think about it."

"Like Colt said, you're welcome here. For as long as you can stand us. Hopefully, that's longer than just the rest of the weekend."

Then the important thing finally surfaced. *Maggie.* "What day is this?"

"Wednesday. Or it will be when the sun comes up."

"I was supposed to go home Sunday. People will be worried. My best friend... she has to be frantic." I kicked aside the sheets, but there was too much masculinity holding them down. "I need to call. Can I get cell reception up here?" The thought of hiking to my car, then driving down that damn bumpy road to somewhere civilized seemed too exhausting to even contemplate. Plus, there was my stuff, my gear... my tent.

"Whoa... slow down." Jericho set a hand on my shoulder, pushing me back against the pillows. "One step at a time. First, what are you going to tell her?"

"I'm going to tell her..." What the hell was I going to tell her? That I decided to just up and move in with a couple guys I happened to have sex with? *Oh, and by the way, I'm a wolf.* "I can't tell her the whole truth. You don't want others... her to know about this, do you?"

There was a moment of silence. Even though I couldn't

read their minds, it was clear there was no debate on the answer to that question. *A big fat no.*

"Yeah... I thought so. No. So I won't tell Maggie the why."

"Wait. You've decided to stay?" There was a little more than a hint of surprise in Jericho's voice. He sat up, turning to face me.

Colt was in a similar state of shock. I glanced at him and almost laughed at the look on his face but didn't have the heart.

"Did you really think I'd leave now?"

"Red, you have to admit this all happened to you so quickly. We don't expect you to stay. We want you to, but..."

"It's a lot to ask." Colt finished Jericho's sentence. "I mean, we want you to know that we understand how you're feeling."

"You asked me, and I accepted. I know it's crazy, all of it... but I also know what I want." I heard my voice speaking the words and wondered what I had just agreed to. It was totally off the wall, totally out of character for me, but then again, nothing about my former life seemed to fit anymore. I was a completely different person—half woman, half wolf—and I knew there was no possible way I could return to life as it once was.

This is where I belonged. With Colt and Jericho. *Between two wolves.*

"There's nothing conventional about my life. I work from home; I write strange stories. I don't have any family—not that no one would miss me, but still. I can work from anywhere as long as I have some kind of Internet access at some point. There are ways to work around that."

"Hey, take a breath." Jericho reached over, putting a finger against my mouth. "One thing at a time. You'll stay?"

I waited until he took his hand away. "Yes, I want to stay."

"You don't know how happy that makes us, Red. Later today, we'll take you out to the clearing. There's a place where I'm pretty sure you can make a call."

"Okay. All right. I'll tell her I met you, both of you. That right there should keep her occupied with questions for about a week or so."

The guys laughed, and I joined them. It felt good to laugh. It felt right.

"After that... I'll think of something."

# CHAPTER 8

I HAD THOUGHT of something to tell Maggie. I told her about Jericho and Colt and meeting them in the springs, and after many prying questions from her, I gave her a play-by-play of exactly what happened in the springs, minus the near-death experience and, of course, no mention of what I had become. She seemed particularly interested in the graphic details of my threesome and asked me a torrent of questions, giggling after I answered each one.

The battery on the phone was almost dead before I got around to telling her I was staying... that I had planned to move into a cottage with my two lovers.

"You're leaving everything behind to go off with these two strangers? That's crazy!"

"I know it seems crazy, Maggie. But somehow, this feels right. I want to be with them, no matter what I have to leave behind." When I heard the streak of pain in her voice, I felt tears well up in my eyes at the thought of losing her. "I would never abandon you. We'll be friends for the rest of our lives. You'll see me again. I promise."

I heard her breathe in a deep sigh and let it out slowly. "Are you happy, Rish?"

"Happier than I have ever been. I feel alive when I'm here, like I've never felt before. I have never been so at home, as crazy as it sounds." I looked out past the edge of the clearing, down toward the river, and beyond. "It's so beautiful here, Maggie. So peaceful."

"Then do what you need to do. I'll be here, always... I love you."

"I love you, too."

Before I could end the call, the battery went dead, and I shoved the phone in my pocket. There'd be a time when I was in town or somewhere there was a signal, and I'd call her back. We'd figure it out. We always did. It wasn't good-bye. That was for certain.

I turned back to the cabin. There were lights on downstairs, voices, scents. I closed my eyes and breathed in all of it. I was exactly where I belonged.

▭

It was a little before dawn a few days later, and I'd crawled into bed in Jericho's room. It had taken me a little while to adjust to sleeping in a different bed every night, never quite sure who was going to show up. Most often than not, it was all of us piled into one bed. I was never alone at night. We shifters were a nocturnal race, and being up until dawn became the norm. I still wrote best in the middle of the night, and the guys were used to prowling around in the darkness. All in all, our lives meshed together seamlessly.

"Well, we aim to please. You know that. If there's anything else..."

I was pillowed on Jericho's shoulder. Colt was still downstairs, locking the doors and windows, closing out the day. I was drowsy, but not ready to fall asleep. Something stirred inside me, a lazy tendril of desire uncurling in my stomach, a flutter of arousal. I didn't think I'd ever get tired of this feeling, of the anticipation of being with Jericho and Colt.

Some of it was the human side of me, the desire to love and be loved—lust and desire—the same feelings I'd had in other relationships. It was familiar, just multiplied times two.

Overriding all that was the wolf in me, and that part was growing stronger by the day. The feelings I had for Colt and Jericho were nothing short of all-consuming, powerful—primal. To say that I would kill for them would be an understatement. I would fight for them, tooth and nail, heart and soul, just like I knew they would for me.

So, add that level of commitment to our love life, and the result was way beyond simple multiplication. I knew the need swirling through me now was going to explode into a white-hot fire, a desire to take and be taken, to mate with Jericho and Colt over and over. To be consumed by my wolves. To be consumed by love.

"Hey, you still awake?" Jericho prodded me, not entirely too gently, poking my shoulder. "You want the bed to your-self?" He started to sit up, but I rolled onto him, my breasts pressed against his chest.

The sheet was caught between us, but it didn't do much to conceal Jericho's erection. I wiggled my hips, loving the feel of it

"Like hell." I smiled down at him. Even in the soft light of the lamp, the details of his face stood out. The blood of his clan was so clear in him, so strong. A wave of sadness washed over me. He was the last of his clan like Colt was the last of his. I was the only chance of survival for either clan.

"Stop thinking about it. It's fine. Really." His voice softened as he reached up to brush back a strand of hair. "You can't change how things are right this very minute. Give it time."

I touched his cheek, then ran my finger down the bridge of his nose. "I know. I'm just... impatient."

"You know we live longer than humans, right? Unless someone like Weatherly comes along again. Otherwise, we've got time. Lots of time."

"Time for what?"

I glanced over my shoulder. Colt stood in the doorway, stark naked. I'd gotten used to that right away. It was one of the perks of living with guys who had no inhibitions and who were used to shifting at the drop of a hat. I still got dressed more often than not.

"Time for her to save us, save our clans."

Colt crossed the room and sat on the edge of the bed. "You're not ready yet anyway, Red. You know that." He leaned down and kissed the back of my head. "You've been a shifter for less than a month. It takes time to sink into this life, to let your body go through all the changes." He tugged at the sheet, the part that covered my ass. "Besides, you haven't shifted yet. We're not sure..." He kissed my shoulder, his hand moving to the small of my back.

"Not sure of what?" I tried to sit up, but Jericho wrapped his arms around my shoulders.

They both had a way of distracting me from pretty much everything.

"Not sure if you're able to yet. We've had this conversation before."

"Yeah. I know. I need to shift." They were right. I did need to shift—or at least try. I'd been, well, hesitant. I'd watched Colt and Jericho, but most of those times had been under less-than-ideal circumstances. In fact, some of those times had been downright terrifying. I wasn't sure I wanted to go through that whole drama—and frankly, what looked like trauma—with my body. But I was supposed to think about it... or something.

"But not right now. Right now..." As usual, Colt read my mind.

He slid his hand over my ass, fingers probing between my legs. I arched under his touch, my legs sliding down over Jericho's thighs. Jericho responded instantly, hips flexing upward, prodding me with his cock. Not to cross my shifters, but I was practically purring under Colt's touch.

"Right now, you need to stop worrying, okay? It's just going to distract you from what's really important."

"And what's that?" I wiggled again, and Jericho twitched the sheet out from between us. It was, as always, glorious to feel his skin against mine. He was hot, as usual. It still amazed me how warm both guys were. I imagined us in winter, me snuggled between them, toasty warm without even needing blankets.

"What's important is us... *this*..." Colt's fingers slipped lower, playing over my swollen folds. "No pun intended, but I get the feeling..." His fingers pushed farther. "This is something you're looking forward to just as much as we are."

"Yeah, well, I am." I drew in a sharp breath as Colt probed, one finger sliding down, rubbing my clit. I made a little yelping sound, something new that had started cropping up in my symphony of noises during sex. I assumed it was part of my new identity. In response, he thrust harder, the palm of his hand cupping me, his thumb pressing into the cleft of my ass. I arched farther, loving the proprietary way he touched me.

While Colt was doing a great job of taking my breath away, beneath me, Jericho was making inroads on a frontal attack, his cock sliding against my inner thigh.

"You two going to fight over who gets there first?" I pushed up against Jericho's chest, letting my knees slide apart on the bed.

There was always a hint of competition between them, subtle, never interfering, mostly good-natured. I'd long ago gotten over worrying they'd come to blows over me. But the game was still there, the hint of it adding a little spice.

"I think I won this time." Colt curled his fingers inside me, finding that magic spot that drove me wild. My body jerked, and I gasped as a primal rush of arousal speared me. Not that I wanted to, but I wasn't sure I'd ever get used to this, the intensity, how everything seemed heightened, my senses sharpened, every sensation taken to the max.

"I think not." Jericho flexed his hips quickly upward, almost flipping me off his body.

Behind me, Colt laughed, his fingers slipping out of me. Jericho grabbed my hips, getting me back into position, the head of his cock taking the place of Colt's fingers.

"Always a pleasure, Red." Jericho's entry was exquisite. He had a way of taking me that was slow and languorous but edged with something raw that sent a thrill through me like no one ever had. It wasn't exactly fear. I knew in every cell of my being that this man would never hurt me, that he would fight for me like I would for him. But still...

Colt was moving behind me, the bed dipping and shifting. He reached out, grabbing my hips, pulling me up and down. I sat back, Jericho's cock sliding farther into me, my thighs tensing against his hips.

Colt moved his hands up my torso, reaching up to cup my breasts. I leaned against him, his broad chest pressing against my back. He nuzzled my neck for a minute, his breath hot, his scent washing over me. I never realized how good men could smell until I got mixed up with these two. I closed my eyes and inhaled, and something coiled inside me like a spring that got wound tighter. And when that spring sprang, all hell was likely to break loose, in a strictly sexual sense.

But until then, until I couldn't stand it anymore and came so hard, I thought I'd break apart, yeah, this was exactly where I wanted to be.

Jericho ran his hands up my thighs, fingers playing over my skin. He moved them higher until he reached the apex of my thighs, until his thumbs reached that certain spot between my legs. He spread the edges of my swollen folds, one thumb circling over my clit. I jerked again, but there was nowhere for me to go. I was held fast against Colt.

He tightened his hands on my breasts, moving from caressing to fondling to practically mauling me. I bit my lip, looking down at his hands, dark against my pale skin, loving the contrast. Behind me was the unmistakable thrust of Colt's erection moving against my ass. For a moment, he rubbed against me, hot and hard. Then he shifted, his cock sliding against the cleft of my ass. This was still uncharted territory for me, and as close as we'd come on several occasions, we hadn't explored this, um... area yet.

"Like the view?" Jericho grinned up at me.

"I like the view very much." I reached up, covering Colt's big hands with my much smaller ones. "Do you like the view?"

"Very much. From here, you look sexy beyond all belief. Good enough to eat... If I didn't have my cock in that lovely—"

"Okay. Okay. I get the picture." I'd never be able to match these guys in braggadocio or their slightly dirty way of looking at the world. I loved it, but it made me blush. *Like now.*

"I love that color on you, Red. You look pretty in pink."

I felt myself going six shades pinker. "You can stop now."

The guys had an instinct for knowing what to say to get under my skin. I think it was a form of foreplay.

"Go easy on her, Jericho. You know when she comes, she

flushes all over. Not just her face." Colt took one hand away from my breast, turning my face to his. "Right? You could light up the night."

Before I could say anything, he claimed my mouth in a messy kiss. I twisted in his grip, wanting more of him. I got it as he thrust his tongue between my lips and the kiss went from messy to wet and over-the-top sexy. It was the kind of kiss I'd always dreamed of having, but never got. Now, with Colt and Jericho, kisses were wild and passionate and sometimes very messy in the best possible way.

Beneath me, Jericho's movements were getting just a little bit out of control, a little bit erratic. It meant he was close, or he was teasing me... again. Or trying to get my attention. I broke away from Colt, looking down at Jericho.

Colt teased his fingers along my jaw, the other hand still occupied with my breast. He'd begun rolling my hard nipple between his thumb and forefinger. Little jolts ricocheted through me, sharp and penetrating, contrasting with the heat building lower.

"Colt, want a turn?"

"Hey, I'm not a video game controller you pass back and forth."

But Jericho was already sitting up. Colt let me go with a little push as Jericho pulled me toward him. I wrapped my legs around his waist, throwing my arms around his neck. We were face to face, our noses almost touching.

"You're a hell of a lot more fun than video games. Besides, I outgrew those a long time ago. I like grown-up games now."

He kissed me, something between rough and gentle, that strange combination that always took me by surprise, threw me a little off guard and back to day one. And I was always the tiniest bit hesitant about how to react. I mean, I reacted to the kiss. My body reacted, melting into Jericho as I always did. But

I never knew if I should go aggressive or play up the gentle. So, I just let him lead the way.

This kiss was anything but gentle. He grabbed the back of my head, pulling me into the kiss. It deepened. Impulsively, I pulled his lower lip into my mouth, sucking briefly. And then I did it. I bit Jericho's lip.

He growled but didn't pull away. I did, tugging his lower lip with my teeth. I opened my eyes to see him looking at me from beneath hooded lids. I bit down just a little harder, and his eyes widened just a bit. Then I chickened out and let go.

Jericho reached up, rubbing his lip. "You're getting better. You still pull your punches, though." He gave me a lopsided grin. "You're a wolf now, Red. You can act like one."

Colt's breath was hot against my ear, his hands moving up my back, thumbs working into the hair at the nape of my neck. "So can I."

Before I had a chance to think of a comeback, Colt grabbed me from behind. With a surprised yelp, I let go of Jericho.

Colt was quick, far quicker than I was. I found myself on my knees, practically falling onto my face. He was already pressed against my ass, his cock sliding between my legs. My body was still humming from Jericho's attention to that part of my anatomy. Then Colt was there, sliding into me. It was different. He was different.

I managed to push up against the pressure of Colt pushing me forward with each thrust. It was a struggle, but I finally got up on my hands. I was panting, from exertion, from arousal. From the desire to want to turn and snap at Colt, to taste him as I had Jericho.

I shook my head, blinking in surprise. Something wasn't right.

"Jericho..." My voice sounded harsh, choked. "Jericho, something's happening."

I saw panic in his eyes, and then he was leaning over, pushing back the hair from my face. Then I was moving, lunging forward on the bed, fingers gripping the sheets. Colt was beside me, trying to stroke my hair. But I shook him off.

"This is it, right? It's happening... But why? I don't want it—"

A force like nothing I'd ever felt shook me. And I mean shook. All I wanted was to curl into a fetal position, to hold myself from splintering into a million shards. It was like every cell in my body was set on some high-pitch vibrate mode. I closed my eyes, gritted my teeth, and tried to hold on.

"I guess this means you're ready." There was a mixture of apprehension and excitement in Colt's voice.

I forced myself to look at him. "I'm not. I am not ready. This isn't... I don't want—" Whatever the hell I wanted to say got lost in the growl that tore from my throat. My voice rose to an almost howl, then cracked, turning into a guttural moan.

"This hurts." I was sweating now, my body running hot, very hot. I uncurled myself, rolling over onto my back. The room spun around me, and for a horrible minute, I thought I was going to be sick. "Fuck, this hurts. Is it always like this?"

Colt loomed up next to me. Everything was distorted, and I blinked, trying to make him come into focus.

He knelt beside the bed. "Yeah. It does, at first. It gets easier. But we'll get you through this, and from then on, it'll be a breeze."

I blew out a breath. *A breeze, right.* My body felt like it was going through a meat grinder, my mind being blown to pieces. There was no way they knew what I was going through. I was alone in this.

*Alone...*

I jerked my head around. "Wait. You'll be there, right? I

can't do this alone." I shot a look at Colt, then to Jericho standing behind him. "You'll be there?"

"We will, Red. Right beside you. But..." I got that grin from Colt, the crooked one, the one that drove me insane sometimes.

"But what?" I gasped out what I was sure were going to be my last human words for now. Maybe forever.

"Well, we can't talk as wolves. And we don't know if you'll be able to... communicate as a wolf."

I gave up trying to understand him and gave in to the pain. Another blast of whatever the hell this was tore through me, and I knew this was it. My arms were in agony, being stretched, bent backward, and torn out of the sockets. I screamed.

"Jericho, we need to get her outside. She can't stay in here."

"She can't walk downstairs. I'll carry her."

There was a roaring in my ears, the pain in my arms traveling down to my legs. I wanted to lie still, very, very still, not be picked up and carried downstairs. But that's what was happening. Colt slid his arms under my shoulders and knees, picking me up easily. I turned my face toward his chest.

For the first time since I'd known him, Colt felt cool against my heated skin. I closed my eyes and hung on as he carried me out of the room and down the stairs.

CHAPTER 9

COLT SET me down on the soft ground beneath the pines. It was blessedly cool, and for a moment, I just lay there, pain wracking my body. It was too strong for me to fight, even if I wanted to.

Something was changing inside me. Not just my body, but something deep inside my core. I wanted this. I wanted to change. I was afraid of the pain, but the desire to be a wolf was growing stronger than the fear.

"Colt..." I tried to sit up, but I could only make it to my hands and knees. I stayed there, head down, gulping in the night air. "Jericho?"

"We're here, Red. Right here. We're not leaving you."

"Will you change with me?"

"We will."

I looked up at Jericho, Colt standing behind him. "Promise?"

"Red, we wouldn't miss this for all the world. We'll be right there beside you, every step."

Some kind of seismic wave of pain took my breath away. I

arched up onto my knees, head back, screaming my pain into the night sky. The sound went from human to wolf and this time stayed there.

Jericho said something. Colt answered, but their voices were muddy, muffled, words making no sense. My hands hurt. The tips of my fingers felt like someone was cutting them open with knives. I made the mistake of looking down.

My nails were splitting, the ends of my fingers widening, shortening, pulling back into my palms. Claws emerged, thick, sharp, wicked-looking. I wanted to scream, but frankly, I was mesmerized. Thick hair appeared, reddish blond, and within minutes, my hands—my feet—were covered. It moved up my arms and legs, and I looked down at my body. I was completely covered.

There was more, more pain, more changes. My jaw cracked, stretching. It was agony, and I threw my hands up to my face, scratching my skin with my claws. The pain was nothing compared to the torture in the rest of my body. I tried to lower my arms, but they refused to cooperate, and I fell forward onto my newly formed paws. I wanted this to end, to be whatever I was supposed to be.

There was another burst of noise in my head, the roar deafening now. Someone touched me, and I turned, snarling, snapping my jaws—and my very sharp teeth—at the hand on my shoulder.

It was Colt. "She's one of us."

The roaring was gone. I could hear everything, see everything, and smell things I could not identify.

I was a wolf.

Something pushed at my other shoulder. I turned, teeth bared. It was a gray wolf... It was Jericho.

"It's okay."

I shook my head. It sounded for a minute like radio static or bees buzzing. But then the noises cleared. The voice was his, in my mind. And he was there, standing next to me, a wolf.

"Think it, and you can talk to me. You'll have to work at it."

I wanted to tell him I was okay—or at least that I thought I was okay. But it was like being in a dream where you want to scream but it's all muffled, like screaming into a pillow. A brief sharp pain lanced through my head, and I whined in protest.

"It's okay. Just take it slow. You can understand me, right? Just wag your tail."

Even as a wolf, he could make me smile. *If wolves could smile.* And wag my tail, right... But there was something behind me, something I could control. I glanced over my shoulder. I did have a tail, a big, lush tail, blond tipped in red. An experimental wiggle of my back end brought a yip from my left.

"Wag your tail, not wiggle your ass. As much as I like that ass..."

I spun around. The big black wolf I'd seen on the trail in the park was sitting, head cocked, watching me with bright-blue eyes. Colt.

I snapped at him.

"You can wag your tail however you want." It was Jericho again, clearer this time.

"Screw you."

Colt and Jericho barked what I assumed was wolfish laughter. "Good job, Red. You got it."

"Leave it to Colt to make you mad enough to talk."

"You feel like taking a walk in the woods?" Jericho wagged his tail and turned. "Follow the leader."

I took a few experimental steps. Four legs and a tail on a woman who had a hard time walking and chewing gum at the same time. But one step led to another and another, and within minutes, I was loping down the path behind Jericho.

Colt followed. I could hear him, every footfall on the pine

needles clear and sharp. I could smell him, too. And Jericho. Their scents were even more intoxicating like this, mixed with trees and foliage and decaying leaves.

It hit me like a physical blow someplace near my heart. *These are my wolves.*

The path I'd walked on before was suddenly full of things I'd never seen or even knew existed. Everything was interesting. I heard something in the leaves and couldn't help pouncing on it. Turned out it was a shrew. I caught it and tossed it in the air. Then I backed away, my mouth filled with something that tasted horrible.

Jericho's laughed echoed in my head. "You'll learn what's edible and what's not. Those are not."

I headed off the path, deeper into the forest. The guys flanked me, never pushing too close, but always there. I snuffled through leaves, listened to earthworms burrowing, beetles moving invisibly under cover. All of it was fascinating. I moved through a clearing, a space beneath the pines. I stopped, taking it all in. It was like a cathedral, a sacred space almost in our backyard. I wanted to come here again as myself... or as my other self.

"Come on. You'll love the river."

Colt veered off, heading down the ravine. I'd never been here, couldn't have ever walked here. It was steep and rocky, but I worked my way easily between boulders and fallen logs. If nothing else, I loved being graceful and surefooted.

The river shimmered in the dark, the surface giving off colors I never even knew existed, sounds I'd never heard with my human ears. I stood, open-mouthed, with what I thought was probably a wolf like grin on my face.

"Beautiful, right?" Colt brushed against my shoulder, a bold move since I'd tried to bite him earlier. But the desire to snap had faded. Maybe I was getting used to being in this new skin.

"Yeah. Beyond beautiful."

"More fun to play in. Come on." Colt nudged me with his nose, pushing me forward. But I didn't need any prodding.

"Race you." I was already sprinting toward the river. I looked over my shoulder, my two wolves right behind me.

I ran into the water. It was cold on my paws, but it ran off my fur. The rocks beneath me were slippery, but I clambered over them with ease. Water hit my muzzle, and I turned. Colt jumped from a nearby rock, water splashing over me. I barked... I think it was something like a bark. It was a sound of perfect joy.

We played in the water for a long time, jumping, splashing each other, veering off to turn over a rock in search of something hidden beneath. I discovered a crayfish, nosing it with interest. Until it clamped one claw on the end of my nose. I pulled back, snorting, shaking my head until it came loose, sailing through the air. I heard it hit the water with a little plunk.

Colt crossed the river, and Jericho and I joined him. We started up the other side, into the park. It was the first time I'd been here since I'd met Colt and Jericho at the hot springs. It seemed a lifetime away now.

We skirted the campsites. The scent of burning wood was acrid, foreign, made me sneeze. Underneath that was the tantalizing smell of food. I lifted my head, sniffing the air, salivating. It was irresistible, and I turned, following the aroma.

Jericho cut me off, a low growl rippling from his throat. I stopped.

Colt stepped up on the other side.

"No."

A single word spoken by both. My hackles rose. I wanted what I wanted.

"We can't risk being seen."

I heard the words, let the meaning sink. I backed down, stepped away. It was hard, but I turned toward the river. The guys followed. And we went home.

## CHAPTER 10

"I NEVER WANT to go through that again. At least not the first part. The rest… yeah, definitely. But not right now."

The guys were hovering around the bed, pacing but looking extremely pleased with me. I was certainly pleased with myself, but I was also exhausted.

"This pacing stuff has to stop, okay? Sit or something. You're driving me crazy."

Colt perched on the edge of the bed. Jericho hovered a moment longer, then sat down on the windowsill. They still seemed full of energy. Annoyingly so.

"It's hard coming down sometimes." Colt reached out, pulling the blanket up over my arms. "But for you, it was different.

"You think?" I turned toward Colt. Every inch of my body hurt, and I winced.

"You didn't grow up like this. We did. But you did good, Red." He leaned over and kissed my forehead. "Really good."

"So, I'm one of you now, for real?" I was having a hard time keeping my eyes open. Colt was fading in and out, Jericho behind him just a big, familiar shape backlit by the light from the window.

"For real. You're a shifter. One of us." Jericho came into view over Colt's shoulder. "You're our shifter, Red."

"Well, your shifter wants to sleep." I pulled the blanket higher, unable to keep my eyes open any longer. And not wanting to. I wasn't going anywhere, and I knew they weren't. "We can do a play-by-play later."

The last thing I heard was Colt's soft laugh and the door clicking shut behind them.

I opened my eyes. It was dark, really dark. The usual sounds were absent, and for a minute, I panicked. The only clock in the house was downstairs, the big antique in the front room that didn't keep very good time. I could just hear it ticking.

*Cell phone.* But I had no idea where that was right now.

Tossing off the blankets, I sat up. A wave of dizziness made me reconsider, but I shook my head. I was still in Jericho's room, but like my phone, I wasn't sure where my clothes were. It didn't matter.

My eyes took almost no time to adjust to the total darkness. I stood up, waited through another wave of dizziness, and then decided it just might be from hunger and not some bizarre aftereffect of becoming a wolf for the first time. The rest of me felt pretty normal, except for the lingering aches in my joints.

I snagged a robe from the bathroom and padded downstairs. Before I'd reached the bottom, I heard Colt's and Jericho's voices through the open door. They were on the front porch.

"Hey, Red. You're back with us." Colt was sitting on the

ancient wicker sofa that seemed on the verge of collapse. He patted the cushion beside him.

Jericho was leaned against the wide porch railing.

I dropped down, thankful for the softness of the cushions. My hips and knees ached, but I was starting to take a perverse pleasure in the pain. It was a badge of some kind.

*Shifter: achievement unlocked.*

"You feeling okay?" Jericho held a beer out to me.

I shook my head. "Not bad, considering."

"You were amazing, Red. Seriously. You did really great for not being born to it." Colt wrapped an arm around my shoulders, rather gentler than usual. He kissed the top of my head. "And you're just as stubborn as any shifter I know."

"And you were beautiful. Wish we could have gotten a picture. But... that's not something we do." Jericho finished his beer, set the empty bottle on the railing, and joined us. "Your coat is like honey and fire, amazing. Can't wait to see you as a wolf again."

I thought about that, about the pain. "Will it always be like that? Will it always hurt?"

"Can't say. You're not born as a shifter. Colt and I were shifting before we even knew what that meant. It's just how we're wired. For you..." Jericho took my hand. "It's a steep learning curve."

"Why did it just happen... out of the blue?"

Jericho laughed. "Might have been the heat of the moment. Your inner wolf gets excited by strong emotions, strong desires. And you, Red, are full of strong desires." He shrugged. "The wolf rises to the surface. In your case, it got away from you."

"It's something you'll learn to use to your advantage." Colt ran his fingers through my hair. They snagged in a tangle, and I cringed, suddenly aware of how unkempt I must look.

"Just take your time. There's no rush. You seem to think

you need to prove yourself to us. Or to yourself." Colt took my other hand. "There's nothing you need to do, other than be here with us."

"About that..." I held their hands, my guys... my wolves. "You said—one of you said—that until I shifted, we wouldn't know if the mating biting thing had worked. So now that I've shifted... that means..."

Colt lifted my hand, kissing my knuckles. "That means you're a shifter, through and through. To the bone."

"I'm glad to know I'm one of the pack."

"What you really want to know is if you have a pup, will it be a shifter? The answer is yes."

I didn't realize I'd been holding my breath until I released a sigh. "Yeah. That's what I really wanted to know." Something heavy and dense felt as though it were lifted from deep inside me. I smiled, a silly, loopy smile that I tried to hold back. I'd wanted this from the start. From Colt's first bite, from the time Jericho's teeth sank into my flesh. I wanted to give them both a fighting chance at having a clan again. And now I knew I could.

Jericho wound his fingers through mine. "Red, hold on. First, we're not asking you to do anything. Not to continue our clans or anything like that. I'd... We'd never ask that of you."

"I know. But I want to... I can do this for you, for both of you. It's like this... It's... I mean..." I stumbled over the words to explain the excitement running through me.

Part of my brain was still working on wolf time, and I had the desire to wag the tail I didn't have at the moment. Or yip and jump. I took a breath, looked between the two of them, at the identical bemused expressions, and shrugged.

"Call it instinct. Or something like that. For the first time, I have a clear idea of my life. And this is it." I smiled. "Now, keep in mind that I'm not the barefoot and pregnant kind of woman. I need to be your equal. In all things."

Jericho held my hand, and Colt held me close.

"You will always be our equal." I turned toward Jericho and saw that his eyes were filled with love for me, and I believed him.

I took a deep breath, letting it out slowly. Time stood still in one of those rare perfect little moments. The sun was rising, as it always did. And it would set and the moon would rise, over and over, again and again. The river would rise in the spring, wash away the pools at the hot springs, and then people would come and rebuild them. Everything kept keeping on.

Something clicked inside me, as if someone tuned on—or off—a switch. The chatter in my mind, meaningless static, disappeared. It was like seeing my place in the universe, touching the great wheel, and for a moment—a beautiful, exquisite, still moment—knowing how I fit into all of that.

And for the first time since Weatherly took me, since they'd come to get me, since they'd made me theirs, I realized not only were they right, but *why* they were right. There was time. Time to get used to this new life, this way of living. There would be time. Time to save their clans, time to do whatever I could, if that's what was going to happen. Everything was going to be okay.

"Okay. No rush." I lifted both of their hands to my lips, nibbling on their knuckles. "But that doesn't mean we can't start now, right?"

▭

The guys pulled off clothes as we made our way up the stairs and down the hall, dropping shirts and pants, on the floor. It took ten seconds for Jericho to untie the sash on my robe, letting it fall to the floor. We tumbled into the closest room and onto Colt's bed, Jericho claiming my mouth with a brutal kiss even before I'd caught my breath. It was right, the harshness of it, the force, the weight of his body pinning me to the mattress. For a long moment, I let him weigh me down, let him plunder my mouth, his tongue sweeping, probing, exploring.

But inside, something roiled and moved, paced and stalked. Someone had called it my inner wolf, and she was on the move. She wanted out. But I wasn't ready for her yet.

The power inside me grew, the urge to bite and snap, but I held it in check, working with her, taming her. I let my wolf know I was in control, but I let her know she was welcome to join the party.

I pushed up against Jericho, rolling him over... or he let me. Either way, it was my turn to pin him to the bed, to straddle his hips with my thighs. I broke the kiss, sitting up, a wave of triumph and arousal flooding my body.

"God, you're beautiful, Red. I can see your wolf... feel her, taste her. Keep her in check, but don't muzzle her."

I leaned down, kissing him again, tugging his lower lip between my teeth. I felt his smile as I bit harder. I held on to him until he made a sound like a whine.

I ran my finger over his lower lip. "You sure about that muzzle? This might get dangerous for you."

"I think Jericho can handle himself." Colt climbed onto the bed beside him.

I looked down at him as he stretched out, all long legs, broad chest... and a very obvious erection. It still amazed me that the guys were comfortable with this, that both were self-confident enough or self-aware enough to be like this with me.

"And we know she can handle both of us." Jericho sat up, tipping me onto my back. "Right, Red?"

I squirmed beneath him, shimmying my legs up his body. His erection slid along the insides of my thighs, coming danger-ously close to where I wanted him to be. I tried to pull him closer, but he was stronger than I was, and he held himself just out of reach.

"Impatient, aren't you?"

"I want you... like crazy. You know that." I was panting, arousal making me hot, hotter than I'd ever been in my life. I wanted Jericho inside me, Colt right after him.

"I do know that." Jericho flexed his hips, the head of his cock grazing my swollen folds. That brief, teasing contact had me crying out as if he'd thrust himself into me to the hilt. If being a wolf-in-training made every part of me this sensitive, this attuned to even the slightest contact, then being with these guys might just challenge my sanity.

"I want you, too, Red." Jericho rolled his hips, sliding into me, inch by inch. I pushed my hips up to meet him, lifting my ass, claiming as much of him as I could, as much as he would give me.

"But I want you on my terms. My wolf wants control."

I snarled up at him, showing him my teeth. A rush of adrenaline shot through me, and for a moment, I felt like I could easily overpower Jericho, rise and take him. The thought amazed me, even scared me for a second.

But Jericho's mind reading must have been fully operational. Before I had a chance to draw a breath, he thrust into me, burying himself to the hilt. I arched up beneath him, my body humming with energy. I was so ready, so close that it took all my willpower not to come right then and there.

Colt was beside me, his lips against my neck. When he spoke, his breath tickled my ear. "Let it go, Red. If that's what you want to do. Your power is endless..." He reached up, caressing my breast, rolling my hard nipple between his fingers. An earthshattering wave of ecstasy flashed through me. And my mind was suitably blown.

I screamed—or howled or both. The sound was otherworldly, but I didn't care. I let loose, head back, body arching beneath Jericho. The strength boiling inside me was incredible, and Jericho wrapped one arm beneath me, hanging on like I was a bucking bronco. I was pressed against him, crushed against his chest, his hips grinding against me. The wolf in my body took over, howling for all she was worth as I let go, as Colt said.

The world around me was spinning like mad. I closed my eyes. My mind was filled with sounds, music, wordless poems, and colored lights. It was crazy beautiful, and I think I laughed out loud.

From above me came the unmistakable sounds of Jericho joining me in this wild dance. I opened my eyes, watching his face, every nuance of what was going on with him clear in his expression.

And then I felt what he was feeling, heard what he was thinking. It meshed with the waves crashing through me, dovetailed perfectly with everything I thought, felt.

There was no choice but to give in and let it wash me away. I lost touch with everything except Jericho and myself. If Colt was there, I wasn't aware of him at all.

After a long, long time, I washed up on some shore, calm, still. I was almost afraid to move, to break the perfect moment. I opened one eye, looking up at Jericho.

Only he wasn't up, he was beside. I turned my head.

"Hey, my sweet wolf."

"That was pretty amazing."

"Beyond amazing." He brushed a strand of hair from my face. "For me, too. Truly. Not just saying that so you'll sleep with me again. That was…"

"Yeah." I touched his face. "It was."

Something warm touched my hip. I turned to the other side.

Colt had his head propped up on one elbow. "You got anything left for me?"

"Always." I rolled onto my side.

"Are you sure about—"

I put a finger to his lips. "You're so beautiful, Colt. Let's find a better use for that mouth besides asking questions."

He grinned.

I slipped my finger between his lips and let him suck gently on it. He swirled his tongue over my fingertip, teasing me, pulling me deeper. I reached between us, finding his cock, wrapping my hand around him. He moaned softly, hips flexing, sliding himself into my palm.

"Is that what you wanted?"

He bit my finger, not all that gently. I pulled it out slowly, very slowly, never looking away from Colt's eyes, stroking him forcefully as I did.

"You aren't going to be satisfied with just this, are you?" I gave him a little tug at the end of that stroke. "I know I'm not. I want more... much more of you. Mate of mine."

Never letting go of him, I sat up and swung one leg over Colt's body as he rolled onto his back. I straddled his hips, holding him, squeezing him. He bit his lip as I brought my body close to him.

"You want this?" I moved again until the head of his cock touched me, touched my wet pussy. Just the soft brush of his hot silkiness sent a wave of desire through me, almost bringing me to the edge again. It also brought my wolf howling to the surface. It was all I could do to fight her back, to keep fangs and claws from tearing through my flesh, tearing into Colt.

"She's powerful, isn't she? Hard to control." He reached for me, hands resting on my hips, moving higher. I leaned into them, letting him cup my breasts. "I love the wolf in you, Red. But it's you I want. And I want you now."

He thrust up as I pulled my hand away. I gasped, throwing my head back as he filled me. It was all new, all pristine, as if this were the first time I'd been with any man. My mate, the wolf who'd bitten me, was claiming me. I was over the moon.

I rode Colt hard, forcing him deeper, beyond any place any man had ever been. I took him, and I loved every second of it. In that minute, everything else faded away, including Jericho. There was nothing in my world except Colt and me, coming together as one. Coming together forever.

My body arched and shook, my hips moving to some ancient rhythm that I seemed to know without even trying. Colt matched every move, every twist, grind, shake, and thrust. We moved in perfect harmony.

We came together, the peak we reached higher than any I'd ever climbed. I closed my eyes, threw my arms wide, and howled my climax for the world to hear. Then it was all too much, and my mind gave in, gave up trying to hold on to reality. I cried out names—Colt's... Jericho's—and then everything went black.

Someone was holding me, easing me onto the bed. I opened my eyes to find my guys looking down at me. I was relieved to find I was in one piece. At least my body felt like it was still intact. My mind, though, was another matter.

I sat up a little too quickly. Colt put an arm behind me, and we rearranged arms and legs until the three of us were sitting against the head of the bed. I looked at the tangle of sheets—some torn—and blankets, most of which were on the floor with the pillows.

"Guess we're sleeping in Jericho's room tonight."

"Yeah. We might have to rethink the bedroom arrangements." Colt looked around at the devastation that was his bed. "If we keep this up, we're going to run out of sheets."

I glanced at Jericho. He looked... fine. But I wasn't. Other than a major case of afterglow, which made me feel sublimely relaxed, I was slightly upset with myself. I took his hand. "I'm sorry. I didn't mean..."

He looked down at me. "Didn't mean to what? Have a hell of a good fuck with Colt?"

I blinked at his choice of words and the smile on his face. "Well, yeah. I mean... it was... different. Not necessarily better than with you, but..."

"Different. And it will be. He's the wolf you're mated to. Can't change that."

"And that's okay with you?" I was having a hard time wrapping my head around this. The sharing thing was still hard enough to grasp, but this was something else.

He shrugged, lacing his fingers through mine. "It's going to be different with you and him. It has to be. I'm okay with that. If I'd been the one to mark you, the tables would be turned."

Colt had been silent. I reached out and took his hand. "So, you two really are okay with how all of this is working out? Really, truly?"

"Cross my heart and pinky swear if that's what will make you happy. But yeah, it is what it is. You have something different with Jericho that I'll never have. And what we have... it's colored by the mark."

"It's not going to change how I feel about you, Red." Jericho leaned close, kissing my cheek. "I love you no matter what."

"I love you, too." Colt kissed the other cheek. "You need to stop worrying about us. We appreciate it, but we're a lot tougher than you think."

For the first time in a long time, I was speechless. Two men, men who'd fought for me, had told me they loved me.

"I love you both so much." I looked between my wolves.

We hung out in Colt's room for a little while longer, talking about everything and nothing, the way people talk when they've just told each other they love them. A little shy maybe, a little tentative. Testing the waters. Which seemed a little odd since we'd just destroyed a bed with our lovemaking. I felt I was already in the deep end of the hot springs, loving every minute of it.

CHAPTER 11

THE SUN WAS JUST COMING up over the top of Black
Wolf on the other side of the river, setting the trees on the ridge
alight. The leaves had changed almost overnight; fall was here.
There was a tang in the air, crispness, like biting into an apple.

I'd never been a fan of autumn. It had always seemed to me
things ended in the fall. The garden my father had loved to
putter around in on weekends was giving up its last tomatoes,
the flowers fading, setting seed. And when I was a kid, it also
meant back to school, the end of the summer. Fall always made
me sad.

But this year was different. It was a beginning. My heart
did that thing I'd only read about in overwritten romance
novels. It swelled with emotion. I'd never felt it before, and it
took me a minute to realize what it was, that I liked how it felt,
that I was comfortable with so many new emotions. And I
realized something else. For the first time in a long, long time, I
was truly happy. I wasn't thrilled about being awake this early,
though. I was more accustomed to going to bed at this time.
But my schedule and the rest of the world had rarely meshed,

and now it was even more obvious, living here with my wolves.

Jericho and Colt were sound asleep. I'd wanted to leave early, do what I needed to do, and be back before dark. Some of my errands were purely chores, getting the last of my things out of my apartment. Maggie had called, and the couple subletting my apartment wanted to move in a week early, willing to pay extra for most of the furniture that I no longer needed. What was left wasn't much, but it was all personal. Books and journals. Photos of my dad. The bare essentials, sentimental and otherwise. My clothes that I'd brought up over a couple weekends, everything else remaining with the sublet. And that included the artwork Harrison never liked.

Colt and Jericho had made the transition into my new life with them a little easier. For one, they'd cleared the path down the mountain so I wasn't continually being hit in the face with branches and underbrush. They'd hacked out a parking space for my car, too, so I could pull off the logging road that led back to the main road.

I headed down the path. It felt strange to be awake in the daylight. It seemed far brighter than I remembered for this time of year. The shifter in me dug through my purse, fishing out sunglasses. The guys had told me there were things that took some getting used to, and I supposed this was one of them.

The car was covered in leaves and pine needles, well camouflaged against the undergrowth behind it. I brushed off the windshield, unlocked the car, and got in. This was the first time I'd started it up in weeks. I crossed my fingers. It seemed to me that my dad had told me cars needed to run on a regular basis or they stopped working.

I turned the key, and the engine purred. Smiling, I managed to turn around on the narrow road heading back toward the city.

It was a very surreal experience, speeding down the interstate. The fastest I'd moved lately had been at a sprint through the forest, not piloting a car at the limit, even though I'd done it thousands of times before. Before my new life.

I took the exit to my street, slowing down as my apartment came into view. Maggie's car was at the curb. My heart did a little jump at the thought of seeing her. I missed her more than I thought possible. We'd blithely assumed phone calls and text messages would be enough. But the service in the mountains was a fickle mistress, and even though I could get a bar or two if I walked out to the edge of the clearing below the cabin, it wasn't reliable. Colt had been amazed there was any signal at all. Not that either he or Jericho bothered much with cell phones or computers.

The light was out in the hallway, as it always was. That was something I wouldn't miss: conversations—more like arguments—with the super, trying to get him to replace the bulb. No longer my problem.

I took the stairs two at a time. Since I'd started shifting on a regular basis and gotten over the whole being exhausted every time, I'd had more energy than ever. Back in my old life, these stairs had seemed insurmountable. Now they were a piece of cake.

"Risha!" The door to my apartment was open, Maggie leaning out into the hall. "You made good time."

"I did."

She pulled me into a big hug, and I squeezed her back. She squeaked out a little sound, and I backed off, forgetting for a minute she wasn't a wolf like me.

"You go away and turn into some muscle woman. You've lost weight. Don't those guys feed you?"

She dragged me into the apartment before I could pick a

question to answer. There was food on the counter, bagels and cream cheese, fruit, juice, and coffee.

"Are you expecting company?" I poured a cup of coffee and took a sip.

Maggie stood, hands on hips, watching. "Only you. All your favorites. And since when do you drink your coffee black?" She nodded at the cream and sugar sitting on the counter. "You're a sugar maven. Have been from the first cup you ever had."

"Guess my tastes have changed." How much else had changed? And how much of those changes could I talk to Maggie about?

"Well, even if you've given up cream and sugar, it's still great to see you." Maggie perched on a counter stool. I'd had them in storage. Harrison thought they were great. I tended to fall off them during dinner. Maggie had brought them back out in her attempt to "stage" the apartment when she'd helped me find a sublet.

"Thanks for finding... What's their names?" I took another sip of coffee. "I really appreciate all your help."

"They're the Spauldings. Deena and David. Sounds like high school sweethearts, our age, married for ages. Fell in love with the apartment as is, down to the art on the walls." Maggie slid an envelope across the counter "Here's all their contact information, the signed agreement, and a copy of the lease. You're lucky there are only a couple months left on the lease. The Spauldings are looking to stay after the sublet is up, so hopefully that works out and they don't stiff you on the rent for the next couple months."

"I trust your judgment. You're pretty good at reading people." I spread a generous layer of cream cheese on a bagel. My stomach had been growling for the last half hour. I took a bite. But something was wrong. I loved cream cheese and onion bagels. But this tasted... off. Wrong. I set aside the bagel.

"Not hungry?"

"I ate before I left." I hated lying to Maggie. But there was no way I could tell her what I suspected, that the wolf in me wasn't a big fan of dairy.

"You okay?"

I glanced up at Maggie. She could read me like a book, knew me better than anyone. *Well, except for Jericho and Colt.* "Yeah. Just... tired. From the ride." But I could read her, too, and I knew she wasn't buying it.

"Risha... come clean. What is it? Is it the guys?" That little line appeared between her brows, the one that told me she was worried. I hated seeing it.

"No... Yes. Sort of. But it's not what you think. It's nothing bad." I wasn't sure what to call it, how to tell her I wasn't the same person she thought I was. "I've made some changes in my life, Maggie. Some really major changes."

"That's pretty obvious. You went away to clear your head, and you ended up moving in with two guys. That's a pretty major change, especially for unconventional you." She gave me a smile, but the worry was still in her eyes. "Are you telling me there's more?"

"It's a different kind of life, Maggie. Radically different." I pushed up the sleeves of my sweater, propping my chin in my hands. "I'm not sure I can explain it."

Maggie reached out, touching my arm. "Is there something you're not telling me?"

*Yeah, there is.* "No..."

"You're scratched... and bruised." Her eyes were locked on my arms. I looked down, then pulled down my sleeves. "Risha, are they doing that?"

"Oh, no. God, no. Jericho and Colt would never hurt me.

We do live in the wilderness, you know. Lots of hiking, fishing, things like that. These are just... sort of a daily occurrence."

She still wasn't buying it. I reached out and squeezed her hand. "Listen. Come up to the cabin. I want you to meet them and them to meet you. You're the most important person in my life. I want you to see that I'm okay up there. Really okay."

After a minute, she squeezed my hand. "Okay. Deal. Before it snows, I'll come up and meet your guys." She giggled. "I still can't believe you ended up living with two guys. It's just so..."

"Wild?" I winked. "It certainly is. But it's right for me."

"I was going to say sexy. But if you want to stick with wild, that works, too."

# CHAPTER 12

MY LAST STOP was the gym. There was nothing there for me to get, but I wanted to say good-bye to Jack. I felt I owed him something, an explanation or a thank-you. He'd been in my life for only a short time, but it was his voice I heard most often. Could be that he reminded me of an older version of my dad, or it could be that he didn't take any of my shit, and I appreciated that.

"Hey, Red. About time you show up. You missed quite a few sessions. Where the hell have you been?"

I leaned on the counter, watching the guys in the ring. Jack came around and stood next to me.

"Yeah. About that. I need to cancel the rest of my contract. I'm moving."

He looked down at me, and I swear the air between us changed. I thought he was going to yell or give me the silent treatment, but after a moment, he broke into a smile. I had to admit it was the first time I'd ever seen Jack smile. He leaned forward, and I tensed, expecting a smack to the back of my head. Instead, he kissed my cheek. I wasn't sure which startled me more—the smile or the unexpected show of something resembling affection.

"About time you found your pack, Red, whoever they are. You'll fit in just fine." He stepped back.

I stared at him, my mouth falling open. *Did I just hear him say what I think he said? Did he scent the shifter on me? Is he a shifter?*

"You heard me."

I stared harder, a ripple of energy rushing through my body, and I felt goose bumps crop up on my arms. I'd heard his words, but I swear his lips hadn't moved.

He simply smiled and walked behind the counter. "Just let me get the cancellation form, and you're good to go." He shuffled papers.

I watched, stunned, a million questions on the tip of my tongue. But I knew I couldn't ask them.

I signed the form he pushed at me.

"Forwarding address? You might have a refund coming."

I shook my head. "Not... really." I didn't think our road even had a name.

"Off the grid. I understand."

"Here..." I scribbled Maggie's address. "My friend. She'll see that I get it."

He glanced at the paper. "Works for me. Listen, Red. You take care of yourself. It's a different life, but if there's ever been anyone who can handle it, it's you. You're one of the toughest broads I've ever had the pleasure of working with."

Someone in the ring called Jack's name. He nodded. "I got a client waiting. Take care, Red." He smiled at me again, and then he was gone.

I was back at the cabin just before sunset, which made the walk up the trail much easier. The boxes from my old apartment could wait until tomorrow, until Colt and Jericho could help me. *My guys... my wolves.*

Even though I'd only been gone half a day, I missed them terribly. Missed their scent, the way they moved, looked... the way they looked at me. Touched me. I was smiling long before I saw the cabin, before I saw Jericho and Colt sitting on the porch.

They came down the stairs, and I got the biggest bear hug. Or I guess wolf hug would be the proper term. Whichever, it was just what I needed.

"Glad you're back. We missed you." Colt kissed me on one cheek, Jericho the other. The kisses might have been chaste, but their hands were making it clear they had something a lot less innocent in mind. And that suited me just fine.

"I missed you guys, too."

"Where's your stuff? Do you want to bring it up? We cleared room in the loft."

"Boxes can wait." I pulled Colt close, kissing him hard, a big wet kiss with plenty of tongue. Before he could say anything, I did the same to Jericho, tugging his bottom lip, putting just enough pressure on him to remind him I'd bitten him before. "But I can't."

"Whatever you want, Red. Inside or out?" Colt spun me away from Jericho, pulling me into his arms.

"Out. And I know a place." I pushed away from Colt, skipping out of his grasp. I ran around the cabin, following the trial we'd taken the first night I shifted. I wanted to be in that space with them.

Colt caught me easily, grabbing me around the waist. I was laughing as he pulled me down onto the soft pine needles that carpeted the ground. It smelled cool and fresh, like Christmas warmed by the sun. I rolled onto my back, looking up at Colt backed by the clear indigo of the coming twilight.

"Your eyes look silver at night. Did you know that?"

"And your eyes shine like diamonds."

"Isn't she the most beautiful thing in the world?" Jericho dropped onto the ground beside us. "You're a beautiful woman, and you make a beautiful wolf."

My face went hot. "You're making me blush."

"And it makes you all the prettier."

"Did we come out here to talk, or did we come out here for something else?"

It turned out we were there for something else.

I let the guys take the lead, my wolf content to bask in the attention and the love. It was darker, but I could still see if I wanted to, if I kept my eyes open. But I closed them, seeing them in my mind's eye as they worshipped my body.

They took turns, moving over me, nuzzling and kissing, sucking my breasts until my nipples were hard and aching. I arched against them, winding my fingers in their hair, holding them against me.

Jericho broke away, moving slowly down my body, leaving a trail of fire on my skin with his kisses, his tongue, his sharp teeth brushing against the edge of my navel. He moved lower, and I gasped as those lips and tongue and sharp teeth brushed against something else, something far more sensitive.

Hands spread my legs, but I was already letting them fall open. Fingers caressed the soft skin of the insides of my thighs, playing over my heated flesh. I grabbed at the pine needles beneath me, crushing them, the smell of pine filling the air. I wanted those fingers to move higher, to touch me at my core. But they only teased me, only fanned the fire they'd started. I could have begged them silently, just with my mind. I didn't. I let them play.

A kiss softer than a butterfly's wing touched me, and I drew in a sharp breath. The kiss was followed by another, lips firmer, pressing against me. Then the flick of a tongue at the edge, closer. But not there yet.

The other stayed at my breasts, sucking, stroking gently in time with the kisses between my legs. I shuddered, slowing my breathing but unable to slow my heart. It bounded and leapt in time with the touch of the man between my thighs, the one at my breast.

And then there was more, kisses becoming deeper, the flick of a tongue circling, testing. Then suddenly, plundering, probing, delving deeply into me. I sighed, ass pressed against the ground, fingers wound through thick hair.

Deeper and harder, licking and sucking at me until I couldn't stand it.

I arched violently, digging my fingers into the earth, but didn't cry out, didn't scream my ecstasy to the sky. I kept it inside, kept the power contained, turning it inward.

My wolf danced with me in sheer joy, feeling everything, I did, loving every second of my pleasure. She wasn't controlled or contained, held back, or held down. Everything was as it should be.

I opened my eyes, watching the stars overhead turning on the great wheel in the sky. I'd touched that wheel, thanks to Colt and Jericho. I smiled, and my wolf did as well.

She and I were one.

# THE WOLVES NEXT DOOR

## A PARANORMAL WOLF SHIFTER MÉNAGE ROMANCE

# CHAPTER 1

*ANOTHER CRAZY DAY of endless shopping*, thought Julie as she dumped her bags onto the floor, struggled to open the front door, and then fought to pick up the heavy bags once again.

That's when she heard a deep voice rumble from out of nowhere. A voice she knew she would never forget.

"Looks like you could use some help with those."

Crushed gravel... warm, delicious velvet, and pure steel mixed with just a hint of smooth, deep bass... *That voice.* Julie caught her breath as the words washed over her senses, her pulse instantly quickening. She was reluctant to look behind her. She already knew who it was. Only one man had a voice that could send such wickedly delicious vibrations through her curvy frame, reducing her to a blushing schoolgirl within minutes, leaving her feeling lightheaded and breathless.

"Come on, let me help you with that. Those bags look awfully heavy *for a girl.*" This time, his voice held humor, and she rolled her eyes before finally spinning around to face him.

"Hi, Caine." She greeted him with a bright smile. "But this girl can manage. Easily."

With a man like Caine, there was only one thing to expect: unapologetic and brazenly hot fire that could melt any woman's heart with just one look. Even a woman like Julie who didn't fall easily.

Yet that's exactly what happened every time she ran into him.

Julie had moved into the quiet neighborhood only a few months ago, and so far, Caine was one of the only neighbors who had reached out to her. Julie didn't mind that so much since the last thing she wanted was to add chaos to her life with nosy neighbors wanting to invade her space and know all about her business.

After all, she moved to the area for peace and quiet and, most importantly, a brand-new start, a second chance. And that involved keeping a low profile, her head down, minding her own damn business.

She looked up, *way* up, at Caine and instantly felt the undeniable heat in the deep blue of his eyes.

It was hard to turn a shoulder to such a beautiful, charismatic man, even if the plus-size beauty felt completely awkward and out of place with him. Perhaps she wasn't used to the attention of such a seductively handsome man, or maybe it was because of her own insecurities, ignited by an ex-boyfriend who made her question *everything* about herself. But as she stood before Caine and his offer to help with her shopping bags, all self-conscious thought was swept from her mind, replaced with a deep, satisfying need to be close to him, to remain in his presence.

His dirty-blond hair and six-foot-six frame in that fitted black T-shirt and low-slung jeans looked casual enough at first glance, harmless even, but you could still imagine him just walking out of a Calvin Klein photo shoot.

*Those jeans, oh, those jeans... They show off all the good parts.*

"Thanks, Caine. I appreciate the help, but I think I'll manage." she finally replied. Damn the ridiculous mousy voice that came from her lips. Every single time he came near her, she felt she should run the other way for fear of further embarrassing herself. But Caine seemed harmless enough—as harmless as a walking sex god could be.

Julie had to quell the impulse to run her fingers through his hair. She hoped she looked okay after a full day of shopping and errands. What could she say? Shopping was her pick-me-up, especially after a rough day—or week. *And I've had more than a few of those lately.*

"Are you sure about that?" Caine prodded, a small smile tilting his sinfully curved lips. Julie tore her eyes away from that beautiful mouth to look down at the bags, which still dotted the floor at her feet, barely maintaining their contents. She figured two trips would be all it would take, and she'd have all her stuff inside. But then she looked up at Caine once again and didn't feel like denying him one more time. Why the hell would she say no? Not to those gorgeous blue eyes. Not to that sinfully flirty smile with those melt-your-heart dimples. What harm would it be anyway, accepting a bit of help from a friendly neighbor?

"On second thought, I really would appreciate your help. Thanks," she replied with a genuine smile. She swore Caine's eyes darkened momentarily as he held her gaze, but then he nodded with a return smile.

"No problem," he replied, his molten-lava voice oozing sexuality, and with one quick movement, he easily gathered up several of the overflowing bags into his large hands.

"Come on in," Julie whispered, though he already was walking through her front door. She hid an inward sigh as she watched him enter what she'd so far considered her personal space.

Her eyes lingered briefly on his retreating back, stretched beneath the fabric of his T-shirt and outlined in muscle, and then down at his perfectly sculpted frame. *No man's ass has the right to look that good in jeans*, thought Julie with a shiver. Finally, she bent down to pick up the remaining two bags. As she straightened, she glanced across the street and let out a quiet groan of dismay.

Julie recognized the woman standing there in front of the opposite house, her thin face etched in disapproval. She had long brunette hair tied back in a severe ponytail, and her gaze was that of sharp daggers and cold steel. *Just what I need.* It was bad enough that she'd been feeling snubbed by the ladies in the neighborhood, but now she'd have to contend with being thought of as the neighborhood flirt, maybe even slut, luring their sexy male neighbors into her love nest.

Not sure what to do, Julie simply smiled and nodded, but the woman merely huffed and turned her back, shaking her head all the way up to her front door, which she slammed shut behind her. *Ouch. Okay, so that's how it's going to be. Well, all the more reason not to socialize.*

With a deep sigh, she retreated into her house, only to find Caine waiting for her, standing in the middle of the foyer, bags still in hand.

"Where do you want me?" He glanced over his shoulder at her, his dimples prominent on his tanned face.

Julie couldn't control the rush of heat between her thighs or the way her nipples suddenly felt sensitive beneath her thin blouse. Stuttering, she struggled to breathe. "Umm, in the... the living room. Just set the bags down on the coffee table, please."

She moved ahead of him, leading him deeper into the house, and he followed close behind, his masculine scent wafting in the air, permeating everything it touched, and she knew she would never be able to walk through the front door again without being instantly reminded of Caine. And she was very certain he knew that.

Caine noted that the bags weren't filled with groceries, but clothing and other fashion items. Some of the bags held insignia from pricey designer stores. Coupled with the way the house seemed so nicely decorated and styled, it was obvious Julie was doing well for herself. Or maybe she had a rich family—or boyfriend.

The thought of any man in Julie's life fired him up, causing him to let out a growl. *Damn.* He didn't want to think about that. Ryan had warned him that they should take it slow. Give her time to adjust to the area, get to know her. It was all part of the process to eventually make her understand that not only had she come into their territory, but she'd staked her claim on the two men destined to have her as a mate.

*Our one and only mate.*

And now it occurred to him that she might not even be single. After all, she was absolutely stunning. Curves in places Caine never even dreamed a woman could have them, and eyes; such a gorgeous, impossibly dark brown he was almost tempted to ask if she wore contacts. And her smile—it had the power to tilt his world on its side, leaving him desperate to cling to reality before he was swept away in some dangerously wicked fantasy. And oh, those lips... deliciously plump and begging to be kissed. When she smiled at him the way she had as she'd thanked him for his offer to help, Caine had felt the strings clench around his heart. Taking things slow with Julie would be the most difficult thing he ever did.

Besides, he wasn't known for his patience. Ryan was the calm and steady one. Dark, brooding, and enigmatic, he was the opposite of Caine's wild, carefree style.

But there wasn't a carefree thought on his mind right then, a frown marring his forehead as he suddenly wondered if the reason Julie always seemed so nervous or wary of letting him close was because she was already taken.

Imagining another man's hands on Julie's body tightened his gut until he could hardly breathe. Yet he couldn't sense another man on her—no masculine scent existed in the room other than his own. Funny how, after only three months since she moved in, he already thought of her as theirs to claim. And though Caine normally didn't like to share when it came to his women, when it came to Julie, Caine and Ryan already had an understanding. There could only be one woman for them, a shared mate that would fulfill their needs as lover, friend, and mother to their offspring. One scent of Julie, and their joint fate had been sealed...

Ryan had found her first.

He'd literally passed by her on the street a short distance away from her house. He'd seen her heading toward him and was instantly taken in by her beauty. Taller than the average woman, beautifully curved, a classic beauty that made you lose your breath for a moment in hungry admiration.

As she'd approached, she'd looked up and met Ryan's gaze, and he instantly picked her scent in the air. She gave him a polite smile and nod and then brushed past him on the narrow pavement, oblivious to the desire she etched into his heart.

A minute later, Ryan spun around, fists clenching, desperate to hold back the urge to claim what he was sure was his. Being a shifter meant there was always a thin line between your primal and human instincts. Sometimes, it was easy to simply give in, the beast breaking through the logic, forcing its desires above all rational thought. As he watched the gloriously beautiful woman walk away, Ryan felt closer to losing control than he'd ever felt since he had originally shifted.

He watched with narrowed eyes as she suddenly moved toward the house nested between his and Caine's. As she let herself in, he realized she was his new neighbor, the woman who had just purchased the Miller house that had stood empty for years. And then a smile had spread over his normally forbidding expression, dispelling the shadows. He couldn't wait to tell Caine the news.

They'd found their mate. Or more aptly, she'd found them, although she had yet to know it. Fate couldn't have been kinder, and Ryan was hell-bent on making sure he seized every opportunity to get to know her, to bring her closer into his circle, and finally, when the time was right, to reveal who she was to them. Their one true mate, forever claimed, possessed by their never-ending desire for her. She would succumb to her own desperate need for them, accepting them as both her leaders and lovers in return, and she would finally be right where she belonged.

# CHAPTER 2

JULIE COULD SENSE that something wasn't right, that Caine was on edge around her, and she wondered why. Was he suddenly unsure as to whether he should have befriended her, especially with the rest of the neighborhood all but ignoring her existence? Maybe he was worried about what people would think if they somehow found out about him being "too nice" to the new girl in town.

But for some reason, she doubted that was the case. She told herself she hadn't mistaken the attraction she'd felt coming off him, and he didn't seem like the type who would care about what anyone thought of him. Caine wanted her. Any red-blooded woman could tell when a man desired her, and she could feel it, the sexual tension hanging thick in the air.

Before that thought could send her into a panic, she laughed inwardly at herself. Caine had never done or said anything disrespectful or suggestive. She knew she had nothing to fear from him. If anything, it was herself she couldn't trust. Caine made her feel... *things*. Things she'd sworn to never feel again, not until she knew what the hell she was doing when it came to men and relationships. Until then, either one was out of bounds.

"Just set them there, please." She directed him, and he turned to place the bags on the nearby coffee table.

When he faced her again, he seemed calmer and his face was clear of whatever had been troubling him. Now, he flashed her that killer smile that made her take a sudden gulp of air, her face blushing crimson red.

"Your home is very nice. You've really done a great job with the place," he replied, shoving his hands in his pockets.

"Thanks," Julie said with a pleased smile. "I've had a lot of fun with it. That's my job... I'm an interior designer."

She didn't know why she'd divulged that information. Why she'd let him in at all. But something about Caine made her feel safe, like he could be trusted. And Julie realized she had been desperate for someone to talk to.

"That doesn't surprise me. You seem like the creative, artsy type. Now me, I'm just a tech nerd. I work in software... programming mainly."

"Wow. Brains and brawn." Julie choked on a laugh, covering her mouth with her hand. *Okay, now that was crossing the line.*

She wasn't sure what he read in her gaze or in the restless way she hugged herself and rubbed her arms as if searching for security in the wave of attraction that took hold of her, but he only smiled, his deep-blue eyes searching her face.

"I get by. But you, well, you're every man's dream. Such an intelligent woman, creative, and... absolutely beautiful."

Julie sucked in a breath, completely caught off guard. His gaze washed her skin in a burning wave of heat, and she couldn't look away, couldn't breathe. He'd called her beautiful —and for the first time in her life, she believed it. Alarm bells should have been ringing in her head. But they weren't.

Instead, she felt a surge of confidence, sensing his genuine desire for her.

*What in the world is happening to me?*

*I should know better than this,* Julie's inner voice warned her. *I shouldn't be going weak at the knees for the first good-looking guy who tells me he finds me beautiful. I came down here for some peace and quiet, to find myself again. The last thing I needed was to get bowled over by another handsome face. Not after the last relationship and his constant abuse and unforgivable betrayal.* She couldn't risk her heart again, especially not with a man like Caine.

She drew in a deep, long breath and tried to think of an easy way to do what she had to do, despite the fact that everything in her mind and body begged her not to. "Look, um, Caine, I'm not quite sure—"

"It's just dinner. My place. I'm inviting a few friends over for a barbeque. Nothing too serious." Caine's words broke in before she could finish, and she paused when he added with a grin, "Come on. It'll be fun. I promise. It's my way of saying welcome to the neighborhood."

*Oh.* Well, dammit. Julie realized just how silly she must look to Caine, assuming he was inviting her out on a date when he was just being friendly, trying to reach out to the new girl in town.

Gulping down her disappointment, she forced a smile. "Thank you, Caine. Sure, I'd love to come over. What time should I be there?"

"Ah, any time after six is fine. And don't worry; it's just a casual get-together amongst friends. Nothing formal." He smiled with enough warmth to light her skin on fire, and when he held out his hand to her, she was certain her fingertips would ignite in flames at his heated touch. "Julie," he rumbled, his voice low, "I'm really looking forward to seeing you again."

Men like Caine certainly had no problem getting women, gorgeous women, to do anything he wanted. *He's just being nice to me,* Julie thought as she accepted his hand and felt the immediate strength in his grip. *It's not like he's desperate to touch...*

But even as she placed her hand in his and decided the gesture was indeed innocent, it didn't feel that way. His large hand closed around her much smaller one, and she felt enveloped by warmth. Julie almost shivered from how much heat Caine seemed to exude.

An instant magnetism surged through her, coupling with a budding sexual awareness. Visions of his nicely heated olive-tinted skin against hers made her heart flutter and her thighs ache. With just this light touch, Julie came full circle with the realization that this man was unlike any other she'd ever met. She would never have believed she could fall so easily for a man's charms or want someone so badly that she barely knew. She needed to get a grip on her desperate hunger for this stranger before it got out of hand and she got hurt... again.

# CHAPTER 3

JULIE HADN'T BEEN sure what exactly to wear, so she went for a simple sundress. You could never go wrong with a dress, especially if its hem skimmed the thighs and the fabric clung nicely to her plentiful curves. It was gray and had cutouts in the back, nothing too revealing, but it gave the dress a feminine slant that highlighted her lines.

Julie considered her reflection and wondered if she should put on any makeup. She didn't want to seem like she was trying too hard, desperate to win attention from her handsome host, though if she were honest with herself, she would have to admit that's exactly what she was hoping for. Besides, if she looked good, she'd feel good, and Julie knew she could use all the confidence she could muster up.

She'd grown up with issues about her weight, her mother constantly reminding her that men preferred "thin" women and if she weren't careful, she would end up miserable and alone. *Perhaps my mom was right after all*, she thought, considering her failed relationships, but still, a part of her fought the echoes of insecurity, drowning out her mother's voice and reminding her that Caine had called her beautiful.

She'd lost her plain Jane persona over the years and learned how to fake a smile and, when necessary, confidence, and if she had to use those tools tonight, she most certainly would. Still, as she stood in front of the mirror, she felt that all too familiar pang of self-doubt. Sighing, she put on some light foundation, mascara, and a flattering shade of lip-gloss to highlight her already puffy lips and fought down any lingering nerves. Just dinner amongst new friends, and in a few hours, she'd be back home, safe within her walls, hidden away from the scrutiny of the world around her.

*Damn him*, she thought as she recalled how her ex, Grant, had tried to break her spirit, but she'd fought her way through until she could escape his torment. Now there was no going back to the weak woman she was. She refused to ever look back again.

Julie couldn't help but smile when she thought of Caine and how he hadn't seemed put off when she'd artlessly said he had brain and brawn. She decided if she had the opportunity, she'd let him take her where he wanted. Was she in any way a woman he'd ever consider dating? There'd been a certain something in those gorgeous blue eyes of his, and she decided to accept it as truth, finally silencing the nagging voice in her head that insisted on telling her Caine Marks could never possibly settle for a broken woman like her.

She found herself standing in front of Caine's door, reluctant to knock and then deciding she had nothing to lose. *Here goes nothing*, she thought.

He opened almost instantly, so her surprised smile was

genuine. He looked hot as ever, his T-shirt rolled up at the sleeves to reveal his inked forearms. His dark blue jeans were deliciously snug and his dirty-blond hair looked freshly washed. Julie stared at him, her mind blank apart from a blur of moving body parts.

He grinned. "Right on time. You look beautiful."

*There's that word again.*

"Thank you," Julie whispered, heat rushing to her cheeks.

He swung open the door for her, and she walked through, pausing for direction. He quickly slid the palm of his hand down to her lower back, guiding her in. She shivered at the way his hand held her back, his grip strong and possessive. As he released her, his slanted grin tugged at the knots in her belly.

"I'm glad you're here. Come on in," he said warmly.

Julie loved Caine's home. The designer within appreciated the open-plan concept of the place, while the furniture was minimalist yet welcoming, even homely.

She was surprised to see that other people had already arrived. Her eyes widened slightly as she came face to face with two of the biggest men she'd ever seen.

Caine was well above six feet and packing serious muscle himself, but these two were absolute giants, both of them very good-looking, their muscular frames threatening to rip through the cotton of their T-shirts. They looked like they could easily be in the army or some special forces team or something. Caine introduced them as Vern and Hawke, friends from childhood.

They regarded her with interest, and Julie was quite sure she caught them sending Caine a nod of approval when they thought she wasn't looking. So much brawn in one room. It was almost surreal, as though she had stepped onto the pages of a romance novel.

Quickly scanning the room, she was relieved to find two other women chatting quietly in the corner. As she made her way toward them, they turned to greet her, one of them handing her a chilled glass of white wine, which she gratefully accepted.

Caine came forward to make more introductions. Two of the women happened to be significant others of the other two men in the room. Jemima was the petite brunette dating Hawke, and Julie couldn't help picturing how the six-foot-plus hunk would look next to the pretty, tiny girl. The blonde, who was willowy with cover girl beauty, happened to be Hailey, who was Vern's fiancée. This was another image of contrasts that intrigued Julie. But it was the clear, unspoken bond between them all that couldn't be ignored, yet they never let her feel like she was the outsider. Julie figured they'd been paired off nicely for the dinner setting, but that was until she got yet another surprise.

"Oh good, Ryan's here," Caine announced from behind her. "Now we can get to eating. Julie, there's someone you haven't met yet."

Julie felt his hand in the small of her back, and she turned around in interest, her glass lifting to her lips. The hand with the glass paused in midair when she came face to face with him.

Caine was grinning. "Julie, meet Ryan. He's like the big brother I never wanted." He joked. "Ryan, this is Julie. She lives in between our houses. She moved in months ago. Remember I told you about her?"

Julie knew she was staring but couldn't stop. She'd never forget that face or that body. It had to be several weeks ago, but the memory was still fresh.

Tall, dark, and handsome didn't begin to describe him. He had "dangerous" written all over him, from the top of his inky-black clean-shaven hair to his dark-gray shoes. The kind of guy Mama and all your friends warned you about. His smoldering dark-blue eyes held hers, and Julie felt swept away.

*Damn.* She was in big trouble.

And she wasn't exactly sure what the heck she had done wrong, but she already felt guilty as hell for the simmering of awareness that bubbled between her thighs.

"I believe I've seen you before," Julie said. She was surprised she could actually piece together coherent words. Thank goodness. She even managed to hold out her hand and then felt tremors rush through her when he swallowed it in his strong grip.

"Yes. I remember," he replied, his voice a deep rumble.

Just three words—combined with that look that could singe off a girl's panties—and Julie decided she was officially losing her mind. She definitely had a thing for Caine, which she'd been looking forward to exploring if opportunity presented itself. So how come she was getting instantly bowled over by Mr. Dark and Deadly here?

Yeah, she certainly remembered him, too. How could she forget? It had been only a few moments, but it seemed set in stone. A week after she moved in, she'd been on her way home from a walk. They'd passed each other on the walkway, but there had been that instant their eyes had met and held. She'd been struck by the fierceness of his gaze and the almost devilish edge to his attractiveness. He had that "bad biker" look and was all lean and mean, with an impressively broad chest and shoulders that would make an Olympic swimmer green with envy.

Finding out he was actually her neighbor and Caine's close friend put Julie in somewhat of a dilemma. Getting equally drawn in by two men she barely knew wasn't something that had ever happened to her before. She certainly couldn't deny the fact that they both made her pulse race and her head swim with deliciously naughty thoughts. And it wasn't just because they were so incredibly good-looking.

She'd dated gorgeous men before, though none of the relationships ever lasted. But this attraction was different. Caine and Ryan got to her in ways she couldn't understand, and as they stood side by side, watching her intently, she realized she could never have either of them. And the knowledge that both men wanted her so badly was incredibly intoxicating.

"Well, it's nice to meet you," Julie said brightly, finally breaking the spell and retrieving her hand from his gentle yet firm grip. *Damn and double damn.* She'd just moved to a neighborhood that had two of the most sinfully gorgeous men living on either side of her, and there was nothing she could do about it.

Strangely enough, once she got that into her head, it made her feel a lot better. Now she could just chill with them and not worry about how they sent the blood rushing like wildfire through her veins. Or so she liked to believe

It had seemed odd, though, that there were three women to the four guys, but somehow in the end, it worked out. Especially since the two best friends took it upon themselves to give her their undivided attention whenever possible.

Dinner was an informal and fun affair. The food was perfect and the presentation as good as anything you'd find at a Michelin-starred restaurant. Ryan chose to designate himself as the chef's assistant and helped with getting the plated courses to the dining table and keeping the glasses filled, while Caine did his thing in the kitchen in between sitting at the table with them and playing host.

Julie was glad she came. She didn't want the night to end. She didn't have to do much talking and instead people-watched her dinner companions and marveled at how much they seemed like old friends, complete with the ribbing and the laughs.

Julie never had this with Grant. Neither of them really had that many friends—none they'd kept around for long. Julie had made her life all about Grant, and her few girlfriends had drifted away thanks to his dark attitude and the way he liked to pick at their faults and why she shouldn't have them in her life. When their romance had faded, there'd been no one to help Julie pick up the pieces. No family, no friends. Somehow, that had made it easier to start a new life.

And now she was here. For the first time in a long while, she felt accepted and part of a special group. Maybe this could be her new "family." Everyone treated her as if she were already one of them. If she could just get over the strange way she was insanely attracted to both Caine and Ryan, she'd be fine.

Julie had never dreamed that the night would end like this.

After all the food and music, the others started to call it a night, until Julie found herself with just Ryan as Caine.

Julie's laughter died off at the end of something funny Ryan had said. She'd never thought she could relax so much around him, but now that it was just them, the atmosphere got charged in the way it only could when a man and woman had something simmering between them.

Julie placed down her wine glass and rose quickly, if not unsteadily, to her feet.

"I think I'd better be going," she said, hoping she wouldn't fall flat on her face in these damn heels. Maybe those after-dinner drinks had been a few too many. But everyone had been having so much fun dancing and joking around that Julie had let herself get carried away. The high point of the evening had been getting to dance with Caine, and then Ryan had come up to steal her away into his arms. It had given the sensation of being the center of attention between two gorgeous men, and that had been such a high she'd never expected or imagined.

Now she was flustered, excited, and worried about what she might do if she lingered. Caine could be heard saying good night to Hawke and Jemima when Ryan rose and closed the space between him and Julie. She instinctively backed away a few steps.

Ryan paused in his stride. "Are you afraid of me?"

Julie's heart was pumping fast, but it wasn't out of fear. Adrenalin mixed in with a massive dose of endorphins whizzed through her core, and she placed a hand on her belly to quell the huge coil of arousal tightening there. She met the dark depths of Ryan's piercing eyes and felt she could fall adrift inside them, tangled up and torn with desire.

"No..." She began slowly, gathering her wits about her, and she couldn't keep the teasing note from her voice as she added, "I don't really know. Should I be?"

Ryan flashed a wicked grin that instantly flooded the crotch of her panties with creamy want. "Maybe a little caution would be wise."

"Why? Because you're the big bad wolf about to eat me all up?" Julie asked with a coy smile.

And then she wanted to slap a hand over her mouth. She had never been good at flirting, yet just today, she'd done it twice. First with Caine and now with Ryan, talking to him in a tone that could only be described as come-hither. Was she out of her mind?

A glow seemed to hit the dark-blue pools of Ryan's eyes, and Julie caught her breath at the way it transformed his handsome face into something indeed feral and untamed.

Before she could stumble back in confusion, he grabbed her wrist.

Just as he pulled her close, steadying her in the enclosure of his arms, Caine came in, and Julie wanted the floor to simply open up and swallow her. Shivering, she strained away from the disturbingly stimulating circle of Ryan's embrace.

"I'm not going to hurt you," Ryan said almost in her ear as his lips brushed close. "You know you're safe with us."

"You can stop frightening her, Ryan," Caine growled as he advanced. "Seriously. I can't turn my back for five minutes."

"He wasn't frightening me," Julie said quickly, coming to Ryan's defense.

His wolfish grin brought the heat to her face as she stared up at him. Pushing into his formidable chest, she came up against a rock-solid wall that wouldn't budge.

"Then why can I feel you tremble?" Caine said quietly from behind her, shocking Julie with his closeness. She could virtually feel his breath rumbling against the back of her neck as his hands came to rest heavily on her shoulders, massaging gently.

Everything seemed to spin in circles within the room. Julie couldn't handle all the testosterone flying around, and she blamed it on all the wine. She usually had more control over her emotions, yet around these two, she felt as helpless as a schoolgirl caught in the crossfire of her first crush.

"Well, maybe because she's so turned on by us both, she doesn't know what to do," Ryan declared, his words spreading the heat from Julie's face down to the apex of her thighs where desperately hot moisture pooled.

Julie knew what Ryan said was true, so she couldn't deny it. Couldn't say she didn't feel the most wanton thrill from being pushed in between two powerful men in this way. The deliciousness in their heated gaze, the hunger in the way they licked their lips, unable to take their eyes from her curvy frame. Why had this never been her fantasy before? Well, that didn't matter; it certainly was now. It felt so good, Ryan's steely hardness pushing against her belly while Caine's equally rock-stiff erection prodded against her lush, round ass.

She felt Ryan's hands slide down her waist to her hips and his fingers dug in so firmly she could feel the imprint of each one. She gasped, unsure what to do, as a myriad of sensations washed over her. Images of a carnal tango with her caught between these two hot men made her mind whirl for a few moments, and she struggled to breathe.

Behind her, Caine carefully brushed aside her hair from her neck, baring the sensitive flesh to his searching lips as his mouth sucked on her skin softly. "Relax, Julie. Let yourself go. There's no reason to hold anything in. We can give you what you need. Everything and more," he rasped, the warmth of his breath in her ear twisting her nipples into tight knots that begged to be kissed.

*More...? How could they possibly give me more?* The thoughts raced through Julie's fuddled brain. Because wishing to be taken by two men was definitely more than she'd ever wanted before. Or at least thought she wanted.

Were they truly serious about this, or was this just some crazy alcohol-induced joke?

She didn't have to wonder for long. The way they held her, touched her, it was clear they both wanted nothing more than to ravish her body.

Perhaps that had always been their plan. Had they set up this little seduction scene from the start?

Julie felt a mixture of consternation and excitement. The very idea of having them claim her had the titillating ingredient that was so taboo and so out of her comfort zone that she was trembling more than ever. Could she? More to the point... should she?

"Will you let us have you, Julie?" It was Ryan who spoke, and she forced her eyes open to meet the mesmerizing heat of his gaze. Her name from his lips sounded like an erotic caress of a suede-lined whip lashing against her senses.

She moaned, clutching the front of his T-shirt, her fingers gripping for dear life. "I... This is all so new. So crazy." Julie breathed, head shakily groggily.

She felt Caine's arm snake across her chest as he gently held her chin and turned her face to the side where his lips waited to claim hers. "You need to trust us, beautiful. Don't be afraid to give in to what your body wants. If you say the word, we're yours."

"Caine." She whimpered, and it seemed all the encouragement he needed to seize her lips in a deep, breathless kiss.

Julie's eyelids snapped closed, and she succumbed to the masterful heat of Caine's lips. He devoured her with a masculine dominance, delving his tongue deep to mate with hers. She felt blown away by the addictive taste and texture, spicy and sweet. She felt safe in his kiss, yet still, there was a dark, wild promise in the way he thrust in roughly with that velvet tongue that made her shiver.

In that same moment, she felt lips tracing her collarbone, bared by Ryan's fingers drawing her neckline off her shoulder. He began a moist, sensual trail that led up to her throat, where he nuzzled, groaning deeply as he inhaled her scent. Julie felt swamped with pleasure she almost wasn't equipped to handle.

Even with Caine's kiss sweeping her senses into mush, she was much too aware of Ryan's hands dipping past the high hem of her dress and reaching up over to the top of her thighs. Feeling his touch on her naked flesh had her groaning against Caine's mouth. The next second, Ryan cupped seeking fingers between her thighs, and his thumb flicked across her clit through her panties. She jerked as if stung by a thousand electric eels.

"Easy, babe," Ryan said softly, lifting his face from where he'd buried it in her neck.

Breathless, she broke from Caine's intoxicating mouth. Before she could think, Ryan's free hand came up to pinch her chin, and he turned her to face him.

"My turn," he growled, his teasing smile a flash of white against his handsome tanned face.

Julie felt her heart pounding in her chest, her body aware of every smooth touch, every graze of their fingertips, every squeeze of their greedy hands.

*This is really happening.*

Ryan closed in for a kiss, and it all became clear to Julie that this wasn't a game. If she let them, they'd lead her to the depths of pure carnal pleasures. Ryan's ravenous mouth on hers showed her he'd be just as demanding and sensually delightful as Caine. They even tasted alike: all hungry, hot, and wild.

Ryan slicked his wicked tongue across the seam of her lips, weakening her knees and sending a trickle of juice down her inner thighs. Then he ran his tongue all over the inside, lapping and probing, drawing her out to meet him in the open as Julie learned to duel with her tongue.

She couldn't tell for sure how they moved to the sofa. All she knew was she felt herself backing up, and then her knees hit the cushions before she was pulled down along with them. Ryan's possessive kiss distracted her from the fact that firm, sure hands—definitely Caine's—were drawing her thighs far apart and pushing up one knee so she had one foot propped on the sofa, leaving her exposed to penetrating, hungry eyes. She gasped, shocked to her marrow. But before she could tug down the skirt of her dress, Ryan gently but firmly found her wrist and guided her hand to his hardness.

Julie's fingers closed around his massive erection straining against his jeans, and another gasp of shock escaped her. Nothing had ever felt so powerfully hard and thick. Unable to control herself, she squeezed experimentally and was rewarded with Ryan's deep groan of approval. Her fingers traced the outline, confined as it was beneath the fabric. Senses alight, she stroked him hungrily and was so caught up in his delicious hardness that when Caine's fingers pushed aside the seam of her panties, she hardly made a move to stop him.

"You're so curvy... so incredibly beautiful," Ryan whispered thickly against her lips as he partially broke the kiss. "You only need to close your eyes and give in to everything you're feeling, Julie. Can you do that?"

Julie's throat felt strangled, and she could only let out a soft, needy mewl as she quivered and shook. Her eyes flew down between her spread legs to find Caine's head lowering to plant kisses up her right knee and straight to the juncture of her thighs. His fingers stroked her from behind the panel of her panties, and she let out an open-mouthed groan. Her folds felt electrified from his touch as he parted her vulva for his tender perusal.

She heard him murmur the words soft, beautiful, sexy, and the heat rose high on her cheeks until she felt robbed of air. Feeling his gaze was so forbidden yet empowering at the same time. She'd never felt so much like a woman until Caine leaned even closer and set the tip of his tongue right at her slit. Bucking, she almost couldn't hold back her cry of desperate, unashamed pleasure.

But even that was just the beginning. Ryan, busy at her bodice, was working on unfastening the tiny bows holding the front of her dress together. He bared her cleavage in seconds, and Julie could only watch with breath bated in expectation as he pushed aside the cups of her lacy bra and freed her full, swollen breasts with their dark-pink nipples.

"You make us so wild for you... so damn hot for your body," Ryan growled, meeting her eyes for that single, earth-stilling moment before he closed his mouth over one thick, rigid nub at her breast.

This had to be a dream. No way could all this pleasure be real. Caine's cool, silky tongue tasting her sweet pussy, making her center a scorching hub, and Ryan tugging at her nipples with teeth both rough and sweet, making her toes curl and her back arch as she gave herself to them. Both men's mouths on her body, teasing and pleasing her, had Julie crossing the line of ecstasy into sublime agony. So good... yet so very bad. She arched her spine until she was bent back as far as she could go, offering herself up to her attentive, dedicated lovers whose groans of approval filled the room.

"You taste so sweet," Caine said, his voice thick and deep. His tongue lapped gently and steadily over her folds and turned her lower body to jelly. "I want to make you come, Julie... Come for us."

It didn't take long before she lost control of all senses but the buzzing vibrations of Caine's skillful tongue lapping against her while Ryan kneaded her breasts and scraped his perfect teeth against her throat, kissing her relentlessly. She struggled to breathe, to think straight, and then gave up trying to make sense of all she felt. The desire for these two beautiful men was both terrifying and intoxicating, but they forced her to let go, to give in to the hurricane of pleasure that engulfed her, pushing her over the edge.

Julie gasped, a desperate cry, her head thrown back as her body heaved against their strong embrace. Caine refused to stop licking and kissing her clit and thighs, moving quickly, as if he had done it a thousand times and knew where every sensitive nerve ending lived. Ryan held her tight in his arms, his broad chest now pushed firmly against her back, cradling her in strong, controlled hands that kept her steady while Caine claimed her as his own.

Nothing could have prepared her for the way these two men made her feel. Every fantasy, every dream—nothing compared to the wild, unbridled desire as wave after wave of hot, sticky sweet pleasure rolled over her. Ryan's thundering growl begged her to just let go, to give in to their want and need for her, washing over her skin, buzzing in her ear. And then it happened.

Her body was no longer her own. It was as though she were merely a puppet in their wonderfully possessive show. She was lost in a maze of ecstasy, falling facedown into a pool of indescribable bliss. The jagged rush of abandon grew and grew inside her until there was nothing left of her being. Around her, the world faded to mist as she flung her head from side to side, suddenly erupting into a rainbow of fireworks.

Julie heard a shrill cry spilling from her mouth, her orgasm slamming into her from the back and torpedoing her into orbit. And then all was dark.

## CHAPTER 4

*WHAT THE HELL HAPPENED?* she wondered, hands pressed against her throat as she stared bemusedly around the dim expanse of her own bedroom. *How did I get here?*

The last thing she remembered was laughing almost drunkenly at something Ryan had been telling her. Caine then came back in to meet them after seeing everyone else out the door. Had she been so out of it she hadn't realized when she'd gotten herself home?

She looked down and saw she still wore her dress. *Thank God.* For a moment, she'd been so afraid that the wild, sexual dream had been real. That she actually did let not just Caine, but Ryan do things to her body that had triggered the most intense orgasm of her life. Now that would really have been something.

She slipped out of bed and wavered on her bare feet as she tried to stand. Okay, definitely no more wine or any kind of spirits for her, not for a good while. Shaking her head slightly in self-reproof, she padded to the large bay window looking out into the night and sighed deeply.

The dream had felt so good. Was she so awful for wishing it had been real?

Deep inside, she ached for a fulfillment that had been denied. She'd loved the feel of Ryan in her dream, his lips bold and hands greedy and possessive as they held her tightly. She moaned softly, remembering how Caine's tongue had felt so delightful dancing over her secret places, bringing her such deep pleasure.

Julie bit hard on her bottom lip as a tremor of desire vibrated through her belly. Her eyes were suddenly drawn to the midnight moon, and she wondered what both men were doing right at that very moment.

Were they thinking of her, longing for her? Part of her felt so ashamed of these new feelings that brewed within, yet another part so desperately wanted to lose herself to these men with complete, reckless abandon. To not care about consequences or what people might think about her. To just give in, to give herself to them completely.

Could she trust herself not to fall too hard?

---

They could see her silhouette outlined in her bedroom window. Even from so far away, they could discern her need, her desperate longing for them. Crouching low in their wolf form, both Caine and Ryan growled, their need for a mate dominating every thought.

*She needs us just as badly as we need her.*

Ryan didn't have to look Caine's way for their thoughts to connect. They'd known each other for so long that they could easily read each other's mind. Now that they'd shifted, all their senses were more heightened than ever, and the unique scent of their mate reached them in sensuous notes dancing in the wind.

Hours earlier, she'd fallen asleep from complete passion-induced exhaustion. Ryan had carried her soft, curvy form back home, aided by Caine, who'd let them into the dark, silent house. They'd gently laid her on her bed, and it had been all they could do to walk away.

Ryan didn't think he'd ever forget the way she squirmed beneath his lips and moaned his name as he'd pulled at her dark-pink nipples with his teeth. She had the softest skin, faintly scented with flowers and musk. Her breasts were exquisitely rounded orbs, firm and youthful. Julie had no idea how close to the truth she'd been when she'd teased him about being a big bad wolf about to eat her up.

Lucky Caine, who had actually had that privilege. He'd dipped his tongue in places Ryan still longed to explore, but he was patient. He knew he'd get his turn to taste her sweet desires. It had given them both immeasurable satisfaction to bring her to orgasm the way they had. But they hadn't had the heart to take things further, to claim her as their own. No, for that, she would have to fully give in... to beg them not to stop.

*She is unlike any other woman I've ever met*, thought Ryan as his gleaming eyes never moved from the shapely figure looking at the moon from her window.

*But we shouldn't have gone so fast*, Caine growled quietly. *When I came in and saw her in your arms, I couldn't help myself.*

*Neither could I. She drove me crazy with the scent of her desire. I could smell it, calling to me*, confessed Ryan.

*We need to take our time.*

They knew that. This wasn't just about sex for them. They could get that easily, from anywhere. It was much more power-ful, much more important than that. She was their intended mate, the one woman they were destined to share for the rest of their lives.

They knew Julie had to trust them first, get to know them. They'd already invited her into their lives, and she'd met their friends. Hawke and Vern, along with their mates, shared one pack with Caine and Ryan. The other two men had found their mates months ago, and both women were human, which meant Hailey and Jemima would know exactly how to welcome Julie into the fold. They hoped that was enough.

Convincing Julie to come to terms with the fact that they were wolves was almost as daunting as having her understand that Caine and Ryan fully intended to share her as their mate.

But this was their way, the way of the clan. It was the only way to survive. They just had to convince her that they could make her happy. Deliriously happy.

# CHAPTER 5

JULIE COULDN'T SHAKE the feeling of being watched.

She seemed to be getting that a lot more lately. Ever since she decided to go on these early morning runs, she had a sense she wasn't alone. But she never saw anyone.

This was the safest neighborhood, so she knew she had nothing to fear. That was the main reason she'd chosen to buy property there, even though it cut a big dent in her savings. She'd needed someplace her ex-boyfriend would never think to look for her.

And lately, she'd needed a way to release all the pent-up energy she seemed to have. Ever since that eventful dinner three nights ago, Julie realized she needed an outlet that could keep her mind off her strange desires. What did it all mean?

She remembered how, at first, she'd considered her attraction for Caine and decided she was going to be more open to his advances. But then meeting Ryan forced her to face the reality that for the first time in her life, she was incredibly attracted to not just one, but two men and that she knew she'd never be able to choose.

*What kind of woman does that make me?*

The two men were so different yet so similar. Ryan was dominant, like deliciously rugged passion that refused to be tamed, while Caine was the firm yet gentle lover who could easily charm his way into any woman's bed. They were both sinfully gorgeous, and when she looked into their eyes, she didn't feel the usual insecurities that a full-figured woman like her sometimes had. She only felt genuinely wanted… appreciated, and it made her pulse quicken and her heart skip a beat as the branding heat of their desire possessively claimed her full attention with every encounter.

But then she'd force herself to break the spell and walk away from their delicious invitations, later scolding herself for not seeing it through, not giving it a chance. She just didn't want to be *that* kind of woman. Whatever that meant.

She was better off keeping to herself. That had always been the plan anyway. God knew she had enough trouble with men in the past.

She suddenly heard pounding feet behind her and glanced back to see a familiar figure with dark hair wafting as he ran with a fluid stride. Ryan caught up with her easily, and the ready flash of his grin made all the common sense flee from Julie's head.

*Stop worrying about the risks of putting your heart on the line and just do it already,* she told herself as she caught his smoldering gaze, his piercing blue eyes nearly blinding her in a wave of lust.

"Mind if I join you?" he asked, though it really wasn't a question.

"Oh. Not at all, Ryan," Julie replied, struggling to sound casual despite what Ryan's unexpected appearance was doing to that crazy libido she'd developed since she'd met the two men.

He easily kept up pace with her, and her sidelong glance took in his muscular, fit body encased in well-fitting running gear. His golden tan was burnished with perspiration she was ready to lick off. Every muscle in his strong arms looked carved from adamantine steel.

"The other night—at Caine's place. I hope we didn't do anything to scare you off," Ryan said, his lips curling into a grin.

"What? No, um... I don't quite understand," Julie replied in confusion, wondering what he meant. She still couldn't figure out what had happened that night and didn't want to give herself away. What if she really had made a fool of herself, thanks to being so tipsy? Had she thrown herself at them? Or worse, passed out from all that wine?

"Okay, good to hear. Because Caine was worried you might be avoiding him, especially with the way the night ended. You running off and everything."

Julie had to conceal her sigh of relief. At least she'd had the good sense to make her escape before she did anything stupid. She could almost relax now.

"Oh, no, nothing like that," she told him quickly. "I've just been really busy working on some design portfolios for a new client, and I've been stuck in my office at home," she explained, the effort causing her to become more breathless than usual, so she ground to a stop.

She leaned against a nearby tree and drew in a deep, refreshing breath. She looked around at the scenery and couldn't help feeling happy once again that she'd moved here. Out there in the city, she'd never had the chance to really exhale. This place made her feel as though she'd found her home base, a place where she could truly relax and feel safe.

"I'm glad to hear that. I, for one, began to think I made you uncomfortable," said Ryan.

Julie found herself getting backed into the sturdy tree trunk as Ryan's thickly corded arm propped near the side of her head while he closed the inches between them enough to give her a whiff of his warm-blooded, deeply masculine scent that did crazy things to her hormones. His startling blue eyes swept over her face like he was committing every feature to memory.

"Uncomfortable, me?" Julie all but squeaked. Her head was swimming. This was one of the reasons she'd taken to running, and now he was right here, impossible to escape.

"Julie, I won't lie. The first time I saw you, though fleeting, really struck me. I haven't been able to stop thinking about you ever since," Ryan confessed, his voice a low rumble of masculine power.

His dark lashes, so thick and lush they made her almost groan with envy, swooped down as he seemed to keep his inner thoughts hidden. His body language, though, told her all she wanted to know. Ryan wanted her, and she was almost hyperventilating from the very thought that she hadn't been wrong after all.

"I don't know what to say," she replied, eyes darting around.

"It's okay to be confused. But when I said you didn't need to be afraid, I meant it. I'd do all in my power to make you feel safe and protected." He lifted his other hand and reached for her cheek, and Julie involuntarily flinched, turning her face away. Ryan scowled, his hand lowering to rest on her shoulder. "Someone hurt you, didn't they? Who was he?"

His astuteness astounded Julie. How could he possibly even...?

She shook her head dismissively. "He was no one. I'm over that. I'm stronger than I look, and I assure you I don't need you or anyone to take care of me." Her eyes met his defiantly, and he nodded with a humorous smile.

"I hear you. Fact is I definitely like a woman who can stand up for herself. You can bet I like a lot of things about you, Julie," he said, eyes twinkling.

Julie had to smile at that. "I bet you say that and all the girls just melt."

"There's only one girl that I want to melt, and each time I look at her, it gets harder to keep myself in check," he said gruffly, eyes gleaming meaningfully into hers. "What is it about you that makes me want to shield you from all the bad, bad things in the world? Yet I can't wait to ravish you myself."

Julie gulped, her throat going dry.

Well, at least he was putting it out there. This was her chance to tell him she just wasn't interested. That she'd just been through a bad breakup and needed to work on herself and not just jump into the next relationship. That the last thing she really needed was a fling, which could be all this hot, sexy hunk of badness was offering.

"Maybe you need time to figure it all out," she said mildly, resisting the urge to bite on her bottom lip, aware he couldn't tear his heated gaze from her mouth.

"Yeah. I do. And maybe you can help me. We could go for drinks later tonight and maybe see what happens. I know a few nice places in town. You should let me show you around."

"You're asking me out on a date?" Julie asked, a smile playing on her lips.

His charm was infectious. And God help her, this man was plain irresistible. What harm could it do? He grinned rakishly and Julie grew wet and hot in places she'd sworn to hold in check. Just because she'd vowed not to get involved didn't mean they couldn't be friends.

"I sure am," he replied with a smile, voice smoky with promise.

Julie knew she was in trouble. She nodded slowly in assent and secretly hoped she'd figure out a way to resist this impossibly handsome man who wanted her more than any other ever had.

# CHAPTER 6

THE BAND WAS PLAYING some nice folksy rock music that Julie couldn't have imagined she'd enjoy, but she did. She liked the bar, too, nice ambience. They had some really great beers on tap. Add to that her gorgeous date, and there wasn't much more a girl could ask for.

She knew they caught a few looks from the other patrons, but it was no one she really needed to worry about. Spending time with Ryan, just talking and drinking, was bringing out a side of him she hadn't expected. She already knew he was funny without really trying to be, especially when he was talking about himself. She learned he was partners with Caine, though Ryan's job was to handle the business end of things, while Caine was the "brains" of the outfit, as Ryan jokingly put it. Julie liked that Ryan didn't take himself too seriously. He had this tough exterior that would make people want to tread carefully around him, but he really was a nice guy.

She was feeling comfortable around him, which both delighted and surprised her. She'd never dreamed she'd feel safe around a man again, especially this quickly. But Ryan, with his protective bearing and rugged charm, made it hard for her to hold on to her defenses. And he did all he could to make her feel desired and special. Julie really liked him and was growing more than just attracted to him. But how could she tell him there was no way this could go any further?

"Would you like another beer?" Ryan asked, breaking off their conversation to nod at her half-empty glass, which she was still nursing.

Julie shook her head, assuring him she was good. She really wanted to keep her head tonight, and that meant drinking responsibly.

One thing she couldn't be responsible about was how she felt around Ryan. The way his large, slightly callused hand would brush lightly over hers as he reached for his beer, the graze of his deep laugh teasing her senses, and the way he looked at her that made her sizzle deep within her folds. She needed—oh, she wasn't sure what she needed. Ryan—and Caine—made her want things she really, really shouldn't. Where was she going to find the strength to walk away?

"Ah, look who's here. Surprise, surprise," drawled Ryan, and Julie looked over her shoulder to see what he was talking about. Something lurched in her chest when she saw Caine walk into the crowded bar, looking as gorgeous as ever.

But he wasn't alone.

A tall, somewhat willowy brunette had her arm tucked into his, and she was certainly a beauty. She wore a pair of snug blue jeans and a shirt unbuttoned low enough to hint at enviably large cleavage. Her swathe of thick, rich-brown hair fell over one shoulder, and she flicked it over her back as she turned to Caine with a possessive, pleased smile.

Julie wasn't sure of the emotion that raged through her belly like fire, but she didn't like it. And she didn't like the way Caine smiled back at the girl and patted her hand on his arm, either. Then he led them to the other end of the bar to order drinks.

"I didn't know Caine had a girlfriend," Julie said before she could stop herself. She'd meant to say something casual but instead stood the risk of sounding like a jealous, scorned twit.

"Oh, that's not his girlfriend. That's just Darcy. She's... Well, maybe at one time she'd have been a love interest, but it never really happened. Now they're just friends."

Julie found that hard to believe, but she didn't voice it aloud. Instead, she nodded and buried her nose in her drink, wishing she wasn't acting so stupid. After all, she was here with someone else. The last thing she should be doing was feeling pissed off at Caine for hanging out with some other girl. A girl who seemed to be leaning far too close to him as they waited for their order.

Just then, Caine looked up, caught her gaze, and smiled in recognition. Ryan waved him over, and he excused himself from his companion to make his way over in easy, long strides.

"My favorite girl," Caine said in greeting as he bent to kiss her cheek, which already grew hot from his presence.

"Oh, I think you already have your hands full," Julie blurted and then chewed hard on her lip in mortification. *Damn, damn, and damn!* Now he'd know she was jealous.

He merely grinned and turned to the equally smiling Ryan. "You didn't tell Julie about Darcy?" Caine asked, eyebrows arched.

Ryan shrugged. "Julie knows deep down that when it comes to her, there's really no competition. But I did let her know that Darcy wasn't anything to worry about."

"Good. But I think Julie knows in her heart how it stands." Caine's smile tilted sexily, and Julie couldn't help the way her toes wanted to curl inside her shoes.

Was Caine for real? He was actually flirting with her in front of Ryan! And Ryan didn't seem to mind in the slightest.

Julie blushed furiously, the heat creeping up to the surface of her dark skin as she thought of that dream and how both of them had taken delight in bringing her to an unforgettable climax. She could visualize it even clearer now, and it sent chills of wanton excitement down her spine. Their strange exchange made her confused, and she wondered if she wasn't beginning to lose it. Her months-long state of celibacy was perhaps beginning to catch up to her. She needed air.

Escape was all she could think of right then, so she quickly stood and mumbled an excuse about needing to use the ladies' room.

"Are you all right?" Ryan asked with deep concern, his arm closing lightly around her shoulders. She nodded quickly, gave him and Caine a small smile, and then rushed from the bar before she made more of a fool of herself. She needed to be in control of her emotions by the time she got back.

▭

Both men watched her go, and it was impossible to hide the glow of need on their faces. "This is going to be tougher than I imagined. I mean, taking things slow," Caine said, not peeling his eyes away until Julie was out of sight. She looked like a delightful treat tonight, wearing another dress, black this time, with two thin straps holding it up. He liked a woman comfortable enough in her own skin to keep things feminine. He could still smell the shampoo of her hair and the cocoa butter fragrance of her skin. He felt his cock stir, remembering how the dusky glow had called out for his lips to trace each contour from her throat to her shoulder.

"I know how you feel, man," Ryan replied meaningfully.

"Breaking the ice is just one step. Getting to convince her she doesn't have to choose will be another."

Both men were astute enough to know Julie was having that inner battle. With all their heart, they longed to explain the truth of their intentions, but she needed time. Especially when it was obvious, she'd been hurt before, maybe even recently. Was that why she'd moved here? There were so many things they wanted to find out about her, but she still kept so much under wraps. What would it take to break down her defenses?

When Caine finally returned to the waiting Darcy, he quirked his brow at the spitting anger in her eyes. Julie had just returned, and from across the room, Darcy and Caine watched as Ryan placed a hand on her waist and rose to kiss her cheek before guiding her back on her stool as if she were some china doll about to break.

Darcy's scowl deepened. "It's getting rampant, isn't it?" She began with a fake smile as she lifted her beer to her pouty pink lips.

Caine chose to ignore her biting tone and instead asked what she meant.

"The way everyone seems to be willing to mate with humans. First Vern and then Hawke. Soon, the whole pack will be overrun and weakened by this trend, which makes me wonder why Alpha Jepson condones such fraternization."

Darcy was in the same pack as Caine and Ryan and, like them, had wolf traits. Like many in the pack, she frowned on them having to mix with humans, and as a female, she felt especially threatened. Once, she'd had a thing for Caine, but then when he told her what they—Caine *and* Ryan—were looking for, Darcy had backed out. She regretted it now but couldn't show it. She'd let the opportunity pass her by, and now it was too late to change her mind.

Caine's face broke into one of his rare frowns. "You, of all people, know that we can't help who we mate. It's nature. And mating with humans could never make us weaker, but stronger. The more we learn to coexist, the better for all concerned along the line."

"Or so it would seem," Darcy said with a curl to her lips. "Well, I guess it's hard to think straight when sentiment is involved. But what makes you think she'll ever want anything to do with your special... arrangement?"

Darcy saw Caine's slight wince and knew she'd hit a sore point. She smiled inwardly. So, it wasn't going to be all cut and dry, then. Maybe there was still hope.

Yes, she knew all about mates and how they were "fated." But then again, mates could also be chosen. She knew that once, Caine had been ready to settle for choosing a mate so long as she met their need for a ménage relationship. Perhaps he would be made to reconsider his earlier choice. But as long as Julie was in the picture, Darcy couldn't see that happening.

Her eyes glowed with intent, which she concealed by turning away to beckon the bartender to refill her glass. Her hidden smile widened as she thought of all the possibilities open to her as mate to Caine and Ryan. Everyone knew they were two of the strongest and most respected shifters in their pack. Either of them could be made alpha of their thriving community, and Darcy knew becoming aligned with them would prove favorable to her clan and, of course, to herself. As their mate, she'd gain madam alpha status, and considering she virtually grew up in the pack, she felt this was more than her due. It was her birthright.

The only thing standing in her way was the wonderfully curvy human usurper who might have seduced the two friends with her innocent, alluring beauty. But Darcy could tell there was more to Julie than what anyone knew, and she was going to do everything in her power to win her rightful place with both Caine and Ryan—even if it meant getting rid of the competition herself.

CHAPTER 7

A MONTH AGO, if anyone had told Julie she'd have not one, but two gorgeous men vying for her affections, she'd have laughed out loud and called them crazy.

Now, reality was turning into a manifestation of her most secret fantasies. At first, she hadn't wanted to believe it. Both men had come at her from different angles. Ryan played the romantic, while Caine took the more indirect approach, getting her sweet on him by showing up to help with her flowers or odd jobs around the house.

Before long, she started meeting both of them for nights on the town, dancing and drinking with friends—always people known to Caine and Ryan who seemed all too happy to welcome Julie into the fold. Julie couldn't say it was always friendly all around. There were a few who showed how little they thought of her budding "friendship" with the popular duo. One to note was Darcy, who Julie sensed at once considered her a rival.

Julie didn't let that get to her, though. Caine and Ryan had shown time and again that she'd won a place in their hearts, and as surprised as it made her, she felt her defenses slowly crumbling.

She didn't understand the vibes she was getting when she was around them, the way they didn't seem jealous of each other and even encouraged her interest in one or the other. It was almost as if they wanted her to get used to having both of them around. Many times, she felt struck by the possibility that they wouldn't be averse to the thought of sharing her. They never came right out and said it, but somehow, she guessed it from their actions.

Julie thought things over again and again and still told herself she was crazy. Caine and Ryan might seem close, but no way could they be "courting" the same girl, right? They were all just great friends, and she was simply getting to know them —together.

*Or... it could be far, far more than that.* But could she let herself consider that deliciously exciting and forbidden fantasy?

Even now, she still flushed with pleasure, thinking how much they seemed to enjoy spending time with her. They were always dropping by her place or her to theirs. And finally, Julie had stopped caring what the nosy women in the neighborhood thought. She'd always be the outsider to them, but with Caine and Ryan, she felt she'd found people she could really trust and who appreciated her. And she wasn't going to give that up for anything or anyone.

It amazed her how well her life had turned out with all she'd been through. She still woke up to nightmares, but they were few and far between when compared to the lust-induced fantasies of wanton threesomes with two powerful men who loved her. Julie was starting to believe she was finally able to put the past behind her, and perhaps she would be able to find happiness.

If only she could have seen it coming. If only she could have known that you can run, but you can never, ever hide.

Everything had been going so well. Julie was feeling like her old self again. She'd made new friends and had a sense of belonging that she'd been missing for so long. For the first time, life was all about her, not some man who tried to dominate her every waking moment. Best of all, she truly believed she was falling in love again.

Yet this was different from any kind of relationship she'd ever known. The woman in her felt awakened, stirred to new heights of awareness and desire. Oh yes, she just might be falling in love. With two of the hottest men she'd ever met. And each day, she questioned her ability to hold back her emotions. They grew bolder, more aggressive, more... compelling.

What would happen if she told Caine and Ryan how she felt? Would they make her fantasies come true and realize, just as she had, the bond that drew them as one? Or would she be the person who tore them apart? She couldn't stand the thought of that.

Julie marveled at her own daring passions. So much had truly changed if she was considering propositioning two men in this way. Still, it went beyond the physical for her. She trusted them, felt a kinship with them that couldn't be denied. What if this was something real? Would she be a fool to keep fighting it and risk both of them slipping through her fingers?

What mattered most was that life truly held such promise now, and she wasn't willing to look back, to lose out on the opportunity for love.

She heard her phone ringing in the living room, and it shook her from her thoughts. She moved quickly to pull off her gardening gloves, exiting her greenhouse and heading back to the main section of her home.

She felt slightly out of breath, trying to catch the call on its last ring.

━━

Caine could tell Julie wasn't her usual bubbly self, and when he glanced Ryan's way, he knew his best friend had noticed it, too. They were having dinner at a secluded bistro, a small, pack-owned restaurant that was very much off the beaten path. The kind of place humans would overlook but was well known by their pack members. They'd chosen the place because of its romantic décor and the fact that on this particular night, there weren't too many people around. They wanted no distractions tonight—for many reasons.

They could tell Julie was still wary and wasn't sure where she stood with them. They were about to put her straight. Yet both men sensed that there was something bothering her. Her hands seemed to tremble as she reached for her glass or silverware, and she had a faraway look in her eyes in the middle of their conversation, as if her mind were somewhere else.

Caine sent Ryan another look, questioning this time, and Ryan gave an imperceptible nod.

"Something bothering you, Julie?" Caine asked gently, his worried eyes resting on Julie's troubled face.

Her expression cleared, and she smiled, but it didn't quite reach her eyes. "Oh, I'm fine. Everything's absolutely perfect. The food, the wine, the music. I also love the candlelight... Very nice touch." She sent both of them warm smiles, and on the surface, it seemed as if she'd regained her composure. But they weren't fooled.

"You trust us, don't you, Julie?" Ryan asked in much the same tone Caine had used.

He rested his hand over hers, and he felt her somewhat convulsive tremor at his touch and had to quell his eyes from changing to silver. He wasn't oblivious to her agitation, and it made him grit his teeth, thinking that anything or anyone could make her so fearful. His shifter senses were tuned in to her every emotion, and his beast was clawing to protect his—their—mate.

"Of course, I do," she said, giving Ryan a quizzical look. "You two are my closest friends now." Her smile struggled to light up her face and almost—*almost*—dispelled the shadows in her eyes.

"The truth is, Julie... we were hoping to be far more than that." Caine spoke up, ignoring Ryan's warning glance. *Now or never, brother. She has to know. We can't keep this up. You're already close to shift mode right now. We can't risk her finding out the hard way.*

"What Caine's trying to say," Ryan whispered, rubbing his thumb tenderly over her slender knuckles, "is that you've come to mean a lot to us. A lot more than you may realize. It's been only a few weeks, but we've known from the very beginning exactly what our hearts long for—and that's you, Julie."

Her lips worked silently for a few moments, her eyes darting from one man to the other. "I'm not sure exactly where you're going with this," she said slowly. She would have pulled her hand from his, but Ryan's grip tightened just that bit more.

"I don't blame you for being confused." Ryan continued calmly. "Caine and I grew up together, and it was pretty rough because we were both orphans fostered by abusive parents. We learned how to stick up for ourselves and each other. When we were old enough, we ran from our foster home and found our way here, where we were lucky to finally find a true family. Here we were able to be with those of our kind who accepted us without question and made us feel right at home."

Her eyebrows arched. "What do you mean your *kind?*"

Ryan hesitated, and it was Caine who said, "Julie, there's no easy way to say this, but I'll try. Ryan and I... we're different. And it's not just us; we're a whole group with similar traits and a bond that links us together for life."

She stared at them both for several seconds, and each one passed like a life sentence. There was no way they could get into her head, not yet. They could sense her emotions, but only on the surface. They knew she was more curious than worried, but they still waited for what she would say next.

"You and your friends... I mean Vern and Hawke and many of the other people I've been coming in contact with over the past few weeks." She began slowly. "You're all part of this... group?"

Ah, their mate was intelligent. She must have seen similarities, qualities that only the very discerning could pick out.

They smiled and nodded.

"Yes, they are members of our pack," Ryan told her, trying to make her see, to understand. "You see, we—"

There was a buzzing sound in the air, and it cut through Ryan's words. Julie looked down at her phone, her face immediately turning stark white as the blood drained from it.

Both men felt the surge of their shifter blood as their fierce protective instincts rose to the forefront.

She suddenly jumped to her feet, and they found themselves springing up in identical defensive stances that gave them a more aggressive look than they'd wanted to display in her presence. She looked startled at how quickly they'd moved and hastily told them she was fine, that she just needed to go to the restroom.

They could tell she simply wanted privacy, perhaps to take the call that had her phone buzzing.

"I'll be right back," she said, her forced smile not fooling them one bit.

But there was nothing they could do. They couldn't figure out what she was hiding, but they wished with all their heart that she would open up to them. That's why she needed to know what she truly meant to them. Whatever trouble she was in, they'd help her through it—protect her as any mate should.

"Why won't she let us be there for her?" Caine asked aloud, sitting back with a frustrated sigh. He shoved his hand through his dark locks, looking in the direction Julie had gone.

"She still thinks she's alone, that she should handle her problems herself as she's done for so long," Ryan said thoughtfully. "Whatever's got her worried, I bet it's something to do with her past. That man who hurt her."

Caine sat up with interest. "Did she ever discuss it with you? About what happened?"

Ryan shook his head. "All she let out was that she was over him. Maybe some guy she was with who hurt her in the process, and now she's trying to get the pieces back together."

"What if it's him calling? What if he wants her back?" Caine said suddenly. His blue eyes had gone dark and then seemed to glow a fierce gold.

Ryan couldn't help but mirror the fury running through Caine's veins at the very notion. "Fuck! No wonder she's so jittery." He snarled. "We can't let him get to her, can't give him the chance to hurt her again after she's obviously fought to start her life over."

Caine glanced at his watch and scowled. "She's taking too long back there. What should we do?"

Ryan paused, his mind working fast. As the older one between them, he was used to making the decisions when it came to vital matters, and right now, he wanted nothing more than to go find Julie and make her realize just how much they wanted to protect her. Wanted to claim her totally. But he knew it was harder for him to rein in his wolf. He hadn't had that much practice since he was so used to letting go and losing it. Caine, however, had always had much greater control.

"You should go after her," Ryan said firmly. "I'll wait here for you two to get back."

Caine nodded his assent and rose to quickly move through the tables to the back of the restaurant. He stood outside the door of the ladies' room and listened in with his supersensory hearing. Nothing. It took only a few moments for him to realize his mate wasn't in there. He felt the immediate sense of danger, and he knew in an instant that she'd left out the back exit.

He moved so fast his surroundings became a blur. But he still made time enough to project to Ryan, *Julie's left the restaurant. Go out the front. I'll check around the back. Now, Ryan!*

Caine knew Ryan would need no second bidding and would move as quickly as possible. He was throwing open the back door of the restaurant, his gaze moving clearly through the dark night. Just down the street from the restaurant, he saw Julie standing beside the open door of an SUV and two men trying to pull her in. She wasn't struggling, but Caine could smell her fear and her reluctance to leave with them.

*Shit.* It was happening. Bones snapping, teeth baring and elongating, skin giving way to bristling coat. His wolf was huge, its golden-brown color making him seem like a flash of light speeding through the night as he flew right for the men trying to steal away his mate. He'd tear them to pieces before he'd let that happen.

The two figures trying to herd Julie into the black SUV turned sharply at the sound of that fierce snarl. Sentiments like,

"What the fuck?" spilled out of the one closer to Caine, while he could see the other one reaching for his gun.

———

Julie looked over her shoulder and saw the massive shape of the wolf bounding straight off the ground, aiming for the throat of the man holding her elbow. Her eyes widened in shock at the sight of the impossibly large wolf, its teeth glinting dangerously in the dim light of the deserted back street. She'd have screamed if she wasn't so out of it.

The wolf got backhanded by the man who had to let her go. But the beast came right back at them, this time for the man trying to aim and shoot but couldn't get a clear target at the wolf that moved like lightning.

Julie stumbled backward, watching the two men fight off the beast. Seconds later she heard the sound of cloth and flesh ripping, and one of her captors yelled in pain, holding on to his mutilated arm. The gun fell from his fingers as he clutched at the savaged arm.

"Julie!" The sound of Ryan's voice pulled her out of her stupor. He was running down the street.

She just stood there in shock while the wolf seemed to be ready to eat those two alive.

The injured one screamed, "Let's get the hell out of here!"

Both men managed to jump into the car, barely evading the snapping jaws of the wolf. Cursing, they slammed the doors behind them as the driver sped off with a squeal of tires.

Ryan rushed forward and caught Julie before she could crumble to the asphalt. He watched the golden-haired wolf race after the speeding car until it sharply turned the corner. Only then did the beast slow down and turn back in the direction of the restaurant.

Ryan's eyes shifted quickly to the woman clutched in his arms. His rage gave way to tender concern as he felt her fingers grab hold of his shirt.

Her lips were forming words, but no sound came out. He held her tighter to him while lowering his ear to her mouth.

"Save me," she whispered and went limp in his arms, her eyelids fluttering closed.

Cursing underneath his breath, he moved her closer to the safety of the shadows just outside the restaurant's back door. Looking up, he saw that Caine had reached them and was already shifting into human form. Luckily, the back of the restaurant was isolated, so as Caine straightened in his nude human form, he didn't have to worry about being seen.

He was more worried about their mate, and he was quick to join Ryan's side. "How is she?" His voice was still harsh with fury. There were bloodstains on his bare chest and jaw, none of it his.

"She fainted," Ryan said in a clipped, worried tone as he brought his arm beneath her knees and back and swept her easily into his hold. "But otherwise unhurt."

The back door opened, and the owner of the restaurant burst out, followed by two of his workers, all three lycan shifters.

"We heard a commotion," Jake, the owner and chef, growled. "Do you guys need any help? What happened?" They looked ready for a fight, noticing the woman Ryan carried.

Ryan quickly explained what had happened. "Some men tried to kidnap our mate. We were able to scare them off, and Caine definitely injured one of them. You'll find his gun somewhere on the road."

Nodding, one of the workers quickly went searching and came back with the firearm in mere seconds.

"I've got friends at the sheriff's office. They'll know how to check that for prints," Jake said. "But you all need to come back inside and make sure she's safe in case those fucks come back. And we'll find some clothes for you, Caine."

"Thanks," Caine said, his mind filled with thoughts of anger and retribution. Part of him hoped those guys would return so he could get a better chance at ripping out their throats. But like Ryan, he tried to stay calm, knowing they'd make better headway if they kept focused on the most important thing right now—taking their mate to safety.

CHAPTER 8

JULIE WOKE with a start and immediately shot up from the pillows. She didn't recognize her surroundings, and that drove her instantly into panic. It was a homely looking bedroom with an oak bed and massive pillows. Across was a window, which took up the whole wall, giving a view of mountains and woods. Julie felt her head begin to spin. How did she get to a house in the woods?

She wasn't going to find answers just lying around. Quickly, she got out of bed. Looking down, she saw she was dressed in a loose white T-shirt, several sizes too large. She plucked at the V-shaped neckline, peeking beneath to confirm that, indeed, she was naked except for her panties. Okay. Now she could really start to freak out.

Padding to the door on bare feet, she opened it slowly and carefully. Once it was ajar, she looked out to find an empty corridor. Inching out of the bedroom, she moved down the hall, her footsteps faltering when she heard voices.

"Whoever they are, they came into our territory and tried

to steal our mate right from underneath our noses," growled Caine's distinctive voice. "We're not going to let that go."

"Definitely not. But until Julie opens up and tells us who those men were and why she was leaving with them, there isn't much we can do. What kills me right now is that she couldn't trust us to keep her safe. Why else would she have agreed to go with those men?" Ryan said bitterly.

Julie felt shamed by the hurt in his voice. She didn't know they cared so much. But what did they mean by "territory" and "mate?" If they hadn't mentioned her name directly, she'd have thought they were talking about something else.

Confused by the tone of their voices and the strange turn of phrase, she stumbled backward and managed to somehow trip over her own feet. The conversation between the two men stopped abruptly, and she heard Ryan call out her name clearly.

Sighing, she gathered more nerve and moved out into the living room area, finding both Caine and Ryan standing there, looking her way. They made no move to close the gap between them as she stood some distance away.

"You heard us talking?" Ryan asked more gently, while Caine gazed at her with a look that made every inch of her start to tingle.

It was a few moments before she could think of what to say. "I heard a bit," she said, not knowing where to look. "Could you please tell me what's going on? Why did you guys bring me here?"

Caine stepped forward, his expression deepening with worry. "Don't you remember? We were at the restaurant and you went to the restroom. I was just in time to see you about to leave with the two men in a car. You fainted, and we brought you here to keep you safe. Whoever those people were, we wanted you someplace they'd never track you. No one knows about this place but us."

He moved just close enough to reach out and touch her, but she backed into the wall. A pained look came over Caine's face, but he cloaked it quickly. "Julie, why can't you be completely honest with us? What kind of trouble are you in?"

"Why don't we start with you two?" Julie said, her voice filled with suspicion. "You say you saw me try to leave with two men, but you were nowhere close to where we were. It was Ryan who came out to rescue me when that monster wolf came out of nowhere and—"

She shivered, wrapping her arms around herself as she relived each moment, seeing that huge, dark golden beast almost rip the men to shreds. She still didn't understand it, but she had a strange feeling the wolf had come out to protect her. *But why?*

Caine paused at her accusatory tone. "I was close, but you didn't see me," he said enigmatically. "I was busy getting help while Ryan rushed out to get you out of harm's way."

Ryan stalked forward, and his dark eyes looked stormy as he searched Julie's face. "Why would you do that? Endanger yourself the way you did? You knew we were waiting back at the restaurant, yet you chose to leave with strange men without saying a word. Do you have any idea how much we care about you?"

"I did it to protect you both!" she cried out, stung by Ryan's fury. "If I didn't go with them, they'd have..."

She shook her head and spun around. She couldn't face the righteous anger she could feel coming off them in waves.

Taking a deep breath, she faced them again, with reluctance. "Look, I'm sorry for getting you mixed up in my troubles. Just give me my clothes, and I'll leave. Thanks for all you've done for me so far, but I can't let you get any more involved. For your own safety, you need to let me go."

Ryan seemed to swallow his anger, his voice gentling with surprising speed as he gripped her by the shoulders. "Don't you think we're more than capable of protecting you, Julie? That's all we ever wanted to do."

"And I told you once before that I can take care of myself," Julie said, hating to do it but shrugging out of his hold. "Please. Just let me go. Forget you ever met me."

"That's not an option," Caine said suddenly, in the harshest tone she'd ever heard him use. "And if you think we're going to let you walk out of our lives, you've got another thing coming. Anyone who ever tries to hurt you or take you away will have to go through us first."

Despite her inherent independence and sense of self-preservation, Julie felt a certain thrill from Caine's words and the blaze of possession in his blue eyes. Ryan looked just as fiercely protective, and she felt that familiar sensation of sinking helplessly into his gaze, now heated pools of blue.

She looked from one to the other, and suddenly, Julie realized just how serious they were about her. Things had gotten real, and they were no longer just the two caring, attentive "friends" she enjoyed hanging out with. Even the sexual tension she normally felt around them had magnified to almost impossible proportions.

Somehow, they'd gotten her alone in this place. It was some kind of cabin in the woods, and she had an inkling they were miles from anywhere. They claimed it was to keep her safe, but was that the true reason? In bringing her out here, didn't they suddenly become the one thing she needed protection from?

To her amazement, Ryan groaned out loud. "I'm sorry if we frightened you. We can smell your fear, Julie, and that hurts more than anything could—knowing you're scared of us."

They could smell her fear? There it was again, the strange terms they used. Why did nothing make sense about them anymore?

"Julie..."

She heard them both call out for her, but she was too busy running back the way she'd come. Suddenly, the bedroom seemed the safest place to be. It was familiar and kept her out of their reach. She dashed down the corridor and back into the room, slamming the door behind her. She thanked the stars there was a key and a bolt, both of which she quickly used. She had her back against the doorframe as she breathed in shallowly, her mind spinning around in circles.

The sound of Caine's voice on the other side of the door made her jump. "Please, Julie. Search your heart and you'll know we'd rather die than hurt you," he said softly, and it was as though he spoke just inches from her face. "You don't have to tell us anything if you aren't ready. But we can't let you leave unless we're sure we can protect you. And I understand you don't like to feel that you need to depend on others for your safety, but for once, believe me when I tell you that we're here for you. You can count on it."

She hadn't drawn a single breath all through his speech and she didn't say one word in reply, though she could tell he was waiting. She heard his deep sigh as, several seconds later, he retreated from the door. Only then did she sag against the frame, back sliding down its length to the ground as she hugged her arms around her knees and rested her spinning head there.

## CHAPTER 9

"I SMELL BREAKFAST," she said, moving forward to the island where Ryan was seated on a barstool.

He grinned, the flash of white filled with relief and warmth. "Caine has kitchen duty this morning. That's why everything smells so good and not burned, as my cooking would undoubtedly have. Why don't you sit down? I'll pour you some coffee."

She nodded and looked at Caine, who stood by the stove. It was definitely the heavenly smells that had led her straight here from her bedroom. She'd had a lot of time to think things through in the past couple hours, and she'd told herself she'd listen to Caine. Trusting her instincts again, she felt sure she was right that Ryan and Caine were the men she needed in her life, two people she could rely on, even with so much hanging in the balance.

"Mmm, this is so good." She sighed expressively after just one sip of the fragrant brew.

Her hum of pleasure sounded somewhat erotic, and when she looked up, blushing, she caught the men watching her, their eyes glued to her full, wet lips. She suddenly felt self-conscious of the fact that she only wore panties and a thin T-shirt, and she wondered who had undressed her, though she was too embarrassed to ask.

Caine soon set out their plates, heaping with delicious food. When she glanced his way, he merely smirked. "If you're going to be eating with us, you'll need to keep up and grow a decent appetite. Now eat, woman."

Julie hid a smile. She liked the thought of eating with them more often. She also liked that they took her well-being so seriously as to whisk her off to their secret hideaway just to keep her safe. Most of all, she liked how it felt to be amongst two people who truly cared about her. Whatever their "agenda," she knew she had no reason to doubt their integrity. And she'd make sure they had no cause to doubt hers.

"For the last several months, I've been on the run from my ex-boyfriend." She began, staring down at her plate. She could feel their joint gaze on her, but she continued without looking up.

"Grant Gaines is a man I've known all my life—well, *thought* I knew. He fronted as a legitimate businessman, but soon after we started dating five years ago, I realized he was nothing more than a thug who runs some kind of crime ring. He was always this cool, handsome guy with good standing in my community. I never dreamed he was into all sorts of shady deals, from drugs to arms dealing and even human trafficking." She shuddered visibly.

Now she looked up to meet both pairs of eyes that never shifted from hers. "Grant is a very powerful man, and somehow, he found me. I picked up the phone just days ago to hear his voice. *Did you really think you could escape me? Did you think I'd ever give up what's mine?*"

Julie shook her head at the memory and how desperately

afraid she'd been to know he was on the other end of the line. He knew where she was and would come after her.

"I wanted to leave the very next day, but I guess I was sick of running. I already had a home, new friends. I had you guys," she said, voice softening as she gazed at them both. "That one time he called, I told him to leave me alone or I'd call the cops. He didn't call again, and I felt relieved. But last night, he called my cell. I went into the restroom to answer it, and he told me he knew exactly where I was at that moment and who I was with. Said he had men stationed outside the restaurant who'd been ordered to shoot my two companions if I didn't do as he instructed. I told him not to hurt my friends and I'd do anything he wanted. That was when he told me to leave through the back and get into the car. I was about to do just that when the biggest wolf I'd ever seen flew at my abductor and fairly ripped his arm off. From the way it didn't try to hurt me, I realized that somehow, it was protecting me. Defending *me*."

She smiled slightly, rolling her fork around her food. "And then Ryan came to the rescue. Everything went blank after that."

"Will you tell us exactly why you left Grant in the first place? Did he try to hurt you?" Ryan asked calmly, though the fist he had clenched on the island looked almost white-knuckled, as if he were reining in his emotions.

Julie let out a deep sigh. "Once I knew the type of man he really was, I tried to leave him, but he always threatened to hurt my friends or the people I loved. I didn't really have anyone else to call my own since he never let anyone stay close to me. I'd already lost my parents when I was in college, and whatever friends or relatives I had drifted away because of my involvement with him. He liked that I was defenseless and, in his power, unable to fight for myself. One day, I did fight," she said with grim satisfaction.

"It was more than six months ago when I packed my bags for the last time. He came home early and caught me trying to leave. He grabbed me by the arms and pinned me against the wall. Promised me he'd show me who was my master and that by the time he was through, I'd be so disfigured and helpless that no one else would ever want me. That was when he slapped me around, ripped at my clothes, and threw me on the floor..." She winced slightly, but then after a slight pause to inhale a steadying breath, she continued.

"Somehow, when he got on top of me, I was able to reach for one of the paperweights that had fallen to the floor during our struggle. I hit him on the head and knocked him out cold."

Julie shrugged and began eating again, saying calmly, "That's how I escaped from him, and I've been running ever since."

"This is where your running stops—for good," Ryan told her firmly. "Grant can't get you here. We'll keep you safe from him for as long as it takes to make sure he pays for all he's done."

Julie slowly swallowed her food and looked from one man to the other. "You both know I can't hole up here with you forever, right? You've got your own lives to lead. I can't expect you to—"

"Julie, you still don't understand, do you?" Caine asked, reaching out and brushing his fingertips gently across her bangs, tucking the longer strands behind one ear.

"Understand what?" she croaked, suddenly turned on by his gentle touch and the way his eyes seemed to melt her insides.

"That you belong with us," he said simply. "You were meant to share our lives, and whatever danger is keeping that from happening, Ryan and I will see to it that it's a thing of the past."

The words "share" and "our" had Julie feeling as though she would start hyperventilating. She dropped her fork and gulped down the still-hot coffee to clear her throat. Ryan, who sat next to her, placed a hand gently on her bare knee, and the warm weight did impossible things to her already mounting state of arousal. The kitchen suddenly seemed to grow smaller as she became wildly aware of that silken web that enmeshed her in the combined need for these two that almost overpowered her.

"You know what we want, Julie?" Ryan asked huskily. "Or do we need to show you?"

Julie gulped. Ryan's hand stroking her knee ever so softly... Caine's fingers forking through her hair with just that bit of sensuality...

No, she definitely didn't need any more explaining. But that didn't make it any less excruciatingly beguiling to suddenly come to terms with what she'd only guessed at and—dare she admit to herself—hoped for.

Instead of responding directly, she simply smiled. "Breakfast was perfect. And talking about everything that's happened has lifted a weight off my chest. You don't know how much it means knowing that, for the first time in a long while, I can feel safe."

She rose and was about to clean up their dishes when Ryan stopped her. "Don't worry about those. Go freshen up. Caine will find something you can change into 'til we can do something about your clothes and whatnot."

"Thank you," she said, feeling strangely shy now that so much was out in the open.

Both men watched her leave the kitchen, and there was no mistaking the barely suppressed hunger in their gazes, mixed with the deepest tenderness. Emotions warred within them, and it was all they could do not to scramble after their mate like horny teenage boys.

It didn't make things easier to know how much her arousal seeped in droplets of honey down her inner thighs, the scent almost driving them mad. But they had to focus on what was most important, and that was protecting Julie from this bastard that had hurt her so much, had driven her away from everything she had ever known. They had to make sure he could never hurt her again, and then she'd be free to move on with her life, to be with them forever.

Their desire made them long to be one with their mate, finally. She was the love of their lives, a woman to be protected and cared for. Her ingrown independence wasn't going to be a problem because they'd show her the many ways, she'd find strength, even in submitting to them.

*One step at a time*, they thought, nodding to each other, no more words needing to be said. They knew what they had to do.

JULIE WAS TAKING A LONG, warm, luxurious shower. Naked beneath the spray, her body tingled so much that each drop seemed to stimulate her every nerve ending.

Closing her eyes brought forth images she'd long denied and needs she'd kept bottled up far too long. Her hands lingered on her throat, breasts, and in between her thighs, soaping sensually and wishing it was a lover's hands that moved over her instead.

Not just any lover. *Her* lovers—two of the most physically irresistible men she'd ever met. Two warmhearted, patient, and exciting men who made her feel beautiful when they looked at her. She skimmed her hands over her belly and up to slightly knead her D-cup breasts.

The rush of the water almost made her miss the sound of the bathroom door opening.

Julie suddenly sensed the lone figure of a naked man joining her in the shower, taking up the space behind her. Hands, large and deliciously warm, came around and tugged her wandering hands down to her sides. Julie gasped inaudibly at the sensation of rock-hard, nude male pushing against her from behind. She didn't look back, but when she glanced down, she saw the arms were dotted with black tribal ink. The next instant, she heard the rumble of his voice in her ear as his lips brushed her lobe.

"Every inch of you is so very beautiful," Caine growled. "Do you like my hands on you, baby?"

Julie let out a soft moan. If he needed confirmation that he could keep going with his exploration of her thick, curvy frame, then Julie thought he could read body language well enough. Even he could feel the way she trembled with carnal response to his fingers feathering under the swell of her breasts, across the line of her nipples, and then sinking down to grip her waist and push her back against his unmistakably rigid manhood. He nestled his unyielding length right between the fleshy orbs of her ass, where he felt right at home.

*Oh my. Oh goodness*, thought Julie. So long without a man and she was all set to disintegrate if Caine drifted his hand much lower and simply flicked her clit.

Fighting for control, she instead rested back against his broad, muscular chest and whispered into the falling shower, "Yes. I like your hands on me. Touch me, Caine. All over."

He groaned in her ear, and a single long shudder seemed to move through his body as his fingers tightened momentarily on her hips. Then he spun her around to face him and kissed her hard, so hard their teeth clashed. She panted, hands gripping tightly to the width of his upper arms. The world faded away, and Julie caught no more of the sounds or smells of the shower. All she could taste and feel was Caine, and she drew herself up toward him with total abandon. He cradled her to him, trailing his lips sensuously from her responsive mouth to trace her lobe and then her neck with his eager tongue. He bent lower to explore the hollow that dipped between her breasts, which he now had scooped together in his hands. Julie felt intoxicated by his touch and the feeling of his lips on her skin.

Her hands traced over his powerfully built body, unable to keep from touching his broad shoulders, muscled torso, the taut leanness of his hips and thighs, and then... Oh God. The length and girth of his cock as she encircled him with both hands made her lightheaded for a moment.

Caine's tongue had begun sweeping over her nipple, and Julie was whimpering with pleasure just as he let out a guttural groan, his hardness swelling in her palms as she stroked him. He felt so good in her hands that she couldn't stop her fists pumping on his impressively long and thick shaft. Just imagining him sliding inside her wet heat was enough to have a low whine escaping her parted lips.

She stroked him further, lost in the sensation of flesh-coated steel, only to feel his hands grab her wrists and draw her fingers gently from him. Julie's heart lurched at the deprivation until she heard him groan in her ear that if she kept touching him like that, he'd lose control before he had the chance to be inside her.

"And I've waited too long to have it end too soon. You ready for me, woman?" Caine asked at the same time he slid one hand down her belly to cup her mound. Julie mewled and thrust her hips, spreading her feet to give him better access to her melting heat.

A deep, feral sound of pleasure rippled through Caine's chest as his fingers came in contact with her unmistakable slickness. He explored her folds with an insistent, knowing touch. Julie almost blacked out from the ecstasy of Caine touching her aching center. He teased her now swollen vulva expertly, and she streamed juices all over his hand, making him growl deeply in approval.

Julie's head fell against his shoulder, and she lowered her

lips to kiss his neck. She savored the scent of his arousal that seemed to escape from his pores. He smelled fierce and wild, the steam rising from his gloriously tanned body. She felt the tension of the muscles in his throat as she nibbled on his skin.

"Harder, Julie. Don't be afraid to bite harder. Your teeth feel so good on my neck." He groaned.

Julie hesitated, longing to give in to her strange urge to break into his smooth flesh with her teeth. What was wrong with her? She wasn't normally a biter, but she almost couldn't help wanting to sink her teeth deep into his flesh, just as he'd instructed.

Just then, he thrust one finger deep inside her, and her response shocked her. Crying out, she opened her mouth wide over his neck and bit, body jerking to the sensation of Caine sliding that one finger in and out of her hot, wet pussy.

Her harsh moans of pleasure were muffled against his flesh, her teeth digging deep enough to break, but not quite managing to. Caine slipped a second finger slowly inside, and now there were two wedged sideways and probing her secret depths. He hooked up into the roof of her tunnel and seemed to release a hidden spring of bliss that had her throwing her head back and screeching as her whole body caught fire with lust.

Caine started with gentle teasing strokes that grew faster, rougher. The sensation of being shredded to pieces by pleasure would be magnified, Julie knew, when he finally claimed her completely, as she soon found herself imploring him to do.

"Please, Caine. I need you buried deep inside me. Now."

"Yes. Now," he rasped in agreement, pulling his two fingers out of her with tormenting slowness and then lifting them to his mouth and sucking hard on them, groaning deeply. "You taste as incredible as I remember. So tight and sweet, Julie. And so ready for me."

Julie couldn't agree more. She was so wet and ready she

was flooding her thighs with her liquid want. For a moment, his words about "remembering" how she tasted had her confused. But there was no time to dwell on it, not when Caine grabbed her thighs and lifted them to wrap them around his waist.

"Grab hold of my shoulders," he commanded in a voice so thick she could hardly recognize it.

But she obeyed quickly, wrapping her arms around him for more leverage as she felt his arms hook underneath each of her bent knees, spreading her wide for his impending invasion. She let out whimper after whimper and clung tighter to him like a lifeline. He was so rock-hard all he had to do was aim his engorged tip to her slit in readiness to plunge into her dripping passage.

For the first few moments, he rubbed his cap against her, tantalizing the soaked bundle of nerves. Staring deep into her eyes, with the water falling through his hair and making it slick and dark, he looked like a beautiful god, and Julie felt a deep accomplishment that such a fiercely perfect specimen desired her so powerfully his muscles stood out in high definition as he fought back his need to rampage right into her depths.

"I love you, Julie," he said clearly, his stormy blue eyes filled with passion, need, and a greater emotion she felt slayed her right through.

"Oh, Caine. I love you, too," she breathed out, heart swelling almost to bursting. She felt overcome with the tumult of powerfully charged feelings that her only available outlet seemed to be once again bending to his neck and biting hard, harder than before, to fight back the rising agony of pleasure threatening to tear her to shreds.

Julie couldn't have foreseen her almost savage gesture would finally send Caine over the edge. He lost control, and with her name ringing on his lips, he gave in to his need and suddenly thrust hard into her.

Her shocked gasp turned into a deep, long moan as her lover filled her with immense proportion. Nails buried into his back, Julie tried to brace herself against his next thrust, sure it would split her in half. Caine withdrew almost to the tip and then bucked forward, pushing deep inside her to the hilt. And this time, he didn't stop, didn't pause to let her catch her breath or her senses. With each moan, each cry and breath that escaped her open mouth, Caine thrust faster and harder.

*Oh... oh. Oh!* She must have cried over and over, the energy of Caine's passion merging and mounting with hers, submerging them in a waterfall of shared enticement. The angle of each smooth, unbroken plunge of his hard, hot cock deep inside her seemed to trigger spasm after spasm of micro eruptions, and Julie sensed she couldn't outlast him.

Fingers inching up to pull at his slick hair, Julie reached for his lips and moaned helplessly into his mouth. Caine's breath became ragged as her walls tightened convulsively on his thrusting shaft. He seemed as close to the peak as she was, and she basked in her power to bring him to the same mindless pleasure he gave her. A fountain of heat already began to rise from her center and echoed through her spine that arched as her body was impaled on his thick shaft again and again.

Caine's pace began to grow desperate, and a maddening scent seemed to come off him in waves, making her senses whirl with intoxication. It was musky and hot and ferocious, calling to her inner animal in ways no lover had ever done. She felt her walls begin to quiver with intense pulses around him, building the pressure that sent her hurtling to meet her orgasm while triggering Caine's.

Bucking wildly atop his slightly bent thighs, Julie exploded in ecstasy. Caine's arms were the only thing holding her up as she lost all control of her limbs, suddenly weak and limp. He stayed deep inside her, filling her to the brim with his explosive eruption of scalding hot seed.

Still, the warm shower cascaded, leaving them awash in mist and a heat that couldn't rival the flames licking at them and welding them as one. Caine didn't set Julie back down on her feet until he was sure she could be steady on them. Then with a flurry of soft kisses, their hands found the soap, which they ran lovingly over each other. Minutes later, they were washed clean, and Caine lifted the now drowsy Julie easily into his arms. Her fingers linked behind his neck and didn't let go even when she felt the softness of the sheets as he placed her gently upon the giving mattress. She was fast asleep moments later, blissfully sated.

Julie had always had sensitive feet and now, feeling fingers begin to massage her instep tenderly, she opened her eyes and stared up at the ceiling for a moment, trying to get her bearings.

Large, warm hands wrapped around her ankles, and she jerked up on her elbows. Her eyes widened to find Ryan spread across the foot of her bed. She felt an irrepressible shiver at the fact that he'd been there all this while and she'd been blissfully unaware of his presence.

She looked around and found there was no one else in the room with them, but that didn't keep her blush from stealing across her face and neck. She was still completely naked, her body temperature back to normal after the heated coupling with Caine in the shower. A glance at the bedside clock told her that a couple of hours had passed, and she groaned. Why had they let her sleep so long?

"I'm sorry I dozed off," she said sheepishly.

The silent Ryan was stroking his thumbs over her soles

with gentle pressure on her soft, sensitive flesh. Her legs jerked reflexively, the light touch of his hands exciting not just her surface nerves, but her secret ones as well. Already, she began to seep from her greedy folds, and she gazed almost wantonly down at the man so casually draped at the end of her bed.

"You needed your rest," Ryan said easily. A wicked glint in his eyes put her on alert and made her heart pound in carnal awareness. The next second, he was trailing an index finger down her right sole, and she whimpered, fighting down a giggle.

"Ticklish, I see," Ryan murmured, glancing up with that dark look of heat she always found so rakish and overpoweringly sexy.

Seeing Ryan's playful side was as thrilling as it was heart-melting. He moved slowly upward, dancing his fingers up her calf until he cupped the back of one knee and lifted her leg so her foot was planted flat on the bed. He skipped fingers upward over the inside of her thigh, and this time, she couldn't help but jump as her belly rippled with unstoppable laughter.

"Ah, definitely ticklish there as well," he said deeply.

Julie's mirth died away as she became achingly aware of the change of atmosphere as Ryan straightened over her, propped up by his arms. He was naked, and so was she. Yet Julie felt no self-consciousness. She felt only like a woman already in her prime and comfortable being sexual.

She hungrily ran her eyes over Ryan's magnificent body. He was pure muscle, with gleaming olive skin and a form that was right out of a sexy male swimsuit shoot. She itched to trace each hard-packed muscle, and a glimpse she sent audaciously lower found her staring at that part of him nestled against his dark, curly pubes. Her mouth parted in a soft gasp, and instantly, dewy moisture formed at her apex. Like Caine, Ryan was gifted with a size that would make a god green with envy. She'd always guessed he'd be huge, but seeing the proof made her feel like her fantasies didn't even do him justice. Her eyes flew up to meet his and found his deep-blue irises almost black, the sinfully long lashes half hooding his searing gaze.

"Julie," he said softly, cupping her face and pressing his lips to the corner of her mouth. "I want you far more than I should."

She trembled, fingers digging into the sheets. "I want you, too." Her breathing matched his, uneven, hurried, as if they were both running at break-neck speed while they remained still as statues.

"Do you?" he said huskily.

His body half rested on hers, and that sensation of being crushed beneath him only made her more turned on. She loved the aura of dominance he exuded that had nothing to do with force or angst. Thinking of Grant in that moment felt like such sacrilege, and she pushed any memory of him to the deepest depths of her mind.

"Yes," she replied with firmness. He nuzzled at her throat, and she arched off the bed, hands slowly lifting to reach around his gloriously muscular frame. Gushes of arousal poured from her center, and she almost whimpered as she said, "I think I've wanted you—wanted this—forever."

Ryan growled deep in his throat, his lower body grinding into hers. The thick, rigid length of his maleness rubbed into her belly, and she could feel the cool, wet trails of his pre-cum on her flesh. That alone was enough to make her inner sheath quiver to be filled and stormed by his granite-hard member.

"I can get a little rough sometimes... but I'll never hurt you or cause you pain," he said on a raspy whisper, each word ringing true in her ears. "Just trust me to take you to heights of pleasure you've never even imagined."

"Oh yes, please," Julie whispered, unabashed by her sweltering desire for this man.

"Now turn over, baby, and let me give you a taste of what I've been thinking of doing to you for the longest time."

Ryan's commanding, husky words would have normally filled her with consternation, but somehow, Julie knew there was nothing to worry about. She chose to trust him, just as he asked. She could never imagine him hurting her, certainly never like Grant had.

Slowly, she rolled over and rested her face against the pillows, her whole-body trembling with anticipation.

"Beautiful," Ryan whispered, and Julie could only imagine the view he was getting—the spread length of her thighs, her curvy bottom, and then the long, supple line of her back. She grew wet thinking he could just see the pulpy mound of her sex in between her slightly parted legs.

"I want to taste you all over. I missed that the last time, and it's all I've been thinking of since then," growled Ryan, his breath fanning her ear.

Julie closed her eyes and focused her other senses solely on the man whose voice and words made love to her in ways that sent chills of pleasure down her back. His hands smoothed over every inch of her, and his lips and tongue traced the same spots as his fingers. It was like a full-body massage but all the more electrifying. She was dripping on herself by the time his lips reached the crevice between her splayed thighs.

"Your scent has the power to drive me crazy," Ryan said thickly, his hands cupping the globes of her ass and spreading them open so he could kiss her labia. Julie moaned helplessly. He inhaled her aroma and let out a rough growl of desire. His tongue came out and quickly swept the length of her slit. The pleasure of that alone had her body convulsing, and she gripped tightly on the pillows.

"Mmm," she purred with shameless delight.

Ryan's mouth there... and there was the most carnal of

pleasures. He licked her to an almost fiendish moistness. He drove that skilled tongue as deep as it would go, using its stiff tip to manipulate the sensitive edges of her inner folds. Reaching his arm beneath her belly, he drew her up slightly so her bottom was arched in the air and his tongue could reach her hooded clit. He teased her with masterful determination.

If Julie cried out any louder or longer, she'd be hoarse. Pleasure became almost agony as her clit came to feverish life beneath his tongue. And just when she thought it couldn't get any more intense, she felt him spear her entrance with first one finger, then two.

"Ryan... ooh," she cried, the sound fading into a half sob. "Oh, please."

"Please what, Julie?" Ryan paused in his thrusting of her depths. "Please stop?"

"No."

"Then tell me what you want. Tell me exactly what you want me to do to you," he said in that voice that was all smooth silk and rough gravel.

"Take me," Julie gasped out, hungry to be filled by him in ways that his probing fingers couldn't achieve.

Ryan had brought her to a point where all reason left her, and something told her he felt the same. Yet when she felt his hands guide her hips even higher, bringing her up on her hands and knees, she felt a slight trepidation. The sheer size of him, claiming her at that angle, might prove more than she could handle.

She felt Ryan's body at her back, leaning over her and covering her with heat and want. His hand gently scooped her hair, and he pulled her head back, just enough so he could seek her mouth and snake his tongue inside. Moaning, she welcomed his kiss, inflamed yet calmed by it. His other hand covered one of her breasts, squeezing passionately and causing her nipples to grow taut and achy.

With his fingers attached to the tingling nub at the tip of her breast and his tongue thrusting into her mouth, Julie almost got distracted from the fact that his big, hard member probed at her entrance from behind. She came to her senses and let out a low whine against his lips.

"Shh, my love. Let it happen. You're already so wet and open for me. You'll love it. I promise." He kissed her again, more deeply and possessively than before. When he drew back slightly, he gazed deeply into her eyes. "You know I love you, don't you?"

"Yes, and I love you."

Julie meant the words with all her heart. This felt so right, without question. It was true that every part of her was molten and ready for him, wetness coursing from her sex. She would take him, all of him, and revel in being claimed in a way that was no-holds-barred, elemental, and uncaged. Moaning in encouragement, she ground her hips back against him.

Ryan let out a groan of appreciation but made no other sound as he rose behind her and seized her hips. In one fluid surge, he thrust, sheathing himself to the neck of her depths. Julie gasped aloud, her whole body almost jolted forward from the powerful impact. Embedded inside her, he made himself known to every inch of her walls. She drew in much-needed air as, for a few moments, he held still inside her. Enough for her to get accustomed to his girth, her muscles stretching to take him as deep as he wanted to go. Soon, her body wanted more, and she moved with sensuous enticement, which Ryan did not mistake.

Without further delay, he began to drive himself in and out of her ready heat until he built a tempo that made Julie go wild. With him so fully encased inside her, it should have hurt, but the slight discomfort was overshadowed by the immense pleasure he gave with each purposeful stroke. Her moans of ecstasy grew louder, earthier, and she could feel they spurred him further. His thrusts came more rapidly, his shaft throbbing with each squeeze of her powerful inner muscles as the sweet delight of their passion rose higher.

Yet each time Julie felt close enough to the edge to fall over into the depths of unstoppable ecstasy, Ryan slowed his rough, taking thrusts, easing into a grinding pace that sent a blinding wave of pleasure over her body.

Time and again, he drew them back from the peak, until Julie felt she couldn't take anymore. Crying out his name, she begged for release as she arched her back, her arms stretched full length beneath her. She heard Ryan's low, thick growl in response to her plea before he reached underneath and maneuvered his fingers to find her pulsing clit. When he coupled his thrusts to match his strumming of her clit, Julie knew she was finally lost.

As she gave in to the flood tide of their relentless coupling, Julie was relieved that Ryan didn't hold back long, letting go just moments after her explosive orgasm ebbed into shudders and twitches. She felt each imprint of his fingers digging into the flesh of her hips as he pounded to a finish, sending a torrent of his hot liquid essence deep into her womb.

In Julie's sated state, she was almost insensible to the fact that when they fell to the bed, they were still linked as one. Ryan had his arms wrapped around her and spooned against her quivering body. His gentle kisses on the top of her head sent her to sleep for the second time that day.

Once Julie's breathing grew low and steady with slumber, Ryan carefully extricated his body from the softness of hers. Leaving his mate lying so tantalizingly in those ruffled sheets was the hardest thing he had to do. But she deserved her rest, especially after the exertions of pleasing both her demanding lovers. From the blissful expression playing on her sleeping features, Ryan figured she had no complaints in that regard.

Smiling, he bent to pick up his clothes but didn't try to put them on as he left the bedroom quietly. It took moments of sniffing the air to know Caine wasn't in the cabin, and he knew where he would be. Tossing his clothes to the floor, Ryan crouched and phased into his glorious wolf form, taking off in the direction of the dense woods to join his brother wolf in an exultant run.

They'd made it past the first stage of claiming their mate. Soon, she'd be ready to take them both at the same time. And in quick succession, she'd be prepared for the final step of being mated to them forever.

# CHAPTER 11

CAINE WAS glad to see the happy smile on Julie's face when she emerged from the bedroom, wearing one of his favorite T-shirts. It hugged all her curves in a way that made his throat dry, stopping just above her knee and exposing her beautifully toned and creamy legs.

She moved easily into his arms and kissed him full on the lips. Caine was rock hard in moments. Fighting back his ever-ready wolf lust, he tightened his arms around her for a moment before releasing her reluctantly.

"Where's Ryan?" she asked curiously, looking around at the den where she'd come looking for them.

"He went back into town. He'll go to your place and bring a few things, your clothes, for one. Although... if it were up to me, you'd be fine walking around with nothing on at all," he growled, pulling her back against him to steal one more irresistible kiss.

"Good thing it's not left to you, then," she said wryly. A deep sigh escaped her, and she began tentatively. "Caine, these last few hours..."

"I know. We shouldn't have put such a strain on you. But we've held back so long, and it was hard not to give in to how we felt. If we tired you out—"

"No, I'm fine," she said, her cheeks looking hot as she swept her lashes shyly down. "In fact, I've never felt so... alive. No, what I truly wanted to ask is... What next? Is this supposed to be some ongoing thing, a relationship, or..."

Caine cupped her face gently and compelled her to meet his gaze. "I'd rather wait until Ryan's here so we can explain what we're hoping for. But I can tell you this isn't some fling or whatever. We're playing for keeps, Julie. It might seem unconventional to the outside world, but this is the way we choose to share our future. With you. Just you."

Julie was staring at him, eyes wide. "When you talk of the future, you mean like marriage? How is that possible since there's two of you? That's um... illegal."

Caine smiled. "Obviously. Ryan's the elder, so basically, you'll wed him, but you'll belong to both of us. Our children, our family will be as one. Can you picture a lifetime of being with the two men who are determined to make you the center of their world?"

"I..." She began, her expression lost. "It's... I never imagined this would ever happen to me. I just don't feel that I deserve you both."

Caine let out a chuckle as he scooped her up into his arms. "You deserve much more than us, Julie. Though, we're hoping you'll give us the chance to earn your love."

"I already love you both." She rested her cheek against his shoulder. "More than I've ever loved anyone."

"I won't tell you that everything will always be easy," Caine said reluctantly. "There's still a lot that you need to know before you agree to stay with us. But like I said, I'll wait for Ryan before getting into that."

She looked up at him then, and her smile was trusting, adoring. Caine felt a pang as he wished with all his heart that she'd always look like that, look at them with trust and love and never doubt they had her best interests at heart. They'd find a way to take care of Grant, and then they'd let her know the truth about their lycan heritage and how she was going to play her part as their mate, lover, and wife for all eternity.

CHAPTER 12

THIS WASN'T EXACTLY how Julie had imagined her life would be, yet she was happier than she ever thought possible, and it was only getting better.

Here were two absolutely incredible men whom she'd fallen deeply in love with and who adored her and wanted a future with her in return. They were working so hard to make sure they could be together with nothing standing between them. Here, in these dark woods, she had spent hours getting to know them better, and with each passing minute, she could see a clearer future with all three of them blissfully happy.

The only problem was what to do about Grant.

"He's never going to stop coming after me. I realize that now," she said in a far-off voice, sitting between Ryan and Caine on the comfortable leather sofa in front of the crackling fireplace. More than a week had passed, and she wondered how long it would be before they would have to leave the safety of their private cabin.

"We're working on a way to bring him down," Ryan replied through gritted teeth. "He may have tracked you to our town, but this cabin is the last place he'll ever find you. In the meantime, it's our goal to link him to the attempted abduction at that restaurant. The prints on that gun didn't match anyone on record, but that's a search narrowed to our area. We know Grant's original base was the city you used to live in, so it wouldn't be hard to prove that he sent his men in an attempt to kidnap you or worse. He already has a motive since you decided to leave him. The police would want to know why he was so keen on getting you back at all costs."

Julie huffed. "Well, it wasn't because he actually cared about me. He just hates to be thwarted. I'm just a toy he doesn't want to let go of just yet," she said bitterly. "I still can't figure out how he found me, though. Maybe I unintentionally left some sort of paper trail that led him to me. I thought I was careful. To think he had his men outside, watching us eating at that restaurant." She shook her head and shuddered. "They had guns and would have used them. You can't imagine how relieved I am it never came to that."

She smiled when both men leaned in, planting kisses on her cheek and nuzzling her closely.

"It will be okay," Caine said, his voice just as strained with anger as Ryan's had been. "I'm just glad you didn't get carted away just to keep them from shooting at us. Because it would have killed us to think of you sacrificing yourself like that for us. Promise us you'll never do that again, Julie."

"I promise," she replied quietly, sighing when Caine's lips shifted from her cheek to her neck.

Her heart pounded in instant excitement as he nuzzled her with a tenderness that grew more passionate, his lips opening over her flesh. As she moaned, her parted mouth was captured in a ravenous kiss by Ryan, his fingers raking through her hair to cup the back of her head. She shuddered helplessly as both her lovers began a passionate assault on her senses.

She couldn't think straight whenever this happened. And it had happened many times over the last week. That night of the dinner at Caine's place hadn't been a dream; she'd only just found out. Ryan had confessed when she'd prodded. Told her that they had been unable to resist giving her a taste of how it could be—but had chosen not to take further advantage. As both men began to kiss and fondle her body, Julie could only groan with desire, allowing her two lovers to claim her as their own.

The heated exchange of lips on lips and hands on flesh grew more charged with energy. Clothes were ripped away, only to fall to the floor, joined soon enough by their entwined bodies. Laid gently on her back on a sheepskin rug, Julie was taken to an all-new plane of carnal delights when both Ryan and Caine teased her heated body like never before.

Her hard breasts were pulled into Ryan's hot, demanding mouth, and Julie let her head fall back to the floor as moans of sweet agony raked through her body. One large hand pushed in between her thighs to search out her wetness and the sensitive button that promised unbridled pleasure. As Ryan stroked skillfully at her breast, suckling hungrily on her left nipple, Caine kissed downward from her right breast to her soaked slit and licked her skillfully to frenzied levels of ecstasy. Just at the moment she would have exploded in a forceful rush, Caine rose over her and drove his thick, long cock in to the hilt, stretching her with his rigid maleness.

"Oh!" she cried, loving the swift, decisive claim.

Her core felt full, and she reveled in the rhythm of each thrust that swelled the raging lust within her to titanic proportions. She opened her eyes groggily when she felt a movement to find Ryan kneeling beside her head. She only had to turn her cheek and her lips would come in contact with his thick, jutting erection, so beautifully carved she felt her mouth begin to salivate, wanting to suck hard and deep on his gorgeous shaft.

She didn't even have to think twice about what to do. Her fingers wrapped around his thick, silky base, and her tongue lashed out to taste his sweet pre-cum. The sound of Ryan's deep groan filled her with desire. Greedily, she opened wide and welcomed his cock into her hot, wet mouth, inch by delicious inch.

"Mmm," she purred, savoring the feel of him expanding her lips with his beautiful cock as she eagerly pleasured him.

Caine stretched her just as fully at the heart of her core, his shaft plowing in and out of her blazing hot pussy. The music of their mutual moans and linked bodies grew louder as their dance became more frenzied, passionate, intense.

"Oh God... It feels so good to be inside you, Julie," Caine growled, leaning close enough to lick her nipple with his hot tongue.

Julie moaned in response, the sound vibrating around Ryan's shaft. He too let out a deep growl of pleasure, fisting her hair gently and using it as a harness to guide her back and forth on his rock-solid length. "And having your beautiful mouth wrapped around me, pleasuring me, is enough to make me go crazy. I'm so close, Julie," he rasped.

"Me, too." Caine agreed huskily.

He sucked hard on a nipple, latching his mouth tightly around it while his thrust ramped to a piston-like tempo. Julie could only whimper, desire washing over her body, buzzing in her belly, her mind blown by a thousand sensations. Ryan thrusting in and out of her mouth at the same pace as Caine grinding powerfully inside her velvet-lined walls had her body dissolving into helpless quivers. Pleasure was the single most cataclysmic entity threatening to rupture her to pieces.

"Keep going like that, sweet one, and I'll be exploding

down your throat. Is that what you want, baby?" Ryan asked, holding Julie's head in place with both hands as he looked deep into her eyes, his expression one that clearly illustrated his incredible hunger for her. Julie's answer was to stroke her fingers faster on his base, dragging in one last breath through her open mouth, which she pushed down on his shaft until she almost engulfed him whole. Her throat muscles worked convulsively, and the vibrations as well as her strongly sucking lips had Ryan letting go of the last shred of his control as he erupted a full stream into her mouth.

The sight of Ryan bursting forth inside Julie's mouth and watching her swallow every drop was enough to push Caine over the edge as he came deep inside her clenching walls, his seed filling her until it was dripping down her thighs. He had to hold tight to her hips, which began to spasm with her ensuing orgasm as his almost manic thrusts sent her into orbit. On and on she climaxed, and just watching her let go for them was a vision they were desperate to burn into memory.

Ryan reluctantly withdrew from her mouth so she could draw in much-needed air, his hands combing gently through her hair as she rested back against the soft rug, her body sated, still twitching with reflexive tremors.

As she lay back, chest heaving and eyes closed tight, her two lovers came to lie on either side of her, their hands and lips gliding over her face, lips, and body to calm her into a pleasure-induced slumber.

"I'll be fine. You two don't have to worry about me. If there's somewhere you need to be, then go," Julie said.

She'd walked in on them talking about some meeting with the "alpha," and though she didn't fully understand what that meant, she sensed that being here with her had been keeping them from certain obligations.

They turned to face her as she entered. She was wearing one of the dresses Ryan had bought her days before. It was flirty and hung on tiny straps, the hem barely skimming past her curvy thighs. She giggled as they ran their eyes over her with unconcealed masculine admiration. It felt as though they were undressing her with those hungry eyes, but Julie couldn't be sidetracked. They'd made love in every room and possibly every position known to man, and still they couldn't seem to get enough of her. The craziest thing was Julie felt an equal rise of excitement coating her inner thighs and knew she'd never get enough of them either.

She marveled at the way her once low sex drive now matched those of her two skilled lovers. She'd become absolutely insatiable, and even her body had become accustomed to the many physical demands of pleasing two highly sexed, powerful men who couldn't get enough.

Still, she kept her attention on the matter at hand. "You guys told me that this hideaway is safe, remember. Which means I'll be perfectly fine being left on my own while you go do whatever it is that you need to take care of."

"It'll only be for a few hours." Caine agreed, advancing to her side and taking her hand to lift it to his lips for a soft kiss. "But Ryan and I have never left you here alone. One of us has always been home to make sure you—"

"I'm not a child, okay? I don't need babysitting," she teased with a smile.

No one had ever come around the place since they'd

arrived nearly two weeks ago. She finally felt safe, and she was certain that nothing would happen to her if left alone in their secret hideaway. She just wanted life to get back to normal, and that meant being able to handle herself without her men hovering around like bodyguards twenty-four hours a day.

"Julie, we bought this place knowing that one day we'd need a location we could make a home with our chosen mate—I mean wife," Ryan explained, also coming forward and then cupping her face in his strong hands, his masculine fingers skimming her heated skin. "Here, we'll be safe from prying eyes and people that just don't understand our lifestyle. But we never want you to get the impression that you're being locked away or imprisoned. For one thing, you have a career, and we respect that. When the time comes, we intend to do what's not just best for us, but you as well." He kissed her lips softly. "We just need time to get some things straightened out, okay? And this meeting will help with that."

Julie nodded, looking from Ryan to Caine with trusting eyes. "I know there's still so much you aren't telling me," she said softly, eyes downcast. "But you can't protect me from the truth forever. Over the past several days, I've overheard you both whispering. I know you're hiding something important from me, and I'm confused. I thought you didn't want anything or anyone to come between us."

Julie glanced up to see them share a quick look. Her heart ached, and she wondered why they felt she couldn't handle the truth, whatever the truth was.

"You have nothing to fear with us, Julie," Ryan replied, looking straight into her eyes. "Yes, there's more you need to know about us, but we promise, all in good time. Just know that we would never, ever hurt you."

Julie drew in a deep, shaky breath and nodded. Somehow, she believed them. She had to. Who else could she turn to? She was tired of running, fed up with being alone. Just this small taste of being cherished by not one, but two devoted lovers wasn't something she wanted to give up. Whatever the cost, Julie vowed she would see it through, that she would give her heart to the most beautiful men she'd ever known. No matter the risks.

# CHAPTER 13

THE LOW, murmuring voices ceased when Alpha Jepson came into the hall. He was closely flanked by his betas, both being at least six five in height and over two hundred fifty pounds of pure brawn. This wasn't a social gathering, but a specially arranged assembly of the top-ranking members of their pack. There was Alpha Jepson's wife, Madame Alpha Agatha and many of the other high-ranking females. There were also other betas and a few omegas, everyone there closely involved in the running of pack matters.

The meetings never took that long, and tonight wasn't any different. Ryan and Caine felt equal relief that within an hour, the issues at hand were discussed and handled. As two of the most powerful members of the pack, they knew they were respectively in line to be voted in as alpha when the time came, which wasn't anytime soon. Alpha Jepson was still in his prime. Though, being alpha was about who was strongest and most capable of leading the pack, and it was getting to the point that Alpha Jepson might find himself challenged in that regard. Ryan and Caine had no intention of defying their alpha's authority for whatever reason, but if the members decided to set a vote into motion, then they wouldn't have no choice but to step up to the plate. Members only felt safe when they were sure their leader was the best to protect them and their interests.

Once the meeting was over, both men approached their alpha to have a quiet word. He grinned when he saw them, his lined eyes twinkling. "I was speaking to Vern and Hawke the other day, and they said something about you finding a mate, in the singular. Are congratulations in order?"

Ryan and Caine looked to each other with small, wry smiles. "Yes, Alpha. We both have a mate—one mate. And that's what we wanted to talk about. Congratulations aren't in order until we can properly bond her to our respective wolf. But she doesn't even know we're lycan yet."

Alpha Jepson nodded in understanding. "So, when are you going to break the news to her?"

"Tonight—when we get back home where she's waiting," Ryan explained.

"Any mate of yours is welcome into our pack, of course," Alpha Jepson said immediately. "You won't find any problems infusing her into the kindred."

"Oh, won't they?" said a female voice from behind them.

The three men shared frowns and turned to find Darcy walking right up to where they stood. Behind her was a handful other females, their expressions set.

"What is the meaning of this, Darcy?" Alpha Jepson asked with more curiosity than anger.

"With all due respect, Alpha, at these meetings, you keep going on about pack security and keeping things running smoothly for the benefit of all," Darcy replied, a small grin playing upon her blood-red lips. "But how can that be if so, many potential alphas are being lost to human mates?"

Ryan let out an impatient sigh while Caine merely shook his head in exasperation. They both waited for their alpha to respond.

"It's not about losing pack males, but gaining human members," the alpha said sensibly.

"Exactly. Human. While many females are left unmated, with their chances of finding a mate growing slimmer, especially when their own pack choose mates from outside the pack," Darcy said bitterly, and the women behind her murmured loudly in assent.

"We don't choose our mates. That's for the fates to decide." Ryan spoke up, his eyes narrowed to slits. "Darcy, we all know this concern of yours is because of what happened between you and Caine. But Julie is our mate now, and there's nothing you can do but accept it and move on."

Darcy's thin lips formed a thinner line. "This isn't some act of a scorned woman, contrary to what you think," she said with dignity. "It's about what's best for our pack. How would the men of the pack feel if more and more pack females were choosing human males for mates?"

"We'll view it as nature taking its course," Alpha Jepson said, his tone cool with reproof as he frowned at Darcy. "What's wrong with you, Darcy? You aren't some green pup. You know how this works. Mating is nature's way for our kind to find the perfect other half that suits our needs physically, emotionally, and psychologically. Now, Julie happens to be the perfect other half for Ryan and Caine. You'll have to accept that, no matter your personal feelings on the matter. Remember, Darcy, everything finds a balance. Bonding with humans through mating can only bring us closer together. Lycan and mankind living as one will give us less desire to want to wipe the other from the face of the earth."

Alpha Jepson's last words were spoken with a trace of

humor, and the others surrounding him could be heard chuckling. Darcy's face froze with anger as she noted the mirth on Ryan's and Caine's faces. She stepped up closer and looked up into them.

"I'm glad you think this is so funny," she said, anger burning in her eyes. "I wonder if you'll be laughing when I tell you that right at this minute, Julie could well be reunited with her true mate, the one who loves her enough to never want to share her."

Ryan looked to Caine, who was equally confused.

Scowling furiously, Ryan grabbed Darcy's shoulders and shook her. "What on earth are you talking about? What have you done?"

"What I felt was best for the pack," she replied with a shrug. "When a man came asking questions at the local pub about you two running off with his beloved, I had to do what I could to help him reconnect with his true mate, of course."

"What... man?" Caine gritted out, grabbing her arm and spinning her to face him.

Her smile was mocking. "Tall, dark-skinned. Quite handsome, in fact, much like a Hollywood actor. And so distraught that his woman went off and left him after a quarrel, moving to this town with no word to her friends or family back home. Her fickle behavior is long forgiven, and he only wants her back so they can get married just as they always wanted. He told me his name is Grant Gaines and that Julie is his one and only true love. How desperately romantic." She smiled wickedly, her lips curled into a sneer. "Imagine his feeling of betrayal, knowing she was now shacking up with two strange men she'd met only a few weeks ago."

Ryan was enraged, but he let Darcy go with a sound of disgust. "Well, he can keep looking. He's never going to discover where she is, and you... you will pay for this."

"So, you think." Darcy scoffed, turning around without another word. The next second, she was pushed into the nearby wall, which cracked from the impact. She snarled, her fangs bared as she stared into Ryan's thunderous face. She was barely shaken by the sudden aggression, but the force of it had brought her hackles up, as did the arm Ryan kept across her chest that kept her imprisoned against the damaged wall.

"And what the fuck does that mean?" growled Ryan, his eyes flashing a dangerous silver.

Curbing her fear and embarrassed by the attention now turned to them by the whole room, she spat out in a surly tone, "A few days ago, you came into town to get some stuff, and I decided to follow you when you headed back into the woods. I managed to do so without you catching my scent, and from a distance, I was able to watch you make your way to a cabin up in the mountains. Well, that's where I told Grant he can find his precious Julie, since I figured she'd be holing up there with you two."

There was a loud roar as Caine shot forward and made a grab for Darcy's throat, but Ryan quickly held him aside. "We have no time for this, Caine. We need to head back to the cabin now. Julie is in danger."

Darcy was smirking when Ryan faced her again. "You better pray we get to Julie in time. Because if not, nothing will stand in my way of making sure you pay for your hand in this."

Her face paled, but before she could speak, Alpha Jepson said, "There'll be no need for that, Ryan. I'll see to it that Darcy gets a just sanction: banishment from the pack. Effective immediately."

A collective gasp rose in the room, and Darcy sank back against the wall.

Both Ryan and Caine had already raced from the great hall, desperate to reach Julie before it was too late.

Alpha Jepson glared into Darcy's face. "Anyone who takes pleasure in causing dissention within a pack doesn't deserve to have one. I suggest you're long gone before they get back, or I won't be responsible for what happens to you."

Without waiting for a response, he turned to his betas and rapped out orders as they quickly left the crowded, shell-shocked room.

CHAPTER 14

JULIE JERKED AWAKE, hands closing around the remote control, which had almost slipped from her fingers as she'd dozed in front of the TV. There were more than enough movies to keep her busy while she waited for Ryan and Caine to return, but even the comedy she'd been watching hadn't been able to keep her awake. She already missed her two lovers so much it made everything she tried to busy herself with feel tiresome. She'd already tried a bath and now this silly movie.

She sighed heavily, then smiled deeply. Maybe she'd make them a nice steak dinner. They sure had a thing for meat, judging by the large quantity of it in the freezer, and she knew just how they liked them—practically rare and very well-seasoned.

Relieved at the idea of doing something that would distract her mind from the longing ache she felt in the pit of her stomach every time she thought of Ryan and Caine, she made her way into the kitchen, when she suddenly heard a strange sound. Turning, she cried out as a shadow of a man came forward, his eyes burning with anger and arousal.

"Grant..." She gasped, barely able to speak.

"Hello, Julie," he replied, coming closer.

She let out a shrill cry and turned to run. He grabbed her around the waist before she could escape him, his strong arms banding around her, forcing her against his chest.

"Now, this isn't the welcome I expected after all these months apart," drawled Grant, pinning her back against him as he whispered in her ear.

Julie struggled against him, but he was far too strong. He grabbed her hair with one hand and twisted it to the side so she could stare into his cold, dark eyes.

"Didn't think you'd ever see me again, did you?" he asked through clenched teeth.

"What did you...? How could you even...?" Julie's face creased in pain as he yanked cruelly on her hair.

"It wasn't easy, mind you. First, I had to find where you ran off to, and that was a bit difficult with you continuously moving and all. But when you settled here, I was able to track you through your credit card records. You never struck me as being so stupid, Julie. Maybe you wanted me to find you. Is that it, baby? You missed me."

"You're delusional, as usual," she spat, her fear suddenly replaced with uncontrollable anger. "Now let me go before Ryan and Caine come back and make you regret this!"

"Ah—your *two* lovers. You've grown into quite the whore, haven't you? Giving yourself so cheaply to two creatures." Grant snarled, fingers tightening in her hair with a punishing grip.

Julie winced at the pain but didn't cry out. "They love me. Something you'd never understand the meaning of."

"Now that hurts. Would I hunt you halfway across the freaking country for over six months if I didn't care?" he growled, a deep scowl darkening his face. "And this time, I'll make sure you'll never escape again. I've got men waiting outside, enough to fight off a fucking army. So, if your lovers show up before I get you out of here, they're going to be in for quite the surprise."

Julie gasped in dismay as Grant turned her head to look out the window. She could see several men dressed in suits, their large hands holding guns as they stood guard. How could she not have heard their cars drive up? Then she remembered how she'd dozed off to the blaring sound of the television. She swore underneath her breath and vowed not to panic, knowing if she stood any chance of escape, she had to remain calm and think her way out of this mess.

"The sooner we leave, the better chance of being gone before those two punks get back." Grant continued, a sneer on his lips. "And now that I know just how sexual you are, having two lovers and all, I'll be sure to liven things up in bed, starting with keeping you cuffed—permanently if need be."

"You think you'll get away with kidnapping me?" Julie replied angrily. "Maybe keep me locked in a dungeon so no one will know what kind of a monster you really are?"

"I always wanted a dungeon," mused Grant, his lips curling derisively. "Now move."

Julie was reluctant to take another step, but she had no choice. She couldn't risk Ryan and Caine coming back and facing the small army that stood outside. Her heart sank as she allowed Grant to push her toward the door. They just got out into the open air when sounds of movement came at them from the woods.

The armed men turned in that direction, but no one could have been prepared for the sight that met their eyes moments later.

"What in the hell...?" yelled Grant as a teeming band of huge, snarling wolves burst from the trees.

"Shoot them!" Grant commanded, pointing to the advancing pack.

Before the men could react, the massive beasts flew at them from every angle. There were screams, yells, and sporadic shooting at nothing in particular as guns went off in hands struggling to fight off immense, snapping furry creatures.

Julie stared in shock at the spectacle of so many wolves overpowering the men who'd encircled the cabin. Swearing loudly, Grant backed into the house again, dragging Julie along with him with an arm pinned around her waist.

Before they got far, they came face to face with Ryan.

"Ryan!" cried Julie happily, but then she yelped as Grant forcefully yanked her by the arm to stand behind him.

"Let her go," Ryan said simply, coldly.

Julie stared at his face and almost didn't recognize him. His eyes had gone a strange light color, and she watched in horror as his bared teeth seemed to elongate and sharpened into edges.

*What the...?*

Her attention snapped back to Grant, who retrieved a gun from his waistband. Seizing Julie by the neck, he pointed the barrel right at her temple. "And you need to back off."

"You won't hurt her," Ryan said with certainty but began to back off slowly as Grant advanced with the trembling Julie trapped in front of his body, gun to her head.

"You don't fucking know me, man," Grant said coldly. "Don't push me. Now move the hell out of my way."

As Ryan silently shifted aside, Grant looked at him with a triumphant sneer before dragging Julie along with him outside to where one of his trucks had been parked.

The next second, something flew into vision, and Julie's

head turned in time to see a familiar-looking golden-brown wolf leap in the air, straight for Grant. He had caught the quick movement and spun with his gun, shooting thrice in quick succession. Julie cried out and tumbled back, Grant's hand falling from around her as he was downed on his back by the monstrous wolf landing on his chest.

"What the hell is this? Get off me!" Grant roared, trying to push off the wolf snapping at his face.

Julie crawled away on her hands and knees before she felt gentle arms pull her up. Sobbing, she fell against Ryan, who helped her to her feet.

Grant shouted again, and Julie looked to find the wolf had ripped at his suited arm. She couldn't be sure, but she guessed this was the wolf that'd shown up to rescue her from Grant's men outside the restaurant all those days ago. She was staring in disbelief, watching Grant struggling to fight off the relentless wolf who snarled and snapped ferociously, its claws ripping at his now tattered suit.

Another shot rang out, and Julie screamed, watching as the wolf bounded off Grant's chest. Grant scrambled to his feet, and instinctively, Ryan pulled her into a tight embrace, keeping her from harm's way as Grant shot at the wolf that leapt away to safety. Grant dashed for the truck, not looking back at the stunned Julie.

She watched in horror as Ryan let go of her, intent on going after Grant. "No! He has a gun, Ryan," she cried out frantically, hand reaching out for him.

"I can't let him get away, Julie," Ryan replied, adding quietly, "I'm sorry."

Julie looked at him in confusion. *Sorry? What does he mean?*

She could only watch in confusion as Ryan took off after

Grant, his clothes ripping from his body as he began the transformation from man into a beautiful, powerful wolf.

Julie's eyes widened with shock as she saw Ryan's now nude form leap into the air, his limbs changing and a coat of black, silky fur sprouting from his back and head. By the time he landed on the ground and bounded into the distance, he was in full wolf form.

*Oh. My. God.*

She was shaking, confusion making her feel weak and dizzy. Suddenly, there was a crunch of branches behind her, and she turned to find a gloriously dark wolf limping toward her. It was monstrous in size and towered over her as it knelt.

She gasped in fear and backed away slowly. But then she saw the wolf pause, a wounded look on its face that seemed strangely familiar. After what she'd witnessed with Ryan transforming into a huge black wolf, she was beginning to question her senses. But then she remembered this wolf had saved her, twice, and she had to push her fear to the side as she saw its front limb.

"You're hurt," she whispered softly and, without thinking, crawled the rest of the way forward, closing the gap between them. She gently lifted the injured limb, amazed at her courage when faced with the most fearsome beast. To her relief, she saw that the injury was just a graze from one of the bullets. But it looked very painful, and she looked up into the wolf's furred face with sympathy and gratitude for his help.

"You'll be okay," she whispered, staring into its eyes and feeling a connection that struck her to the core. Suddenly, her mind cleared and she gasped. "Caine?"

The wolf made a deep growling sound of assent as he nuzzled her hand. Julie caught her breath, his warm touch reassuring, loving.

She looked up to find a pack of wolves moving to surround

them, and without thought, she instinctively wrapped her arms around Caine's wolf.

One of the wolves came forward, nodding in their direction. It was dark gray with white tufts along the top of its large head. Julie felt a wave of relief wash over her as she realized the wolves weren't threatening.

Moments later, Ryan's wolf returned, and Julie felt herself breathe again, realizing just how terrified she was that she had lost him. She watched in amazement as Ryan seemed to communicate with the dark-gray wolf that she assumed was the leader. The gray wolf silently nodded and, the next minute, was leading the many other wolves back into the woods.

Julie watched them disappear into the trees the way they'd come. By the time she turned back around, it was to find two naked figures crouched on the ground. Ryan looked up and straightened, helping Caine up as he held his injured arm close to his body. Julie was speechless, but she was no longer afraid. And when Ryan held out his hand, she didn't hesitate to accept it, allowing him to help her up to her feet.

"Everything's going to be okay. You're safe, Julie," Ryan murmured, pulling her into his arms.

Julie nodded. "And... Grant?"

Ryan grimaced. "He lost control of the truck and rammed into a tree at the side of the road. He's still alive but unconscious. His men are dead... taken out by members of our pack. The police will be here soon, so we'll need to prepare. Are you okay?"

Julie looked deep into their eyes, and from the quiet, sober tone in Ryan's voice, she knew they were afraid she would never be able to accept who they really were.

"Yes. I'm more than fine... I've never been happier in all my life," she replied truthfully, trust and love shining brightly in her eyes. "So... this is the big secret you were waiting to tell me?"

Ryan and Caine shared rueful looks.

"Yes. We're from a clan known as lycan," Ryan explained. "Which means we can shift into wolves at will but can also live as humans. We're part of a large pack. They are the wolves that came to our aid tonight. And, Julie..." He paused only briefly, his eyes fiery with desire, and Julie could see just how much he truly loved her. "Once you mate with us, you'll be part of the pack, too. Forever."

They watched her face for any sign that she wouldn't be able to accept their truth, but she simply smiled, acceptance shining in her blue eyes. "I want nothing more than to be your mate... forever."

"You have no idea how happy you've made us," Ryan replied, grinning widely, overcome with the emotion that shone on her face. "But we intend to show you... every day of your life."

He reached for her, crushing her into his arms. She wrapped her hands around his neck and kissed him, her lips melting against his.

Then, suddenly remembering, Julie let out a dismayed groan and glanced with concern at Caine's injured arm. She was shocked to see the bloodied graze already fading to nothing more than an angry bruise.

"I'll be just fine." Caine chuckled, and Julie laughed as he pulled her from Ryan's arms, carefully wrapping her into his own strong, warm embrace. She breathed in his intoxicating scent and decided there was no place she'd rather be.

"Just think. A few days from now, you'll be bound to us both for life," Caine murmured low, his voice thick with desire. He kissed her softly on the lips and then nibbled a path down to her neck as she burrowed into their warmth and strength.

She felt the hardening bulge in Caine's jeans and giggled. "I can live with that."

———

IF YOU LOVED **CLAIMED BY HER TWO ALPHAS**, you're going to devour **CLAIMED BY HER WOLF!**

**GET A FREE SEDONA VENEZ BOOK!**

https://sedonavenez.com/free-book

# SNEAK PEEK AT CLAIMED BY HER WOLF

## CHAPTER 1

The morning sun broke through the horizon, just as Jade's car crested a hill, spreading pale pink, and gold light over the mountains. The snow-colored hills, which had been an enigmatic blue-white, blushed prettily, as the light touched down on them, taking on the warm glow of the breathtaking sunrise. This time of day was magical, and she couldn't help but smile at the memory of her childhood in this area.

Wanting to capture the moment, Jade stopped her car at the top of the hill to take another sip out of her Styrofoam coffee mug, and just breathe. She watched the sparkling light continue to spread over the treetops, and the blankets of snow on the ground, casting it in what looked like a shimmer of diamonds. The view took her breath away.

She couldn't help but compare her surroundings from her life in the city. This was far more tranquil and picturesque than Los Angeles could ever hope to be, and it was times like this that she regretted giving up the sights and sounds of nature, in favor of the hustle and bustle of Hollywood. But as she shifted the car into gear, and slowly coasted down the hill, her car skidded on a patch of black ice, and she abruptly remembered why she'd been willing to give it all up, and get the hell out of Dodge.

Fear shot through her like a bullet, and she instinctively started to slam the brakes before remembering what her grandpa, Emilio Garcia, had once told her. Fighting against the panic and confusion, she focused her eyes on the road, as she eased her foot off the accelerator and waited until the car gained traction before gently accelerating again.

"Phew." She resisted the urge to swipe the back of her hand across her brow. Instead, she kept both hands firmly on the steering wheel. Los Angeles roads rarely had ice patches—hell, snow was practically unheard of. Sunny weather and clear skies were the norm with temperatures rarely going below freezing even in the winter, and that was just how she liked it.

As Jade rounded a corner, the sign for the Snow Drift Resort, her grandpa's ski lodge, came into view. The nostalgia that had been creeping up on her all year came back in full force, and she sighed. Maybe she liked Los Angeles better for day-to-day living, but she missed the snowball fights of her childhood winters where she ran around the outside of the lodge with her cousins, building forts and snowmen and chucking snowy missiles at each other. She missed stomping inside afterward, soaked and covered in snow, and receiving a huge mug of hot chocolate from her grandpa, thick with marsh-mallows and topped with whipped cream. She remembered how she would snuggle up and sip on the heavenly drink, as she thawed by the fire.

In the end, those memories were what made her return to the resort year after year. She longed to spend time with her loved ones and reconnect with her roots. Back in LA she was Jade Garcia, hot shot advertising executive, but here... she was just a little girl surrounded by the wonder of nature, and the warmth of family.

The winding road continued for a little while further, but eventually the thickets of trees on either side of the path gave way to the sprawling resort. Cabins dotted the snow-covered landscape on either side of the road, available for people who wanted a more private experience. Ahead, the lodge loomed looking like a rambling gingerbread house, with its frosted windows and snow-covered rooftops. Twinkling Christmas lights dangled from the eaves, and along the railing that wrapped around the porch, and Jade could make out two gigantic wreaths hanging from the double doors.

Beyond the house and further up the hill, Jade could see the ski slopes, still empty given the early morning hour. She knew by the number of cars parked outside the lodge that they would be full in just a few hours, though, and it made her glad that the resort continued to be popular amongst the locals.

Parking the car and making her way up to the front porch, Jade found her grandmother Annabella already standing outside waiting for her.

"Jade, my darling. It's so good to see you." Annabella's face was wreathed in smiles as he embraced her, the scent of cinnamon and green chili enveloping her. "I'm so glad you made it. I was starting to get worried when you didn't arrive yesterday, as expected."

Jade pulled back, and kissed her grandmother on the cheek. "I'm sorry, Nan. I ended up stuck at work trying to finish up a project last minute, and didn't leave until really late." She stifled a yawn. "I only slept a few hours, though, because I was so excited to get here."

Annabella's dark eyes widened in shock. "Don't tell me you drove all night?"

"That sounds like my girl," interjected the rich baritone

that was her grandfather Emilio's voice.

The wooden stairs behind Jade creaked, and she turned to see her grandfather walking up the steps to the front porch, dressed in a heavy flannel jacket, snow pants, and a fleece hat with ear flaps. His dark eyes sparkled as Jade flew into his arms, and he wrapped her up in his embrace, still as strong and comforting as when she was a child.

"Oh, I missed you so much," Jade murmured into the red and black plaid of his jacket. He smelled of wood smoke, tobacco and clean, fresh snow. "You've already been up at the slopes?"

His handlebar mustache twitched, as he grinned at her. "Someone's gotta keep this place running, my dear," he said in that gravelly voice of his. He then moved passed her to lift one of her hefty suitcases. "Here, let's get you inside to your room."

Jade grabbed the other suitcase before her grandfather could, and then followed her grandparents into the lodge. The foyer was just as she remembered it—cozy groupings of couches and chairs and bear rugs in front of multiple fireplaces where people could hang out and talk, plus a bar towards the back where guests could order beverages and snacks.

Overhead, the ceiling soared and Jade could see the garland-covered balconies of the three floors above where guests stayed. Christmas music floated from hidden speakers, adding charm to the already festive atmosphere, and reminding Jade of the unwrapped presents in her trunk.

The one thing Jade did not see in the middle of the foyer was a ten-foot tall Christmas tree. Her heart sank a little as she remembered her grandfather's words from a couple of days ago —even though business was doing okay, they'd come upon a lot of unexpected expenses recently, and money was tight. Usually the tree would have been up by now, and there would have been presents under it for all the staff from her grandparents, as they did every year. Instead, there was a much smaller tree standing near one of the lounging chairs off to the right, decorated with a modest amount of Christmas ornaments, and with only a few fake presents sitting atop the tree skirt.

A sigh escaped Jade's lips. She was going to have to do something about the lack of presents, if she could.

Jade waved at Gabriel, her cousin, who was checking in a guest at the front desk, and then hurried passed to keep up with her grandparents. Emilio bypassed the huge, carved wooden staircase toward the rear in favor of the single-elevator, which they'd had installed about ten years ago. They rode up to the third floor where her grandparents kept a suite of rooms. Though they could have lived in any one of the cabins, they preferred to live in the lodge so as to stay close at hand in case they were needed.

"Here you are," Annabella said, smiling as her and Emilio showed Jade to her room. It was the same room she always stayed in, just outside the main living room. The cozy interior was adorned with hand-carved oak furniture and Indian-style blankets and rugs. "Do you want some breakfast? I was about to whip up some huevos rancheros, and maybe some pancakes?"

The idea of a plateful of eggs, beans, salsa and guacamole served on one of her grandmother's freshly made tortillas did sound appealing. But the queen-sized mattress's call was stronger, and Jade wasn't able to suppress a yawn.

"I'd love some, but maybe after a nap?" She asked, running a hand through her long brown curls.

Her grandmother's dark brown eyes scanned her critically. "Well, you do look healthy enough," she relented. "I'll feed you after you've slept. Sleep well, *nina*."

Jade smiled as her grandmother closed the door behind her and tugged a little on the pink sweater she wore. Abuelita hadn't meant anything by what she'd said, but there was no denying that Jade was a curvy girl. Her thick, curvy shape was a far cry from the svelte figures that populated Hollywood, that was for certain, but she didn't let it bother her at all. She felt beautiful, regardless of the number on the scale, and she wasn't going to ever worry about it. Counting calories was never going to be something she was willing to dedicate her time to – life was too damn short for that nonsense.

Shaking her head, she pulled off her gloves, jacket and boots. Then she curled up under the thick, welcoming covers, laid her head against the pillows, and promptly fell asleep.

"Jade? Jade!"

Jade groaned at the sound of her grandfather's voice. Cracking open her eyelids, she looked at the digital clock by her bed, and then jolted upright when she saw that it was two o'clock. *Jesus, where'd the time go? I must've been asleep for at least six hours!*

"What is it?" She asked, jumping out of bed to pull open her bedroom door. Her grandfather's troubled expression told her it wasn't something as simple as missing breakfast. "Is something wrong?"

Emilio sighed. "Rachel's car died on the way up here, and Gabriel has to head out. I hate to ask this of you so soon, but..."

"You want me to cover the front desk." Jade smiled, and patted her grandfather's shoulder. "No problem at all, grandpa. Just give me a few minutes to freshen up, and I'll be right down."

"Thank you so much, Jade... I really appreciate it." He enveloped her in another one of his tight bear hugs that she loved. "You're the best."

Jade changed into a new pair of jeans, and a dark green

sweater that brought out the color in her eyes. With no time to shower, she settled for scrubbing her face over the sink until her cheeks were rosy, then quickly touched her face up with some make-up before heading down the stairs.

Gabriel was standing by the reception desk, already buttoned up for the snowy weather outside. "Thanks so much for helping out," he said, giving Jade a quick hug.

"No problem." Jade smiled up at him, amazed at how much taller the 19-year-old had grown since she'd last seen him. "I'll have to catch up later with you and your Aunt Margo, yeah?"

"For sure. Looking forward to it, cuz." He gave her a quick kiss on the cheek, and was gone.

Sighing, Jade settled behind the counter and re-familiarized herself with the computer, the register and the drawers. Her username and password from the previous year still worked, so she logged in and pulled up a game of solitaire so she'd have something to do since the lodge was mostly empty, its guests already checked in and out on the slopes.

Ten minutes later, the door opened, and a gust of cold air whooshed in behind it, distracting Jade from her game. She looked up as a tall, dark haired man dressed in a thick, heavy woolen jacket with a fleece-lined hood and dark jeans entered the lodge. He stomped his snow-encrusted boots on the rug before looking up at her, causing her breath to catch in her throat, as his deep silver gaze connected with hers. Frozen to the spot, she could do nothing but stare as he approached, and the closer he got, the more his eyes pulled her in.

*Damn, he's gorgeous.* Thick, wavy black hair dusted with flecks of snow framed his tanned, oblong face. The tight jeans he wore showcased long, muscular legs, and though the jacket was thick and padded, it didn't hide the breadth of his shoulders, or his trim physique. She bet there were muscles under there, too, maybe even a six pack.

"Excuse me?" His deep, slightly gravelly voice drew her gaze back to his face with a snap—*and it is a gorgeous face*, she thought with an inward sigh. His silver eyes were thickly lashed, his mouth firm and sensual, his cheekbones razor-sharp. A five o'clock shadow dusted his strong, square jaw, and there was a cleft in his chin she was dying to flick her finger against. "I'm here to check in?"

"Of course." Flustered, Jade dropped her gaze to the computer, and pulled up the guest reservation portal. "Umm, what's your reservation date?"

He arched a brow, a slight smile playing on his sculpted lips. "That would be today."

Heat scalded her cheeks. "Right," she muttered, wishing she was in private so she could smack some sense into herself. *Why was she tripping over her tongue like a fool?* She'd lived and worked in Hollywood long enough to get fully desensitized to masculine beauty, so he shouldn't have affected her just because he was hot. But, for some reason, he was making her pulse skyrocket, and her hormones fly into overdrive, and she wasn't sure whether she liked it or not.

"What's your name so I can look up your reservation?" She pasted on a bright smile as she said it to cover up her awkwardness. She was not going to mess this up any further.

"Dawson McKinnon." A smile tugged at the wicked curves of his lips. "And you are?"

Butterflies tickled the lining of her stomach. "Jade Garcia."

"Jade," he murmured. "Just like your eyes."

*Oh God.* She was going to combust if he kept talking to her like that in that deep, sexy voice of his. "I've found your reservation," she chirped. "You're here for the month?"

"Yes, ma'am." He slid his credit card over the counter so that Jade could charge it, and their fingers brushed. Electricity raced through her nerves, and she snatched her hand back as quickly as she could without being rude.

"That's nice." She swiped the card, then laid it back on the counter. "With friends?"

"No." Something flashed in his eyes that spoke of bitterness. "No friends. Just me, and the wilderness."

"At Christmas time though?" She couldn't stop herself from asking the question, even though she knew better than to pry. Still, something about the look in his eye tugged at her heartstrings. "Seems like a strange time to want to be alone."

His lips curved, and he crossed his arms over the counter, leaning forward. "Oh, I never said I wanted to be alone," he said, his husky voice like rough velvet. "Just that I haven't managed to find any company yet."

"Oh." The sound came out as a squeak, and Jade wanted to kick herself. She was acting like some mousy little girl! Straightening her shoulders, she tossed her curly brown hair over her shoulder, and smiled. "Well, I'm sure you'll find many people here you can enjoy the slopes with. We're usually packed this time of year."

"I'm sure," he agreed, but he didn't increase the distance.

Seconds ticked by as they stared into each other's eyes, and the skin beneath Jade's sweater grew uncomfortably warm. After a few moments, he straightened up, and Jade sighed in both relief, and disappointment. But his next words threw her off balance all over again.

"I'm also sure you'd make for some great company. And if you're not too busy, I'd love to take you out on the slopes tomorrow, and teach you how to ski."

***

**Devour CLAIMED BY HER WOLF!**

# WANT FREE SEDONA VENEZ BOOKS?

Sign up for Sedona Venez's Newsletter and receive FREE BOOKS. In addition to the free stories, you will also get special pricing, exclusive previews and news of new releases.

## GET A FREE SEDONA VENEZ BOOK!

Join Sedona's mailing list to be the first to know of new releases, free books, special prices and other author giveaways.

https://sedonavenez.com/free-book

## ABOUT THE AUTHOR

USA TODAY BESTSELLING AUTHOR SEDONA VENEZ lives in New York City with her hot ex-military hubby—hooah—and their fur babies. She loves writing sizzling, sexy intricate stories about strong but broken characters who push limits, overcome their fears and risk it all for love.

*Sedona loves to connect with readers!*
www.sedonavenez.com